CENOTAPH OF BONES

Threads of Fate Book Four

MICHAEL HEAD

This book is dedicated to all of the men and women who have served and are currently serving in the military. Thank you for all you sacrifice.

"Without heroes, we are all plain people, and don't know how far we can go."

- Bernard Malamud

PROLOGUE

What Comes

A woman sat in a cushioned chair; legs propped up on a matching ottoman in front of a roaring fireplace. The chamber she was in wasn't what most people would consider a room. It was closer to a wall-less cube floating in a vast nothing than anything else, but even that was a poor description. Calling it a spot of reality forced into existence by a willpower so indomitable that it was capable of creating something out of the nothingness of the ether was more accurate of a description. Still not quite the truth, but near enough to consider it as an acceptable description. The woman was sipping on a fluted glass filled with a dark blue liquid, her perfect marble-white skin and flowing white hair providing a strong contrast with the brown leather upholstery. The difference between her white skin and empty black eye sockets was even more striking. Despite the lack of eyes, the woman was nonetheless paying close attention to the creature standing off to her side, beside a matching chair that sat empty.

The creature was a twisted abomination, its rubbery flesh giving off an oily sheen in the light of the fire. It was humanoid-shaped, but its shape was the only thing human about it. If a mad sorcerer were to combine the features of an octopus, spider, cockroach, and black slime mold, it would probably look closer to what the woman was looking at. While it didn't have what most would consider a mouth, it somehow managed a gritty-sounding voice that formed a recognizable pattern of speech.

"The Great God of the Dark Horde has bid me to speak with you, false god of anger." The malformed mass of corrupted flesh seemed to quiver in amusement. It must have thought insulting the woman was funny. It clearly wasn't capable of reading a room. "I have been given a message by the most holy of holies, and he demands a response." The creature held up a scroll of black hide, clearly made from the skin of an abomination very similar to the messenger. As it made to pass the scroll over to the woman, she held up a hand to stop him from approaching any closer.

"Why don't you just tell me what Hastur, the disgusting mass of tentacles and eyestalks playing at being a god, has to say, *nox*?" The creature made a hissing sound at the insult to the creature it considered its god and attempted to just toss the scroll at the woman. The scroll merely stuck in the air a few inches in front of its outstretched tentacle arm, as if caught in the invisible strands of a spider's web. "You would do well to remember where you stand, messenger of a pretend god. This is not your home dimension, and your continued existence only lasts for as long as *I* allow it." She didn't raise her voice, merely stated her threat as a fact for the warped perversion of nature to contemplate. "Now, read the scroll to me, and make sure you recite it word for word. I would rather not have to touch that filthy thing, and I am sure your 'god' wouldn't want his 'divine' words to be twisted any more than they already are, coming from his mouth."

"Fine." It grumbled a bit as it plucked the black leather from the air, then proceeded to unroll the scroll and began reading. "Gods of Light and Sin, you have broken the accords. I demand recompense. You willingly broke a seal to circumvent the Wheel of Reincarnation and allowed us entry into a gated world. By our laws, this maintained the balance. Your recent actions broke this balance. When one of your representatives destroyed a gate, fairly created by my agents, it resulted in the destruction of the greater portion of my forces staged for entry. This goes beyond what is acceptable. Their deaths were not allowed until they crossed into the gated world, and as such, have led to a greater tilting of the scales. Balance in all things, and that balance you have broken. I demand—"

"Enough." She interrupted the creature with a wave of her hand, its body frozen by a small flex of her will. "Your pretend god of the dark is trying to lecture *me* on maintaining the balance? What of the hundreds of realms you hold in your vile grasp, tilting those 'precious' scales so far to your side that they threaten to rip apart the frail fabric of reality?" Something within the black expanse of her eyes rippled under their surface of darkness, causing the room to tremble in response. "No, I think I will not listen to *his* demands. He lost, fairly, and with no direct action on our part. If his dark priestess didn't reinforce a gateway correctly, that is no fault of ours." She took another sip from her glass before waving her hand, freeing the creature from whatever hold it had been under. "Return to your general and tell him we will not concede anything to him just because he lost this round. And remind him that we are fully aware of the greater balance, and how far he and his dark brothers have pushed it. There will be no more easy worlds for him to consume."

The dark creature just stood there, shuddering in rage instead of humor. "My lord shall reap your world like the ripe stalk of grain it is, just like he will reap all you and yours have sown!" It raised a limb to point at her, its voice raising in volume. "There will be a reckoning, and when it comes, I will be waiting!" It raised up to the tips of its limbs, like a human standing on its toes to seem taller. "I swear, you will regret this, and—"

Whatever else it was going to say was cut off by another

wave of the woman's hand. She was humming quietly as the pile of ash that used to be the abomination was swept into the fireplace by a gust of wind. A man, who could have been mistaken for the twin brother of the woman, suddenly appeared in the empty chair next to her. He seemed to be made of white marble, with a robe so pristine it was nearly blinding. The only difference between the two were his eyes. His were glowing an opaque, solid blue that seemed to glitter like sapphires in the dim light cast by the flames in the fireplace.

"You could have handled that better, Wrath." The man was pointing at the dusty remains of the messenger. "He won't be able to tell Hastur anything you said now."

She snorted and looked at him with an arched eyebrow. "I think he will get the message, one way or another." The ashes finished tumbling into the hearth. "Besides, I didn't see you stepping in to help with the situation, Pride."

He grinned, not denying the accusation. Instead, he waved a hand to open a window on the non-existent wall beside the fireplace. "Actually, I was taking some time out of my incredibly busy schedule to look in on our favorite little pet project." The scene on the other side of the window was of a small ship fighting to stay afloat on a dark and stormy sea, ice coating the rigging as frozen spray washed over its decks. "It looks like they are finally getting close to the mountains." Tiny figures could be seen rushing about on the slippery vessel, the occasional flash of light hinting that not all was well onboard the struggling ship. "If they can make it to shore, that is."

Wrath watched the events unfold for a moment before waving her hand again, making the window fade back into the ether. "If he can't reach land with just the few minor inconveniences they face now, there is no way he and his friends could handle what is hiding under the mountains."

Pride shrugged his shoulders, obviously not caring either way. "I already positioned everything for their arrival. Once they make it to the mountains, they will quickly find their way into the path of the disturbance. We should be able to focus our attention elsewhere for a time."

"Good." Wrath stood up, her chair fading from existence. "I have another project of importance to check on, anyway. One I have been ignoring for long enough."

With that, she turned and walked off into the empty expanse of nothingness, quickly fading from view.

CHAPTER ONE

Minor Inconveniences

Today was my sixteenth birthday. Really, it was more like my 656th birthday, but I like to think age is more about how you feel than an actual number.

Yeah, that was a total lie. Right now, I felt like I was closer to a thousand years old, with how tired I was. This was far from my favorite birthday, given the current situation. Not my worst birthday, of course. That honor was held by the birthday when I accidentally killed millions of innocent people and doomed all life on my planet to a slow and terrible death. The gods had seen fit to allow me a chance to correct my mistake, but correcting it was far from easy.

Currently, I was trying to do three things at once, which wouldn't normally be *too* much of a problem, given my level of experience. Steering a ship, reading the earth qi detecting equipment that was keeping us from running aground against the rocky coast, and helping to provide enough wind qi to propel the ship through a winter storm wasn't overly taxing. The thing making it difficult was the giant crab monster trying to crush me in its claws.

"Team three, focus! You need to make sure they stay out of

the rigging, not help team one keep them from coming over the starboard rails!" The ship's captain turned to look back at me, his eyebrows rising in surprise. "Where in the hell is Artus?! He is supposed to be protecting the helmsman!" Considering Artus, the first mate, was lying behind me in two pieces, I didn't think he was going to be much help. The captain saw it too, his face falling for a moment before directing some assistance my way. I didn't know how long the two men had been friends, but from his reaction, I was certain his death hit the captain hard. "Reserve team, go protect the helmsman! Get those stars-damned crabs off of him!" With that, he turned to join team two in clearing the port rails. They needed the help, seeing as how there were already several sailors bleeding out on the deck.

I wasn't in any particular danger at the moment, but the shield formation plate protecting me from the crab was quickly running out of stored energy. Those things must have had some serious crushing power in their claws.

The creatures were some version of the dreaded Pilum Crab, hulking man-sized creatures that roamed the coastline in search of easy prey. These had a thicker than normal exoskeleton, with one claw much larger than the other. To make matters worse, they seemed to be very good at instinctively using water and earth qi to help them fight. Evidence of that could be seen by all the experienced sailors they had already brought low. The Pilum Crab currently attacking me was using its oversized claw like a vice, squeezing the shield around me hard enough to cause the formation plate to shoot out the occasional spark from the copper runes as the metal started melting, threatening to burn out the carved symbols.

When the reserve team showed up to help, I was relieved to see all my friends were okay. Donny, Valerie, Chu, and Jamila were all in various stages of undress. This attack had been a surprise, the sailor in the crow's nest either not seeing it, or asleep on the job. None of us had enough time to get ready beyond grabbing what weapons were nearby and rushing to our posts. Since I had already been at my post, I had just enough time to throw down a shield plate and keep trying to increase our speed. If I could get us out of the Pilum Crabs' territory, they might break off the attack.

"Don't hit Jim's shield! It looks like it can't take much more damage!" Donny was shouting orders to the others, his axe already working to clear the Pilum Crabs climbing over the rear railing of the ship. "Jamila, you know what to do!" She didn't even acknowledge the statement, already sprinting on the icy deck in my direction.

As soon as she reached me, a thin loop of wire wrapped around a protruding eyestalk. One smooth jerking motion later, and the crab forgot all about me. The squirt of blue blood and viscera from the severed eyestalk made the creature spin about, claws clacking as it searched for the source of its pain.

Jamila, of course, was already gone. She had made room for Chu to come in, mace swinging sideways in a devastating blow that sent the crab through the railing and back into the ocean. Valerie found herself standing in the middle of a melee taking place on deck, weaving around the fighting while trying to shoot any vulnerable spot she could find on the creatures as they made their way farther up into the rigging. Somehow, the Pilum Crabs must have understood that tearing up our sails would slow us down long enough for them to finish us off. Considering how poorly we were faring against the surprisingly intelligent creatures, they might even pull it off.

"Donny, they need us down there!" Chu was using his mace to point toward the port side, where the ship's captain was struggling against three Pilum Crabs all by himself. There were only a few of team two still standing, and it wouldn't be long until they were overrun.

"I see it! Valerie, you get over here and do what you can. The rest of us, let's push these bastards back into the sea!" Donny put action to his words, leaping forward into the fray.

With my friends joining in the action, they seemed to turn the tide. Pilum Crabs started to jump back into the ocean, most giving up on the assault. The ones in the rigging did plenty of damage before Valerie could knock them down, their thick chitin shells cracking as they fell onto the deck below. Both masts still had plenty of sail up, enough to allow us to maintain the necessary speed to not get swamped by the frothing stormy seas. That was pretty much the only good news.

There was a round of cheers from the survivors as the last crab fell to the captain's curved saber. Unfortunately, the number of people cheering was outnumbered by the groans of the wounded. The dead, of course, didn't make any sound.

"Get the injured below! Anyone with a talent for healing still on their feet, get to work. We don't have much time before they bleed out!" The captain's shouts were instantly obeyed, and his warning of limited time was readily apparent to everyone. With the way the crabs attacked, there were either gaping wounds or severed limbs that required immediate attention. Those massive pincer claws were devastatingly effective.

I watched as all four of my friends went below. Each of them had a high enough level of cultivation to handle wood qi, otherwise known as life qi, and their ability to heal might manage to save several lives. Especially Chu, as he was even better at healing than he was at cooking. And Chu could make one hell of a good stew.

My own abilities at healing could certainly be of use, but the captain hadn't sent anyone to relieve me yet. I couldn't just abandon the wheel, and there didn't seem to be enough able-bodied sailors left to come and take over.

The captain was directing the few sailors not needed to shuffle wounded below up into the rigging, ordering them to get the ship back to rights. Just then, a flash of lightning lit up the sky. The storm was getting worse, and I could swear I felt the temperature drop another five degrees. It was already cold enough to freeze the sea spray onto the deck in thin sheets, making any chance of sure footing impossible. The rigging wasn't much better, and the groaning sounds from the masts because of the added weight of all the layered ice on the ropes was exceedingly ominous. Which, of course, was when things had to get worse.

A hard shudder went through the ship, and I lost all tension in the wheel. Something had disabled the rudder. The ship whipped hard to port, throwing everyone topside in a slide across the deck. The man in the crow's nest went flying overboard, the whipping motion all the way at the top of the forward mast too strong for him to hang on. The storm was loud, but he was louder. His scream was silenced as he impacted the water. At that height, it was like slamming into stone. He wouldn't need to worry about apologizing to the captain about not spotting the crab attack anymore.

Surprisingly, the men in the rigging were able to hang on. The captain, who had only been saved from a watery death by the waist-height railing, looked at me like he was about to kill me for executing such a stupid maneuver. All I did was give the wheel a light flick, sending it spinning. He instantly got the message. We were rudderless in a winter storm, less than half a mile from the rocky shores of the Northern Mountain Range, where even a ship that *could* steer carried the risk of being beaten into splinters against the underwater hazards. Like I said earlier, not the worst birthday ever, but it was sure trying.

"They're coming back!" A man up in the rigging pointed toward the rear of the ship. Our forward momentum had been cut in half, and a churning wave of Pilum Crabs was quickly catching up. A massive claw latched onto the railing only a few feet away from me, and the one-eyed crab monster pulled itself back on deck. For it to get here this fast, it must never have let go of the ship. Was this creature intelligent enough to know that cutting the steering ropes running along the rudder would cripple the ship? I guess it didn't really matter at this point.

Now that trying to direct the ship was a pointless endeavor, I could concentrate on the crabs. Nobody wanted an infestation of crabs, that was for sure. My first move was to activate the spear function of my spirit wood ring. I spun a little extra qi into the shaft, extending it out past its normal length to something more like an eight foot shaft. The extra foot would help keep the monster farther away from me.

I closed the distance between the crab and myself as it was trying to get all of its legs over the railing. I jabbed forward and the point stabbed into a vulnerable spot at the forward leg joint, sending the creature reeling. It got caught in the railing, falling backward and wrenching two of its ten limbs in the process. They were near their breaking point, wedged between the railing and the edge of the ship, with the full weight of its body bearing down on them. I decided to give it a little nudge.

Two quick pokes in the thick joints, and the limbs tore free. I looked over the side to see it fall into the ocean, its one eye stalk seeming to stare me down as it crashed into the churning wake of the ship.

It also gave me a great view of the ridiculous number of crab monsters coming straight for us. I let the spear return to its ring form. Was it weird that I was suddenly hungry? Because I could totally go for some crab legs right now. Not these crab monsters specifically, of course. They seemed a little too sentient for me to eat. But some regular crabs? That would do the trick.

The sudden arrival of the captain snapped me out of my daydream. He looked over the railing and went pale, his tan skin going almost as white as bleached parchment.

"We need more speed, and we need it *now*!" He was shouting back over his shoulder at where the first mate normally stood. When he didn't get a reply, it took a second for him to remember why. He didn't have a first mate anymore. Shifting his focus to the wheel, he ran over to test it for responsiveness. Just like before, there was no tension. I could have told him that. It took me a moment to realize, but the man was panicking.

The ship's captain and crew had held themselves apart from us for the majority of the trip. They weren't exactly happy with us, considering we were the reason they were forced to travel northward up the Western Province's coastline during the end of fall-year and beginning of winter-year. They had to brave the

Ocean of Tears during some of the worst weather a sailor would ever need to face. It also meant this wasn't the first time we had been attacked by sea creatures on this journey. Unfortunately for them, orders straight from the gods superseded any wishes they might have. Well, they didn't know it had been orders from the gods, but their employers had lent me the use of their ship. Which was basically the same thing as far as they were concerned.

Since they hadn't done much more than assign us to teams and put us in the work and fighting rotation, it took me some time to recognize that it wasn't just the captain running around frantically. Pretty much the entire remaining crew was losing it.

"I need wind qi in those sails, now! Everything you have! No holding back!" The captain was shouting at the crew working on deck. He wasn't even going to wait for the people in the rigging to get clear. Didn't he realize that adding speed without being able to steer was just asking for something bad to happen?

Before I even had a chance to say anything, there were over a dozen massive blasts of wind qi directed straight at the sails. The ship, without a stable rudder to direct its path, shuddered and groaned under the pressure. The keel was following the edge of the waves, forcing the ship to dip lower into the wave troughs than was safe. For a moment, I thought we were going to get swamped. Finding out how deep this portion of the ocean was—in the hardest way possible—wasn't on my list of things to do this week. Luckily, the buoyancy of the ship won out, and we shot out over the top of the next wave like an arrow loosed from a bow. It was almost like we were flying. Until we weren't.

The ship slapped back down on the surface of the ocean hard enough that I heard—and felt—something snap amidship. The impact stole any of the extra momentum the quick burst of wind qi gave us, and we were right back where we started. Except for the ship being even more broken than it was before. Yay for us.

Our impact also had the unfortunate side-effect of jarring

everyone in the rigging loose, causing a veritable rain of sailors to fall onto the deck. While some people might be into that sort of thing, I didn't think the sailors were happy about it. There were probably more than a few broken bones, which meant we now lost the majority of the people able to fight off the still-approaching Pilum Crabs. The captain was no help either, since all he was doing was spouting orders that were clearly counter-productive. It was time for something drastic.

I started pulling out small bags of poppers. Donny and I had been busy over the past month, doing our best to restock on our supply of formation plates and other items. We had managed to build up quite a stockpile, so carefully shifting them around until I had a sack with one hundred poppers barely put a dent in what I had stored away.

Poppers were a little invention I had made a while back. They were basically pebbles with a few runes lightly carved onto their surface. When they impacted with something hard enough, it activated the sequence. The runes formed a bubble of compressed air barely larger than the size of a fist, and less than a split second after forming, the bubble would 'pop,' causing a small shockwave of mostly harmless air to be force-fully expelled. We had learned the hard way that when they were in large bunches, the shockwaves they caused were anything but harmless. Which was the effect I was going for right now.

"Captain!" I shouted to get his attention as soon as I had my bag ready. "You need to get everyone you can off the deck! This is going to get loud!" He just looked at me, not understanding what I was saying. His level of panic and shock was too far gone for me to get through to him. Oh well. I tried.

I ran to the back railing, looking out at the approaching mass of Pilum Crabs. Another flash of lightning illuminated the skies, showing me several hundred of them quickly catching up to us. There were probably even more under the surface. Near the front of the approaching horde, I saw a familiar-looking crab with only one eyestalk that was missing a few limbs. This thing could really hold a grudge. I guess I knew who was volunteering to be my target.

The shouts from the captain bellowing orders behind me—who finally snapped out of his paralysis—fell on deaf ears. I needed to focus. If this throw didn't hit just right, my sack of poppers would just splash into the ocean and do nothing. I spun the sack a few times to build up momentum, trying to time it with the rise and fall of the waves. Giving the sack one last spin, I released it just as the ship crested a wave. I watched as it landed a little short of the one-eyed crab I was aiming for, splashing just under the surface and smashing into the barely visible outstretched claw of a monster right in front of it. The resulting explosion wasn't quite what I was expecting.

Instead of causing a massive explosion on the surface like I had intended, a giant bubble formed underwater. When it 'popped,' it sent a visible shockwave through the water, and an eruption of sea water that shot as high as the ship's masts into the sky. It seemed as if even the storm was shocked, thunder and lightning pausing for a moment, like they were gauging their competition. The storm replied, lighting up the skies with a wave of sheet lightning that brightened the ocean like a sunny summer's day. I wasn't sure if it was the explosion of the poppers, or the lightning that answered it, but it seemed to shake the ocean as if it was in the midst of a seaquake.

The damage the explosion did to the horde of Pilum Crabs was on a scale I had a hard time wrapping my brain around. From what I could see in the split second before the shockwave hit the ship, it looked like I had managed to kill all of them. And by kill, I meant rip them apart. Violently.

When the underwater shockwave hit our ship, it was like being slammed by the hand of an angry god. The already damaged vessel was thrown forward, riding a circular wave that originated from the accidentally awesome eruption I had caused. Everyone that had managed to stay standing up to this point were thrown off their feet, and I couldn't stop myself from being slammed into the rear railing. It let loose an ominous crack, but held.

I managed to get my feet under me and move away from the edge of the ship, back toward the wheel. Which was when I noticed the earth qi detector going crazy. I looked up just in time to see a fresh flash of lightning illuminate a pointed spear of rock jutting from the ocean waves. Then there was a crunching impact when the ship ran aground, and I was sent flying straight into unconsciousness.

CHAPTER TWO

Dark Places

The shock of waking up into a dream was always an adjustment. I had gone from feeling my collarbone snap against the mainmast to suddenly standing at the edge of a dark cavern lit by the faint blue glow of bioluminescent lichen, and the pale green light emitted by obviously poisonous mushrooms. It was a *bit* disorienting.

I knew I was standing in a cave because of all the human-sized stalagmites and stalactites. The blue-green glow provided just enough light to see in the stifling darkness, and the oppressive air felt thick and heavy, even in my dream lungs. It was like the maw of some giant monster, its heavy breath wet and stinking, with its teeth ready to smash down and rend my flesh and bones. The dark cavern was bringing out darker thoughts. The foreboding atmosphere was only enhanced by the heavy presence of metal and dark qi permeating the area. Considering I was underground, it should have been earth qi filling the space, not death and darkness. Which was probably why the gods were showing me all of this in the first place.

I moved deeper into the cavern, taking my time to cast out my senses as I shuffled forward. Even though I was here only in spirit, something was telling me I should still be careful in a place like this. As I moved forward, I realized this was more like a very long and wide hallway slanted downward than a normal underground cave. Considering I wasn't an expert in underground geography, I just kept going instead of investigating further.

There weren't any clear paths to take deeper into the field of stalagmites, so I just followed the thickest flows of qi. It was a steady trickle of energy that seemed to be drawn down into the depths of the earth. I kept going like that for a while, my sense of time skewed by the monotonous landscape. This was definitely the longest tunnel I had ever seen, but I had never heard of such a large underground space before. No memories from my first life could clue me in on where I was, or how deep I might be.

Eventually, the downward slope started to level off. The stalagmites and stalactites were almost touching here, and they were thicker than the ones I had been seeing. This area must have been older or saw more moisture over the passing centuries.

The trickle of metal and dark qi started to speed up, as if whatever pull was drawing it in was getting stronger. I picked up my pace to keep up with it, still doing my best to stay quiet. It also started to get brighter, as if someone had purposely encouraged the growth of the glowing lichen. I started to notice the stalactites and stalagmites were becoming more uniform, as if they were sculpted instead of forming naturally. I began to suspect this place had been engineered by someone over centuries of effort, without using the tell-tale smoothness brought about by an earth qi user.

After what felt like another hour of stalking the flow of qi, I finally reached the end of the long tunnel. I also confirmed there were people living down here. At least, at some point there had been.

The forest of stone spikes had ended abruptly, opening up into a city-sized cavern. I found myself at the edge of a long, downward-sloped ramp, with an even longer vertical drop on either side. It was too far down to see in the dark cave, but I could hear the rush of water from an underground river coming up from below. Across the chasm, I saw a large wall that blocked any further advance into the cave system. At one point, it had probably been an imposing sight to anyone with ideas of invading the local underground residents' homes.

The ramp led to a walled ancient city, with a badly crumbling stone portcullis that blocked a gate barely large enough to fit a standard freight wagon. Not that a wagon could make it through the area I had just walked, unless the stalactites and stalagmites had formed *after* the civilization here had died out. It all felt *old*. I was certain it predated the founding of the current empire, meaning it was probably the remains of a culture that had died out millennia ago. It was hard to tell, given the faded and pitted walls, but a carving near the gate appeared to be a fox with several tails, surrounded by very short people. I couldn't tell if they were trying to capture the kitsune, or if they were venerating it.

The lowered portcullis wouldn't stop anyone from entering, considering the breach in the wall to either side of the free-standing gatehouse. The walls were pockmarked along their full length, either showing signs of advanced age, or lasting evidence of a massive battle that had ended many centuries ago. There was no sign of life from the uniformly square buildings I could see through the gaps, and there were no lights or smoke coming from deeper within the city.

It was reminiscent of how my own clan had designed Roh City. The buildings appeared to all be square, laid out in a grid-like pattern to maximize available space and keep street traffic from bunching up too much in one place. I was only making an educated guess, but it looked like they could fit over thirty of the buildings inside the cavern. The darkness kept me from seeing all the way to the back of the cave.

Following the ramp down, I noticed that the stream of qi had once again picked up the pace. I wasn't sure why, but a feeling of danger seemed to push down on me. Which was when I finally noticed that the city wasn't actually abandoned.

Amidst the rubble beside the gate, I saw a single man standing watch. I hadn't noticed him before, because his armor blended in so well with the gray stone. Even his skin seemed gray. And I couldn't help but notice that he wasn't moving. Not even to breathe. Ah, crap. The undead. There was either a dark curse in this place, or a metal qi cultivator had embraced the death aspect of the element so much that they must have figured out how to animate the dead. There might be a necromancer down here.

Before I could investigate further, I was yanked backward into a blinding white light.

CHAPTER THREE

Picking Up the Pieces

I opened my eyes to find Chu standing over me, a glowing formation plate held high over his head. The storm was still raging, forcing me to blink away the falling sleet that fell into my eyes. Stars, it was cold.

"Jim! Thank the gods you woke up. I wasn't sure if your talisman would be able to fix what was beyond my own healing abilities or not. Head injuries are always a tricky thing to deal with." He held out a hand to pull me back to my feet. "How are you feeling?"

It would have been easy to just say 'bad,' but I shuffled around a bit to check if everything still worked. I had a splitting headache, and my shoulder felt like there was ground glass in the joint, but that was all. I pulled a healing pill from my belt, swallowing it before I answered him.

"I'll live." He grinned at my response but didn't comment further. "What happened? Where are we?" Looking around, I realized we were in a rocky cove next to the ocean, with no one else in sight. "And where is everybody else?" He let out a sigh, looking over his shoulder at the empty beach. It was impossible to see very far, given the weather.

"They are further down the beach, trying to salvage what they can from what's left of the ship." He waved a hand to indicate the rocks all over the area. "We hit a spur of rock pretty hard, and the ship broke apart faster than you might imagine. The sailors elected a leader, and he wants them to find as much as they can before the tide changes." Chu put his hands on his hips, and I finally realized how tired he looked. "Donny and I helped the people still below decks, and the girls managed to save the horses. We healed those that weren't too far gone. Everyone that made it out of the wreckage, anyway. I saved the people I could see, but everything happened so fast…"

I understood. Sometimes, there wasn't much you could do, no matter how powerful or skilled you were. "They elected a leader?" I fought to connect the thoughts bouncing around in my aching skull. "I take it the ship's captain didn't make it, then?"

Chu shook his head. "No, he never made it to shore. The crew voted for the ship's boatswain to lead them. He was the most senior person that they have left." He looked at me for a second before continuing. "I wanted to warn you, the crew is pretty divided in their opinion about what happened. Some of them are saying you saved us all, and others are convinced the shipwreck is your fault. That's why you are all the way over here, and not back at the camp with the others right now. Once they gather what they can from the remains of the ship, there is going to be a trial."

"A trial? For what?" Right after I asked, I realized how the events of the last few minutes might come across to someone that didn't know the rudder had been disabled. It might appear to some that I had just given up on steering, and instead done something to blow up the Pilum Crabs and the ship at the same time. Which, now that I was thinking about it, I kind of did. I had a feeling the Auction House was going to be upset with me when they found out I wrecked their ship. On accident, of course. How was I supposed to know an underwater explosion would be so, well, explosive?

"They are going to decide what to do with you, Jim." I opened my mouth to argue, but he held up his hand to stop me. "I know, I get you didn't wreck the ship on purpose. They are willing to hear your side of things before they determine what to do." I felt frustrated, but there wasn't much I could do about it right now. "The first step was to see if you even survived, so they will need to see what options they are going to have at the trial. My guess is, the worst they would decide on is to tie you up and take you to the nearest magistrate."

"It doesn't matter. We aren't going with them, no matter what they decide." Chu stared at me with a confused look on his face. "We need to get to the mountains and make our way underground." Now he was even more befuddled. "Message from the gods, possible animated dead people, it's probably going to suck, you know, the usual." He sighed, shrugging his shoulders in defeat. I knew how he felt.

"Either way, we need to comb the beach further up this direction, and then go back to let them know you are still among the living. No one else has tried this way, and I thought we could give it a shot." I nodded in agreement, and we started walking north along the shore.

While we were stumbling along the frigid beach, trying to see through the falling mix of sleet and snow, I couldn't help but think about what had brought me to this miserable and barren rocky coast.

My friends and I had left the Western Provincial Capital after a crazy scramble to arrange a ship with the branch manager of the Auction House. I had made sure to message my parents to let them know I was okay, and check if I had anything from back home.

There had been plenty of correspondence from my parents, not to mention messages for my friends from their families. Chu's father, a merchant, was already expanding their small business to meet the demands of the trade deals Chu had been arranging while we traveled. Donny's father had taken a position in the Roh military after the coup attempt and had quickly risen to the top of the rank structure, elevating my family in the eyes of the clan. It had been welcome news, especially after the damage to our reputation my Uncle Hu and his son had managed to inflict on our small family branch. Not to mention my own escape from Roh City, which had been far from peaceful.

Both Jamila and Valerie had received the best news, however. They finally had permission to marry. It had made the most recent part of our trip awkward somehow, now that the engagements of Donny and Valerie, and Chu and Jamila, were official. We didn't have time to go to a shrine during our rush to leave the city, so the four of them were on pins and needles about the whole thing. I had thought about asking the ship's captain to just marry them, but they wanted it to happen in a shrine to the gods to make it more official. Having met a few of the gods, I didn't understand the hang-up.

The most important message for my mission, however, was the one from Wisp. I had hired him to bring Kory to a healer and get him back to Roh City. He had accomplished it, thankfully, and apparently Kory was on the mend. The relief we all had felt was palpable. Kory was already eager to rejoin our little group, but we all sent him a message to remind him to take it easy.

I had sent Wisp a message to find me a way into the good graces of the General of the North, which was the fancy title for the King-ranked cultivator that was the Northern Province's version of a King. I was headed that direction after figuring out the situation with the problem in the mountains, and having him help pave the way for me would speed things up a bit. It would also be a good test of Wisp's abilities.

Once I had solved the problems in the north, I couldn't help but hope I might have the chance to finally start tracking down Ming, the man whose betrayal had caused all of this. He would answer for his crimes. Well, future crimes, but it wasn't like I was willing to let him off the hook. It was only a matter of time until he started destroying the lives of the people he saw as play-things. Which was basically everyone.

"Look!" Chu's shout brought me out of my thoughts. "There are some barrels that made it!" He was pointing farther up the beach, where we could barely see what looked like a pile of wreckage. A swirl of snow hid it from sight before I could see what it was for sure.

We picked up the pace, shuffling through the slurry on the beach. As we got closer, I could see it wasn't just barrels that had made it ashore. There was a large piece of the prow of the ship that was already half-buried on its side in the sand. How had it been buried so deep already? The answer was a simple one. This wasn't from our ship.

"Those aren't barrels, Chu. And they can't be ours, they're too old. Let's check them out." Chu and I approached slowly, as if one of them would jump up and try to bite us or something. It didn't feel like we were being too cautious, considering we had no idea what might be in the area.

A closer inspection showed them to be at least several years old. Whatever had done this had been pretty stars-damned powerful. The severed edge of the wooden prow had been cut off by someone, or something, with an incredibly sharp weapon or claw. And it had struck from below. It was an almost perfectly clean cut until it reached where the deck would have been. There, the break was jagged, as if something had snapped the wooden planks like toothpicks. It was probably from the weight of the ship itself as it had filled with water.

From its size, I imagined this had to have come from at least a three-masted merchant vessel, and I was looking at the front quarter of all that was left. Any identifying marks had long-since been worn away by time and weather, if it even had any in the first place. There were plenty of unmarked pirates and privateers that didn't like to be identified. It was just another risk you ran when sailing the Ocean of Tears.

"Jim, you aren't going to believe this. Come look!" While I had been inspecting the damage, Chu had actually climbed inside the preserved cross-section of the hold. I found him standing in front of a door. Considering the prow was sideways, the door wasn't something we could just open and walk through. "Check out the lock on that thing! What do you think it's protecting? Treasure? Jim, did we just find lost treasure on a pirate shipwreck?"

I couldn't help but laugh. Inspecting the lock, I noticed it was definitely a heavy-duty piece, with carved wards to prevent anyone from just picking the mechanism.

"We don't know if this was a pirate ship or not, but we might have found some treasure. If they used something like this on the outside, maybe they did something to preserve the things inside."

Chu was practically vibrating with excitement. "Okay, then open it up and get in there. Let's find out!"

I knelt down to get a better look, with him literally breathing down my neck the whole time. "Why don't you look around at the rest of the wreckage?" I looked pointedly at him over my shoulder. "It would give me a chance to concentrate." He gave me a sheepish grin and backed away without saying anything. Seeing him go into a different area, I got back to work.

After a few minutes of poking at it, I realized I was wasting my time. The lock was definitely top of the line and must have been made by a Grandmaster craftsman. It was far beyond my skills from my first life. I would have needed to risk damaging whatever was on the other side of the door by just blasting it apart, or going through the side of the hull now that it was on dry land.

This time around, it wasn't necessary. I had a way to cheat. A thin sliver of light qi sliced through the locking mechanism, splitting the runes before they could even activate. There was a slight backlash of escaping qi, but it didn't do anything besides ruffle my clothing.

Which made me realize how beat-up my poor clothes were looking. I would need to change to the self-cleaning clothes I got before killing the Chancellor back in the Southern Provincial Capital. Their only downside was their blue color, which symbolized they were from the Southern Province. Not exactly the best thing to wear when walking around the Western or Northern Provinces. It tended to draw extra attention from those who cared about such things. I guess being stuck in the deserted wilderness would make it a non-issue for now.

The door fell inward after I gave it a push, providing me with a ramp down into the room. It was a disaster. At one point, the walls must have been lined in shelves loaded with trade goods. They didn't handle the crash very well. Most of the wood and ceramic in the room had been shattered into splinters and shards that turned the floor into a dangerous mess no one would want to walk through barefoot. I could see scraps of molded clothing, rusted metal, ruined sailcloth, and bundles of brittle rope mixed in with the worthless pile. Why did I open this door again?

"You got it open? Great! Let me get in there and take a look." Chu must have finished searching the remains of the other decks, because he was standing right behind me. I moved out of the way so he could see into the room.

"Sorry, but it looks to me like the most valuable thing here was the actual lock I just ruined." His face fell, so I motioned him into the room. "But if you want to make sure, you are more than welcome to look through all of that mess." He perked right back up, and shot past me into the room. "Just be careful in there! I don't want you getting cut by some rusty hunk of metal and getting the lockjaw disease. The herbs to heal that are rare in the north, and wood qi only heals it slowly." From the sounds of him throwing stuff around in there, he didn't seem to hear me. No surprise there.

It took him almost five minutes to find the first thing worth keeping. I would have given up far sooner, but he was determined to discover that imaginary treasure. He started tossing items through the open door in a pile that quickly grew larger by the moment.

There was a coil of long rope that was still in good shape, a few coin pouches, an impressive pile of loose jewelry, and several blocks and rods of wood that were covered in carvings. At first, I didn't understand why he was saving those. I picked one up to get a closer look. I realized it was similar to the expandable raft I once had, but lost during a fight with a kraken. It looked like these were meant as emergency replacement sections for the ship, meaning this ship had been owned by a very rich person or group. It wasn't spirit wood, so it would weaken as the qi expanding it ran out, but for emergencies it would be perfectly acceptable. The rods were probably designed to work as masts or spars in case the original ones broke, while the blocks could be used to plug any leaks in the hull. It was an impressive tool. Too bad it hadn't saved the original ship.

"Jim, you should probably take a look at this." Chu's voice was subdued, as if he were sad about something. I quickly ducked into the room to see what was wrong. In the back corner of the room, still partially buried under all the fragments, were three skeletons. Two were adult sized, with a smaller one wedged between them. They were still in the remains of their clothing, which looked to have been of high quality. The little one was wearing a blue dress, made from the same fabric of the dress one of the adults had been wearing. It had been a family. Chu was kneeling next to them.

"There isn't anything we can do for them, my friend." He looked up at me, his eyes moist. For some reason, the scene had also hit me as incredibly sad. "The best we can do is provide them with a better final resting place than this old wreck." Chu stood silently and began to finish clearing off the bodies. I walked over to help him. He finally broke the silence once we had them uncovered.

"I was so concerned with the idea of treasure that I didn't even think of what this all represented." He looked around the room before his eyes settled on the remains of the little family. "This shipwreck marks the deaths of a lot of people." He sighed before wiping at his eyes. "I think we should finish up here, and then burn what is left. Give the ghosts of the crew some rest." I patted him on the back.

"That might draw some unwanted attention to the area, but it sounds like a fine plan to me. We can finish grabbing what we can use, bury these three farther up the beach, and then burn this thing." I picked up a roll of sailcloth. "Help me wrap them up so we can move them."

We carefully moved the remains onto a stretch of fabric, the two of us being as gentle as we could. I noticed a signet ring on the hand of the man, along with a storage ring on the opposite hand. It was a diamond hammer surrounded by flames made from chips of ruby. The woman had a broach with a similar symbol, and the child had a necklace. I put all three in my storage belt, and the storage ring in a belt pouch. If we could figure out what clan they came from, we could at least return the items to any living family. I would inspect the storage ring for more clues later.

Once they were wrapped up and secured, Chu and I moved the bodies out to the beach. Then we both went back to make sure we hadn't missed anything. There were a few more blocks of the expanding pieces of wood, and a few more pieces of rope and sail cloth that were still in decent shape. At the very least, we could use it to fashion tents for everyone.

Chu let me store everything instead of splitting it between us, even the valuable items. He must have really been affected by the bodies for it to cause him to turn down any form of wealth. Or maybe it was a sign of how he was changing as he grew older.

We carried the wrapped bodies farther away from the ocean, and found an area of tumbled stones that would do nicely as a gravesite. Chu used his qi to open a deep grave, while I used a strand of earth qi to move and shape three stones as markers. I didn't know any names to put in place, so I copied the symbols that had been on their jewelry. They were deeply carved, to help preserve them from the damage that sea winds would undoubtedly do as the years passed by. It was better than many on this unforgiving world would ever receive.

Chu laid them in the grave, and we both covered them with several layers of protective stone. I turned to leave but he stayed for a minute longer. His head was bowed, and he seemed to be praying. I left him to it. I had met the gods, and from what I had seen, none were likely to listen. Maybe there were some other gods out there that cared about the three lost souls we had laid to rest. A small part of me still hoped there were.

While he was praying, I made my way back to the ship-wreck. The weather had changed from a mix of sleet and snow to mostly just snow, which allowed for a slight increase in visibility. I watched the cold waters of the steel-gray ocean for a time, letting the cold seep into my body. The melancholy mood seemed to fit well with the upcoming tasks I knew I had to face.

CHAPTER FOUR

Big Problems

Figuring out a way to deal with the sailors was the first step. I didn't want to have to fight my way free if I could avoid it, and parting ways amicably would probably put me in a better position with the Auction House.

After handling them, I would have to find a way into the cave system that contained what I had seen in my dream. The shudder that went down my spine didn't have anything to do with the cold. Dealing with the animated dead was never fun.

Sometimes, cultivators could have something that set them apart from their peers. They might have an extra meridian or two, have an oversized core, or even gain an almost unnatural affinity with a specific element. I had been born with an oversized brain core and one extra meridian, which was what made me the powerful cultivator that basically destroyed the world. There were others, though, that were just as capable and dangerous as I had been. Will be. You get what I mean.

The cultivators that had a deep connection with a specific element could do much more than even I could manage. Wood qi was also called life qi for a reason, and when a cultivator had a strong enough attachment, they were capable of instant self-healing, communicating with nature, and even bringing the freshly dead back to life. There were even tales of cultivators that were so connected with life qi that they were functionally ageless, not just immortal. I didn't believe such tales, but who knows what the creator of this universe might allow…

Every element had some similarly advanced power. For example, those deeply connected to earth qi could build an entire palace with nothing but a thought, or even manipulate the forces of gravity around them with only a minor exertion of will. Cultivators with a strong attachment to fire qi could burn any opponent to ash, or create flames so hot that they seemed to burn cold. There was a bard that claimed a fire cultivator was what sparked the forges of creation, somehow bringing forth new life that populated barren continents halfway around the world. I could go on and on about all the fanciful stories spread around a campfire, but it was metal qi, sometimes known as death qi, that was my current problem.

A death cultivator could manipulate the flesh of the dead the same way someone using earth qi could manipulate sand. I had witnessed a particularly powerful Sage create a creature of bone from the site of an ancient battlefield. The creature had looked like the dragons seen on the tapestries in the Emperor's throne room, magnificent and terrible. It had been a display of power that haunted my dreams for a long time.

If they had enough practice, a death cultivator could control dozens of animated dead, using the bodies of the fallen to kill their enemies without raising a finger. I also heard that while the initial qi investment of raising a dead person was substantial, it only took a trickle of power to control them. If it weren't for the fact that a death cultivator—otherwise known as a necromancer —had to actively control their flesh and bone golems, they would have long ago ruled over the living. They were a small army unto themselves. Who also happened to usually smell really bad.

The problem with what I had seen in my dream was that I hadn't seen the cultivator controlling the dead sentry near the entrance to the ancient underground city. Every necromancer I had ever come across had needed to be able to *see* their creations to be able to manipulate them like the disgusting and rotting puppets they were. That meant this was something new. If a death cultivator had managed to find a way for their creatures to become self-aware enough to perform a task by themselves, they could threaten everything. Given sufficient time, the necromancer could build an army that never needed to eat, or sleep, or even dig a latrine. It would be nigh unstoppable. I could see why this had the gods concerned.

I hadn't heard of anything like this in my first life, meaning this was certainly brought about by the *nox* problem. One of the more intelligent demons must have bonded with a death cultivator, and found a way to adapt their abilities into something much more dangerous.

"Are you ready?" I had been deep in thought, and hadn't noticed Chu walk up behind me. "I think it's past time for us to head back." I turned to face him, and saw that he already had a formation plate out. He saw me nod in silent agreement, so he activated the plate and tossed it inside the wooden wreckage of the ship. It only took a few seconds for smoke to start billowing out of the cracks in the wood. "I put enough of my qi in that fireball trap to burn up what's left twice over. Let's get out of here."

We started making our way back down the beach, the heat from the burning wreckage warming our backs. It was a welcome reprieve from the cold, even if it only lasted a short time. The pillar of smoke it sent up also brought some familiar faces running along the beach toward us.

"We can't leave you two alone for a few hours before you manage to burn something down!" Donny's grin stretched from ear to ear. "It's good to see you up and moving, Jim. We knew Chu would be able to get you back on your feet in no time."

"He really should have more faith in himself by now." Jamila was already moving to stand next to her betrothed. "It's something I am more than willing to help him with. Any warrior worth his salt should have some self-confidence in their abilities." Chu opened his mouth to argue, but she silenced him with a look. "Don't argue with me, mister. You and I can talk about this some more later."

I traded a look with Donny that told me the irony of the situation wasn't lost on either of us. Poor Chu. He never even had a chance. Jamila was steadily becoming less shy and more assertive as she grew into her own, which left Chu in a rather precarious position. The uplifted corners of his mouth told me he loved it.

"So, you going to tell us what the two of you were up to out here?" Donny was starting to walk closer to the fire, so I reached out and stopped him with a hand on his arm.

"Chu and I found an old shipwreck. The remains of a family were inside, so we laid them to rest and burned everything that wasn't of use." I started walking back in the direction we had come, wanting to change the subject. "Where is Valerie? And how is the situation back at camp?"

"Oh, she's watching the horses," Jamila answered before Donny could speak. "None of us trust the sailors alone with them. They might steal them and try to ride for the nearest village, even though it would mean weeks of travel by land. Not only that, but—"

"Not just that." Donny seemed excited, talking fast before Jamila could finish what she was saying. "Right before we came to see what you two were burning, the ship's captain just wandered into camp!" Both Chu and I looked at Donny. "I know! Crazy, right? We all thought he was dead, but he rode the floating carcass of a Pilum Crab to shore, and just washed up farther down the beach. He had a few more of the crew with him as well, so they were still getting organized again when we left. Valerie should be able to tell us what to expect from them when we get back." Chu looked over at me, waiting for me to talk. When I didn't say anything, he decided to speak up.

"Either way, we won't be joining them." He subconsciously twirled the ring on his finger, which held his heavy mace and armor. When Donny and Jamila looked at me, I finally explained.

"The gods showed me where we need to go. The enemy we are hunting is in a huge cave system." I looked behind us, to the north. "And I don't think this one will be easy." They all looked at me, their concerns evident. "We are going to be facing a death cultivator. A necromancer. And this one is different somehow. Stronger in a way I can't figure out yet. The worst part is, I don't know how deep we have to travel underground. Or how extensive the cave network is. This could take us a *really* long time to figure out." Everyone traded glances, but I was pleased to see them lose some tension in their body language. What I didn't say was how handicapped I now felt. Considering that the element of surprise was our biggest advantage against the rogue necromancer, I couldn't use dark qi unless I was willing to give it up. They might sense me using the hidden form of qi, considering nothing else in nature seemed to do so. That meant even using light qi might be a risk, or a way for them to know something out of the ordinary was nearby.

"Jim, don't worry about it." Donny waved his hand to indicate the landscape. "We don't have a lot of other stuff going on right now. We might as well help you save the world." That brought a few chuckles out of everyone.

We finally saw the campsite the crew had set up on the beach a few minutes later. Even though I was concerned about the crew's ideas of how much blame for the shipwreck rested on my head, the thought of getting to warm up by the roaring fire sped my shuffling steps. I was surprised to see how many people had made it ashore. There had to be over twenty shuffling forms tiredly moving supplies around, meaning the vast majority of the remaining crew had survived. Chu held up a hand to stop me.

"Why don't you wait here and let the three of us go first?" He looked toward the camp. "Just in case they are thinking of doing something we would all regret." Everyone agreed, and I used a quick flex of my will to pull a camp stool out of my belt to sit on while I waited. Its legs sank into the sand a bit when I sat down, but it was better than just standing there.

The wind had really picked up, making me shiver as the snow somehow made its way inside the collar of my shirt. Funny how it always seemed to be able to do that when it was snowing. I would need to look through my storage belt to find some furs to keep warm. Now that we were on land, using a trickle of fire qi to keep myself warm might alert a nearby predator there was a possible meal running around. Until I got a better understanding of what creatures were in the area, I didn't want to risk attracting anything.

Since the fates absolutely hated me, just as I had that thought I felt a spike of energy come from the camp. Didn't these people understand they needed to keep a low profile? Their huge fire was bad enough, but the heavy snow would make it invisible after a few hundred yards. Throwing qi around could be felt for miles by a powerful monster. This wasn't the open ocean, where heavy and unpredictable qi flows covered up all but the largest of power expenditures. Or a city, where there were walls and guards to protect everyone from the creatures that roamed the land. This was the wild, where anything was possible.

I felt another flare of power, this one familiar to me. Donny was showing off his Low Saint aura to the sailors, most likely as a way to show them they shouldn't take him lightly. Our little group was far more powerful than most people our age, making it necessary sometimes for us to show what we were capable of doing if provoked. We kept to a steady training regimen that even the strictest of sects would find onerous, and my abilities at alchemy gave us an edge even the children of the four kings would see as advantageous. Not that those spoiled pukes ever worked a day in their lives. Ugh. I hated those snobby rich kids. They weren't all bad, of course, but that was like saying not all squirrels were secretly evil. Sure, one or two might be decent, but we all know the vast majority are constantly plotting the downfall of humanity.

There was an answering flare of power that had to be from the captain. He was the only member of the crew that was at Middle Saint, making him an equal match for my own current cultivation level. I honestly believed that Donny could take him if it came down to a fight. We had a remarkable amount of combat experience, and our weapons and armor were of a very high quality. But, considering the average age of a Saint-level cultivator was about one hundred and fifty years old, and Donny was only twenty-four, the captain might have enough surprises up his sleeve to balance the playing field. It was best to not risk it.

I put away my chair and started walking toward the fire burning in the distance. As I got closer, I started to hear angry shouts coming from the camp. I picked up my pace, wanting to get there before it came to blows. It was tempting to unleash my own aura as a distraction, but it might only make things worse. Backing people into a corner was never a good idea. Unless you *wanted* to fight them, of course. The shouting paused the moment I stepped into the firelight.

"I see the murdering psychopath has decided to join us!" Ouch. I'm not going to say the captain was entirely wrong, but his accusation didn't quite apply this time around. I tried to ignore the hunks of Pilum Crab being cooked over their fire, the smell somehow making me a little ill. Eating intelligent creatures never sat well with me. I focused back on the captain.

"Look, I understand why you are upset, but you need to calm down and rein in your aura." I spoke softly and had both hands raised, trying to show I meant no harm. "We don't know what could be waiting for us farther inland, and you are ringing the dinner bell right now."

"Are you trying to give me orders?!" The captain's aura flared even brighter, sending a few of his own men to their knees. An angry Saint could pressure a cultivator pretty hard. "You destroyed my ship, and now you have the *gall* to tell me what to do? Men, throw him in irons. We are going to have us a trial right now!"

Stars-dammit, this was going all wrong really quickly. How was I supposed to know an underwater explosion would have such a massive shockwave? To make matters worse, I could sense all four of my friends off to my right start to spin up their own qi in response. This was about to go from bad to worse. Which, true to form, was when it got even worser. Yes, worser. No, it's not a real word, but it certainly fits this situation.

A suffocating, wild aura unveiled itself a few miles to the south, opposite the direction from where Chu and I had burned the old shipwreck. If it was that strong from this far away, all I knew was that I didn't want to mess with whatever creature was now aware of our presence. It had to be at *least* Duke-ranked, maybe King. Since it was a beast and not a cultivator, that would make it nearly impossible to defeat without a dedicated team of warriors trained and prepared to fight overpowered beasts, as they tended to have special abilities and strengths that humans did not. Which, currently, wasn't the case. Even my friends were really only prepared to face other cultivators, not something like this. The animalistic fury of something similar to what we were feeling was beyond us. It was hard to tell over the roaring of the fire and the blowing of the wind, but I could have sworn I heard the roar of anger from something big. Like, wow-that's-a-nice-building kind of big. We only had one option.

It was time to go.

CHAPTER FIVE

Finding a Path Forward

The captain, along with everyone else, instantly retracted their auras. It was too little, too late, but I appreciated the effort. Everyone turned to look at me, even the captain. I guess warning them this would happen raised my worth a few notches. My friends were already scrambling to collect whatever gear and supplies they could fit in their storage devices. I started to do the same. I was happy to see my friends prioritizing food, so I made sure to grab every barrel of lamp oil, boxes of glow stones, and crates of candles I laid eyes on. They remembered we were going to be spending a lot of time inside some caves soon, and had acted accordingly. Even though I still had a good supply of glow stones, I knew having light to see by underground would be essential for survival.

Seeing the five of us quickly move into action seemed to snap everyone else out of their stupor. The weakest of the group were helped to their feet by the sailors that could still stand under the weight of the aura we were now being subjected to, its distant pressure making a few of them have difficulties breathing under the stifling assault.

As if in response to our need, the snowstorm picked up in

fury, further reducing visibility. You could barely see more than fifty feet in any direction. It might be enough to save us.

"Head north, and start angling more inland. If we can reach the forests farther away from the beach, we might be able to lose it in the trees!" I was shouting to my friends, but everyone else seemed to think it was a good idea. Having someone shout a plan seemed to galvanize the sailors into a more determined speed. In less than two minutes, everything that had been salvaged and brought to shore was either stored away or loaded into makeshift traveling packs.

Valerie jumped on Scout and took off. The tracks she left behind were our guide through the snow. Jamila wasn't far behind, her own horse, Cloud, seemed to be excited to race after being cooped up on a ship for so long. The two of them working together should be able to find us a safe path through the rocky coastline.

Donny and Chu took the lead, the two of them setting a pace that was more of a jog than a run. Everyone else followed, splitting into a double line that ran in their footsteps. At least they were smart enough that we didn't have to explain why it was a good idea to follow directly behind the man in front of you. The rocky beach could easily hide stones the perfect size and shape for a man to roll his ankle, making it important to try to step in the footsteps of the person in front of you. A broken leg or sprained ankle would require healing, which would slow us all down. And slowing down would equal death.

I waited for everyone to start moving before bringing up the rear, already shuffling through my stockpile of formation plates and traps. I needed to find something to slow down the beast following us, otherwise there would soon be a lot of dead sailors. While they might want me dead for wrecking their ship, I didn't particularly hold a grudge against them. They hadn't even had time to hear my version of events, and I knew at least a few of them already suspected that my actions had saved their lives.

"I don't exactly like this, but I am man enough to admit

when I am in over my head." The captain was jogging alongside me, his eyes forward on his men to make sure none of them were showing signs of flagging. I hadn't noticed him at first, considering I was trying to concentrate on the contents of my belt. "You warned me this might happen, and I didn't listen. I might know the risks a person faces on the sea, but the wilderness is as mysterious a threat as any I have faced. We will follow you and your group until we reach some semblance of safety. After that, we can revisit your role in the destruction of my ship."

"Fine with me." I glanced over at him, finally noticing how worn and tired the man looked. I couldn't blame him. There had been a lot of trials he had faced in a very short period of time. Riding the carcass of a dead crab creature to shore couldn't have been fun, and it was admirable that he had saved so many of his men in the process. "You have to know that I didn't wreck the ship on purpose. Something—one of those crabs, I think—cut the linkage rope to the rudder. If they hadn't done that, we would still be sailing north, instead of running from some monster." He didn't answer me, instead picking up his pace to corral a sailor that was drifting too far out of line.

Having everyone in two equal lines had given me the opportunity to count just how many people managed to survive and were with us. Including my friends and I, there were thirty-six people that made it to shore. Considering the ship had been carrying fifty people, I couldn't help but be impressed. The Auction House employed capable people, even if they weren't the best in combat. I also noticed several were still injured, including more than one still missing a hand or arm. They hadn't had time to ingest the pills to regrow them, or maybe they didn't have any. I might be able to make a few with the ingredients I was carrying, but it would take several hours to create them. It would be another way for me to help make amends for blowing up the ship, which I felt would help balance the scales a bit.

I started dropping proximity traps as we ran, pausing to

pour some bottled liquid qi on them to maximize their longevity. Most of the plates were stone spike traps, with a few quicksand traps to keep the monster guessing. It would probably only slow the creature down, but right now, that was exactly what we needed. I could feel its crushing aura getting closer, which had the negative side-effect of slowing us down even further. Too many of the crew weren't strong enough to withstand the mental and physical effects of the oppressive aura.

To make matters worse, I started to notice the landscape change. We had already traveled well over two miles from the campsite, and the quickest path forward had unfortunately been straight north along the beach instead of angling more inland. The gradual shift from rocky shoreline to steep cliffs meant we were slowly becoming trapped. On our left was the ocean, and to our right were sheer rock walls that were only getting higher. It might have been my imagination, but it even felt like the beach was getting narrower. If there was a spur of land farther up ahead, we would be trapped.

The muffled thundering of a horse at full sprint reached my ears, the heavy snow distorting how far away the rider must be. We came to a quick halt as Jamila appeared out of the storm in front of us.

"Bad news! The beach runs straight into the cliffs less than half a mile up ahead." Stars. I hated it when I was right sometimes. It was like the gods could hear my thoughts, and kept providing me with the worst possible outcomes I could think of. She continued to talk to Chu and Donny in a voice loud enough that we could all hear. "Until the tide goes back out, we're pretty much trapped. Some of us will have to stand and fight while the rest try to climb the cliff walls." There was some muttering from the sailors, but the captain silenced them with a shout.

"I'll stay! The rest of you, get moving! I don't know how long I can hold back the beast." That was when I felt a trio of traps I had placed go off, their triggers linked to my brain core through their proximity runes. The answering roars a moment later told me I had at least made it mad. This time, everyone else heard it too. Whatever the beast was, it had to be huge. More than one person turned whiter than the snow falling from the sky. Even the captain seemed less sure of volunteering to face the creature.

"No, we stick together!" I stepped forward, moving to the front of the line. "If we can get to a place narrow enough to restrict its movements, we might have a chance!" They didn't seem to believe me, but no one spoke out against my idea. I already had a plan forming in the back of my mind that might work, but it would all depend on what the landscape looked like farther up the beach. "We need to hurry if we want time to prepare!" Jamila, not waiting to see if everyone agreed, was already spurring Cloud back up the beach. Everyone else soon followed, this time running all out.

If we were going to get out of this, I needed to find a better path forward.

CHAPTER SIX

Making a Stand

The next several minutes were a blur of frantic breathing and blowing snow. Visibility was getting even worse, each person just focusing on the tracks directly in front of them. It was like traveling in a white tunnel, with no beginning and no end. The cold temperature made everyone's breath come out in a pale mist, leaving white streamers behind us like a ship leaving a wake on the ocean. I was back at the rear of the line, doing my best to motivate everyone to keep up the pace.

Another roar indicated the creature had found the second set of my traps. The next one was going to be the quicksand trap. I was really hoping it would buy us some extra time, because it was most definitely gaining on us. I would need at least a few minutes to get everything arranged, and right now I wasn't going to get it.

"You better have a good idea, kid, because otherwise we are all dead." The captain had worked his way back to me, grabbing a few of the heavier packs off the backs of his men. I could feel him cycling his qi to increase his strength in order to carry all of them.

"Don't worry, I am pretty sure this will work. All we need is a narrow spot of beach to restrict the beast's movement." I glanced behind us, but all I could see was a white wall of snow. "If this storm keeps up, there is no way the creature will be able to figure out my plan." He didn't say anything further. I guess seeing me wipe out an entire cast of crabs in one blow tended to get me a little leeway.

Suddenly, the earth shuddered as if we were in an earthquake. We were all thrown off our feet, most of us skidding several feet through the rocky sand and snow. The guttural roar of anger that came from behind us was loud enough to shake some rocks loose from the cliff to our right. I think my quicksand trap must have tripped it. Just how big was this thing?

It did provide us extra motivation to get back on our feet and start moving. This time, there were no neat and orderly lines. Everyone was sprinting as fast as they could along the steadily narrowing beach, clustered up and tripping over each other. I stopped to help a sailor back to his feet after I saw him stumble to his knees. He was leaking blood from his nose, ears, and eyes, the aura from the beast proving to be too much for his poorly reinforced body to handle. I threw him over my shoulders and took off, cycling my heart core to boost my strength.

It was only a few hundred yards farther up the beach until we finally reached the area where Valerie and Jamila were waiting for us. The spur of land jutting out into the surf was like a wall in front of us, and it was almost as high as the cliffside to our right. Well over a hundred feet of vertical rock hemmed us on two sides, with the rough ocean waves boxing us in. We had nowhere to go. Perfect.

"Okay, Jim, now would be the time to reveal your great plan!" Donny was forced to shout to be heard over the crashing waves of the beach and heavy thudding footsteps of the quickly approaching beast. "We are running out of time here!"

I handed off the man I was carrying to the captain as he approached. It looked like he wanted to talk, and I didn't have the time. Tossing a person at someone tends to be a good distraction.

"Who here is good at manipulating earth qi?" All of my friends raised their hands, but they weren't who I wanted working on this. Just in case, I wanted them to have full qi reserves. Luckily, two of the sailors tentatively raised their hands. "Good! You two, start forming a narrow depression into the side of the cliff. We need enough room for everyone to stand far enough back that you can drop a thin layer of stone they can hide behind. Just like a hidden room, or that smuggler's section you had at the rear of the hold on your ship. You know, the one with the false wall?" Over half the crew looked chagrined, and the captain was spluttering in fake outrage. I didn't actually know if their ship had one, but they were so common that I would be genuinely shocked if their former ship *didn't* have a secret compartment.

Instead of arguing, the two sailors instantly got to work. They used their earth qi to shift the stone inward, making a deep curve into the cliffside. I felt my fourth and final series of trap plates go off, meaning we were almost out of time. The creature was less than a quarter of a mile away, and it would be able to see us through the snow soon enough. I looked back at the progress, and saw there were already people moving supplies and packs into the space.

"Hey! Don't forget to leave a gap at the bottom for air flow when you make the false wall." I saw my friends clustered off to the side, each of them clearly engaged with looking through their own storage devices. They were probably taking stock of their own trap plates. "And make sure to leave room for the horses!"

Donny walked over to me, clearly nervous about the approaching creature. Its footsteps were causing loose pebbles to come tumbling down the cliff face. We still didn't even know what it was yet, and everyone was already scared. Stars, *I* was a little scared. Only a complete idiot stops feeling fear.

"You know it will just keep looking for us, Jim. Hiding inside the cliff won't work for long."

I nodded in agreement with Donny. "That's why this is only

the first part. I need you to keep everyone quiet, and make sure they don't let loose their auras." I looked over at the spur of land jutting out into the ocean. "If I'm not back in a few hours, wait longer." He opened his mouth to argue, but I was already gone.

I pulled out one of the replacement masts we had found in the old shipwreck as I ran. I was headed for the place where the spur and the cliff met. The intent was to put my back to the spur of rock with the expandable mast wedged into the corner. I was going to make the monster mad, and then activate the chunk of wood as it charged, impaling the beast and ending the fight before it really even had a chance to get started. As long as everyone else stayed hidden, it would hopefully avoid them entirely.

Getting in position, it was only a few more minutes of waiting until I finally got a glimpse of the beast. It seemed to materialize out of the snow, its massive bulk making the earth shudder with every step.

We were totally and completely screwed. It was a rock troll.

Rock trolls were dangerous because of a mixture of just how quickly they could regenerate from an injury, and their limited intellect. Not smart by any means, but they certainly had more intelligence than an unthinking beast. They had deep connections to both earth and wood qi, allowing them to heal from even the most lethal of blows. Their skin was an actual layer of rock, making them very inflexible and slow. I only knew of one weak spot, and that was their joints. Even those weren't exactly 'weak,' they were just the only place you might manage to hurt one enough for it to really notice.

If a rock troll made its way down from the mountains, an entire platoon of soldiers was assigned to fight it. And they would be lucky if even half of them made it back alive. Rock trolls were fortunately very rare, and only seen in the deepest of winter, when the sharp cold of the high mountain peaks forced them out of their caves. It was still months away from deep winter, so seeing this monster along a beach near the foothills of the mountains was certainly out of character. Something had chased it from its home.

This wasn't just any rock troll, either. I hadn't seen one this big in my entire life, and I had lived a *long* time. It had to be close to seventy feet tall, making my earlier comments about it being building-like more accurate than I would prefer. It also meant my idea of using the wooden mast was pretty much useless. There was no way a big, dull wooden spear could penetrate the thick rocks protecting its vital areas.

The giant creature was stumbling a bit as it walked, and it took me a moment to figure out what was going on. My quicksand trap had worked as intended, turning a ten-foot wide and five-foot deep circle of beach into an almost liquid slurry that hardened to solid stone after a few seconds. It was supposed to hold whatever was trapped inside it, keeping it in place. For a creature this size, it had accidentally formed a donut-like boot around one of its feet. If it weren't for the whole, 'this thing could crush me to death entirely by accident,' I might be laughing at how ridiculous it looked. The rock troll started sniffing, searching for a scent. It was most likely zeroed in on the horses, and it wouldn't take long for it to figure out where they were hiding. I was going to have to do this one on the fly.

"Hey, rock-for-brains!" I used a quick wind qi construct to enhance the volume of my voice so I could get its attention. "You looking for me, stumpy?!" It whipped its head around much faster than something its size should be allowed to move. Its eyes seemed to smolder in anger, as if the lava from a volcano was hidden in their depths. The rock troll's limited intelligence might not entirely understand what I was saying, but it was at least smart enough to know it was being insulted. "Yeah, you, big-for-nothing! Why don't you come over here and I can show you that size doesn't really matter?!" It looked at me like it was confused. Wait, what did I just say?

Giving up on figuring out whatever nonsense I was spouting, it let loose a roar that blew out my ear drums. Which hurt. A lot.

I dropped to one knee, a sense of vertigo hitting me hard. The unexpected shock of pain to my brain had thrown me for a loop. I could feel blood leaking out of my ears, and my whole body was trembling. I glanced back up at the rock troll, and realized I wasn't trembling from pain, but because it was stumbling toward me as quickly as it could with the sandstone donut stuck to its leg, which was causing the ground to shake. I needed to move before I was forced to perform my first and only impression of a meat pancake.

My wood qi healing talisman, still hidden in my waistband, finally fixed my ears. It seemed to be having problems functioning under the oppressive aura the rock troll was exuding, so I let loose my own aura, that of a Middle Saint. It felt like I was trying to stand under a waterfall, the constant pressure making it hard to even get back to my feet.

I managed to stand just as the rock troll got close enough to stomp me flat. It raised its unburdened foot off the ground, holding it over my head for just a moment. Figuring now was as good a time as any, I activated the wooden mast that I had wedged into the rock behind me. It expanded rapidly, growing upward out of the rock almost as fast as an arrow shot from a bow. The tip of the emergency mast missed the foot of the troll, but it managed to slam into its upraised thigh, just behind where it was bent at the knee. It didn't have enough impact to hurt the troll, but it did cause it to abandon its plan to crush me like a bug.

It teetered backward on one foot, unable to drop its other leg because of the massive pole that was now wedged in the back of its knee. The donut of sandstone around its other leg made it even more unstable, the awkward shape keeping the troll from catching its balance. It let out a sound I could only describe as a 'huh?' before toppling into the surf onto its back, once again shaking the ground hard enough to cause a few minor rockslides from the cliffs around me. The wave it caused on impact was reminiscent of the accidental shockwave I had caused when I threw that bag of poppers at the Pilum Crabs.

Not waiting to see how long it would take it to get back up, I started climbing up the cliff wall as quickly as I could move. If I could reach the top of the rocky cliffside, I might be able to lure it far enough from the beach to allow my friends and the ship's crew to get away. Any thought of killing the rock troll was immediately discarded. Such a large creature would be almost impossible to bring down, as any wounds I could inflict would be healed in moments. Even though I was a Saint, I still had a long way to go before safely taking on something that size.

As I made it to the top of the cliffside, I looked back to see how the rock troll was coming along. I was just in time to catch a ship's mast to the face.

It was a glancing blow, but that was still enough to shatter my jaw, cheekbone, and tear off most of my cheek. I was thrown backward in a spray of blood, spun around, and flopped to the ground, the snapping motion of my head impacting with the edge of the mast nearly breaking my neck. If I hadn't been reinforcing my body with layers of qi nearly every single day since my reincarnation, that would have been instant death.

My healing talisman started to repair the damage, but it wasn't going fast enough. I spun my cores hard, using my internal qi to help fix my disfigured face. I was in agony, and I was feeling an immense amount of rage at the creature. Forget running, and trying to play it safe. It was time to kill this troll.

CHAPTER SEVEN

Trolls are Bad

I could only see clearly out of one eye, but what it showed me was enough. The rock troll appeared to be laughing at me, shoulders jumping up and down as it made chuckling sounds reminiscent of a rockslide. Okay, asshole. I got something for you.

Reaching out with my senses, I found the mast it had thrown at me. I used a strand of earth qi to drag it close enough for me to touch it, and I activated the runes to shrink it back down to the size of a thick walking stick. Perfect for throwing.

Standing still felt like a bad idea, so I formed a whip of air qi and wrapped it around the pole. Then I used one of the qi batteries in my belt to dump more energy into the mast's qi matrix. I felt a stronger connection to it now, meaning I could manipulate the runes on its surface with just a flex of my willpower. It could only hold about half of one battery, so half the power of a Low Saint cultivator. That was a lot of power.

I sat up enough to give me room to move my arm, and whipped the expandable mast right back at the rock troll. Just before the mast broke connection with my qi whip, I activated the growth runes embedded in its surface. The cracking sound of the whip flying forward was covered up by the bellow of surprise from the rock troll, as a column of wood almost three times the size of what it had thrown at me thundered into its chest. There was a loud 'bong' sound as the huge piece of wood vibrated from the hard impact. Then, the qi matrix overloaded from the stress, and the mast exploded.

Once again, I was thrown backward, this time over a dozen yards from the edge of the cliff. The concussive force from all that energy escaping was more than I had expected, meaning it must have already held a large amount of qi before I added my own. If there was another powerful monster or two in the area, they would certainly come and see what all the commotion was about after that little show.

I just laid there on my back for a few minutes, allowing my body to heal. I could only hope the rock troll was as damaged as I had been, because wearing down its internal stores of energy so it couldn't heal itself anymore was going to take some time. I was debating on whether or not to finally go and see how things were progressing down there when my blood suddenly ran cold. That explosion might have exposed my friends!

Jumping to my feet, I ran the dozen yards to see what was going on down below. I let out a sigh of relief as soon as I saw the smooth section of stone that marked my friends' location. Somehow, the thin layer of rock had held. There might be a few cracks running along its surface, but they were still hidden from view.

Another earth-shaking roar came from where the rock troll was trying to get back on its feet, the donut of sandstone around its leg still giving it problems. The regenerative powers inherent to all trolls was in evidence, as it seemed to be perfectly fine. There was a swath of pale-looking stone across most of its front that indicated where it had needed to repair the damage done by the explosion. And if I wasn't mistaken, its aura felt just a tiny bit weaker. I had struck a hard blow, but I had a long way to go.

I wished I had taken the time to make more gravity plates,

but they were very resource-intensive and took weeks to make. There had always seemed to be something more important to do. One of those right now might have made all the difference. I made a promise to myself that I wouldn't be without one or two from now on, just in case I came across something like this again.

It was shaping up to be a long, drawn-out fight, so I needed to play it smart. Right now, I held the high ground, so I might as well take advantage of it. I threw out another of my stone spike traps a few yards away from me and activated it. Twenty spikes the size of my leg shot out of the ground, very reminiscent of the stalactites I had seen in my dream. I ran over and broke them all off at their base, then quickly got to work.

Using a plain stiletto knife, which I strengthened with metal qi, I began scratching runes up and down their lengths. I focused most of the carvings around the sharp stone tips, with a corkscrew-like pattern of runes trailing back toward the thicker base. I made sure to layer all eight elements of qi into the runes, quickly emptying my lower core as I powered them up. I had just finished carving the sixth one when a rock the size of an ale barrel smashed into the edge of the cliff, spraying me with stone shrapnel.

I looked over the side to see the rock troll rip another stone out of the side of the cliff almost directly below me. It was making itself handholds so it could climb up! The troll looked up and saw me, letting loose a growl that I felt rumble in my chest. Ever had a building growl at you? It tended to put your insignificance in such a larger world in perspective. I wasn't a fan.

The troll leaned back and threw the rock it held up at me, this time clipping the edge of the cliff a little low and to my left, causing it to ricochet high into the air. It tumbled back down to earth, creating a small crater in the sand. I guess that meant it was my turn.

Normally in a fight, I used the qi stored in my oversized brain core to adjust my perception of time and give me an edge in battle. This time, I spun the qi in my heart core, increasing the power of my body. I now had more than enough strength to pick up one of the heavy stone spikes without straining. I leaned over the edge to look below me, lined up my shot, and let go. Gravity did the rest for me.

The spike didn't hit it on top of the head like I wanted, instead impacting it on the left shoulder. The runes I had carved activated, blasting the troll into the ground sideways hard enough that it bounced. I only knew it bounced because of the double shockwave it made, almost causing me to lose my balance and fall off the edge of the cliff.

I had carved the same runes used to make a popper, just bigger. And I used more of them. A lot more. If a stone the size of a copper coin could create a fist-sized ball of compressed air, imagine what a stone the size of your leg could do. The answer was, a *lot*.

The intent was for the spike to pierce the troll a little bit before going off, hopefully doing the same kind of damage the sack of poppers had done when they went off underwater. Unfortunately, it didn't look like the spike had sunk in very far when it went off. Otherwise, at a minimum its arm would have been blown off.

As the rock troll made it back to its feet, I could see its healing abilities in full once again. The shoulder had been wrenched almost five feet lower than the right one, but it was quickly moving back into place. I could hear the grinding of stone as the limb finally got back into its proper position, and the troll gave it a few ponderous test swings to make sure it was functioning correctly. The look it gave me made the hair on the back of my neck—that wasn't matted down in my blood—stand on end. I think it was finally starting to take me seriously.

It started swiftly climbing back up the wall, so I ran to grab another popper spike. Pop-spike? Popike? Spike-pop? Spiker? Ah, that's the one. Spiker. Why do I always worry about this kind of thing at the worst possible time?

Anyway, I grabbed the next spiker and ran back to the edge.

The troll was already two-thirds of the way up the wall, so I wasn't as careful about aiming this time. I just heaved it over the side, and hoped for the best. And sometimes, *sometimes*, the gods smile on you.

The rock troll tried to catch the spike as it tumbled past him. It would have missed entirely if he hadn't stuck his three-fingered hand out to grab it. Maybe, in its tiny brain, it wanted to snatch it out of the air and throw it back at me, as a way to get some retribution for the first one I dropped on it. Instead, the closed fist of the troll was blasted into bloody gravel. It just stared at its missing hand for a moment, then let loose a surprisingly high-pitched scream before toppling off the cliff wall and back onto the beach. It was the first time the ground shook and I didn't have an accompanying jolt of fear attached to it.

It laid there on its back, holding its maimed limb against its chest. As it regrew, I was positive this time the heavy aura was less than it had been when I first felt it. Apparently, replacing lost body parts required it to use a good portion of its stored qi.

Not one to look a gift horse in the mouth, I rushed back to grab another spiker. This time I put the completed ones in my storage belt, that way I didn't need to go back and forth to pick them up every time.

I made it back in time to see it struggling to rise on its hands and knees, the beach not giving it the firm footing it was accustomed to when living in the mountains. That, and the thick stone ring still attached to its leg was still giving it fits.

This time I took a second to line up my shot, tossing the spiker a little further from the cliff since the creature wasn't right up against the wall. The contraption hit true, smashing the rock troll back into the beach. It landed right between the shoulder blades, directly on the spine. It didn't blow off any body parts, but the high-pitched scream told me it had still hurt.

My next spiker hit it a little lower, near the small of its back. It must not have been as heavily armored, because it formed a bloody crater when it went off. The rock troll rolled onto its back, waving around its arms in an attempt to protect itself.

This time, when it looked up at me, I saw fear in its eyes. I had hurt it.

When I pulled out my fifth spiker, it started scooting backward down the beach. This time I had to use three qi strands to help me throw it far enough to reach the troll. It tried to swat the spiker away, causing it to once again get slammed back into the sands of the beach, further expanding the crater its fall had caused. It was missing a good portion of its freshly-healed hand and forearm afterward. I watched closely as its healing replaced the lost tissue, rock, and bone. It took much longer than it had the first time.

As I pulled free the sixth and final spiker, the rock troll finally managed to get back on its feet. It glared at me with its fiery eyes, opening its mouth to let loose another roar. I hefted the spiker like I was going to throw it, and the troll abandoned its attempt at intimidation. It turned tail and ran, the shuffling gait enforced on it by the awkward sandstone donut making it almost comical. If it hadn't been a terrifying monster of destruction, I might have even summoned the energy to laugh.

I lowered my last spiker and let out a sigh of relief. Its aura was down to about half of what it had been when we first started fighting, but that was still many times my own power. Beasts and monsters already had several advantages over cultivators, and one that powerful made the retreat a roaring victory. If it had continued to try to kill me, it would have been a race to see if I could keep it off the walls long enough to carve more spikers. And the qi required to make them was no small amount. I had no doubt that on level ground, things might have turned out much differently. As its aura faded away in the distance, I leaned over the edge of the cliff and formed a tube of wind qi aimed at where everyone was hiding.

"Hey, guys! It's okay to come out now!" It only took a few seconds for the false wall to sink into the ground, and everyone to come pouring out onto the beach. They were shouting up at me, but I couldn't make out anything they were saying. "I'll let you guys figure out a way up here! I need to rest!" Someone shouted up something in reply, but I was already headed back to the pile of uncarved stone spikes. Just in case it came back, I wanted more than one spiker at the ready. I sat down on the cold and snowy ground to make some more. It would be a good bit of time before they could all join me anyway, so I might as well be productive while waiting.

If that rock troll wanted to try me again, I planned on being prepared.

CHAPTER EIGHT

Names

I had just finished up the last of the spikers and arranging things in my storage belt when I heard the sounds of a horse clomping on stone. Valerie appeared through the snow, the light of a small fire I had made illuminating her like a shadowy apparition come to visit me in the night. Full dark had fallen while I was waiting, and the temperature was quickly dropping to dangerous levels.

"Are you okay, Jim?" She was looking me up and down with a concerned look on her face. "You are covered in a lot of blood."

"Really?" I looked down at myself and realized just how much damage the troll had done to me. "I'm fine now. My healing talisman did its job."

"You have taken a lot of damage in a very short period of time. I don't care what you say, I want you taking it easy for a little while." She was glaring at me with an arched eyebrow, a tell-tale sign that she would brook no arguments about it. "Even you have limits, and there is no sense in pushing them."

"You won't hear any argument from me, Val." I stood up

and brushed the snow off my pants. "I'm ready to let you guys take over fighting the giant monsters for a while." She laughed like I was joking. I was most definitely not joking.

"What do you think about moving farther inland and setting up a camp?" She hopped down from Scout to warm her hands by the fire. "I found a copse of trees a little farther back that would help break up the wind a bit. Everyone else should reach it by the time you and I get there."

"It sounds good to me. I used up most of my qi making more of the spikers, so warming myself with fire qi isn't an option for much longer. I was about to switch over to a formation plate." I shivered as a gust of wind hit me. "A bigger fire and warm bedroll would help keep the cold at bay. And a hot meal with friends would be even better."

"I haven't had the chance to say it yet, but it's good to see you made it off the ship in one piece, Jim." She looked out over the dark cliff. "The rest of us didn't really talk about it, but losing you would be a disaster. Stopping the *nox* isn't something we can manage without your help." I walked over to put a hand on her shoulder to reassure her, but Scout tried to bite me. Stupid horse.

"You don't need to worry. I'm not that easy to kill." She didn't say anything at first, just got back on her horse.

"We all know that you are holding something back from us. The powers that you use sometimes aren't normal, Jim. All of us can feel how different it is." Valerie finally met my eyes. "You know you can trust us, right? With everything? We only want to help you."

She was talking about my use of dark and light qi. Ever since I started giving them cultivation pills with the two unknown forms of qi contained in them, it had made them stronger than their peers. It had apparently also given them a sensitivity to the elements. Meaning they might be able to tap into them soon. If they didn't do it properly, I had fears it could very possibly hurt them. It looked like I was finally going to have to take the final leap of faith and trust them with the secret.

"When we have some time without prying eyes and ears around, I promise to show you what I know." She gave a sharp nod of agreement and spurred her horse back the way she had come.

I had been avoiding telling them about the two forms of qi not just because trusting people came hard for me after what Ming had done, but also because as soon as they knew it, all four could become targets of the powerful. Most sect and clan leaders would sacrifice their own children for an increase in power, and gaining access to two new types of qi would certainly fit that mold. But she was right. If anything *did* kill me, the four of them would be better off if they could use it. Especially if they intended to keep fighting the *nox*.

The trail she left was easy to follow, and I quickly reached the small grove of trees she had talked about. Both Valerie and Jamila were digging around in the snow, trying to find enough wood to start a fire. I left them to it and moved to the center of the copse, where I pulled out a stone that could put out heat if fed enough qi to power it. It would help warm the area faster, and give whoever was cooking a steady temperature to cook on. I hadn't used it earlier, because once it was hot, moving it was problematic. I poured a vial of liquid qi on it, and activated the runes. The dense snow in the tree limbs above us would help contain the heat, making the night much more bearable. I sat down nearby to cultivate and try to replace some of the qi in my cores.

It was just starting to warm a few degrees when the rest of the group came stumbling in. I hadn't set up any lights yet, considering my use of dark qi allowed me to see as if it were a moonlight night under the dark canopy of the trees. I had noticed that Valerie and Jamila weren't having problems seeing either. The pills must have really been helping them.

"This way, everyone. Get closer so you can warm up." The

sailors stumbled through the dark undergrowth and eventually got seated as close as they could around the stone. It wasn't much longer until a fire was crackling a few feet away, finally providing a modicum of light. I was still doing my best to refill my cores, and my half-spent qi battery, when my friends finally came over and sat down next to me. Chu was the first one to speak up.

"So, are you ever going to tell us how you beat that thing?" He cracked a smile. "We couldn't see much, but it sure sounded like one hell of a battle."

It took the better part of half an hour to recount everything, and I even pulled a spiker out of my belt to show it to everyone. By the time I was finished, the ship's cook was serving food from a large pot sitting on my heating stone. A group of five sailors brought each of us a bowl of the surprisingly tasty stew, followed by the captain. He waited for us to start eating before sitting down across from me.

"We heard you tell the story of what happened with the rock troll. I just wanted you to know that we are all thankful to you, for saving us. Your skill with formations explains why the Auction House holds you in such high esteem. At your age, to be this skilled already, I would make sure to gather ties as well. You have a bright future ahead." I nodded and went back to eating my food. He could certainly think that was the primary reason for my connection to his employers. It had been a long couple of days, and I was too hungry to explain everything that tied me to the Auction House. Instead of getting up and going back to his place next to the fire, he hung around for a bit longer.

"Is there something else, captain?" Donny had finished his food, so he was the first to talk. "Or do you just enjoy our company so much you don't want to leave?"

"My men and I have been talking, and we know when we are in over our heads." He motioned to the area around us. "None of us are the least bit aware of what dangers we face out here, and the nearest village would be over a week away by foot. After what happened today, we know that would be a death sentence." More than a few of the sailors listening in were silently bobbing their heads in agreement. "Now, I know we might have gotten off on the wrong foot here, but—"

"The wrong foot, captain?" I cut him off before he could say anything else. "I don't even know your name. The moment we got onboard your ship—which I didn't knowingly sink, by the way—you have kept us at a distance. Sometimes, it felt like the only reason you didn't throw us all overboard was because we were able to help with your 'teams' while we sailed." He opened his mouth to say something, but I talked right over him. "I'm not saying you can't come with us, but you should know right now that we aren't traveling south. We are going deeper into the mountains."

"Deep-deeper into the mountains?!" He spluttered a bit, struggling to speak. "In winter-year?! Are you crazy?" The murmurs from the crowd behind him told me they felt the same way. "Why in the stars would you do something like that?!"

"For the same reason we started on this expedition. There is something in those mountains pushing the creatures that normally live there deeper into the empire." I pointed back toward the beach. "That rock troll that almost killed us? He probably had three or four mountains as his territory, deep in the northern range. Do you think he left it of his own free will? No. Something chased him out of there. And if we don't stop it, all kinds of beasts will come flooding out of the mountains. They will decimate the empire. Kill hundreds of thousands— maybe millions—of innocent people." I slapped my fist into my open palm. "We intend to stop it, and save all those who are in danger."

"That sounds like a job for the Elemental Guard, or maybe even the Emperor's Enforcers!" One of the sailors near the fire was on his feet, his eyes widened in fear. "What can you five do about something like that?!"

Chu answered for me. "Do you see the Elemental Guard?

Last I heard, they haven't left the Imperial City in over a decade. We have been all over the Southern and Western Provinces over the past few years, and I haven't seen even one. And from what I've seen, the Enforcers normally travel in teams smaller than ten cultivators. They don't ever announce their presence, either, unless they are serving as an executioner for a magistrate. That's just common knowledge. How would you find them? And would they even listen to you if you did? Most of you wouldn't believe someone if they told you they had seen a rock troll this far south before winter-year even started getting truly cold." He gave everyone a long, slow stare. "You could even help us. It might be *your* family, *your* loved ones, that those beasts kill when they come out of the mountains. Will you show the courage necessary to stand up and fight? Or will you run and hide, like cowards?"

I decided to cut in, before he could insult their mothers or something. "We are the only people in a position to stop this, so stopping it is what we are going to do. You can try to make your own way south, or you can come north, with us. Neither option is safe, but at least going with us, you might make it to one of the Northern Border Forts. That's our next stop, after the end of our mission."

Silence was our only answer. The captain stood, turning around to look at his men. He spoke over his shoulder to us, refusing to look us in the eye. "My men and I need to talk things over. Please, give us a few moments."

"That's fine." I stood as well. "You have until morning to decide. The five of us will stand first watch, while you figure out what you want to do." I walked over and deactivated the heating function on the cooking stone. It was still hot, so I used the small storage ring on my finger to put it away instead of picking it up and putting it in my belt, then healed the burns it caused. I didn't want them running away with it while we were out of sight. "Next shift is in three hours. Don't be late with our relief."

We spread out through the trees, each of us taking an equal

area of ground to cover. Near the edge of the copse, the snow was still falling heavily. The wind had picked up again, forming deep drifts along the tree line. As I climbed a tree to get a better viewpoint, I could hear the faint shouts of the crew arguing about what to do next. Just as I got settled, I realized something.

I still didn't know the captain's name. What a jerk.

CHAPTER NINE

Competition

Our relief was thirty minutes late. Not long enough to reasonably get upset about, but certainly long enough to let us know they didn't care about keeping things fair between us. That was fine. It let us know exactly where we stood in their eyes. Even though we had just saved their lives, they still didn't want to show us respect. It also told me they were planning to go south, while we went north. That suited us just fine. Figuring out a way to feed all of these people would have been a nightmare underground anyway.

The five of us huddled up during the night next to the horses, my heating stone keeping all of us warm enough that we didn't have a problem sleeping the rest of the night through. I was awakened by the sound of hushed whispers not far away from where we were sleeping.

"I think it's only fair. We let them keep the supplies they took on the beach, and we take the horses. It isn't like they are going to need them where they are going. We would practically be doing them a favor."

"I don't know. Didn't you hear the youngest one fighting

against that giant? Trying to force them into anything seems like a bad idea to me."

"That was some unthinking beast. We are smarter than a monster that spent its whole life up in the mountains, hiding from cultivators that actually know how to fight. Why, I bet I could beat any of those brats in a straight-up fight any day of the week."

I honestly wasn't sure what was more wrong in that last statement. That he could beat one of us, or that he was smarter than the rock troll. Either way, rock trolls everywhere should feel insulted.

Not willing to listen to any more of their nonsense, I sat up and looked straight at them. I also started running a thread of earth qi out of the meridian in the small of my back, just barely under the surface of the snow. One of them blanched when he saw I was awake, and took a step backward. The other lifted the corner of his mouth in a sneer.

"Good morning, you lazy bums. We were about to start taking bets on how long it was going to take you to wake up!" His sneer turned up a notch. "When you are ready, the captain would like to discuss some things with you five. He's waiting by the fire."

"How about this?" I snapped the thread of qi up around his ankle, tightening it enough that he wouldn't be able to slip free, but loose enough that he couldn't feel it through his clothing. "You go and let your captain know that you won't be taking our horses. In fact, you won't be taking anything from us. I can already guess what your plans are, and that suits us fine. You all just go right on ahead and leave. I'll be sure to leave a message with the Auction House about how great our pleasure cruise was when we get to the nearest fort."

He took a step forward, raising a fist in a threatening manner. "You better watch that smart mouth, before I—"

I yanked on the thread, dumping him on his back as I got to my feet. "Before you what, bleed on me? I could rip you to shreds without even trying. Now go do as I say. And make sure you and the rest of your crew are gone by the time I finish my breakfast. I don't enjoy the company of cowards." He tried to splutter out a reply, but I pulled out a spiker and set it base-down on the ground between my feet and leaned on it. That shut him up quickly. "I meant now."

He scrambled back to his feet and took off, his friend right on his heels. I didn't bother listening in on what they actually said to the captain, but by the quick flare of his aura I could tell he wasn't happy. I didn't care. Dealing with these people was getting on my nerves, and I needed to find an entrance to the caverns where the necromancer was building his forces. Taking a closer look at the area around us, it almost seemed darker than normal as well, like it was tainted with something. Or the sun just wasn't as welcome in this region. Maybe it was just exhaustion.

Ever since I saw the undead sentry while dream walking, I had felt a sense of time running out, like the future of the empire was teetering on the brink of destruction. Whatever was different about this death cultivator than any of the others I had come across in the past, it put everything in danger. I only had to figure out what it was, before it killed us all.

My friends and I collected our things and took a few minutes to sort what we had in our storage devices. We had a lot of food from the ship, along with our own food stores. The horses would be able to eat for months off of what we had spread between us, and if we absolutely *had* to, I could make some alchemy concoctions with what I had in my belt that would give us all the nutrients required to survive. I didn't like doing that, because you still *felt* hungry, even if your body didn't actually need any food. It tended to make people a little grumpy.

By the time we had everything sorted, the captain and his crew were already gone. I was surprised there hadn't been another confrontation. It had been an up-and-down experience with them. One minute I thought we were friends, and the next they were planning on taking our horses. I guess saving them from the rock troll had made them abandon ideas of a 'trial' for sinking their ship on accident, but not going to the south with them had strained our relationship too far.

I couldn't help but wonder if the captain was one of those people that seemed to have uncontrollable waves of emotion, where they were perfectly happy one moment, and incredibly angry or sad the next. I had dealt with people like that many times before, and it had seldom gone well. It was almost like their brains didn't work like everyone else's. I had been accused of having my own mental problems from time to time, so it was never a good thing when someone like me mixed with a person dealing with uncontrolled waves of emotions. It usually led to unnecessary fighting, and all kinds of internal strife. Like I said, dealing with them was exhausting.

Since we now had the copse of trees to ourselves, we sat around the remains of the fire and ate a quick breakfast. It quickly turned into a planning meeting, led by Chu.

"Okay everyone. Since we looked at what food we have, I think our biggest problem is fresh meat." Chu was our cook most of the time, so none of us were willing to argue. "I think we should all spread out as we move north, to increase our chances of getting some wild game."

"Yes!" Valerie pumped her fist. "I love hunting! I've got two gold that says I get more meat for the cookpot than the rest of you combined."

"I'll take that bet." Jamila rolled a shuriken across her knuckles. "You aren't the only one that can sneak up on something."

I couldn't help but smile. Two gold was nothing to them after the adventures we had been through, not even counting the coin each of us had made trading across the Southern Province. The fun of the competition was what drove them. It was also what helped push them further through their cultivation. The need to keep up with one another made all of them train their hardest, and focus on their qi manipulation more than any sect or clan I had ever come across in all my years. That, and knowing the fate of the world might depend on your actions. It was a pretty solid motivator.

"Jim, are you in?" Donny broke me out of my thoughts with a tap on the shoulder. "Do you think you can get the most meat?"

I gave him a grin. "Oh, for sure. Let's do this." I got to my feet, cycling my qi to stretch my core walls a bit. "But let's make sure we don't get too spread out. It's still dangerous to be running around by ourselves. That rock troll is still running around somewhere." Everyone agreed, and we got moving.

The farther we traveled north, the denser the trees became. We started off spread out in a line far enough apart that we could barely see each other. As the scattered clusters of trees got closer together, and the open rocky regions gradually grew into large trees with needle-like leaves, our separation from one another slowly turned into only a few hundred yards between the people at the farthest points.

Each of us had taken down several animals, mostly rabbits, and one large buck felled by Valerie. Chu was the only exception. His weapon for long-distance attacks was a blowgun, which wasn't the best choice for something like this. The darts I had made for it were intended to punch through qi shields, not take down small game animals. He was grumbling about how unfair it was when our competition was suddenly put on hold.

We were near a large boulder at the edge of a small clearing, when Valerie held up her hand to stop. "Does anybody else hear that?" Everyone stopped to listen, and even the horses following close behind us held still to try and hear what had piqued our interest.

At first, I didn't notice anything. Then I started to feel the ground trembling, and there were faint shouts coming from the south. All of us looked at one another. Whatever it was, it didn't sound good. And it was headed straight for our location.

"I'll get the horses behind the rock, and try to form some shelter for them. Jamila, Valerie, find a good place in the trees to set up an ambush." They immediately split up and went in opposite directions. "Donny and Chu, you can get on top of the rock to draw whatever this is out in the open. If there is time, I will join you." They started scrambling up the rock, both of them swapping out their long-range weapons for their shields and a pair of spears.

The horses seemed to understand the situation and followed me without prompting. Sometimes, it scared me how smart they seemed to be. I had even checked to make sure they weren't possessed by a *nox* at one point, but they were just exceedingly intelligent creatures. I used some earth qi to form two walls from the rock, extending them out far enough to provide cover from the sides. I felt Donny shaping a roof that connected the two, and both him and Chu moved to stand on it. The flat surface would give them much better footing. I didn't close in the rear portion of the makeshift enclosure, just in case we needed to run.

I spun up my heart core to help me jump the thirty feet to the roof, using just enough qi to enhance my body for the leap. Donny and Chu made room for me in the center, so I got in position, pulling out my silver bow and nocking an arrow. The ground was rumbling steadily now, and the shouts were getting close enough that I could almost make out what they were saying. Finally, it clicked in my brain. I knew what we were facing. Before I could say anything, I heard Jamila shout from a treetop that was a bit higher than its neighbors.

"Stampede!" The girls came tumbling out of the trees on either side of the clearing, and took off at a dead sprint toward the horses. Both of them had a wild look in their eyes. Whatever they had seen must be pretty bad to scare the two of them like that.

The three of us on the rock turned and jumped, the thirty foot drop well within our ability to handle. I backed up into the recently created alcove beside my friends, who had already put their shields away and were doing their best to extend the walls enough to fit all of us. Before they could do more than add another foot or two, the sounds of breaking branches and shattering trees started to reach our ears. Valerie and Jamila reached us at nearly the same time, and I could tell they were worried.

"There has to be thousands of them! We need to fortify this as much as we can, or they will turn us into paste!" Valerie was shouting to be heard over the sound of the approaching creatures. Jamila just nodded in agreement, so all five of us got to work, throwing around earth qi with zero regard to conserving any energy in our cores. In less than a minute, the large rock had nearly doubled in size. Instead of being a normal boulder, we were now hunkered down behind something that looked like a giant stone cone lying on its side. Almost as if an ancient tower had fallen over, and the roof was all that remained. We were still trying to deepen the area we were hunkered down in when a familiar face flashed by the clearing. They let out a shout of surprise, and turned to run inside our enclosure. It was the captain. A few seconds later, most of his crew were trying to crowd in with us as well.

"Thank the stars!" I could barely hear him shouting over the rumble of the approaching stampede, but the sudden influx of people meant we were shoved tightly against one another. He was practically standing on my toes. "I wasn't sure how much longer we could have kept running! We already lost some of the weaker members of the crew to those things!" I was jostled to the side before I could ask what had happened.

The ship's crew were still trying to force their way into our alcove when the stampede hit. Two of the sailors near the edge were swept away, their panicked screams barely audible over the sound of thousands of hooves pounding against the ground. They died rough.

I finally got a look at the creatures, which were something I had only seen once before. They were called Angry Murder Goats, and rare would be an understatement. At less than one hundred pounds and usually shorter than waist height, a single goat was never an issue. The problem was, there was never just one. Angry Murder Goats traveled in packs. I don't know why I know this, but a pack of goats is called a 'trip.' A trip of goats was about to kill us all. We were taking a trip straight to hell. This trip was never in our plans. A trip like this could only end poorly. Why does my brain work this way?

The goats had four curved horns, with four eyes to match. Their coarse hair was a dark blue, with sharp black hooves that were just as dangerous as their horns. Individually, they were ranked at either basic or common level beasts, nowhere near as threatening as something like a Sky Raven or Red Spring Wolf, but when there were hundreds, maybe thousands, you had to raise their threat level quite a bit.

Since I was right at the edge of the rocky outcropping, I was able to lean out just far enough to see how much trouble we were in. There were definitely thousands of them, with no end to their numbers visible through the trees. That explained why the ground was shaking so much. Their combined mass was creating an actual earthquake, causing Scout and Cloud to whinny in fear.

The stampede parted around the cone-shaped rock for the most part, with only a few of the smaller goats able to run up the rounded sides. They were passing by swiftly, the Murder Goats in back not able to see there was no one to chase anymore, so the momentum continued forward. I was about to lean back into the safe confines of our crowded alcove, when I felt someone shove me from behind, straight into the flow of the Angry Murder Goats.

I had been tripped into the trip.

With jokes like that, maybe I deserved it.

CHAPTER TEN

Rematch

I was instantly rammed in the gut by a blue goat. Instead of going under its hooves and being trampled to death by the goats following behind, I held on to its horns and let it carry me for several yards. My weight was too much for it to hold up for long, so as it started to topple, I cast a thread of wind qi into the surrounding trees to pull myself off the ground. I managed to snag a low-hanging branch just past the edge of the clearing, and ended up dangling just a few feet over the passing horns of the Angry Murder Goats running beneath me.

The forest was suffering from the occasional goat that wasn't good at dodging, their hard impacts knocking loose chunks of bark and wood from the bases of the trees. Hanging here was definitely not a safe long-term option.

Not only that, but the four-eyed creatures could see me dangling from the branch, and tried to treat me like a children's birthday celebration toy, jumping up and slamming into me to see if any candy would come out. Their hard horns weren't damaging my Saint-level body very much, but it would start to add up if I couldn't get somewhere safe. A particularly large

Murder Goat managed to crack a horn against my knee, causing me to grimace in pain. It spurred me into action. I pulled myself up onto the branch, and used another qi strand to swing into a neighboring tree.

I made my way back to the edge of the clearing, a little behind and to the side of our rock formation. I could barely see into the alcove, where everyone was still huddled in a cluster, waiting for the stampede to end. I wasn't able to see who had shoved me, and the lack of violence meant my friends probably hadn't even seen it happen.

Considering the trees were all in really rough shape by this point, I finished circling the clearing so I could make the leap onto the side of our cone. The goats might see me sitting up there, but they would mostly be forced to move forward by the momentum of the rest of their trip. I made sure to prepare a shield formation plate in case I was wrong about them not making it up the side, and jumped.

I had to scramble a bit to make sure I didn't slip off, but after some frantic arm-waving, I managed to stick the landing. By now, the stampede was starting to feel less dense, and the ground wasn't shaking nearly as much. I was just about to sit down to focus on healing my injured knee when I heard a familiar roar in the distance. It was the stars-damned rock troll.

The last time I had faced it, I had the advantage of the cliff height to keep me out of easy reach. There was no such advantage now. This rock would only reach to about its chest, meaning I was incredibly screwed. I needed to prepare the battlefield now, before it got here, if I was going to even have a chance to survive this.

Reaching into my storage belt, I pulled free all the stone spike traps I had left. I threw them out in an arc in front of me, creating a hedge of three- to five-foot spikes to keep the troll from rushing me head-on. It also had the happy effect of killing dozens of Angry Murder Goats. Those crazy little kill-happy bastards deserved it.

Next, I fished out my Dagger of Boom. It could hold qi attacks in a storage matrix, and release the pent-up energy all at once. I started emptying one of the qi batteries on my belt into it. My hope was I could use it to stab the troll in the head, killing it instantly. At the minimum, I was pretty sure it would at least hurt the creature enough to start the process of forcing it to use up its qi, slowing down the dangerously-fast healing process.

I made sure all my remaining quicksand traps and spikers were easily accessible in my belt before finding my last trick. I had thought about what I could have done better in the last battle, and this was one of the things I had come up with. It was a gray substance, held in a small glass vial. I only had three of them, and I hoped they wouldn't be necessary. It was an alchemical solution I called 'stick-um,' and it was a type of sticky foam that expanded rapidly upon contact with air, before hardening into a material that was reminiscent of sandstone. If worse came to worst, I would use it to slow the creature down long enough that we could all get away. Well, my friends and I could escape. The rest of them weren't going anywhere until I knew who pushed me into the stampede of goats.

Wow. Never thought I would need to find the answer to that question. My life was weird.

The goats eventually started to taper off. The stampede had felt like it had gone on for hours, but it was probably closer to ten minutes from start to finish. There were still an incredible number of goats running around, and I had no idea why they were down here instead of up in the high mountains where they belonged. Maybe they followed the rock troll out of the region for the same reason. What else was the necromancer pushing down into the empire? And how was he even powerful enough to threaten robust, powerful creatures? I had a sinking feeling I would be dealing with the repercussions from the situation for a long time to come.

In the distance, I heard the unmistakable roar of the rock

troll again. Judging by the way its footsteps were shaking the ground, it would reach the edge of the clearing within a few moments. The already-weakened trees were swaying with every footstep, making it seem as if I was in the middle of a storm. The footsteps paused just before it came into sight. It must have sensed I was waiting for it. The troll let loose a roar—big surprise—and came stomping toward me.

That was when I remembered I had forgotten something. I hadn't bothered to let anyone hiding know that I was up here, and I had prepared some defenses to help.

"Gods, no! It found us again!" The shout came from a sailor that had peeked around the edge of the stone wall and caught a glimpse of the creature. "We need to get out of here, before it kills us all!" They came stumbling out of the alcove and took off running in a gaggle. A few of their braver members paused to fire a few qi attacks before sprinting to catch up to their friends.

My favorite qi construct came from a rather burly, barrel-chested sailor. He had paused at the far edge of the clearing, opposite where the troll and I were standing. Raising two hands above his head and interlocking his thumbs, he used a mixture of fire, air, and metal qi to form what looked like a dozen palm-sized butterflies. As they launched toward the rock troll, he shouted out the name of his attack at the top of his lungs.

"Kiss of the Butterfly Sting!"

Everyone stopped to watch as the fast-moving attack slammed into the chest of the rock troll. The qi constructs broke apart in a colorful burst of light, doing absolutely zero damage to the monster. I wasn't the least bit surprised. I mean, come on. Butterflies don't have stingers. Or lips, for that matter.

It did accomplish the task of redirecting the ire of the rock troll. Instead of focusing on me, it let loose another roar and started taking its ground-churning strides toward the sailors fleeing across the clearing. They were all running as fast as their legs could carry them, but for one man it wasn't enough. The troll grabbed a fallen tree branch that was thicker than my leg, and hurled it at his retreating back like a spear. The impact made the man disappear into the undergrowth, causing me to lose sight of him. I was glad. I really didn't want to see what he looked like after that.

The rock troll stepped around the arc of spikes I had laid out and kept chasing the ship's crew. I decided to do nothing to stop it. Considering one of their number had just tried to kill me, I wasn't feeling particularly well-inclined toward them at the moment. Which, of course, is when Chu and Donny rushed out of the alcove to fight.

Donny had his tower shield and axe at the ready, but it was Chu that really got its attention. His mace was heavy, and I had intended it to be used on something just like the massive creature he was facing when I made it for him. That was probably why, when he sprinted to catch up to the troll and slammed it into the rock troll's heel, it certainly changed the focus of its ire once again.

Chu's downward blow landed hard enough to make the stone skin shatter, and the bladed mace head cut deep into the flesh underneath. It stumbled forward, dropping to one knee and making the already weakened trees groan with the sudden earthquake they were subjected to. By the time it got back on two feet, the injury was already healed. The troll turned back around, and had to nearly put its oversized chin to its chest to look down on my two friends. It let loose a growl that caused both Donny and Chu to take an unconscious step backward. Yep, they definitely made it mad.

"Don't just stand there! Run!" The shout from Valerie made everything seem to happen all at once. Both of the girls had exited the alcove already on horseback, and they swung wide along either side of the clearing in an attempt to flank the monster. Chu dove between the creature's legs, narrowly missing a downward swipe from its massive fist, and sprinted the same direction the sailors had gone. Donny, unfortunately, tried to move back toward the alcove instead of running for the cover of the trees. It isolated him in open space, with only his shield as cover.

As I said before, rock trolls have a limited intellect, making them more dangerous than a beast that would fight on instinct alone. It was certainly smart enough to recognize the girls as a pointless distraction it would never be able to catch while they were riding horses. Even a well-placed arrow from Valerie that hit it in the back of the knee didn't cause the troll to lose focus. Donny was the only viable target at the moment, so that was exactly who it went for. One deceptively-quick shuffling step and the troll punted poor Donny like he was a child's toy.

I felt Donny use a massive amount of qi the moment before impact, but he was sent flying before I could see what he had done. The kick sent him sailing back between the trees, smashing through the already-damaged trunks of several before he came to a rolling stop. His shield had been bent almost in half, clamping around the troll's foot in a weird misshapen lump.

The troll moved to follow, but an enraged Valerie had already jumped off of Scout and was somehow climbing the side of the creature like an angry spider monkey. Which, of course, made it impossible for me to attack with a spiker, otherwise I would risk hurting her. Scout—the crazy horse that he was—had followed right behind her, fearlessly rearing up and slamming his enchanted hooves straight into the troll's backside.

Those enchanted horseshoes must have had some kind of offensive runes carved into them, because that was the only way to explain how much damage he managed to do. The insane equine managed to knock an impressive chunk of rock from the troll's butt, sending it stumbling forward in surprise.

It served as enough of a distraction that Valerie was able to make it all the way up to its shoulder. She somehow managed to pull a spear from a storage device, and rammed it directly into the rock troll's closest eye. The attack meant Scout got to live, but Valerie took a solid slap from the creature in return.

The blow sent her flying in the same general direction that Donny had been kicked. She was lucky enough not to hit a tree or three like Donny. Still, it must have hurt just as much when she hit the ground with bone-jarring force. A lesser pair of culti-vators most likely would have been killed instantly. If we hadn't spent so much time focusing on reinforcing our bodies with qi, they certainly would have been.

I saw Chu already making his way through the trees toward their downed forms, his instincts as an amateur healer sending him to their aid. Jamila was throwing glowing shuriken at the troll to distract it, but they weren't doing much against its rocky skin. This battle was proof that we needed to work more on how to take down single enemies that were much larger than us, because none of this was working well. Luckily, it was plenty distracted by the six-foot spear sticking out of its eye anyway. I mean, as far as distractions go, it was a pretty good one.

The eye was healed only a second or two after it plucked the spear free, but the troll still rubbed at it as if struggling to see. It took a step toward Jamila to end her annoying flurry of throwing stars, but the clanking sound of metal on stone caused it to pause. The shield still wrapped around its foot was stuck, so it bent down to pull it off. I saw the opening I was waiting for.

Pulling out three spikers from my storage belt, I spun the qi in my cores as hard as I could. Instead of using thread wrapped around the spikers to throw them, I just held them in tube-shaped constructs I formed in front of me just long enough to aim before slamming a wave of wind qi into them, launching the stone spikes like bolts from a crossbow. The troll was bent over, so he didn't even see them coming.

All three struck at the same time, hitting the monster in the head and shoulders. It was blown backward by the impact, flip-ping through the air head-over-heels, spraying gravel and blood in an arc that reached higher than the treetops. I felt a moment of strong vindication as it took its own turn being thrown through several trees, its rolling tumble sending it through a dozen conifers before crashing to a halt. I jumped down from my perch before it could get back to its feet and ran over to where Jamila was trying to grab Scout's reins.

"Jamila!" Her head snapped around to look at me. "Get the

others out of here! Head straight north toward the mountains, and get inside the first cave opening you see!" I pointed to the sun that was moving steadily closer to the horizon. "I am going to lead it west, back toward the coastline. Make sure you leave me an easy trail to find, in case I can't kill this thing. It won't be able to follow us through the tight confines of a cave." Jamila gave me a sharp nod in return.

"We'll find something." She glanced at the mountains in the distance. "It'll be close to dark by the time we reach the foothills, so I will have to use glow stones to mark our trail. Don't waste too much time catching up. By the—"

She was cut off by a tree sailing over our heads, raining its green needles down on us. When I said tree, I don't mean a little one you might see around the fringes of a village. I mean a *tree*. Like the kind you use as a mainmast on a merchant ship, or the central supporting pillar in a really nice house. It crashed into the rock formation we had built for cover from the stampede, shattering one side of the alcove everyone had used to hide. We both spun to see the troll—already healed—struggling to pick up a second tree, this time choosing one a little bit smaller. If it had just used a tree it could handle easily, the troll would have probably been able to hit us. Which would not have been fun. I shouldn't have taken my eyes off the stars-damned creature, but getting my friends to safety had been higher on my priority list.

Jamila, not a stranger to dangerous moments like this, had already spurred Cloud toward the rest of my friends with Scout following close behind. I had faith in her to lead them to safety. While she wasn't as good of a scout and pathfinder as Valerie, she was a very close second. She could be a force of nature when provoked, and may the gods help anyone that got in her way. All four would be fine.

Now that they were out of the line of fire, I needed to make sure the rock troll stayed focused on me. It had just managed to get the tree lifted over its head, so I took that as the perfect opportunity to launch another spiker at it. This time my aim was a little off, hitting it in the abdomen instead of the face. The blow still made it drop the tree right on its own head, causing the troll to fall forward onto its chest.

I was down to eleven spikers, and the energy coming from the monster told me it wasn't even down a third of its internal qi. Last time it had only taken five spikers to bring it to half. Had it grown stronger in the short amount of time between our fights? If that was the case, I might be in trouble. Stronger meant faster, and faster meant running away wasn't going to be easy. I needed to hurry.

While the troll was struggling back to its feet, I ran over to the arc of spikes I had formed in preparation for the fight. I started snapping off the spikes and dumping them into my storage belt as fast as I could, goats and all. I might need to carve more spikers on the run, and I probably wouldn't have the time to form more if that was the case.

I had just finished breaking off the last stone spike when I sensed another heavy aura moving straight for us. Had we attracted another powerful monster with our fighting? I stored the spike—and its accompanying three impaled goats—in my belt, and turned to face the creature on the other side of the clearing. The rock troll had made it back to its feet, and it looked mad. The approaching aura didn't seem to worry it in the least. Instead, it leaned back to let out another roar in a challenge to whatever was closing in on the small forest clearing.

That was when I finally realized my mistake. The approaching creature let out a roar in reply, and it sounded almost exactly like the rock troll I was currently facing. It stared at me with a smug look on its rocky features, but that might have just been my imagination. It hadn't been a roar of challenge. It had been a message to another rock troll, letting it know where it was located. The troll I had just fought didn't have a sandstone donut around its ankle. I was dealing with two of them, which explained why this one wasn't going down as easily as it should have, especially given the damage from my last fight. Just my luck, a mating pair of extremely powerful rock trolls.

I took a deep breath, and let it out slowly. This was going to be a tough one. I felt the corners of my lips turn up in a small smile. On the bright side, all the goats I had just put in my belt meant I had won our competition for who collected the most meat. Valerie was going to be pissed.

CHAPTER ELEVEN

Run

I spun up my cores again and sprinted to the edge of the clearing, heading straight for the troll. It hadn't expected the move, so it was slow to react. Dodging the swinging arm required me to dive into a forward roll, but I managed to pop back up to my feet and pass right by its side. I dropped a quicksand trap as I ran out of its reach, and activated it with a thread of qi just as it got in range.

In a strange twist of fate, it stepped into the quicksand with the same foot that still had Donny's shield wrapped around the end of it. I deactivated the trap before it could lift its foot back out, meaning it was a smaller circle of stone than I would have preferred. It hadn't had time to fully form its normal ten-foot circle, instead leaving it stuck in a ring of stone only about four feet around. The troll jerked its foot up from the ground, once again bringing the newly-formed sandstone with it.

This time, it wasn't centered on the foot. It was just on the edge of the ring, making it seem like the troll had one giant foot, and one regular-sized appendage. I couldn't help but laugh at how ridiculous the thing looked. The troll heard me, and it wasn't very happy about it. It stumbled after me, forcing me to turn and sprint away.

The current terrain definitely favored the trolls. While I had to run between and around trees and heavy undergrowth, they could just take their giant strides straight for me. Only the biggest of trees forced them to adjust their pursuit. That was why I was headed for more open ground near the coast. It would even the playing field a bit.

I hadn't seen the other troll yet, but I could feel the ground shaking harder as it quickly closed in on me. Since I was headed west, it had the chance to get an angle on me and close the gap between us faster. I started using my internal qi to boost my speed with my heart core, burning precious energy to make sure it couldn't get in front of me.

My friends' auras faded as we moved farther away, meaning at least one part of my plan was working. The trolls were entirely focused on me, and they were safe for the time being. Now, to just figure out how to get back to them, sans giant and angry monsters.

Keeping in front of the troll that was tearing through the forest behind me was proving difficult. If it hadn't been for the sandstone boot I had given it, I might have been in for a world of hurt. It slowed the troll down just enough to give me a chance.

As it currently stood, I would run out of internal qi before sunset, and then I would have to depend on the energy stored in my belt. I had already used one of the two batteries to charge the Dagger of Boom, meaning I had the equivalent of the energy stores of a single Low Saint cultivator. It wasn't exactly terrible, but I was dealing with two creatures that were each at the power of a Duke, two full levels above my current cultivation rank. Basically, I needed to end this before I ran out of internal qi, or I was as good as dead.

Well, maybe not dead, but I would be forced to use either light or dark qi to kill the creatures. That was still an absolute last resort. I was getting closer to the necromancer, and it could obviously use at least dark qi, meaning it might be able to sense it if I used some. I didn't want to give it the warning that I was on my way if I could avoid it.

The second troll finally caught up with us about five minutes later. It had gotten used to moving around with a giant sandstone donut wrapped around its ankle, so it wasn't slowed nearly as much as I would have liked. At least I got a little bit of good news. Its aura wasn't as strong as it was during our first fight, which meant it hadn't been able to fully recover from the damage I had inflicted.

I decided to spend some precious qi to form two more qi threads. Whipping them up into the tree branches in front of me, I catapulted myself high into the air. I needed to get a better look at the terrain, and try to see how far I was from the coast.

As I cleared the top of the trees, I saw that I hadn't been going as directly west as I would have liked. I had been drifting more northwest, meaning I was farther away from the edge of the forest than I thought. I did, however, see something almost as good. There was a cut through the forest almost directly north from my current location that ran east to west, which I took to be either a river or canyon of some kind. Either way, it might give me a chance to change up the current dynamic.

There were also some ominous-looking clouds moving down from the mountains, meaning we were in for another snowstorm. This one looked like it was going to be much worse than what had moved through the area yesterday. It almost made me wish I hadn't broken the weather-controlling table the Southern King used to shape his District. Knowing the region well from my first life, I expected this storm was likely to drop several feet of snow in a short period of time. Finding the cave my friends were hiding in would be nearly impossible. If I couldn't find them before it blanketed the area in snow, it might take me weeks of searching to figure out where they had gone. I didn't have time to see anything else before gravity brought me back down to the ground. I used a thick tree branch as a springboard as I fell, throwing myself toward the north and gaining some breathing room between the monsters and I.

The two trolls, who I decided to call Donut and Boot to make things easier for me, were not expecting my maneuver. They came to a skidding halt, taking out a few trees in the process. Donut was able to get back up to speed first, with Boot trailing a little farther behind. Now that I had about fifty yards between Donut and I, the option to use trap plates was back on the table.

I first tried dropping another quicksand trap, but we were moving too fast through the forest for it to work. Donut managed to clear the trap before it could finish forming, and the gap between him and Boot meant that it had already hardened by the time it got there. I tried a few wind blade traps, but the trolls didn't even seem to notice when they got hit by them. Finally, I just decided to throw a spiker at Donut and see if it could dodge.

As I pulled one out, I heard Boot give a roaring shout of warning to Donut. Both of them started trying to keep at least a tree or two between us, making it impossible to hit them. They fell back another ten yards or so, but they spread out more to either side so I couldn't run away. Stupid trolls and their even stupider brains! Too dumb to give up on the chase, but too clever to let me kill them quickly. Ugh, so frustrating!

I was at a little more than half of my core capacity by the time I reached the canyon. It had a small swift-running stream at the base, with the sides dropping down at least forty feet to the bottom. The gap was well over one hundred feet from one side to the other, meaning it was a little too far for me to jump across with just some qi enhancement from my heart core. The trees grew right up to the edge of the canyon on both sides, with plenty of exposed roots poking through the dirt and stone walls. I could work with this.

Boot was the first to catch up to me, since Donut had swung out a little wider. It just stood there, slightly hunched over so it could dodge if I threw the spiker still held aloft by a strand of air qi. I was okay with that. I used the time it was giving me to run a few strands of wood qi from the meridians in my feet underground. I activated the shield function of my spirit wood ring so the troll couldn't see me pull out a vial of stick-um from my belt. The shield was pretty useless for blocking a blow from something the size of a house, but I didn't want Boot to warn Donut that I had another trick up my sleeve.

When Donut made it to the clearing, I ran out of time. It charged straight at me, arms spread wide to keep me from getting away. Boot started closing in from the left, just a half-step behind. Instead of trying to run between the two, I jumped backward off the edge of the canyon as I tossed the spiker into the air in front of me. The wood qi I had infused into the roots of the trees poking through the side caught me in a secure net, and then pulled me against the wall as the spiker hit the ground.

I hadn't been this close to one of them going off before, so I had underestimated just how powerful they really were. It shook the whole side of the canyon, and a rain of dirt and stones fell on my head. The confused roars of Donut and Boot were exactly what I was hoping for though, and when they peeked over the edge of the canyon to see what had happened to me, I couldn't hold in the smile that crept across my face.

Tree roots rose from the ground, wrapping up the two rock trolls and slamming them together. They were too heavy to throw over the edge, and the drain on the qi in my cores was extreme. It was worth it. Their chests and heads were shoved together, and I used another thread of qi to lift the vial of stick-um right in front of their faces. A quick flex of willpower crushed the glass vial, and the substance splashed over them.

Stick-um was very fast-acting, and in less than two seconds their heads and chests were liberally coated in expanding foam. Two more seconds, and it started to harden. Their prodigious strength meant they were able to break free of the branches, but the damage was already done. It hardened into a gray rock-like substance, locking the two monsters into a permanent embrace. They stumbled away from the edge of the canyon, and I could hear the sounds of them struggling against one another.

I pulled myself back up onto the ground, and made my way over to where they were trying to pull themselves apart. Since they were so close, they couldn't get enough leverage to break free. Now Donut and Boot looked like a two-headed, eight-limbed monster only a demented god from one of the darker planes of existence could imagine. Their combined mass was too heavy for me to even attempt to move, so I used the qi from my last battery to start shifting the earth at their feet toward the cliff edge.

Both of them felt the shift, and their struggles only increased. Donut tried to run left, and Boot tried to run straight so it could continue to attack me. All they managed to do was help me move them closer to the edge. I think Boot must have been the smarter of the two, because it seemed to understand what I was trying to do. It started smashing its fist down on top of Donut's head over and over again in an attempt to break itself free. Donut didn't appreciate that very much. It started to return the favor, and they completely forgot I was slowly shifting them toward the edge of a cliff.

I reminded them I was still around when I launched two spikers into their ribs, blowing them off the cliff and into the canyon. I ran over to check what had happened to them, and when I looked over the side, I could see them wedged up against some rocks a few dozen yards downstream, laying on their sides. The canyon wasn't deep enough for the drop to kill them, obviously, but it was certainly enough to trap them. For a little while, at least. As I watched, the water from the stream was already starting to build up against them, as if they were a rather unnatural dam. They were still struggling to stand, but I think the water, mud, and slick stones were making it difficult for the trolls. In a few minutes, I would find out if trolls could drown, or if their healing worked on that as well.

Unfortunately, with the storm moving in, I didn't have time to rest and watch the show. I was low on qi, I didn't know where my friends were, and everything was about to be buried under several feet of snow. Why did it feel like I had just lost, even though I was the only one still standing?

CHAPTER TWELVE

Bonfires

While it would have been nice to stay and watch to see what happened with the trolls, I needed to get moving. I jumped across the canyon with a helpful boost from the tree roots throwing me across, landing on the opposite ledge. Then, I climbed to the top of the highest tree in the immediate area to get a better idea of where to go next.

Looking around, I saw the most likely direction my friends went. There was an almost arrow-straight path leading north that the Murder Goats had made, which would make travel for them much easier while on horseback. I started heading that direction at an angle which allowed me to intersect with them quickly, doing my best to refill the qi batteries on the belt as I ran. I could have filled my own cores first, but I wanted to make sure I had the batteries recharged before going underground. It would be more difficult to collect all of the elements down there, and the batteries required a strict balance to keep them stable.

It only took another fifteen minutes for me to reach the trail. I was able to find the glow stones they were leaving as the sun started casting longer shadows through the forest. I made sure to collect them as I went. Considering we were going to be underground for a long time, every one of them might be important. The shift in the weather was darkening the skies, bringing on an early night. By the time I reached the edge of the foothills, it was already starting to snow.

Visibility was cut down to less than a hundred feet, and quickly getting worse. I gave up on collecting the glow stones, instead just sprinting past them as fast as I could. I would have used my qi thread trick to let me fly like a ballooning spider, but the wind was blowing in the wrong direction. The path left by the Angry Murder Goats had veered east, making the trail of glowing spots that were unevenly spaced in the snow the only thing I had to follow through the forest.

The infrequent glow stones led to a narrow ledge that worked its way up the side of a steep hill. It would have been called a mountain in some areas, however with the highest mountains in the empire towering over it, this was certainly a hill in comparison. The trail of glow stones stopped about halfway up the path, but seeing as there was only one way forward, it wasn't a problem.

As the ledge curved around a rocky outcropping near the top, I finally saw a large cave opening wide enough that the horses could fit through. The snow piling up in drifts along the narrow trail made any tracks there invisible. I thought I saw light flickering from deeper within the cavern, spurring me to move faster. I carefully shuffled toward the opening, and took a moment to look back toward the forest. The storm was in full swing now, reducing visibility to almost nothing.

Just as I turned around, a strong gust of wind swirled the snow around me, and made a clear spot down to the base of the hill. It was impossible, but I could have sworn I saw a two-headed, four-legged monster trying to struggle up the narrow trail.

There was no way. Nope. Those trolls couldn't have figured out a way to get here so quickly. The roar that shook a minia-ture avalanche down on my head proved my thoughts to be false. Either they had figured a way to get out of the ravine, or two more trolls had found me. I wasn't sure which was more unbelievable. I was beginning to feel herded in this direction, like some higher power was forcing my friends and I into these particular caves. I even paused to listen for the tell-tale laughter of a certain goddess to see if she was somehow listening in on my thoughts again, but I didn't hear anything this time. Maybe it was just fate, and not the interference of the gods. Or maybe I was just being paranoid.

I turned and sprinted the rest of the way into the cave. There was no way I wanted to fight a regenerating creature that could crush me in one blow during a snowstorm. Especially since I couldn't risk using light or dark qi this close to the necromancer, and when standing on a narrow path with no room to maneuver. If I had more qi, I might have been able to smooth away a section of the trail, but that wasn't in the cards. And, it could potentially shift something in the mountain and collapse the caves my friends were sheltering in. That was a recipe for disaster, no matter how skilled I might be.

As I entered the cave, my skin started tingling like ants were crawling all over me. Getting out of the cold wind and blowing snow made me realize how low the temperature was dropping outside, and my healing focusing stone was telling me that I had been close to freezing off some very important parts of my anatomy. You know, like my fingers and toes.

The cave entrance was barely large enough for the horses to have made it inside. The tunnel floor near the opening was covered with a thin layer of dirt and dead leaves, which slowly tapered off to clean stone. There were signs of it being recently disturbed, meaning I had most likely found the right place. It was certainly too narrow for the rock trolls, and I felt a tension in my shoulders I hadn't realized was there begin to relax. Even if they managed to get up here, they would have to scoop out the tunnel to fit. We should be safe from them.

As I kept moving forward, the tunnel made a sharp turn to the left after a few dozen yards, which was why I couldn't see anything more than a flicker of the light from the roaring bonfire that was relatively close to the entrance from outside the short tunnel opening. When I rounded the corner, I saw Chu fiddling about with his cookpot near the far edge of the light, in a cavern that was far too small to have such a large fire. Donny had his back to me, trying his best to guide the horses around the flames and deeper into the cave. It wasn't going well, considering Scout had clamped his teeth on Donny's ear, and was instead angling him toward the fire. Cloud was impassively watching it happen, like a regular horse would. I wasn't sure which one I preferred—the creepy-smart horse, or the relatively normal one—but I did know I was glad Scout wasn't after *me*.

"Donny, quit messing around and get over here!" Valerie stepped into the light, and Scout immediately released Donny's ear. "I swear, you can't take anything seriously!"

Donny only managed to splutter in reply. He looked around, as if seeking help from a witness that had seen what really happened. That was when he finally noticed me standing near the cavern entrance. "Jim! We were starting to think you had gotten lost! What took you so long?"

I snorted. "Took me so long? You're kidding, right?" His grin was answer enough. "The better question is, why did you build such a large fire? You can barely walk around it."

Chu piped up from the other side of the fire. "Because we didn't build it, those idiots did." He motioned behind him with a thumb, pointing at the darkened section of the cave behind him. "They decided to make it as big as possible, with fire qi enhanced wood, in the hopes that it would warm them up faster. Instead, they nearly killed themselves with the smoke and heat. Jamila had to use her wind bracers to clear out enough of the smoke so that we could actually breathe again."

"Yeah, and then they yelled at me for helping." Jamila walked out of the darkness and sat down next to Chu, immediately starting to chop up some type of root vegetable to add to the pot. "After I threatened to kill one of them, they went deeper into the cave to make another camp away from us." She gave me a small smile. "I don't think they like our group very much."

"Who? The sailors? They managed to get here too?" I tried peeking around the fire, but the angle of the cave didn't let me see any deeper. "I don't know if you saw it or not, but one of them tried pushing me out into the stampede earlier. Having a talk with them is pretty high up on my to-do list at the moment."

"Really? I would like to hear what they have to say as well. There are only seven of them here though, but I'm sure more of them managed to find a place to weather the storm in some other caves around here." Donny pointed past the fire. "They weren't very organized with their retreat. It might be best to wait until we find all of them before you go asking any questions. You wouldn't want to scare them off."

I grimaced, remembering them scramble for their lives through the forest. It had been pretty unorganized. Donny was probably right. "Did you guys find out what caused that stampede that drove them right back to us?"

"From the small amount of information they were willing to tell us, it seems like they tried to kill a goat or two for either some fresh meat, or maybe just for sport." Chu was now measuring out spices from a myriad of small containers he pulled from a storage ring while he talked. "As it turns out, that massive herd of Angry Murder Goats belongs to the rock troll. Or one of them follows the other around, maybe. Either way, it made the troll mad, and it started after them for killing a few goats. Then, the herd freaked out and started that stampede. They had been running for an hour or two by the time it reached us."

"That explains a few things. I can't say I am very surprised that they got into trouble." I pulled out my bowl, considering the stew looked to be almost done. "By the way, I am pretty sure I won the hunting competition. There is a whole lot of goat meat in my storage devices at the moment." That brought about a round of objections and complaints, with the most vocal unsurprisingly being Valerie. After the past few days, sharing a meal and bantering around the fire was a welcome and familiar comfort for all of us. So was just having a warm meal. The temperature was still dropping quickly, even noticeable with the bonfire.

"I'm just saying, that wasn't hunting, that was more like trapping." Valerie was leaning over her bowl, the oversized and enhanced fire forcing us to sit farther apart than we normally would have. "We should have a separate category for animals killed in a trap."

"Speaking of traps, does anyone else think this place feels weird?" I was pulling in qi from the meridians in my feet while we talked, doing my best to replace what I had lost. The energy felt sluggish, like it wasn't used to being disturbed. "Were there any signs of animals living in these caves before you got here? Because the qi feels like there hasn't been anything in this place for a long time."

"We didn't see anything, but Valerie says these caves go on for a long way, much too far for her to check by herself at the moment." Donny was scraping the last of his food out of his bowl as he talked. "There must be a whole underground network hidden in these mountains."

I nodded in reply. I was about to tell them that I was pretty sure there was even a hidden city somewhere in these caves when another roar shook the cavern from just outside the entrance. Why couldn't I just catch a break?

"Stars! I thought you killed that thing?!" Chu had jumped to his feet, knocking over the stew pot in the process.

"I was going to tell you what happened, but I haven't had time!" I moved toward the source of the noise, pulling the Dagger of Boom from my belt as I went. "If those two get in here, we are going to need to go deeper into the caves, to somewhere narrow enough they can't crawl through!"

"Did you just say 'those two'?" Donny's voice seemed to be a little higher than normal. "When did a second one show up?!"

"Less talking, more fighting!" Jamila shouted as she blasted past us, swords already in hand. We followed quickly, everyone rounding the corner at the same time. Which was why we all ended up flying backward into a heap when a massive fist came shooting through the cave entrance.

"Ouch." Valerie let out a muffled groan from the bottom of the pile. She had been in the rear, prepping her bow, meaning she got to be the cushion for the rest of us.

Jamila had it the worst, though. She had caught a giant knuckle straight to the face, and now looked like she was wearing a mask of blood from a deep cut along her hairline. Instead of taking it easy, however, she was already struggling to free herself from the pile and get to stabbing.

Chu finally managed to roll backward off of us and into the cavern, which allowed the rest of us the chance to get back on our feet. The healing pendant around Valerie's neck let out a soft glow as she used one of the charges it contained to heal herself, meaning she was already firing arrows at the giant arm trying to smash us all into meat paste.

I still hadn't managed to gather enough qi to do much. Luckily, the Dagger of Boom still had a full charge. Since Jamila was already stabbing the forearm of the troll repeatedly, it would be too dangerous to use the dagger in such close quarters at the moment. She wouldn't have enough room to back away when I used it. I looked toward the entrance to see the other three arms of the trolls digging furiously at the cave opening, gradually widening it so the stuck-together monsters could get deeper into the tunnel. The cave ceiling let out an ominous crack as the trolls slammed against the wall, making the three of us still in the tunnel pause to look over our heads. Jamila didn't even stop attacking to see what the danger was, just kept stabbing into the gaps between the plates of hard, rocky skin on the creature. She appeared to be somewhat upset.

"I don't think this is going to end well!" Valerie was already backing away, while Donny moved forward to grab Jamila. "We need to get deeper into the caves!" She fired one last arrow before following her own advice, moving to join Chu back in the cavern.

Donny had to physically remove Jamila from the fight. It was a little out of character for her to lose tactical awareness like this. She hadn't even paused to wipe the blood from her eyes. I could see how getting punched in the face made her a bit angrier than normal, but this was a little extreme. What was wrong with her?

We made it out of the tunnel and into the cavern just as the ceiling let out an ominous groan. The trolls had done exactly what I hadn't expected them to do. They had managed to open up the tunnel entrance some, and then started trying to crawl deeper inside. Since they weren't used to being double their normal size, it wasn't working very well for them. Given their level of determination though, it would eventually get to the point that they either managed to widen the entrance tunnel enough to reach us, or collapse the mountainside down on their heads. I was leaning toward the second option happening first.

"We need to get deeper." I gauged our situation while I spoke, seeing that everyone but Jamila was in reasonably good condition. Her eyes seemed a little unfocused, but Chu already had a hand on her shoulder to help steady her. "Start shuffling around the edges, and find a path leading deeper into the mountain." We were backed up against the flames of the bonfire, which still hadn't died down enough for us to easily pass deeper into the cavern.

"Are you sure you want to go farther in? We don't know if there are worse things than the trolls down there." Donny was already moving around the flames as he asked. He had heard the ceiling groan in distress as well. He was just confirming I was sure of my decision.

"Oh, there are certainly worse things deeper in these caves." Chu was on the opposite side of the fire, dragging Jamila with him. "Otherwise, why would the gods have sent us here?"

Donny gave him a thoughtful nod. "That's a fair point." The four of them hurried along, doing their best to grab any loose items we had left out as they went. I knelt to grab the cookpot before joining them when a sizable rock fell out of the swiftly cracking ceiling, landing in the bonfire and throwing the burning logs all around the room.

I was engulfed in the inferno, forcing me to roll clear of the flames before it did more than singe my clothing. Since it was fire qi enhanced wood—I still had no idea where they even got the stuff—it was more than hot enough to hurt me, even with my body strengthened to the resistance levels of a Saint cultivator. I ended up back into the entranceway, less than ten feet from the lovely Donut and Boot, who were still furiously digging their way deeper into the tunnel.

The shouts of my friends were barely audible over the sounds of the crackling flames and the scrabbling of the trolls, making it impossible for me to know what they were saying. Considering their level of competence, I was more than sure they would have a way through the flames figured out quickly.

I just didn't know if it would be before or after the trolls had crushed me.

CHAPTER THIRTEEN

Infection

My next move was to spin up my cores to full speed, only adjusting my perspective of time slightly to reduce my qi expenditure. Since I wasn't even back to a third of my capacity, I needed to be careful. Considering the situation, I went in a direction I didn't normally choose.

Making a qi construct was much easier than my normal style of fighting, but it was far less versatile, and frequently used more qi. This situation happened to be straightforward enough that it wasn't necessary to use my qi thread techniques, and the particular design I thought of wasn't very qi-intensive. I formed the outline of the construct I wanted to make out of wind qi, and then filled the hollow container with water qi. The result was a pillar of water the thickness of my waist. I limited it to the height of the tunnel, then coated it in swirling blades of ice and invisible spikes of air. The attack was named something ridiculously dumb, 'Pillar of Winter's Absolution,' but I just called it what it was—a really good monster blender. I could have tried to use it to make a path through the fire, but it would have evaporated entirely too soon to do any good. Instead, I utilized it exactly the way it was intended.

Using my will to direct the construct, I shoved it straight at the rock trolls. Their instinctive move was to try and smash it, which was exactly the wrong decision. The trolls' limbs passed straight through the water pillar, only knocking free a fine mist of the central portion of the construct. While their fists moved through the column of blades and spikes, it dug deep grooves into their stony flesh. It didn't do nearly enough damage to counteract the trolls' extreme regeneration abilities. That wasn't the point. What my attack did accomplish was to cause the monsters pain, which distracted them from digging any deeper into the tunnel.

The next few minutes were an abject lesson on the definition of insanity. Doing the same thing over and over again, but expecting a different outcome. The trolls just kept swinging against the construct, gouging free chucks of themselves against the pillar over and over again. They clearly didn't understand that punching water didn't get you very far. Their roars of anger and pain were loud enough I was afraid they would collapse the tunnel on my head, even with the distraction.

After a full two minutes of the nearly constant onslaught, the trolls wised up enough to back away from the pillar. I cut my connection to the construct, meaning it would eventually run out of energy and dissipate, but it had enough qi to last for another ten minutes or so.

My concerns about the tunnel collapsing due to all the noise were well-founded. When the trolls backed out of the tunnel, large sections of the ceiling started cracking. Apparently, the trolls had shifted enough stone and dirt that the structural integrity had been compromised. Their presence in the tunnel had been why it had stood up for so long, their mass inadvertently holding up the tunnel.

I watched a long crack run across the ceiling over my head, then another low groan of shifting stone made the ground shudder and dust fall from the ceiling. I was going to have to either try and make it through the room of fire, or risk half the hill falling down on my head. Trying to reinforce the tunnel would only buy me a few minutes of time given the state of the damage, and ultimately just drain me of all my qi.

The gods must have decided once again that I was overdue for something positive to finally happen to me, because that was the moment Chu came striding through the flames, his skin covered by a layer of conjured metal qi.

"Well, it looks to me like you might be in need of some assistance!" His metallic grin was gleaming in the firelight, making him appear more menace than hero. I was happy to see him anyway. "Care for a ride?"

"Don't you dare, Chu!" I tried scrambling back a step, but there was nowhere to go. He scooped me up into a princess carry, forcing me to wrap my arms around his neck. "Why are you like this?"

He chuckled as he sprinted back through the flames, limiting my exposure to the qi-enhanced flames as much as possible. "You can't blame me for having a bit of fun at your expense. After all, you did beat us in the hunting competition. Just call this karma for making us pay you for stopping the Murder Goats."

We were both chuckling as he cleared the flames, his metal qi covering quickly disappearing as he cleared the fire. I was only lightly singed, but my clothing was little better than crispy rags at this point.

"Do you think we're safe from that thing now?" Chu was still holding me as he walked down a series of short tunnels. "We moved back into the second cavern just in case."

"I think we should be fine. They are going to have some problems getting through that tunnel." I shifted to look him in the eye. "And you know you can put me down now."

"Put you down? And miss the looks on everyone's faces when they see me carrying you like the hero I am?" His stupid grin stretched from ear to ear. "I don't think so!"

He set me down just a few seconds later, as soon as we got back to where my friends were standing. I didn't even have a chance to try and struggle free from his grip. Jerk. Everyone did seem happy to see me, except for Jamila. She was glaring at the flames, as if she could see the trolls through them. Chu was bragging about how amazing his rescue was, and poking fun at me while describing the way he carried me through the flames. Jamila seemed to be completely unaware that we had even returned. I held up my hand to silence everyone, and took a step closer to her.

"Jamila? Is everything okay?" I took a closer look at her, and noticed that her aura was in turmoil. I sensed a darkness to it that reminded me of what I had sensed in the captain yesterday, before our groups had gone their separate ways. "You aren't acting like yourself."

Her eyes darted to my face for a second before returning back to the tunnel that led to the rock trolls. "I'm fine. I just want another shot at those trolls." The anger coming off of her was palpable, and her voice deepened into a growl. "They need to pay for hurting me. No one gets away with hurting me."

"Don't worry, they can't hurt you again. They are stuck out there, and we are in here." Chu put his hand on her shoulder to reassure her as he spoke. "Let's push deeper into the cave and try to—"

He was cut off when Jamila grabbed his arm and flipped him onto his back with no warning. "Don't *touch* me!" she screamed in his face, and gripped the hilt of her sword hard enough to turn her knuckles white. "Don't *ever* touch me *again!*" Her rage was a physical force as her aura erupted from her in a sharp wave. The hurt on Chu's face at her actions caused her to pause for a moment, and she took a step back. "I'm… I'm sorry. I don't know what came over me." Chu got to his feet and backed away from her, clearly in far more pain from her words than from having the breath knocked out of him. "Chu, I didn't mean it. I overreacted. There wasn't any reason to lash out at you like that, and…" She trailed off as he turned and started walking deeper into the cave, his shuffling footsteps loud on the stone floor.

Donny was the first to break the silence left by his departure.

"I should follow him. We don't want him running off and getting lost down here." He pointedly didn't look at Jamila as he started to walk away. "Try to find a place to make camp, and we'll be there shortly."

The shock of how quickly things went badly was clear on all of our faces. Jamila seemed the most shocked out of all of us. She silently went to grab the horses so we could move deeper into the cave system, but they balked at her approach. Even Cloud, the horse that she spent the most time with, backed away from her outstretched hand. Now *that* was too far from the norm for me to handle.

I was low on qi, but I used it like a child spends coppers in a candy store. Empowering your aura was usually pointless, as it didn't do anything beyond enhancing your sensitivity to your surroundings. It also made you stand out like a beacon to anything that could sense qi nearby, which wasn't normally a good idea given our current location. Most people found it to be very rude and intrusive as well, making it a seldom-used technique.

Usually, the only people that would inject qi into their core and meridian walls to empower their aura were either people trying to intimidate others, or healers trying to diagnose a rare illness or injury a patient might be suffering from. The latter was pretty much what I was doing now.

My aura became a tangible weight that I focused against Jamila. As it flared against her own aura, she reacted in a similar manner to Chu putting his hand on her shoulder. She had her katana halfway out of its sheath, and was striding toward me with fiery and bloodshot eyes. "You think you can just—"

Valerie was there in a flash, slamming her hand down on the hilt of the katana and forcing it back into its sheath. "What is wrong with you?" She clamped down hard on Jamila's wrist to keep her from trying to draw the sword again. "We are not your enemies, but you keep acting like we are!"

While they were scuffling about, I was doing my best to

inspect the darkness in her aura I had sensed earlier. It was subtle, but I definitely noticed a 'tint' to her normally bright energy field. Like looking at her through smoked glass, it was making her appear more dim to my senses. I walked over and grabbed her arm as she hauled back to smack Valerie. "Jamila! Snap out of it! I need you to concentrate." The suddenness of my command stopped her struggles for a moment. "When did you first start feeling angry? Was it in the forest, or after you made it into the cave? You are certainly intelligent enough to recognize how different you are acting. You even hurt Chu, the man you are supposed to marry!"

She took a step back from us, and we both let her go. After taking a deep breath, she nodded in agreement. "You're right, something feels off. I'm not… My thoughts are… wrong." She clutched her head, as if trying to hold it together. "What is happening to me?"

I approached her slowly, taking the time to try and see if I could sense where the problem was originating from. I saw that her cores were showing signs of strain, and her meridians seemed swollen, as if they were infected. That shouldn't even be possible. "Do you remember exactly when this started? It might be important."

"I'm not sure." She was still holding her head in her hands, so she didn't see Chu and Donny come back around the corner. They must have come back when they heard us yelling. "What is wrong with me?"

"It started around the same time she had to use her wind qi to clear out the smoke from the bonfire." Chu's voice made Jamila spin around to look at him while he talked. "That's when I first noticed her starting to get irrationally angry."

"Chu, I… I'm sorry. I didn't mean those things." She backed against the cavern wall and slid down to sit on her heels. "It's like the worst parts of me are pushed to the front, and there isn't anything I can do to stop it." She ended with her voice barely above a whisper, but it carried easily in the quiet cavern. "What's wrong with me?" Chu didn't say anything, and I could see the pain still reflected in his eyes.

"She's not lying." Everyone turned their eyes on me. "There is something wrong with her aura, and it is clear enough that the horses sensed it." The weight in Chu's eyes seemed to lessen a bit. However, my words weren't much comfort to Jamila.

"So, do you know how to fix it? Have the gods shown you anything to hint at what it could be?" She stood back up, and the concern on her face was clear. Chu stepped over to comfort her, and this time she didn't throw him on the ground.

"I will have to take a closer look when we get settled in somewhere more secure." I looked around, pointing at all the various tunnels that intersected with the small cavern we were currently standing in. "We need a location without so many places where unwanted visitors could find their way inside. And I would like to put a little more distance between the five of us and those rock trolls. Just because we *think* they can't get in here doesn't mean they won't find a way."

Everyone agreed with me, and we started on our way. Valerie led us deeper into the caverns, while Donny and I took charge of the horses. Chu and Jamila were bringing up the rear, taking silent comfort in each other's presence, letting the quiet heal some of the recent wounds.

While we walked, I tried to figure out what was going on with her, and how it could have affected her so quickly. It didn't make any sense to me. It was reminiscent of what I felt from the ship's captain right before they had left, but that was the only time I had felt such a taint in someone's aura. It wasn't close to the same as the miasma aura developed by the dark sects. This was more subtle, and clearly had a direct effect on a person's personality. The people that joined dark sects already had a negative attitude, and the aura was built around that. This was more like a sickness. An infection of some kind, maybe. But what could infect an aura?

CHAPTER FOURTEEN

Revelation

It took us several hours to find a suitable cavern to set up camp. Finding tunnels that were wide enough for the horses to get through was difficult, to say the least. Several times we had to backtrack around narrow spots, and everyone was tired and grumpy by the time we stopped.

The situation wasn't improved by the seven sailors we came across that decided to tag along. They had run deeper into the caverns from the sounds they heard when the trolls had first appeared at the entrance, and had found themselves thoroughly lost once they made a few turns deeper underground. All of them absolutely refused to actually join our group, but they were certainly fine with following us around. Once we set up in a cave large enough to comfortably fit the five of us with the horses, they set up a little ways back down the tunnel we used to enter. There was only one other tunnel leading deeper into the underground labyrinth of caves and passageways, so we felt safe enough to post just one guard. If something came in behind us, the screams of the sailors would alert us. I also set up several alarm and trap plates, so it would take either a swarm of beasts or one very powerful one to get to us from either direction.

Since we were too deep underground to start a real fire—because smoke is a thing—we piled up a few of our brighter glow stones around the qi-powered heating stone in a close imitation of a campfire. Valerie pulled out some feed and a water trough for the horses, and set up a place for them to rest off to the side. Chu risked a minor cave-in by shifting a small section of the floor into a funnel shape, so any manure and such would stay in one location. After that was settled, it was pretty clear everyone was focused mostly on Jamila instead of setting up the camp. Donny had tied the same knot in a tent line three times already without realizing it.

"Okay guys, let's figure this out." There was a collective sigh at my announcement. "Jamila, why don't you lie down next to the heating stone and get comfortable?" She rushed to comply, quickly getting into position. Everyone crowded around behind me, and I could feel them spin up their own cores to watch what I was doing.

I started with a scan of Jamila using a pulse of wood qi. It didn't reveal anything out of the ordinary, which meant this wouldn't be a simple fix. I spun up my brain core a little more and observed the flow of qi through her body, and that was when I finally started to put it together.

The problem wasn't with Jamila. It was the environment. The entire region was just like in my dream walk, heavy in metal and dark qi. She must have inadvertently absorbed a large amount of dark qi after helping with the bonfire fiasco when she refilled the qi in her wind blade bracers. There was only a tiny amount of light qi in her body from the pills I had given everyone, and the influx of dark qi had thrown off her cultivation system. How that affected her mood and tempera-ment was still a mystery to me, but at least I knew how to fix it. It also meant I would have to finally take the leap and tell everyone about dark and light qi, before everyone else started to go through the same thing Jamila had been experiencing. I also realized why the ship's captain had been so irritable. He must have been particularly sensitive to dark qi for it to have affected him so strongly when still on the surface. This was going to cause me all kinds of headaches.

It also meant I was going to need to carve a ridiculous number of formations into the walls of the cavern to stop any form of qi from escaping. Otherwise, the necromancer might notice when I started using light and dark qi. There wasn't going to be much sleep for me in the near future. I couldn't hold back the sigh that escaped, thinking about how tired I already was.

"The good news is, I know what is wrong." I took a deep breath before continuing. "The bad news is, to bring your system back into balance means I have to put you in extreme danger. And I need to prepare this cavern, otherwise it will most likely alert the necromancer to our presence."

"Danger? What kind of danger?" Jamila sat up, and seemed to be excited about the idea of a fight. "I'm not afraid."

"Not just you." I stood and took a few steps so I could look at everyone. "This will put all of you at risk, for the rest of your lives."

"I'm willing to do anything to help Jamila, you have to know that." Chu's determination was plainly written on his features. He looked ready to try to crush a mountain if that was what it took to save her.

"We all feel the same." Donny spoke up, with Valerie giving a sharp nod of agreement. "Whatever it takes. Besides, what could we possibly have to face that is worse than what is already in front of us?" His joke lightened the mood a bit, causing everyone to crack a grin.

"The danger comes from the knowledge I am about to pass on." Everyone's smiles dropped. "What you are going to learn is something that even the emperor would kill half his empire to obtain, because to him and people like him, power is all that matters." It was quiet, but no one raised a word of dissent. "Why don't the four of you get some rest while I carve the runes into the walls? This is going to take a while."

They quickly agreed, and finished setting up camp while I

got to work. Since I was still trying to top off the qi in my cores, I pulled the Dagger of Boom out of my belt. It had a full charge still, and it cut through the stone walls with ease, using only minimal willpower to hold back the massive explosions I normally utilized it for. The layers of runes I was using would block any qi from leaving the area, similar to the plates I used to collect condensed liquid qi. The difference here was that I wasn't drawing any extra qi toward the formations. It was like dropping a stone in a river, instead of a magnet into a pile of iron filings. The intent was for the surrounding qi to just flow around us, leaving the rest of the energy undisturbed.

Anyone paying close attention might notice a slight change in the ambient energy levels, but even I wouldn't interpret it as something deliberate. If the necromancer noticed, they would hopefully think it was just a passing beast disrupting the normal flow of qi at the periphery of his domain. It should be small enough that they wouldn't even notice it in the first place, but I didn't want to underestimate their abilities.

After almost three hours of work, I was finished. It was as good as it was going to get, and I was finally back to full power. The batteries on my belt were also filled, and the dagger was drained to about half of its capacity. I had been worried about walking around with it at full charge. I quickly nudged everyone awake, and we gathered once again around the pile of glow stones and a recharged heating stone.

"Now that everything is prepared, it's time to get started." I took a moment to look everyone in the eye. "There is no going back from this point forward. I don't expect you to back down, but you need to understand this is the biggest decision you have ever made."

"We understand." Valerie looked toward Jamila. "This, whatever *this* is, is necessary for us to move forward. None of us are afraid."

A clatter from the tunnel where the sailors were staying caused me to stop what I was about to say. "Hold on. Even here, we need to take precautions against eavesdropping." I pulled out a shield formation plate and made some adjustments to the runes on the surface. Now, it would stop even air from passing through its thin membrane. No one would be able to hear or see us. I would either need to talk fast, or we would have to take breaks to let fresh air inside. I should have thought of it while carving the cavern, but nobody said I was perfect.

"Okay, you have to know that the suspense is killing us by now." Donny was drumming his fingers on the stone floor hard enough to cause a small pebble to bounce with each impact. "Can we please get on with it?"

I activated the shield, causing a white film to appear in a large circle around us. "Remember, I did warn you about how dangerous this is going to be. Every person with even a modicum of power will hunt you mercilessly for what you are about to see." I took a deep breath, and pushed past my issues of trusting others. This group had proven themselves to be my friends, over and over again. I held out my hands to either side and formed a small orb of dark qi in one, and light qi in the other. "I have hidden this from you for so long because I wanted to protect you. There is no going back after this. I know you have seen this before, but I have never explained it, and you have never asked. These are two hidden forms of qi. They are the primary source of my ability to fight and kill those more powerful than myself, and the reason why I have seen such drastic increases in my fighting strength." I lowered the balls of energy until they touched the stone at my feet. "Each one has its own benefits and hazards, and balancing the two is vital to your stability and survival." The dark qi bubbled as it touched the stone, burning a pitted circle out of the ground as if it were acid. The light qi did the same, but instead of acting like acid, it incinerated a perfectly clean circle from the floor. I brought my hands together, and I absorbed them back into my body as they touched. "Now, let's get started."

CHAPTER FIFTEEN

Honor can be a Pain

The look of astonishment on their faces was pretty universal. It took several more examples of the elements before they finally seemed to grasp the importance of what I was showing them. This was, after all, knowledge that would turn the cultivation world on its head. It was another thirty minutes before everyone was settled down enough for me to start working on fixing the imbalance Jamila was suffering from. First, I deactivated the formation plate blocking all sound to refresh the air inside the dome. After reactivating it, I sat down across from Jamila and crossed my legs in my preferred meditation style.

"Here we go. Normally, I would make you do this on your own, but right now I need you to return to a balanced state as quickly as possible." She gave me a sharp nod of agreement. "Once you feel the energy I push into your meridians, I need you to cycle it through your cores as quickly as possible. Make sure you evenly distribute it throughout your body to counteract the dark qi already there. Everyone else, make sure you pay close attention to the energy flowing through her system. Now that you know about it, the two hidden forms of qi should be easy for you to pick out from the others if you focus hard enough."

"Are you sure?" Donny had a confused look on his face. "Wouldn't thousands of cultivators have noticed it before, if it was that easy?"

"Well, I wasn't going to bring this up yet, but the thing that bridged the gap for all of you is because I made a little mistake. The cultivation pills I have been giving you include an equal amount of dark and light qi. You have been absorbing it for a long time, all without noticing. Now that I have told you, it should be easy to pick it out from the others." They looked at me with a mixture of confusion and anger. I shrugged my shoulders. "Hey, I'm only human. Another important thing I have noticed is that trying to combine the two while they are still inside your cores is… volatile. Make sure you separate them with some other form of qi as a buffer." I didn't tell them the elements I used as a buffer, because I wanted to see if they could figure out something better. If any problems arose, I would tell them exactly how I separated them.

After that, it took less than an hour for Jamila to return to a state of balance, with me trickling in the necessary light qi as I drew some in from my batteries to replace what I used. I could clearly see her relax, the tension in her body melting away.

"I think that's enough." She got to her feet, and I could feel her extending her senses. "I don't want to know what happens if I go too far in the other direction."

"Ha! I didn't even think of that. A very angry Jamila is scary, but I'm not sure we could handle an extremely happy Jamila." I also got to my feet, but much slower than she had. It had been quite a while since I last slept. "Anyway, now everyone should know what to look for when cultivating. This place is extremely dense in dark qi, so it will be very important for all of you to be careful." I deactivated the shield before placing it in my belt. "It will be important to make a bright campsite every time we stop to increase the available light qi, and ensure we all maintain the necessary balance. Cultivation pills can only help so much."

"Not just that." Donny was rummaging through a sack he pulled from a storage ring. "If we are in a prolonged fight of any kind, we will need to light up the area to keep safe. I think I know enough about runes to make a formation plate that works like a really powerful glow stone." He set out several tools and laid them out in a semi-circle around him. "While I work on that, why don't you try to get some rest? We have a long journey ahead, and you being exhausted won't help anyone."

It was hard to argue with that logic. I moved over to a clear spot and pulled out a mattress to sleep on. Considering how hard the stone floor was, the hassle of putting it back in my belt was well worth it. As I was lying in bed, I noticed that all four of my friends were doing their best to cultivate in a deliberate and measured manner. If the speed they were doing so was any indicator, there was certainly already some progress being shown by all. I was also relieved not to feel any negative emotions sent my direction.

The revelation of me keeping a secret from them for such a long time had been something I was worried would drive a wedge between us. I guess I needn't have worried. They genuinely understood the gravity of the information I had given them, and they certainly didn't hold it against me for trying to save them the burden of keeping such a secret. Knowledge was power, and they now had more than any sane person would want.

Thinking about everything made my head start to throb. It was definitely time to get some rest. My head barely hit the pillow before I was off to sleep.

Which lasted all of ten minutes.

"Help! Please, help us!" I was a bit groggy when I came to, but seeing my friends already brandishing weapons and moving away from me had me on my feet quickly. The person calling for aid came from the opposite direction of the sailors staying in the tunnel behind us. It was barely audible, but it was clearly someone in need of assistance. Whoever it was, they had made it deeper into the caves than we had. The shouts seemed to echo, meaning there was no telling how far away they might be. I quickly stuffed my mattress back into my belt before I ended up losing it somehow. The realization of just how comfortable it had been made it much more valuable than a bunch of other stuff I was holding on to.

"Stay where you are!" Jamila was the first person to reach the tunnel opening. "Don't go any further in this direction until we say! We need a moment to disarm our defenses!"

There was no answer, so we deactivated just enough traps to let us through. I made sure to stagger the gap, so anything charging straight into the chamber would still run into at least a few surprises.

"Let's take it slow." Chu had moved into the lead, since Donny had lost his tower shield when fighting one of the trolls. "We don't know who that could be, or what they are running from."

"Sound advice. Now get moving." The bluntness of Jamila's words was tempered by the quick squeeze she gave his arm. She might not be completely back to normal, but she was getting there.

I looked back at our cavern, and remembered that we still had Scout and Cloud to worry about. "Someone needs to stay behind with the horses, in case they get around us, or there is more than one side tunnel that leads into this one." I turned to look at Valerie. "Your bow would work better without all of us in your way. Why don't you stand guard this time?"

"Fine. I don't like it, but I agree we can't just leave them here alone." She glanced back toward the far side of the cavern. "And I still don't trust those sailors hiding in the other tunnel." Everyone gave a sharp nod of agreement. We all knew that they were untrustworthy, but now, with the dense dark qi in the area, they were even more likely to become a problem. It was only a matter of time before they were affected the same way Jamila had been.

We made sure Valerie was ready to go before we started moving out. It was less than thirty yards before we ran into another tunnel that bisected our current one. One led up and to the left, and the other down and to the right. They were both much smaller than the one that continued straight onward, so we decided to just drop a few alarm and nonlethal trap plates before continuing.

After passing through another intersection, we finally heard sounds of fighting coming from around a curve in the tunnel. There wasn't much room for tactics, but we spread out as best as we could. I activated the shield function of my spirit wood ring, and moved to stand next to Chu. Donny pulled a long boar spear from a storage ring, while Jamila had a katana in one hand and three shuriken in the other. It wasn't until just now that I realized I was still wearing the threadbare and scorched clothing from earlier, while everyone else was wearing the brigandine armor I had made them. As soon as I could, we were all getting upgrades. And I was going to change into something that didn't make me look like a homeless vagrant. Or, considering all the dried blood, a deranged murderhobo.

"Quick! Fall back, while we hold them here!" The person shouting was none other than the lost ship captain. For a brief moment, I thought about just letting them deal with whatever they were fighting on their own. Then I shook it off and kept going. "They can't keep this up forever! We just have to find someplace where they can't follow!"

The four of us rushed forward, rounding the curve and finding ourselves on a ridge above a tall and steep-sided cave. It was like a bowl, and we were standing on the rim. In the bottom, we could see where seven tunnels led into the chamber. At all but one of those tunnels, there was a sailor fighting something out of sight. I could see the captain standing at the largest tunnel opening, where he was dashing forward to swing a cutlass at the unseen attackers before darting backward, out of their range. In the center of the bowl, with their backs to the only unguarded tunnel, were ten or twelve sailors that held a mixture of torches and glow stones high over their heads.

"Captain, we can't leave you!" I didn't recognize the sailor at first glance, but once I heard him speak, I recognized the boatswain. He was a capable man on the sea, but it was clear the current situation was a bit outside his normal wheelhouse. And he was looking a little worn out. "You won't have any light!" Despite his words, he was slowly backing toward the open tunnel. That was when I finally got to see what they were all fighting. Fanged Cave Crickets.

The Fanged Cave Cricket was a relatively common creature found all over the empire. They were little more than a nuisance in most places, as even the weakest of cultivators could crush one underfoot with ease, given they rarely got larger than an adult's thumb. I had actually never seen one in a cave before, as most often they were found in the dark spaces under houses, or in similar places where light didn't frequently reach. Most places didn't have caves, after all.

Their bites weren't venomous, but they clamped on hard enough that you were probably going to lose whatever they got their fangs around. In most cases, that meant you might lose a tiny chunk of skin. I had never really thought of them as a threatening monster. Apparently, that was because I hadn't seen them in their natural habitat before. Losing a small piece of skin wouldn't be the boatswain's fate if he wasn't careful, considering these Fanged Cave Crickets were the same size as a large dog. Maybe a small horse.

The first one out of the tunnel attacked the hand holding the torch the man held aloft. It snipped the limb free at the elbow with a loud snapping noise, causing the man to scream as if, well, he unexpectedly had a limb cut off.

Before the torch and severed limb could even hit the ground, the man was already dead. A swarm of over twenty of the monsters came pouring out of the tunnel, and he was gone. The first one to react to the scene was Donny, who threw a rectangular sheet of copper straight into the undulating mass of bugs. I felt him exert a small flex of willpower, and a brilliant orange light erupted from the pile of creepy-crawlies. They let out a screech of pain, and retreated *en masse* back down the darkened tunnel they had come from. I was worried at first that he had used light qi—somehow figuring out the runes for his new element while I slept seemed like something he would do—but thankfully, the orange color meant it was some form of fire qi.

"Up here!" Chu was waving his hand to get their attention. "This way is clear!" Everyone not blinded by the bright light Donny had thrown down into the cave quickly started scrambling up the walls toward our position. I still had mixed emotions about saving the sailors, but I couldn't fault Donny or Chu for doing what felt honorable. I just hoped we didn't quickly come to regret stopping the freakishly huge crickets.

"Go! They hate the light!" The captain was shoving the sailors that had been blinded toward us. "Climb as if your life depended on it!"

They struggled up the steep incline, so Donny quickly dropped a rope to help them climb. It was going to be close, because the light was already starting to dim and the crickets were *not* having problems with the steep incline.

"A little help would be nice!" The sailor that shouted up at us was familiar. I wouldn't bet my life on it, but I was pretty sure it was the same buttnugget—yes, I was still using that one—that tried to take our horses after I had first fought Donut the rock troll. "Any day now!"

"Oops." I *accidentally* nudged a fist-sized rock off the ledge that tumbled down the incline and smashed the offensive man in the face. "Sorry, didn't see that there." My friends all looked at me as the man tumbled halfway back down the steep wall, only stopping himself right before he reached the snapping fangs of the giant bug creatures.

"Really, Jim?" Donny was looking at me with a raised eyebrow. "Maybe right now isn't the time."

"Fair enough." I spun up the qi in my heart core to give me

a boost of strength. "I'm tired of getting knocked around anyway. It's time to show these people why it's a bad idea to mess with me."

The spirit wood spear led the way as I charged down the steep slope, stabbing into the first cricket with a sharp cracking sound of broken chitin. The blow struck just below the head, where a neck would be if it was a human. It jerked back from the sudden pain, causing it to tumble back down to the cavern floor.

I shifted the spear into its shield form to defend myself from a leaping cricket, deflecting the creature to my left, directly into the path of two more creatures. All three toppled down into a heap, so I tossed a fire whip formation plate to finish them off.

My actions had allowed all but the slowest of the sailors to reach the ledge, and caused the Fanged Cave Crickets to split their focus between the captain and I. He was still on the cavern floor, near the tunnel opening he had been guarding earlier. Which, of course, was the opening opposite our path to escape.

"Go! I can hold them here while you escape!" He was shouting up to his men, completely ignoring my presence. "Get the wounded to safety!" His cutlass was a blur as it held back the creatures that were slowly closing in around him, his cores too depleted to use any qi constructs. It wouldn't be long until he would be taken down by the sheer weight of numbers.

I contemplated just letting it happen, but the thought of having to deal with the other sailors without him there to unify all of them into one entity was not a good one. I guess I was going to have to save the ungrateful jerk.

"Get down!" I shouted at him as I jumped off the sloping cavern wall, already spinning up my brain core. "And cover your eyes!"

Time seemed to almost stand still as I reached the apex of my jump, my brain core ramping up my perceptions to the maximum amount I could currently manage. I used all thirteen meridians to spin out threads of fire qi, and then concentrated the energy to be as bright and hot as possible.

The threads whipped through each of the crickets like they were barely even there. I tried to make sure they separated heads from bodies as cleanly as possible, to make collecting their beast cores easier. Not all of them would have one, but it was almost impossible to tell with so many of them clustered together. The extreme heat made the slaughter almost bloodless, as the wounds I created were almost instantly cauterized. Might as well make it easy on myself.

To finish the fight, I tossed a formation plate at each cave entrance. It was a mix of various effects, but all of them were lethal. The crickets would fill the tunnels with bodies before they managed to make it past them.

I released my hold on time, and landed heavily on a pile of monster bodies. My cores were still over half their capacity. Stars, it was good to be a Saint. Not long ago, a fight like this would have exhausted me. I looked over to the captain, who was staring at me with a mixture of surprise and concern. "I think we have enough time to get everyone to safety. Those creatures are going to have a hell of a time getting through the traps I laid down." Instead of answering me, he swallowed hard and quickly made his way to where the last of his men were climbing to safety. I guess I had finally made an impression.

CHAPTER SIXTEEN

Down

I made sure to collect what I could from the crickets. Their fangs were heavily laced with qi, making them useful for alchemy formulas that required a dense qi catalyst. I didn't know any recipes that actually called for their use, but I was sure I could come up with something. There were a total of seven beast cores in the corpses, so I cleaned them off and collected them as well. All but one were earth qi aspected, with the last one being metal qi. The lack of dark qi was a relief. It meant not everything that absorbed qi was able to process the hidden form of energy. Either that, or these creatures were relatively new to the area. I was really, *really* hoping for the former option.

The bodies of three sailors were mixed in with the dead, but only the boatswain had anything of note. A quick scan showed he had a storage earring, so I made sure to grab it. There wasn't much inside beyond several tools that looked useful for maintaining a ship, so I left them in the device. It joined the small collection I was building up in my belt pouch, which reminded me, I still needed to check what was in the ring I had found on the old shipwreck. Maybe I could look through it once we got the sailors settled alongside their friends.

We made good time going back up the tunnels. The sailors were pretty subdued, with more than one of them glancing at me with a fair bit of trepidation. They hadn't actually seen me fight the rock troll on the beach, so I guess my battle prowess wasn't real to them yet. Now, they had to confront the fact that I wasn't going to be shoved aside, or sit still for any junk trials. I was paying particularly close attention to anyone who seemed exceptionally nervous. Whoever shoved me into the stampede might already be dead, but I was still holding out hope I could have a conversation with them about it.

When we finally made it back to our 'base,' the sailors hiding in the tunnel were overjoyed to see that they weren't the only ones to survive. We allowed them into the main chamber, and they went off to the side opposite the horses to talk amongst themselves. After reactivating the traps, we settled in to try to get some rest.

I was starting to feel a little worn around the edges, which wasn't the way to be when in an unknown and dangerous environment. I finally took some time to clean myself up, and change into a set of the blue clothing that was self-cleaning. We had earned it during a tournament in the Southern Provincial Capital, and I had been resistant to wearing clothing that identified me as being from the region. Considering the alternative —going in the buff—I decided it was just time to suck it up and put them on. They weren't as high-quality as my old set, but they were still better than regular clothes. I mean, laundry just sucks, no matter how powerful you are.

The captain finally approached our little camp to talk. His aura was somehow diminished, as if he had lost a cultivation level. While that was certainly possible, it was almost unheard of. He must have experienced something that shook the foundations of his reality to the core. It was considered rude to deeply inspect the cultivation base of anyone besides your closest friends and family, but I did it anyway. I almost gasped aloud with the damage I saw to his meridians. How the man was still standing was a mystery to me. All but his hand and foot meridians were almost completely blocked by the corruption of improperly cycled qi. It would take weeks of focused meditation to return him to his former strength.

"As you can see, I'm in no position to make any demands." The captain was looking straight at me, clearly having noticed my inspection. "Something about this place makes it extremely difficult for me to cycle my qi, and I am at a loss as to why." I could see as he tried to cycle the qi in his lower core, and it looked like it was trapped. He couldn't get it to cycle through his body, causing it to roil like boiling water. The captain winced in pain at the backlash. "I would still ask if you would be willing to escort us back to the surface, so we can leave this horrible place."

"Let us talk about it." I glanced back at my companions. "We'll let you know what we decide." His face reddened in anger, the tainted aura around him seeming to pulse in time with his heartbeat. Then he winced in pain, and backed down.

"Fine. We will await your decision." He turned and walked back to his remaining crew. I paid close attention to how the other members reacted as he spoke to them. More than one already had a similarly tainted aura. It wouldn't be long until they all had anger issues, and difficulty cultivating.

"Is it because of the dark qi?" I glanced over at Jamila, who was looking over the sailors the same way I had been. "The problem with his cultivation. Is it because he doesn't know how to cycle out the dark qi?"

I nodded my head. "Yes. At least, I think that's what the problem is." I gave her system a quick scan to confirm her meridians were clear. "He should be able to clear it out with enough time and focus." She opened her mouth to say something, but I talked over her. "Telling them about dark qi would just damn them to a short life of torture at the hands of a powerful sect or clan. And how long would it take for them to talk about the people who told them about dark and light qi? We would be hunted within hours of them being questioned. Why do you think I kept it from all of you for so long?" She stood quietly while thinking about it. I could see the realization of the truth come over her features.

"Okay." She gave me a quick nod of agreement. "We won't tell them anything." She turned sharply and sat down near the glow stones, where everyone else was already sitting. I could tell she was still bothered by the choice to let them suffer, but considering the alternative was our death, there wasn't anything we could do.

"Does anyone else feel like it's a good idea to get them back to the surface?" Donny was trying to carve some formation plates while we sat. Which reminded me. I needed to see how he had created that bright light using fire qi earlier. If I could do the same thing, but with light qi, it might damage the death cultivator's puppets. Or I could even try it with dark qi, and create a lightless zone that would blind enemies. The dark qi idea wouldn't be much use down here, but once we returned to the surface, I could imagine several ways it could be helpful.

"It's better than keeping them with us, and just waiting for them to lose it like Jamila did." Chu's voice broke me out of my thoughts. "Especially if more than one of them go crazy at the same time." There were murmurs of agreement from everyone.

"Alright, so we get some rest, and then try to find a different path to the surface." I stood to go let them know. "Donny, try to make some more of those flare trap plates, then show them to everyone else. I have a feeling they are going to be something we need more of before this is all over."

I walked over to inform the captain of the decision, but he and his men had already fallen asleep. They hadn't even bothered putting a man on watch. I guess the relief of finding out they weren't the only ones still alive, coupled with the extended fighting, had worn them out. I returned to my own mattress to get some rest.

Instead of falling asleep immediately, I stared up at the ceiling, thinking about what I was going to do. I was a Saint cultivator, but I felt like my gains were too slow, given the knowledge I had. The lack of advanced cultivation aids and body cultivation materials was my true problem, but there wasn't anything I could do about it at the moment. Stopping the death cultivator was my first priority, and then dealing with whatever problems he had caused after that. I was also missing Kory. He was a good friend, and I hoped he was faring well.

When I woke up, it felt like my head was stuffed with wool. I cycled some qi through my body to help, and decided to take one of my weaker alchemy pills to give me a boost. It wasn't as qi-infused as I would have liked, but it was certainly better than nothing. Saving the good ones for a real emergency was more important.

After that, our first order of business was trying to find a way to get back to the surface. Jamila and Valerie took the smaller side tunnel we had found on our way to rescue the captain and his crew, while the sailors sent a group of four back up the way we had come to see if the rock trolls had left. The rest of us followed the captain back to the bowl-shaped cavern, so he could show us the tunnels they had used to get here.

All of it was pointless. The rock trolls had gone, but not until after they had collapsed half the hill onto the area. The tunnel leading up became too narrow for a human to pass through after only a few hundred yards. And of course, the captain and his crew had no idea how to find their way back to the surface. Their running battle with the giant crickets had them so turned around and twisted that it would have taken weeks to figure out how they had made it to the bowl-shaped chamber. Weeks that we just didn't have to give.

"Well, it looks like we only have one real option." All of us had met back up in the basin of the bowl, with only one tunnel opening wide enough that the horses could fit. I was peering into the darkness, trying to use my senses to detect any fluctuations in qi. "The only choice is down."

CHAPTER SEVENTEEN

Darkness

You might say there was a minor amount of pushback from the ship's crew at the idea. In fact, you might more accurately say, there was a *lot* of pushback.

"Go deeper into this rat's nest?! Are you crazy?!"

"I'd rather just die now, and get it over with!"

"This is ridiculous. Why don't we just start tunneling through until we find a way out?"

"They just want us to die, so no one hears about them sinking our ship!"

"*Enough!*" The captain quieted his men with a flare of his aura. Which was now darker than ever. Fantastic. I was *sure* that wouldn't be a problem later. He relaxed as soon as they quieted down again. "Did you forget what happened when we tried to find our way out alone? There is safety in numbers." He turned to the sailor that had asked about just tunneling out. "Did you suddenly learn something about mining that I didn't know about? These mountains are riddled with tunnels. You risk bringing the whole mountain down on our heads, or drowning us in an underground lake. Shifting around large sections of earth will kill us all." His stern stare swept over his men. "We *will* work together to get through this place, and I don't want to hear another word about it from anyone." The captain's voice was firm, brooking no further arguments from the crew.

"We aren't saying that we won't help you get out of here." Valerie was standing next to the opening that would allow us to go deeper into the cave network. "All we are saying is that we need to keep going down. Sometimes, the only way to get out is to go through." She turned and started walking, holding a glow stone high above her head to light the way.

Donny was close behind, with the rest of us following shortly after. Jamila and Chu were leading the horses, with me bringing up the rear. I could hear the captain shouting at his people, and the shuffling footsteps of them trailing us soon echoed down the narrow tunnel. It was going to be a long couple of days. At least, I hoped our time down here would be best measured in days.

The tunnel we were in kept going for what felt like hundreds of miles. It probably wasn't nearly that long, but the pervading darkness and slow pace made it seem like it was. It had several slow curves, meaning we couldn't see very far, even when Valerie tossed a few glow stones farther in front. Several side tunnels branched into this one, but some exploration showed that all of them either became too narrow for a human to pass through, or they circled back into this larger one.

I was at a loss as to how this cave system was formed. We were deep underground, and I was pretty sure we were headed more east than north. I wondered if these ran the full length of the northern ranges, and if so, how it was that I had never heard of them. The caves and tunnels didn't seem to be natural, but there were no tool marks to suggest it had been man-made either. Unless, of course, a group of mad earth cultivators spent their entire lives down here, slowly forming this maze of corridors and caverns. If that actually was the case, the length and size of the stalagmites and stalactites meant it had been a very long time ago.

We spaced out our travel to match the time it took to

recharge the several formation plates most of us were using for illumination. Glow stones didn't require additional qi to function, but their pale green light tended to cast deep shadows, and they were unnerving after a few hours. The more normal light cast by the fire qi in the plates was a welcome reprieve, and the heat they gave off was welcome in the damp cold. Every other recharge cycle we would stop for a meal and short rest, with a break for sleep every third meal. Time continued to pass in a blur, and our haggard group made steady progress as we pushed deeper underground into the mountains. Well, the sailors were looking haggard. My friends and I were doing okay.

Eventually, after what felt like a week of traveling, the tunnel we were in began to level out. By now, we had to be deep under the mountains that bordered the north of the empire, but I had no way of knowing exactly where we were, or how deep we had gone beyond my general impressions. I had also noticed the air starting to feel a little thinner, and the temperature was slowly getting warmer the deeper we went. It was still cold, but we no longer had to depend on the heat from the formation plates to keep from freezing.

"I think I found something." Valerie had come sprinting back to our main group after scouting further down the tunnel. "It looks like we aren't the first ones to reach this far underground. Not by a long shot."

We picked up the pace, excited to see something besides rock and more rock. A few minutes later we ran into a cavern large enough to hold a small village. Which was exactly what was revealed as soon as Valerie tossed a few more glow stones deeper into the area.

"It looks like it has been abandoned for a long time." She was almost whispering, as if talking too loud would disturb the former residents. "I can't be sure, but this might have been an outpost of some kind."

I agreed with her. The village was in a slight depression against the far wall of the cavern, with a dry moat surrounding it for protection. There was a low wall, about five feet high, that encircled a cluster of ten two-story buildings. They were arrayed like spokes of a wheel around a central well, with each building lacking any ornamentation or details to let us know what their original purpose might have been. I thought they looked similar to barracks, but there was no way to be sure. Their doorways seemed a bit shorter than the norm, but still within acceptable limits for a person to walk through standing upright. The walls had a gate almost directly in front of us, the wooden beams long since turned to dust. There was another gate opening on the opposite side of the outpost, which led into another tunnel that was choked with rubble from a collapse.

"Have you checked inside any of them?" Chu was holding his glow stone up to the wall, inspecting the stonework. "That might give us a clue as to why this place was abandoned."

She shook her head. "No, I wanted to wait for the rest of you before I went inside. There is no telling what could be hiding in there."

Any further discussion was interrupted by the group of sailors pouring into the cave. There were exclamations of surprise, and they flooded into the little outpost. They didn't even wait to see if it was clear of monsters or traps. I couldn't help but feel like they were practically asking for a good shel-lacking.

"Well, I guess we should get in there and try to figure out where all of this came from." Donny let out a sigh. "*Before* they manage to destroy any clues this place might hold."

We all nodded in silent agreement and started working our way down to the gate. It had clearly been formidable at one time, with the dry moat making the relatively short walls far more effective than their five feet would normally allow.

"This looks like it was probably a guard post of some kind, instead of just a regular outpost for some kind of an early warning system." Chu was measuring off the thickness of the walls. Almost three paces thick, making them almost twice as wide as they were tall. "Which begs two questions—who were they a guard post for, and what were they guarding against?"

"I don't know, but considering our luck, we will probably find out soon enough." Donny was inspecting the giant hinges, which were all that was left of the gates. "An even bigger question is, what made them all leave?"

"That doesn't matter right now." I spun up the qi in my brain core to help expand my senses. "We need to utilize this place to our advantage. Turning this into a base of operations would let us leave the horses in relative safety, while the rest of us explore deeper into the caves." I tried to sense if there were any threats in the area, but I didn't find anything. The dense levels of dark qi weren't making it easy, and the stagnant feel of the energy was still pervasive. It felt like there hadn't been anything living in this region for a very long time.

"What about the sailors?" Jamila had her hand on her katana, her knuckles white from gripping it too hard. "We still haven't found out who pushed you. And I don't trust any of them with Cloud or Scout."

"We could secure an area near a gate with wards, and if they tried anything the horses could just run away." Donny opened his mouth to say something else, but jumped as Scout bit him on the rear. We all tried to keep a straight face, but Scout seemed to immediately regret where he had bitten Donny. I had never seen a horse spit before. He shook his fist at the horse in anger. "Or they could just stay here and get slaughtered for meat!"

We all burst out in laughter at the exchange. It was a welcome reprieve from the pervasive gloom and darkness pushing down on all of us. Even Donny didn't seem that upset by the whole thing.

"Okay, I get the horses wouldn't want to run, but giving them the option seems like a good idea." Valerie started walking over to the first building as she talked. "I'll clear out the sailors from this one while the rest of you get started on marking out another area for us."

I pulled out the Dagger of Boom again. It was still holding a bit more than half a charge of qi I could use to carve with. "I'll set up a ring of wards around the building like the ones in the last cavern." I made eye contact with everyone, to make sure they understood not to cultivate light or dark qi outside the wards. "It will give us a chance to balance ourselves, before moving deeper." They all gave me a sharp nod, and we spread out to perform our tasks. Chu and Jamila used already carved plates several yards away from the building, while Donny was able to freehand designs to best fit the space between the gate and our temporary new home.

The focus required to make the carvings along the base of the foundation meant I lost track of time. When I finished, I looked up to see my friends circled around the warming stone while Chu was working on frying some flatbread into thick circles. I quickly cycled some qi through my meridians to relieve the pain in my back from being hunched over for so long before approaching them.

"Glad you could join us." Chu flipped a piece of bread, poking it to confirm it was cooking properly. "We were wondering if you were ever going to finish."

"Next time, I'll let you guys make the rune barrier that hides us from the evil guy who uses dead bodies like puppets, and I can sit down near the nice heating stone." I spun the now empty Dagger of Boom across my knuckles before popping it back inside my storage belt. "I wouldn't want to take away from your practice time, after all."

Chu looked around wide-eyed, not seeing any signs of support from anyone sitting around the makeshift campfire. "Now, I didn't mean—"

"Before my future husband puts another foot in his mouth, I actually have a question." Jamila cut him off, holding up a formation plate designed to concentrate qi into a liquid form. We set them up every time we stopped for longer than an hour to increase our supply, and it was a form that all of us could carve in our sleep by this point. "Why don't we just make something like a stamp? Have each of the runes you carve already pre-made, and just use some earth qi to soften up the stone a bit to allow the stamp to form?"

I paused for a second to think about it. There were tools already made like she was talking about, but they were usually constructed from extremely rare materials to ensure they could handle the influx of qi through their structure over and over again. "I don't think we have the materials necessary to make them. A metal or gem that conducts qi, and is stable enough to hold its shape over and over again, would be very rare." She nodded, but had a thoughtful look on her face.

"What do you think about taking a few days to work on securing this place, and maybe working on our stockpile of these new flash plates?" While he talked, Donny was carving one onto a small plank of wood. "You could even finally work on making us new armor and weapons, like you keep talking about." Everyone nodded in agreement with his idea. I *had* been talking about doing it for a long time now.

"Okay. We can take two or three days to figure out some replacement gates, explore this place better, and improve our gear." I looked back at the building we had commandeered. "Is there enough room inside for me to set up my mobile forge?"

"Yes." Donny gave me a sharp nod. "It's basically just one big open space. The second story must have been made from wood, because it is gone, just like the gates."

"Well, we have a plan then. I will get started as soon as we wake up, and the rest of you can work on the gates." I pulled out one of the expanding blocks of wood I had gotten from the old shipwreck. "If you need this, just ask. I can—"

It was my turn to get cut off. A huge wave of dark qi came washing over the far wall, through the area, and blanketed us in complete darkness. There were screams from the direction of sailors, and I felt all my friends spin up their cores. Starsdamnit. I had been really looking forward to eating that bread.

"Can anyone see anything?" Valerie's voice was steady, even if the energy she was putting off wasn't.

"Let's move inside the building, it should provide us with

some protection." I was already walking that direction, so I used some threads of air qi to help guide my friends to the nearest opening. The dark qi made pushing them out of my hand meridians feel like I had to force them through something thick and viscous, similar to dragging a stick through honey.

As we stumbled into the building everyone started pulling out weapons, and we could instantly see again. Somehow, the horses had already beaten us inside the building. They must have felt the disturbance coming, and sought shelter immediately. Smart horses.

The darkness was all-encompassing outside the wards, but the runes forced it to flow around the building. I extended my senses to try and see what was happening to the sailors. Unfortunately, the dark qi didn't let that happen. It was too thick and dense for me to penetrate.

"I'm going to try something." Donny walked over to the nearest window and tossed out one of the formation plates that flashed out a bright light. As soon as it hit the ground, there was a sound like tearing cloth, and the darkness around the doorway seemed less dense. I could even see the glow stones around the warming plate. They were very dim, but I could still see them.

Almost as suddenly as it had come, the wave of dark qi swept past us. I watched as it flowed toward the lowest point, where the well was located. It acted just like water, and drained into the opening, with a few puddles of qi that were left behind. As I moved to get a closer look, they were already dissipating, disappearing like it had never happened.

Had this been a natural phenomenon? Never, in all my years, had I experienced something like this. If an area was regularly flooded with this much natural qi, it would have surely been a haven for cultivators everywhere. But, unless they could find a way to balance all the dark qi with light, it would eventually harm anyone foolish enough to absorb that much of this single type of energy. If it was natural, this might explain why the qi was so still in this area. Nothing living would be able to stay here for any length of time.

"That was crazy!" Chu had already put his mace away and was walking back to the warming plate, where the chunk of bread he had been frying had burned. "Could that be why this place was abandoned? I wouldn't want to live somewhere I was blinded without warning at random moments."

"Who knows? Either way, we need to prepare for it to happen again." Jamila was already placing tons of qi-collecting plates around the immediate area, trying to capture the puddles of energy before they dissipated. "Everyone put out your condensing plates. If we can bottle that stuff, it might come in handy someday."

With a sharp nod, everyone followed suit. After tossing out my plates, I went over to check on the sailors. There were a few people laid out on the ground, and I could see some scorch marks on the buildings near their area that hadn't been there before. I approached the captain as he was directing his people to move into a few of the buildings.

"I take it that things didn't go very well for you over here." The captain looked over at me, clearly not happy to see me. I could see he was shaken, but he was doing his best to ensure his men didn't notice.

"Some of my people overreacted, and it caused a few injuries. Nothing we can't handle." He flicked his wrist, making a roll of herb-infused bandages appear from a storage ring. "We will be ready to continue in a few hours."

"Actually, that's part of why I came over here." I motioned to the walls surrounding the area. "This is clearly part of a larger civilization. One that most likely had a way to reach the surface. My group and I were thinking it would be best to fortify this area, and you wait here. We could move faster with a smaller group."

He paused to think for a moment, gauging his people's appearance. "I can see the benefits of your plan. But what about that massive wave of darkness? It was unnatural, like a dense fog of evil."

"I don't think it was necessarily evil. However, I wouldn't

recommend trying to cultivate if it happens again." I looked over to the rear gate, near where they had set up. "If you could figure out a way to block that entrance, my people will handle the other side."

He gave me a sharp nod, and turned to bark orders at his men. While they jumped to work, I returned to my friends. It looked like Chu already had a fresh batch of bread on the warming plate, and everyone was waiting for a piece. I hurried over to get my portion before Chu could eat mine.

CHAPTER EIGHTEEN

Empty Tomb

After wrestling my piece of bread from Chu, who still looked longingly at it, the others settled down to get some sleep. I volunteered for the first watch, and decided to explore the ruins for any clues to the origins of the builders. If I could gather some information about who they were, it might help me figure out some way to plan for the fight against the necromancer hiding in the larger city.

The first thing I did was look over how the walls were constructed. They looked as if the stone blocks were first quarried, and then fused with the blocks around it. The tool marks were barely noticeable, meaning they were extremely skilled at their job. Since the blocks were fused together, it also meant they had fine control over earth qi.

Next, I went to inspect the buildings. They were almost all the same, with only minor variations in each. One had a much larger door opening, with half-walls lining one side. It appeared to be some kind of stable, but for what type of animal I could only guess.

Another building had the remains of a counter inside, meaning it had most likely been either a store or bar. That was a good clue, because it meant this place was more than just an outpost. It might have been a village.

My next stop was the well, to see if I could tell where the dark qi went. When I looked down it, all I could see was darkness. I pulled out a glow stone, and dropped it over the rim. As it fell, I could see the remnants of a ladder along one side. The glow stone quickly disappeared into the darkness, but not because of any dark qi. It was just really, really deep. Maybe it wasn't even a well. The opening in the floor could have been a means of escape to a lower level, or a way to transport excavated ore. If this was part of a mine, it must have gone empty long ago. There were no signs of precious metals or gems in any of the side tunnels we had inspected.

The last building I checked was lined on the interior with rows of stone benches. It reminded me of a temple, but without the normal alcoves to venerate each of the gods. The building was also missing the stone floor for a second story, leaving the space more open and airy than the other buildings had been.

As I inspected the area where an altar or statue would have normally resided, I noticed a place where the floor was uneven. A closer look revealed a rectangle of flooring that wasn't seated properly. I spun out a thread of earth qi to prod it, and discovered a short stairwell leading down. Great. A basement inside a temple. I'd never been through *that* before.

I used the thread to lift the lid, and pulled a short spear out of my belt. Just in case. The staircase was a steep spiral that led down into another chamber. I used the meridians in my knees to spin out some fire threads. They provided light, and gave me another weapon if I needed it.

The bottom step was carved and inlaid with silver. It looked like a pattern reminiscent of the constellations, but more stylized into spiral patterns. It was familiar to me, but I couldn't quite place where I had seen it before.

Each wall was covered with shelves, cut into them like some sort of deep bookshelves. Poking around revealed a small bronze plaque on each shelf, with pre-Imperial writing. They were lists of names. I was in a burial chamber. An empty one. The memory of a dark temple deep in the southern forests had me feeling a little on edge. There were definitely similarities between the two, but I couldn't tell if it was due to them worshiping the same twisted powers, or if it was just a coincidence.

The back wall had an obelisk covered with name plates. A monument to the dead. A cenotaph, surrounded by empty graves. Looking around at the floor, I could see footprints in the dust. They originated from the room. The only footsteps leading into the hidden burial chamber were my own. The dead had gotten up and walked out of here on their own. A quick count of the shelves gave me an even two hundred missing bodies, and that was only if each shelf held only one person. There was certainly room on the deep shelves to hold several corpses. I felt a chill run down my spine. If there were more places like this, there was no telling how many bodies the death cultivator had animated. They could have an army by now.

I closed the chamber behind me as I left, and used some earth qi to seal it in place this time. It might be too little, too late, but the names on the cenotaph deserved to remain undisturbed from now on.

After finishing my search of the area, I was now positive that this had been some kind of mining village. What they had been mining, and why they had left, were still a mystery to me.

Knowing that there were at least two hundred desiccated corpses running around down here, I thought it would be prudent to light up the area better. I moved along the top of the wall, placing a glow stone every ten steps for the entire circumference of the village. It was just enough to banish all but the deepest of shadows. Now, one person keeping watch on top of any building would be able to see an approaching zombie horde. It also cut into the number of glow stones I had left, but I felt it was worth the cost.

I still had an hour left on my watch, so I decided to finally look inside the ring I had found on the skeleton in the old shipwreck. It was filled with the normal goods you might expect from someone wearing the clothes and jewelry they had been wearing. Several changes of fine clothing, a few bags of coins, and more than one bottle of fine wine paired with rich food. The unexpected find was all the ingots of precious metals. Not to mention an extremely nice set of blacksmithing tools.

The last item in the ring was a bit unexpected. It was a thick notebook, filled with the scrawling notes of its former owner. Part journal and part blacksmithing manual, it gave details on the life of the family we had laid to rest.

I flipped to the end of the book, looking for some clue as to what had ended their voyage so violently.

Today Hadad said he saw the great monster under the ship again. Mari and I are convinced he is just nervous about his apprenticeship with the main branch of the Burning Forge Sect. Such an auspicious beginning for a young man is certainly not what we expected, but his connection to the metal element is so strong that even their Elder Smith seemed jealous after the testing. My own father was shocked at their extravagant offer, considering how miserly they normally were during the selection process. The gods must know how badly we could use the gold, and Hadad will certainly bring fame and fortune to our clan name. With the dark stars falling from the midday sky on the day we left port, I knew this was going to be a journey to remember. Taqa is jealous of her brother leaving home, but she is sure to follow in her mother's footsteps. I have no doubt her sharp temper will serve as a fine foundation for a spearmaster. I will have her begin practice for the trials as soon as we return home. There is a storm moving in, and I am needed on deck again.

That was the end of the entry. If they were attacked only a short time after the *nox* entered the world, it was a fair bet that it was a dark mana demon who sunk their ship. The boy, Hadad, might have attracted a *nox* searching for a powerful host. I had a sneaking suspicion I now knew the identity of the necromancer. If it was just some kid, he might not even realize what he was doing when he agreed to join with the demon.

I tried skimming for more information throughout the journal, but I didn't see anything else I could use other than their clan name. At least I would be able to return some of the items to the surviving family members.

For a moment, I thought about my own children. There were still a few hundred years before they were supposed to be born, which meant I had time to figure out how to handle what to do. I had a strong suspicion that the gods tinkering with my brain during the reincarnation process to remove the madness of floating in a thousand years of nothingness might also be a reason as to why I wasn't more worried about them. I was aware of them, and the possibility of them not being born again if I didn't play my cards just right, but the intense worry I should have been feeling wasn't there. It was concerning, to say the least. What else had the gods done to me?

"Jim? Why are you crying?" Donny had sat down next to me without me even noticing. Some guard I was being.

"It's nothing, don't worry." I scrubbed my eyes with a sleeve. "I'm going to get some rest. Wake me when it's time to go."

He watched me leave, my quiet footsteps the only sound in the underground cave. It wasn't just the chamber under the temple. This whole place was an empty tomb.

CHAPTER NINETEEN

An Army

————

I opened my eyes to pure darkness. There was an instant of panic before I realized I could feel the flow of dark qi brushing over my skin, and I was standing on my feet. I was dream walking again.

Knowing that the wave of dark qi would pass, I just waited until it moved on. Once it cleared, I followed it through the tunnels it was flooding as it passed. Since it obscured everything in front of me, I didn't realize I had reached the underground city I had seen in my last dream until I almost walked off the edge of the cliff.

When I looked down, I could see the orange glow of a river of lava deep in the depths of the dark canyon. From this height, it looked like barely a trickle, but it was impossible to gauge its true size and depth. A second river, this one of water, cut through a smooth channel halfway up the side of the cliff, clearly engineered to pass near the city. It must have been their water source. In more than one place, the water ran over the edges of the path cut into the stone wall, falling to the lava below. It must have eroded its way through after the city was abandoned. Given a few more years, the water would wear through the channel completely and reach the lava below. The resulting steam would most likely destroy the cavern in short order.

Looking up, I noticed the walls had changed since the last time I was here. There had been some recent construction to repair the ancient damage, and it now had a makeshift gate instead of the stone portcullis. It must have been raised out of the way. There was still a large gap to either side of the gate house, so I crossed the narrow stone bridge to see where the wave of dark qi was going.

As I approached, I once again saw a sentry standing in the opening. The bluish-green light from the lichen and mushrooms was almost non-existent this close to the walls, but it was enough to let me see the guard was certainly no longer alive. It looked more like a piece of jerky wearing ancient armor than an actual person, but its grip on the spear it was leaning against was firm. I couldn't feel any aura coming from it, which was a mixed blessing. Normally, a death cultivator had to imbue their flesh puppets with a bit of their own power to make them mobile and strong. That wasn't the case here, meaning it would probably be weaker than the traditional versions. It would also make it impossible to feel the zombie approach, as it had roughly the same energy footprint as a rock. Definitely some bad news.

Moving by the guard was uneventful, beyond it stirring a bit as I walked past. It might have sensed a disturbance, probably because my presence made the qi in the region shift. The energy here was almost as dense and still as everywhere else, besides the steady flow of dark and metal qi still traveling in a stream deeper into the city. Suddenly, the reason for all the stagnant qi took on a more sinister twist. It must be because there wasn't anything living down here. It seemed the cave crickets had just been passing through, after all.

I lost sight of the wave I had been following, but there was only one place it could go. The temptation to pick up my pace was strong, so I tamped it down by trying to memorize as many details of the city as I could. There was no doubt we would be fighting here soon, and any information I could gather now might be the difference between life and death for my friends and I.

It was clear that this place was older than the small village we were staying in. The buildings were more stylized, with things like steps and paths showing the passage of thousands of feet over centuries of time. They were also thicker, with more narrow doorways. It was a hint that this place was first built with defense in mind, meaning it was probably the origin of the underground civilization—the place they had built their beachhead to explore around the area. Normally, such a place would have been closer to the surface, with the exploration delving deeper into the mountains. This seemed to be reversed. Had they originated from within the ground somehow?

I had to stop worrying about the mystery of the town, because I eventually discovered what had drawn in the massive wave of dark qi. It was the necromancer, and he was holding something very familiar to me.

Getting a good look at Hadad was impossible, due to the heavy hooded robes he was wearing. Seriously though, could I ever get an enemy that was something besides dark and dreary? I mean, would it kill these guys to wear something with some color? Anyway. The important bit was what he was using. It was a six-foot staff, with a three-pronged claw on either end. It was gathering the dark qi into a condensed ball on one end, while the opposite end remained empty. The silvery metal it was constructed from reflected the dim light with an oily sheen. It was familiar, because I was looking at the bigger version of the scepter I still carried in my storage belt. The scepter I had found in a temple meant to be a way to access the power of the only thing worse than the *nox*. The devourers. The *vorare*.

Before I could get closer, I was pulled backward. Not by a

wave of light. This time, I fell back into a wall of pure black. Just as it washed over me, I caught a glimpse of what was waiting behind the man holding the staff. Thousands of skeletons, animated corpses, and moldering beasts stood in ranks, awaiting his orders. And all of them were looking right at me.

CHAPTER TWENTY

Alloys

I woke to the sound of shouting and explosions. It wasn't the first time, and it most likely wouldn't be the last. That didn't make it any more fun to deal with, and I scrambled to fight my way free of the blankets covering me to see what was wrong. Stupid mattress.

Jamila and Chu weren't inside, and Donny and Valerie were already on their way out the door. I took a shortcut and dove through the empty window next to me, and rolled to my feet at a sprint toward the rear gate, where I could sense qi being used in rapid fashion.

The sailors were all along the wall, with a few standing in the gap where the gate should be. Three of them were blasting the blocked tunnel with qi attacks, so I spun up my heart core to help me leap on top of the wall.

"What's going on?" I asked the nearest sailor, who was frantically searching the dim cavern, whipping his head around to try and look everywhere at once. "Did you see something?"

"I didn', bu' Bruck did!" He pointed to one of the men throwing qi constructs at the collapsed tunnel. "He seen eyes peekin' o'er the top o' them rocks, an' Bruck ne'er lies!"

"Cease fire!" The captain had finally shown up, and he was waving his arms to get their attention. "I said *cease fire*, stars-damn your souls!"

I jumped down and approached the captain as he got his men back under control. Before I could suggest we go and inspect the tunnel, he was already marching off with a small contingent of his men.

"Well, that was exciting." Chu had jumped down from the opposite side of the gate, and was still holding his mace. "Should we go and see if there actually was something there?"

"No." I shook my head, and turned to go back to our area. "Even if there wasn't something there this time, it's only a matter of time." He hurried up to catch up to me, so I slowed my steps a bit. "I had another dream, and it wasn't a good one. There is a whole undead army down here, and I need to help us prepare for it."

"An army?" He stumbled a bit, but still kept pace with me. "When you say army, do you mean a small army, or, like, an *army*-army?"

"I didn't have time to count, but I would guess somewhere in the three-thousand range." We had reached our building, and I went inside and pulled out my mobile forge. "So, I guess you could say an army-army."

"Stars…" He looked back outside, where the rest of our group was returning. "I'll tell the others. We'll get to work on the formation plate stockpile, and make sure our gate is sealed up. You do what you have to do."

I gave him a sharp nod, and started pulling out ingots of metal. We were facing a new kind of threat, one that I didn't have a good idea of their full capabilities. The sheer number of enemies we might have to face meant my friends and I would need full-body coverage. Getting swarmed by greater numbers meant I couldn't leave gaps in our armor, like I had before. I would need to incorporate everything I had done thus far, and maybe throw in something new.

The metal would need to be an alloy, one that used the qi-dissipating effects of orichalcum, without blocking my friends' ability to use qi when fighting. I needed it to be strong enough to withstand most physical attacks, so it had to be resilient, yet flexible so it didn't crack if hit with enough force. I also wanted to incorporate the qi shield ideas I had used on the buttons during our fight in the Western Capital, to protect everyone long enough to escape if we were surrounded or swarmed. Basically, the perfect armor. This might take a little bit.

The style of armor would have to be similar to the set I had already made, a brigandine. It would allow me to use a layered approach of smaller pieces, and improve flexibility. Instead of small rectangles, I would use long horizontal strips that overlapped. I could also use a base of leather to attach them to, and have spare pieces ready to replace any parts that were worn or broken. The rivets that held them onto the leather would be big enough to hold the runes for the shielding, and I could inlay grooves where liquid qi could be poured onto them to activate the different types of shield before we went into battle. It would be small, and burn through the energy quickly, but in an emergency it might give us the time needed to heal, or recharge our cores enough to keep fighting.

My early experiments combining orichalcum with the oily adamantine were not good. They were like, well, oil and water. Mixing seemed impossible. Orichalcum was hard to deal with, and it was brittle if heated up too much. Getting the adamantine to a malleable state was exhausting, as it used huge amounts of qi and required extremely high temperatures. Pretty much exact opposites. I didn't see a way to get the two metals to work together. I thought I had something that would work, but the ingot exploded in my face when it started to cool down. Scout's chuffing laughter didn't help. Stupid horse was lucky I didn't need any glue.

The seventh attempt was almost perfect. I even got it formed into thick strips to start making it into a greave, but the moment the metal touched my bare skin, it messed up the flow of qi in my body so bad I had to take an hour break just to get back to normal. Definitely not something you want happening in a real fight.

So, I was forced to change things up a little. I had a decent supply of mithril, especially if I included what had been in the ring of the dead man that had been in the old shipwreck. Initially, I had thought about returning all of it to their clan, but I had a continent to save. I needed to use everything at my disposal to make that happen. Mithril wasn't as strong as adamantine, but it was pretty close. It would have to be close enough.

I tried combining mithril and orichalcum, and thankfully it worked. Five ingots of mithril with one ingot of orichalcum turned out to be the perfect mix, and it diluted the effects of the qi-blocking material enough that it wouldn't disrupt the internal use of qi when it touched bare skin. We would still be limited in our external attacks. All the qi we absorbed or used would have to happen through the hands and feet only, but that would be the only place someone could hurt us with qi as well. I would have to make everyone new weapons that allowed us to easily enhance them with various elements, to make up for the lack of versatility we usually enjoyed. A massive qi attack or construct might still be able to get through the armor, but it wouldn't be nearly as damaging.

Mithril was normally a silvery metal that reflected light with a pale and beautiful sheen. Now that it was combined with orichalcum, it had a red tint that cut down on the mirror-like effect. It would make it less visible, which was certainly a positive, but I would need to polish it with something coarse to cut down on reflections even more.

Once I had the alloy figured out, I went and took measurements of my friends. I had lost track of time, and they already had a massive pile of formation plates and popper stones ready to split between us.

Donny was even experimenting with new combinations, and testing them by tossing the plates over the wall. As I watched, a column of stone shot into the air before exploding, sending shards of sharp rocks raining down all over the area. "Nope, not concentrated enough. It needs more energy in the explosion, and less in the vertical expansion…"

I left him to it after collecting his measurements and axe. Everyone else had handed over their main weapons as well, except for Valerie. She had kept her bow, but handed over three quivers of homemade arrows.

"I like my bow just how it is, but if you can improve these somehow, I would appreciate it." They were thicker than the arrows I would normally use, but the arrowheads were still the same size as a regular arrow.

"I think I can come up with something." I stored them in my belt as I walked back to the forge. I had been cultivating as much as possible while taking a break, since the progress I had made so far had drained more than three-quarters of my core. At this rate, I would need to take another break after figuring out an alloy to enhance our weapons. On the upside, all this cultivating still went toward improving my overall level, and gods knew I needed to be as strong as I could be. Literally. The gods had told me that.

There wasn't enough mithril to make both the weapons and armor, so I went back to the adamantine. I still had a ridiculous amount of the metal, making it my best option. A quick experiment with malachite—which made qi usage easier—showed it suffered from the same high heat issues as the orichalcum had, so I would need to do something else. Since I only had a limited amount of malachite, I decided to just inlay it into the weapons. A thin strip of the qi-enhancing metal would allow for a minor increase in the six main elements, and adamantine already allowed for the easy passage of light and dark qi. Just like with the armor, it wasn't perfect, but it was better than the plain steel versions of the weapons that everyone carried right now.

After deciding what I was going to do, I sat down on the floor and started to draw out the plans for each person. Jamila, in particular, wouldn't like how restrictive this armor design would be, but it would be necessary to keep her from getting ripped apart by the death cultivator's minions.

"Rea'y fo' some foo'?" Chu walked in while chewing on a mouthful of food and held out a plate of meat skewers on top of a large piece of flatbread. I raised an eyebrow at him in silent judgment as he swallowed. "What?"

"I guess I should just be happy some made it to me." I grinned and accepted the plate with a nod of thanks. I decided not to give him a hard time about talking with his mouth full, especially considering how good it smelled.

"You have been at this all day." Chu leaned over my shoulder to check on my progress. "It wouldn't be a bad thing if you took a break."

"I can work on these while eating, and cultivating to refill my cores." I took a skewer off the plate and turned back to my sketches. "We need to get moving, before the necromancer can mobilize his forces against us. That means I need to finish with these as soon as possible."

"Do you think you can finish this by tomorrow?" He looked around at the massive mess I had made. "I mean, our old armor is plenty serviceable."

"No, it isn't good enough." I pointed to the drawing of an armet, a full-face helmet that hinged along each cheek and had a visor that dropped in place to hold the sides against the head. "This will cover you better than what we currently have, and provide better protection from qi attacks across your entire body." I then pulled out a piece of parchment with my rivet design. "And each rivet will provide you with a small shield, like the buttons we used before."

He bent down to look them over. "Why do they all have that deep groove along the edges? Wouldn't that make them weaker, where the metal is thinner?"

"Yes, but it's worth the trade-off." I held up my first attempt, and pulled out a vial of liquid qi. "Watch. When I pour this over the rivet, instead of it just running over the top of it, the liquid collects here, along the divot." A sixteen-inch round shield of shimmering qi formed around the small piece of metal. "It is only enough to power it for a minute or two, but that's all we'll need."

"Okay, but why not make a socket? Liquid qi evaporates quickly, and a beast core is just concentrated qi." He poked at the shield, causing the runes on the small rivet to flare brightly. "It just seems like the liquid wouldn't last long. Or, you could just put the runes on the armor itself."

"You know, that isn't a bad idea. Not the runes on the actual armor—that would weaken the plates, and I want those to be easy to swap out anyway—but cores could work." I pulled out a common core. "The only problem is, they would need to be some really big rivets. And, the shield would be made of whatever element the core was aspected toward. That would make them weak to at least its opposite element."

"So, just make a single socket to power the rivet shields, and we can swap out the cores as needed. No protection is going to be perfect." Chu tapped the designs. "This is still going to take a long time, no matter what you do."

"I know, and I could use your help." I pulled out the designs for the leather base and cloth lining the armor would need. "If you and the others could work on these, I would really appreciate it. I'll try to figure out some way to get the core idea to work."

He took them from me and headed for the door. "We can handle this part. You get the rest finished."

Chu was out the door before I could say anything else, so I got back to work. The forge had to be powered by my qi, and I also had to infuse the actual metal with my qi while shaping it. Pretty soon, the sounds of a hammer ringing against an anvil filled the building.

After making enough of the alloy, I started shaping the various pieces into the necessary parts. It took much longer this time around because I couldn't just make a mold. Each piece required a different shape, and I made two of each so everyone had a spare section if something broke. At one point, I heard shouting coming from outside, but I just ignored it and kept working. It sounded like people complaining about the noise I was making, and not an attack. They could just deal with the lack of sleep. It was my friends and I going out there, not them. The sailors were going to stay here and turtle up inside these safe walls—well, as safe as they could be—while we put our lives on the line to save them.

I reworked the design so we could use cores to power the shields. It required a thin wire of malachite running from the socket in the back of the helmet running along the leather backing to each rivet, but it wasn't hard to manage. Core-powered armor shielding wasn't exactly unheard of, but most found the costs to be too extravagant. Considering the materials I had on hand, I wasn't very concerned about costs. There was a low risk of a wire snapping or burning out if the qi drain was too sharp, but something that hit them that hard would just punch through the shields anyway. We would just have to make sure to swap out cores frequently.

It took the better part of the rest of the next day to finish, but when I finally popped the pure mithril rivets in place, the end result was worth it. I felt as though a Grandmaster black-smith would be proud to wear it, even if it was light on enchantments.

The five sets of armor and weapons were far from identical, but they all looked brutally effective. I had made Donny's new axe thinner, and Jamila's dual katanas longer. The mace for Chu was almost the same size, but the handle was a little thicker to manage the weight of the heavy end of the mace better. I had also added a brutal three-sided pyramid-shaped spike at each end of the eight-bladed mace, to give him more versatility and reach. Valerie now had a wide selection of arrows, including heavy armor-piercing tips, barbed tips for maximum damage, and some broadhead tips that were sized properly for the larger arrow shafts she had given me. For myself, I had made a dozen new spears made of solid adamantine, as well as several improved throwing knives that I could use with my whips. The rows of runes that mimicked several trap plates that ran along the hilts and blades would be very useful in the coming battle.

Finally, I had designed new tower shields for everyone. Instead of the massive door-sized steel versions, these would only reach our shoulders if they were set on the ground. I had used plain adamantine, without any of the modifications. They were the last item I had made, so I didn't have the qi left to do anything fancy. The top and bottoms had a row of short, thick spikes, and the edges were sharpened like an oversized axe blade. They were good for both offense and defense, and should prove especially useful in these tunnels.

"Wow." I turned around to see my friends lined up across from me. "That's some impressive work, Jim." Donny approached and picked up his new axe. "Why don't you get some rest, and we can practice with this new gear for a few hours? It looks like it's going to take a little getting used to."

"Yeah, get some sleep. You look dead on your feet." Jamila glanced over at me while checking out her armor. "It's going to take more than a *little* getting used to this armor. I have no idea how I'm going to fight while wrapped up in this metal cocoon."

I didn't bother arguing, I just stumbled to bed. It had been a long two days, and despite being a Saint cultivator, my meridians were still sending spikes of pain through my body. It was a reminder not to slack on reinforcing my cultivation system, and to keep up with my daily exercise regime. I had been neglecting it since we had been shipwrecked, and a few rock trolls were no excuse for falling behind.

As I finally laid down to sleep, it finally hit me. Why would a *nox* be using a tool that helped open a doorway to the *vorare*? I didn't like any of the answers my brain could come up with.

CHAPTER TWENTY-ONE

Just Breathe

I couldn't be sure of what time I finally got out of bed, but it *felt* like morning. The smell of meat frying on a pan was good motivation to get on my feet and try on my new armor all at once. Since I had made it, I didn't have any problems slipping it on and fastening the sides. I left off the helmet for now and put it in my belt, alongside my newly forged weapons.

"About time you got out of bed!" Donny poked his head in one of the empty windows, his helm open and showing off my cousin's stupid grin. "You ready to go? I can't wait to try this stuff out in a real fight!" He disappeared before I could answer. I guess at least he was happy with the new gear.

The meat Chu was cooking wasn't the bacon I was hoping for, but the thinly sliced pieces of Angry Murder Goat were pretty tasty. Well, if you were hungry, it was close enough.

We made sure to pack up everything except for a few days' worth of feed for the horses, and then double-checked our wards. Donny and Chu arranged things with the captain, and made sure they knew not to approach the area we had claimed. The threat of unknown traps would hopefully keep them from trying to eat the horses—or doing something equally stupid—for a day or two. Okay, probably just a few hours, but the first layers of traps weren't really that lethal.

Our first task was to clear enough rubble from the tunnel collapse to allow us room to get through. It took longer than normal, mostly because we were all getting used to our new armor. It made us a little stiffer, but I insisted. The only thing we didn't have on was our helms. They restricted airflow more than I would have liked, and we all had been getting winded quickly. The death cultivator was still alive deeper into these caves, so I knew the air was still breathable farther down. Of course, that didn't preclude the possibility of a section between us and his location that wasn't safe, but we would burn those bridges when we got there.

Eventually, we finished clearing out a path. The sailors had done a good job wrecking the entire area when they had gone a little crazy. To their credit, we did find signs of the dust being disturbed on the opposite side of the rubble, meaning there probably had been something watching them. The trail died off rather quickly, as the dust gradually gave way to areas wet with moisture, mold, and lichen.

We were finally getting deep enough to see small patches of the blue luminescent variety, but it wasn't enough of a light source to allow us to see without using other items.

"I don't care how much it costs, when we get back to the surface, the first thing I'm doing is getting rid of all these green glow stones and picking out a different color." Valerie was walking next to me at the rear, letting Jamila get a turn taking point. "These make us all look washed out and sickly."

"Believe me, I understand." I had my glow stone fastened on the end of my spirit wood walking stick. If I needed to shift it into a different form, it would just fall to the ground at my feet and allow me to still have some extra illumination. "Green used to be one of my favorite colors. Now, I'm getting pretty tired of it."

"Shhhh!" We both looked up to see Donny with a fist raised. It was our universal symbol for freezing in place. It also meant enemies were nearby.

I gestured for everyone to don their helmets. Jamila was still out of sight farther down the tunnel, so we all readied weapons and started to spread out. I didn't see why Donny had stopped us, but I had no reason to doubt him.

Soon, I finally heard what he must have noticed. There was a subtle grinding noise coming from somewhere. The tunnels made it hard to figure out where it was coming from, beyond somewhere up ahead.

After a few minutes without anything happening, we started moving forward again. The grinding sound was still intermittently audible, so we made sure to stay as silent as possible. That was another shortcoming of the new armor. It wasn't exactly the greatest equipment for sneaking around in. We were forced to take agonizingly slow steps to keep ourselves from making a lot of noise.

Catching up to Jamila was now the priority. Until we could identify what was making the grinding sounds, we needed to stick together. I was even doubting our normal tactic of having a scout pushed forward so far. We needed to at least keep one another within sight at all times.

We finally caught up to her when we rounded a gentle curve in the tunnel. She was down on one knee, and leaning against the wall. Chu rushed forward to help her, so we quickly followed behind. As he got close to her, the grinding noise suddenly happened again, and a fine mist sprayed out from a thin crack in the walls. He instantly started coughing, and was soon stumbling.

Jamila must have triggered some form of trap left by the former residents. I had already released the spirit wood back into its ring, and started spinning out some threads of wood qi to drag them back, when a thin crack opened up in the ceiling above us. The grinding sound was much louder, and the crack widened into an inch gap that stretched as far as I could see in either direction. Not good.

"Run! Our only chance is to get clear!" I spun out two more threads of wood qi, then tied one on the left wrist of each person. Despite their hands and wrists being accessible, the armor still tried to make them fizzle out and disperse, so I had to reinforce it with more energy. Then, I forced out a bubble of air qi around my head to try and filter out as much of the mist as possible. My own armor made it even more difficult, but I was able to push through. It was going to drain my cores quickly, but I had to manage it. And, I had found *another* problem with the new armor. Maybe I wasn't quite the Grand-master smith I thought I was.

Donny scooped up both Jamila and Chu, while Valerie helped guide him. I only took a breath when I had to, so I was still standing a few minutes later when all four of them were barely on their feet. My air qi filter wasn't perfect, but it was better than not breathing at all. The wood qi I used was trying to heal them, but without concentrated focus it wasn't doing much beyond slowing the effects of the gas. I used the tethers to start pulling them behind me. They did their best, stumbling and coughing as we tried to get out of the area. There was still no end in sight, so I just put my head down and started walking. I felt it as each of my friends fell to the ground one by one, and I needed to pull harder as the weight increased. The smooth and damp surface made it easy to keep dragging them, at least.

I don't know how long I kept going like that. Time seemed to stretch on for days, but I knew it couldn't have been nearly that long. At some point, I dropped the air bubble and focused entirely on healing the damage to my lungs. The strain was too much for me to do the same for my friends. All I could do was hope that the slow trickle of life qi would keep them alive. The gas was only corrosive to our bodies, meaning its long-ago creator had wanted anyone who triggered the trap to still leave their items in one piece when they found them. It was insidious, and spoke to a strong understanding of alchemy. I lost myself to the cadence of putting one clanking foot in front of the other. We weren't going to die down here. Not from some ancient trap whose owner was nothing more than a memory long forgotten.

I snapped out of it when I walked helmet-first into a wall, causing my shield to flare in the darkness. Looking around, I realized I was clear of the crack that spewed the gas from the walls. My cores were almost completely empty, as were the batteries on my belt. I must have drained those by reflex while my brain was on auto-pilot. I looked up, expecting to see a dead end. Instead, I was greeted by proper stonework.

It wasn't a regular tunnel wall, but the wall of another outpost. This one had much more damage, like it had seen heavy fighting. I followed the curve of the wall to the opposite end of the much wider tunnel, and found a small gap where something had smashed in a section wide enough to squeeze through.

Since I was almost completely out of qi, I decided to physically drag each of my friends through the gap individually. I was completely exhausted, and I would need to set up some light sources before cultivating to maintain enough balance in my cores. The dark and metal qi was even stronger here, and I was too tired to try to cultivate without the assistance a large amount of light would provide.

Once I had everyone inside, I took the time to search the area. They were already starting to come back around, thankfully, but I wanted to make sure we were safe for the time being.

This outpost was much smaller than the last one, and most certainly was meant as more of a checkpoint or stronghold than a village. There were only two one-story buildings placed in front of each gate. The gate on the wall we had entered through wasn't visible from the other side, but it was plainly marked once you were inside the compound. It was a cleverly hinged section of stone bricks, which was probably why it still stood. The other gate was a more traditional archway. The metal portcullis had long ago rusted into near uselessness, and the wooden doors had moldered into large piles of rot. It wouldn't even stop a determined Angry Murder Goat from getting through, but at least we would hear it knocking down the portcullis. I dropped a few trap plates in the gap we had crawled through before helping everyone limp into the nearest building. It was completely empty inside, with no windows, and a short door on each end. Probably a barracks, or possibly a storage area.

All of us were in pretty bad shape. Any time someone tried to talk, it just ended in hard coughing. Whatever that trap had contained, it had been both a sedative and a corrosive. Maybe the armor had been a good choice, because any exposed skin was going to need some healing to recover from the blistering.

I had just set up some wards and a few of our brighter lights so I could start cultivating when I heard a strange scraping sound coming from the other side of the main gate. I had to walk outside to see what was going on, and I instantly dropped to my stomach as soon as I saw what was making the noise.

The scraping I had heard was the sounds of hundreds of bones as they shuffled along the cavern floor. The bones of the feet of a very large group of skeletons that were currently shambling past us, without realizing we were here. Behind them was a contingent of the desiccated remains of what I assumed were the former residents of the underground city. They were all wearing rusted armor, and carried weapons that looked to be made entirely of black and red obsidian. Several corpses that were more, well, *squishy*, moaned behind the silent troops. I even saw a few dirty uniforms from the captain's crew, but not nearly enough to account for all of the people at the outpost. These must be the missing crewmembers they hadn't found yet. There were also a few in the armor of the Imperial Army. Not the Elemental Guard, but the regular conscripts that were forced into service for not paying taxes, or displeasing some lord or another. The smallest group, composed of monsters made of the more normal high mountain pass varieties, brought up the rear. But it wasn't even these that had really caught my attention. I lost count of all of them, but not because there were millions. I lost count because I was shocked at what came next. It was much worse. In the very back of this last trailing element of foes were my hated enemies.

I now knew what had happened to Donut and Boot.

CHAPTER TWENTY-TWO

Stand

It took some effort not to try to kill the damned things immediately. Now that they were dead, the ridiculous regeneration speed would be gone. I hoped, at least. Usually, flesh puppets could be healed, but only by the necromancer using his own qi to regenerate lost tissue and bone. Since these weren't the normal version, I had no idea if that would still hold true. Rock trolls that couldn't feel pain and still regenerated at their ridiculous rates would be a nightmare to fight. Either way, now wasn't the time to find out.

After the procession disappeared down a tunnel on the other side of the cavern, I went back and rejoined my friends. They seemed to be mostly recovered from the mist trap. I took a few minutes to convey what I had seen, and then I sat down to try and recover. The past several hours hadn't been easy on me.

While cultivating, I noticed the qi in the area wasn't as stagnant now that we were deeper underground. The pull of the dark qi was stronger, and the increased flow made it feel more natural. It made refilling my cores much easier, and in a little over four hours I was almost fully recharged. I would still need to refine and condense the qi to turn the quantity of energy into quality elements that evenly distributed through my body to help my advancement, but it was good enough for right now. And I had a feeling we were going to be doing a lot of fighting.

"I'm just saying, that trap was nasty." Chu's voice broke me out of my thoughts. He was cooking a meal near the entrance to the building, and talking to the others while they worked on cleaning the trap residue off of their new armor. "Who in the world would make something like that?"

"From the grinding sound, I am pretty sure it was an old trap." Jamila seemed subdued. She had been the one to trigger the trap, and was probably still beating herself up about it. "It was probably left behind by the same people who built all this stuff."

"If that was an old trap, I would hate to see what it looked like when it was brand new." Donny was checking for any damage to the finish on his chest piece. "How long would it have taken for it to melt us into goo?"

"Does it matter?" Valerie was already done cleaning her armor, and was carving something into a circular piece of stone. "We didn't die, and there is a bigger concern out there. An army of dead things is walking around outside, and we need to figure out a way to kill it, before it kills us." She frowned at the disk in her hand. "I give up. Donny, you see if you can figure this thing out." She tossed it to him, and he studied it intently.

"I see what you were trying to do here, but the runes are in the wrong order. Have Jim try to fix it." He looked up and saw I was done cultivating. "Here, see what you can do. It's a pretty good idea." Donny slid it across the ground to me, and I picked it up to look it over.

The design used a lot of air and earth runes, with a touch of fire added at the end of the rune sequence. I hadn't seen anything like it before. Even my own formation plates tended to only use one or two elements. The more complicated the design, the higher the qi costs. It also increased the chances of the plate just not working, or outright exploding at the wrong time.

"I wanted to make something that would cling to the undead, to slow them down." Valerie walked over and dropped a sack full of the stone disks in my lap. Ouch. "See if you can fix it. I'm tired of messing with the stupid things. I'm going to try to make some of those rune stamps we had talked about."

After using a swirl of wood qi to my lower half to fix the damage, I pulled out a blank disk and started working. Good thing I hadn't needed to speak, because talking in a slightly higher tone could have been a bit embarrassing. I could see what she was going for, but there was too much air and not enough fire runes. As I ate my bowl of stew Chu brought over, I finally put together a sequence that might actually work. I quickly carved a few more examples so we could test them properly, and looked up to show Valerie what I had done. She was gone.

"Hey, where's Valerie?" She wasn't near the others, and the building was just one empty room, so there was no place for her to be hiding.

"Oh, she went to see where that big army you told us about went." Chu pointed with his spoon out the door. "She should be back in a few minutes." I felt a tremor pass through the qi flows in the direction the undead army had gone. Stars-damnit.

I scrambled to my feet, storing the new stone disks in my belt as I headed for the door. My intuition was telling me this wasn't good. Everyone else saw how I was acting and quickly stored any items we had out. Another tremor swept past, this time strong enough that the others felt it too.

"That can't be good." Donny spun up his cores, so we all followed suit. We then pulled out weapons, and made sure our armor was tightened properly. "We should hurry."

"Make sure you get your helms sealed up." I fastened my own in place while I talked. "If you get swarmed, you don't want to leave yourself exposed with unpowered shields." They all did as I asked while we moved to the gate. We all used small bursts of qi to help us jump onto the top of the wall, just in time to see Valerie come sprinting into the cavern.

"They're right behind me!" She paused to turn and loose a qi-reinforced arrow into the tunnel at a target that was out of sight. "Get ready!" Her platinum hair waved behind her like the tail of a comet as she turned and streaked toward us.

Valerie's feet had barely touched the top of the wall when the first of the walking skeletons stumbled into sight and advanced into the open area between the wall and the entrance. It was barely held together by the most tenuous remnants of dry sinew and reinforced by metal qi. A swirl within the deep shadows of its empty eye sockets was evidence of the dark qi animating the human remains. It stopped and lifted a short recurve bow that looked almost petrified with age, and loosed an arrow in our direction.

"What in the world happened?" Donny steadied his fiancée with one hand, and tossed a handful of poppers at the tunnel entrance with the other. "How did they even know you were following them?"

Valerie took a swig of watered wine from a jug she pulled out of her storage ring before answering. "They were waiting for me when I got deeper into the tunnels. There was this giant cat thing that dropped down behind me, and while I was fighting it, a whole bunch of those skeletons came up behind me. I managed to take down the cat, but there were too many of the other ones for me to fight by myself." A group of about fifty skeletons and at least twenty of the desiccated corpses grouped up behind the lone archer, who had been blasted most of the way back to the entrance by Donny's poppers. I had hoped it would have just been knocked into a pile of bones by the small explosions. We weren't that lucky.

"Well, how about Jim just throws one of those big spike things?" Chu motioned for me to get on with it. "That would probably fix this pretty quickly."

"Are you crazy?" Jamila glanced at him before turning back to face the oncoming enemies. "That could bring this whole place down!"

"Donny, Chu, and I form a shield wall at the gate. Jamila,

you be ready to provide relief. Valerie, get your helm in place, and then take out any archers you see. Everyone, be sure to call out if you see one of the bigger creatures come through that tunnel." I pulled out my new shield and strapped it on my arm. "This is going to be a slog, so conserve your qi as much as you can. Make sure any formation plates you toss out don't go off too close to the walls. We don't want to create a gap for them." My tone conveyed how serious I was, and everyone else followed suit. Nearly fifteen to one odds made this a significant fight.

As we got in position, I was more than a little concerned to see our opponents doing the same. They were spreading out into orderly ranks, with about fifteen archers lined up behind them. Valerie would have her hands full.

"Hey, Val, catch!" I tossed up two of the new formation stones to her. "Try to get those to the archers hiding in the back!" She gave me a sharp nod and I felt her spin up her cores.

"Here they come!" Donny's shout made me refocus on the line of skeletons coming toward us. Their front line also had shields, most of which looked to be old and rotted enough to fall apart if they were jostled too hard. The swords and spears mixed in still looked dangerous enough though, and I still didn't know what kind of powers the undead themselves might be able to unleash.

The sudden eruption of lava from the ranks of the archers served as a nice distraction. Not in a way that helped us, though. All five of us stared dumbfounded as a fountain of molten rock showered over their back ranks. The skeletons, however, didn't react in the slightest. Before we could properly link shields and completely block off the gateway, the enemy was on us.

My head was rocked by the impact of an obsidian axe. At the last second, the skeletons had opened ranks and allowed the desiccated corpses marching behind them to step through in a shocking display of tactics.

They were clearly more powerful than their bony brethren,

and I wasn't the only one who had to take a few steps back to reset. By reflex, I had formed a fire whip of qi in my right hand, and I was already swinging it forward at my attacker.

The shield-bearing skeleton that had stepped aside lunged from the rear to take the blow. It destroyed the rotten wooden shield—and most of the skeleton's arm—but the corpse was swinging for me again before I could capitalize on my attack. I was able to catch the blow on my shield this time, and the obsidian axe head shattered on impact.

Without a weapon, my attacker jumped on me. I smashed it with the sharpened edge of my shield, but it accepted the blow to its side and instead clamped down on the arm wielding my whip. Then, of all the odd things a walking corpse could do, it tried to bite me.

Its teeth shattered on the vambrace protecting my forearm, but I was genuinely shocked by its actions. Why would it bite me? Whatever the reason, I didn't like it. I swung my arm hard enough to throw the surprisingly light undead off of my arm, and it knocked down the three skeletons that were almost on me.

"Don't let them bite you!" I wasn't able to look over to see if anyone had acknowledged my shout, considering the growing number of enemies I was now facing demanded all of my attention. "No idea why they want to bite us, but it can't be good!"

I reabsorbed my whip and instead pulled out one of my new spears. It was solid metal, and would do well as both a club to crush bone, and a pointy bit to stab the hollow skulls that contained the dark qi animating the undead. It was time to crack some skulls.

CHAPTER TWENTY-THREE

Feelings

"Get *off* me!" Almost a dozen skeletons and one corpse had slipped around us already, and they had all piled on Jamila. Her katanas were a whirlwind, removing limbs and heads as soon as they got within range. Except for the corpse hanging on her back, gnawing on the top of her helm like a crazed monkey. "Can somebody help me out here?!"

Before I could do anything, an arrow surrounded by a haze of wind qi blasted through the head of Jamila's attacker and embedded itself in the stone floor a few paces away. She gave Valerie a sharp nod of appreciation before returning back into the fray, swords spinning in a dance with no music.

I slammed my shield into the ground in front of me, and the spikes along the bottom held it in place. When I took a step back, the newly placed obstacle forced the undead to part around it to get to me. I spun the solid metal spear like a staff, and then got to work.

Three skeletons came from my right, and a quick slash from the spearpoint separated skulls from spines. Their bones collapsed into a jumbled pile, creating another obstacle to slow the enemies approaching from that side. I had to enhance my strength with a slight boost from my heart core, but the drain was negligible.

The two corpses that rounded the shield to the left were blasted back by an errant wave of wood qi unleashed by Chu. They let loose a screeching sound that somehow managed to be both dusty and loud at the same time. It was also the first time they had made a sound that showed they could feel pain. The life qi didn't truly harm them, but it must have interacted with the death qi holding their bodies together. I would take any advantage I could get.

"They don't like wood qi!" I shouted to my friends while coating my spear in a thin layer of energy. "Use it to push them back!" I used the butt of the spear to smash into the chest of the closest corpse, and spun it horizontally to bring the spear-point into the temple of the second target. The first one got tripped up by the falling body of the second, and I used the shaft of the spear like a stickball bat to remove his head. It got some pretty good distance.

With the sudden burst of violence and change to wood qi, we quickly knocked them clear of the gate and I got a quick count of their remaining numbers. The undead were diminished to somewhere around thirty. Such a hard hit to their numbers should have made them hesitate, however the loss of so many didn't seem to faze them. Their actions so far told me they might be able to operate without direct supervision and grasp a modicum of tactics, but they didn't comprehend a losing battle. The death cultivator's creations would fight without stopping, no matter the odds. I just had to make sure the odds always favored us.

As the remaining undead reformed into orderly ranks, another explosion of lava erupted from their midst. Valerie's formation stone took down another six and made a great opportunity for us to attack. I plucked my shield from the ground, and readied my spear in the opposite hand. Valerie jumped down from her place on the wall and fell in behind

Donny. Without needing to say anything, the five of us quickly closed with the enemy.

I boosted my speed with another burst of qi. It gave me the momentum to slam through the first two skeletons, sending limbs and rib cages flying. I would have kept going if it weren't for the next target in line being one of the tougher desiccated corpses. It held just long enough to get a spear through the eye socket, and the energy keeping it together couldn't withstand the tearing motion of me spinning sideways. I now had a very disgusting decoration on the end of my spear, so I clubbed it into the skull of the next corpse in line. It made a sound like two coconuts bonking together, and I had to fight the strong urge to laugh at the random moment of silliness. Battles were funny like that sometimes.

The head decorating my spear didn't hold together after I tried to repeat the same action, but it did manage to send both of the skeletons to true death. A swipe with the sharp edge of my shield to the shoulder of another skeleton cleared out the immediate area around me, and I saw we were down to just a few enemies left standing. I managed to kill one more of the corpses by crushing its skull with the butt of my spear, and then it was over. They were dead. Again.

"Well, that was fun." Chu was inspecting his gear for damage, but none was immediately obvious. "What was up with them trying to bite us? I had one drop his weapon in favor of getting a bite in, but it was obvious by that point none of them could get through the armor. I don't get it. Do you think they have orders to bite people or something?"

"Whatever it means, it can't be good." Donny was wiping the dust of dead things from his axe blade with a scrap of cloth. "I have a bad feeling about this. We should get back to the others, and let them know about the army marching around down here."

"I hate losing all the progress we have made, but I have to agree. Let's finish up here and head back." I quickly picked up any weapons and items that survived the battle, but there weren't many. I snagged a few obsidian weapons I wanted to look at later, so I made sure to store them in the copper stud I was using to hold all my coin and valuable jewelry. I did find it odd that there wasn't a single valuable item anywhere left on the remains. You would think at least one or two of the bodies would have something on them. "Okay, let's go. And be ready for that gas attack."

We had to take our time going back, mostly because we hadn't cleared any of the side tunnels after setting off the trap. And there were a *lot* of tunnels. Like before, most of them either circled back to the main tunnel, or were dead ends. Two of them ran into natural caverns, and the damp from the water dripping down the stalactites had destroyed any evidence of what they had been used for by the former inhabitants. I did find a rusty old pickaxe head that fell apart when I tried to pick it up. If there had been a handle, it had long since rotted away to nothing.

Finally, we reached the area we had already searched, and our pace picked up. It was hard to gauge time down here, but I think it was something close to four hours since we had fought the undead before we saw the light of the cavern. The haze of smoke in the air as we approached was definitely a bad sign.

We were greeted by the sounds of the injured screaming in pain, and the smoky remains of the makeshift gate the sailors put up were covered in the bones of formerly ambulatory skeletons. There were only a few spots of blood, meaning the captain and his men had suffered only minor casualties.

"Hey!" A shout from atop the walls alerted those inside of our approach. "They're back! And they ain't dead, neither!"

There were intelligible shouts from within, and by the time we reached the gates, the captain was there to greet us.

"We didn't think we would ever see you again. Not after what we saw, anyway." He pointed at the piles of bones and bodies surrounding the area. "We barely held them back, and we had defenses to help us." He was leading us deeper into the abandoned village, so I pulled him into an empty building to question him.

"What happened while we were gone?" I took off my helm, grabbed a chair from my storage belt, and took a seat. Everyone else copied me, and we were soon sipping on some kind of qi-enhanced wine Chu produced from somewhere.

"A few hours after you left, we all heard your horses start neighing and carrying on, like there was a pack of wolves near-by." He pointed through the empty doorway, back toward the gate. "Then Shoop heard some kind of rattling noise coming from the tunnel you went through. We went to check it out, and a whole bunch of death cultivator puppets everyone hates to see came into the light. Only we never saw a death cultivator controlling them. He must have been hiding in the dark some-where. I don't understand why, though. This has to be the most powerful death cultivator I have ever heard of. There must have been two or three hundred of them. I had everyone get behind the walls, and we fought it out for over an hour."

"That sounds a lot like what we went through." I pulled out one of the obsidian axes the biting ones had used. "Did you see any of them using these?"

He took it from me, but shook his head. "No, I don't think so. They all had old weapons, except for the one we knew."

"The one you knew?" Jamila leaned forward in her chair. "What do you mean, the one you knew?"

"It was Kurban, one of the men who didn't make it up the mountain. When we saw him, we didn't know what to do." He handed back the obsidian axe, and leaned back in his chair. "That's when the strange got even stranger. Shoop ran out to try and save him or something, I don't know. It was pretty clear Kurban was already dead. But Shoop ran out there anyway, and he fought through a bunch of those bone puppets until he made it to him. Never seen him fight like that before. It was almost like a single blow would knock down a skeleton, and they wouldn't get back up until after he passed. When he got there, Shoop was so tired he could barely lift his sword. Instead of killing him, Kurban bit Shoop in the neck. It took out a big chunk, and we didn't think he was going to make it back." The captain pointed to where the neck met the shoulder, to indicate where his man had been bitten. "Shoop managed it though. He slipped right through them, almost like he wasn't there. We managed to get the bleeding stopped, but he hasn't said a word since. I think the whole thing broke his mind."

"We would be happy to take a look at him if you would like." I pointed to Chu. "My friend is a very skilled healer. Not formally trained, but I would put him up against any Expert."

"I would appreciate it." He gave Chu a sharp nod. "Now, if you all will excuse me, I need to see to getting the gate repaired, in case they come back."

"What do you mean, come back?" I was suddenly on my feet without realizing it. "Why would they come back?"

"Well, that's the other strange thing." He put away his chair and turned to leave. "Not long after Shoop made it back, they gave up and left. There were still over a hundred of them out there. We were lucky they stopped when they did, otherwise we might have been overrun."

As he left, my friends and I looked at one another. Something wasn't right. The undead we had fought were completely dedicated to bringing us down, until none were left standing. They never even tried to retreat, even when it was clear we were too strong for them to win. Like Donny said earlier, I had a very bad feeling about this.

CHAPTER TWENTY-FOUR

Answers

"Chu, Valerie, and I will go check on the injured." I pointed to Valerie's medallion, which held three healing charges. "We might need that to help. Donny and Jamila should check on the horses, and make sure our defenses are still standing. We'll join you when we finish doing what we can to help."

"Sounds good." Donny stored his own chair and started heading for the door. "Yell for us if you need something."

We split up and went our separate directions. When we got to the area the sailors were using, it was immediately obvious to us where the injured were being held. There were eight men with deep wounds lying on cots, and one that sat in a corner mumbling to himself. Jamila and Chu immediately got to work on the regular injuries.

The rusty blades the skeletons had to have been using could make a person very sick if not treated quickly. The lockjaw disease was a terrible way to die. It started with the injured person having trouble opening their mouth, and ended with their breathing becoming more and more ragged, until they died. No cultivator was immune to the disease until they reached Sage, when their body was reforged in the crucible of advancement.

While they worked to heal the injured, I went to check on Shoop, the man who had been bitten. He was rocking back and forth slowly, hunched over with his knees to his chest. Before I could reach out and lay a hand on his shoulder to inspect him with qi, the captain appeared at my side.

"He's been like this ever since we got him in here." He pointed to a smear of blood on the floor at Shoop's feet. "At first, he was drawing something on the floor in his own blood. He wouldn't say anything, just kept making these swirls and mumbling about his core."

"How long has it been since he was bitten?" I crouched down to look into Shoop's eyes. They were glazed over, and he was sweating. "It looks like he has a fever."

"At least three, maybe four hours." He looked back at the other wounded. "We did what we could for them, but since we are sailors, most of the men are good at wind and water qi. The only cultivator truly efficient with wood qi was my boatswain, and he died when those bugs attacked us." He shook his head, remembering what had happened. "I understand what is wrong with the others, but Shoop is a solid man. He normally doesn't act like this."

"Well, we will do what we can for them. I'll let you know if we figure out anything." He then turned and left without acknowledging what I said. Still a jerk.

I reached out to touch the injured man, but he flinched back. Okay then, it would cost a bit more qi, but I didn't need to make physical contact to inspect him. A quick spin up of my cores allowed me to extend a small net of wood qi, and I cast it over his head and shoulders. Which caused an immediate reaction.

Shoop punched me in the face hard enough to rock me back on my heels. He was screeching like a Wind Banshee, and I had to strengthen the net to hold him in place. I heard a commotion behind me as people rushed into the building to see what was going on, but I stayed focused on what I was doing. I had to, because I wasn't just being attacked physically. There was an infection in the bite mark, and it immediately tried to jump into me through my net. It was something I had never seen before. An infection, *in* the qi.

A disease that attacked the host through their cultivation? That shouldn't even be possible! I could feel it crawling up the qi threads, slowly twisting them into a new shape that tried to expand and reverse back on me. I immediately cut off my connection to the construct, but it didn't dissipate like it should have. Instead, it jumped at me. I rolled backward, avoiding the attack, and it scuttled on the floor after me like a net-shaped spider. It was growing, and doubled in size in a heartbeat, from about the circumference of a dinner plate to that of a shield.

Luckily, an arrow from Valerie flew over my shoulder and spiked it into the ground before it could jump after me again, but Shoop leaped over it and landed on my chest. I was still in my armor, which mitigated most of the damage. I still had my breath knocked out of me from the impact. I don't care how tough or advanced you are, getting the wind knocked out of you still hurts.

I grabbed Shoop by the wrist and elbow, and twisted my hips to throw him off of me. I used my hold to lock out his arm and guide his face straight into the floor. The impact smashed his forehead against the stone, and he went limp. I quickly got to my feet and looked back at the abomination still trying to break free from the hunk of pointy metal holding it in place. A quick burst of fire and wind qi created a fireball that engulfed it in flames. The hissing sound it made as it crisped into ash made my skin crawl. It didn't sound like it was in pain, it just sounded angry.

"What in the stars-forsaken realms of madness was that!" Chu was already by my side, a wave of wood qi from him passing through me to check for injuries. He was holding my hand to do it, since our armor stopped him from healing me normally. "Was that—*thing*—inside him?"

"I have no idea what that was." I cut off the flow to the fire, and the acrid smell of whatever that thing had been burned my nose. Another burst of wind qi, and I pushed the smoke outside the nearby empty window. "And it wasn't inside him. Well, it was, but it wasn't." Chu looked at me like I was spouting nonsense. I guess I was. "It's hard to explain, but that certainly wasn't natural." I pulled out one of the sets of orichalcum chains I had in my belt. "We need to secure this man, and separate him from the others."

"The hell you will!" The captain was walking through the door, his face a thunderhead of anger. "I will not have you shackling my men. You were supposed to help him, not hurt him!"

"Captain, this is for his own protection." I waved my hand at the pile of ash around the arrow still embedded in the floor. "He has some kind of qi infection I didn't even know was possible. I think... I think it might be sentient."

"There is no such thing as a sentient infection. *Or* a qi infection. I don't know what you think you saw, but it wasn't that." He moved to separate us from the unconscious man. "You can go now. We can take care of our own."

"You're making a mistake." I indicated the ash spot on the ground again. "At the very least, separate him from the others, and post a guard. Doing that wouldn't hurt him."

"Fine." He waved a hand toward the door. "Now go." As I started to walk out, he spoke again. "When you find a way out of this place, come and let us know. Until then, it would be best for you to stay away."

I left, my fists clenched in anger. His inability to see what was right in front of him meant an enemy I had no idea how to defeat was left to still threaten us. This could only end badly.

The three of us returned to our area in silence, considering the eyes and ears that were still nearby. A sailor seemed to be positioned at every turn along the way by happenstance, funneling us straight out of their side without giving us the opportunity to circle back. More than one glared at us, fingering weapons as we passed by. I got the distinct impression they didn't like us very much.

It only took a few minutes to get to our side of the small village. The walk felt much longer, considering the circumstances. Once we entered the building we were using as a camp, Donny and Jamila immediately got to their feet.

"What happened?" Jamila rushed over to Chu, and I could feel her spinning her cores in preparation for a fight. "We felt you doing more than just healing over there, but then it just stopped."

"We were debating about going to help." Donny placed his axe back into storage and sat down. "But when it stopped, we were afraid rushing in there would only make things worse."

"You made the right call." I started pulling off my armor and stacking it so I could look it over for damage. "The two of you rushing in there, ready to fight, would have probably escalated things."

"I don't even know why we are bothering with these people." Jamila started copying me, removing her own armor with the help of Valerie. "They only make things worse at every opportunity."

"Their ship was destroyed because of us, and none of them would even be here if we hadn't asked the Auction House to provide us with transportation to the Northern Province." Valerie was having problems getting the side clasps on Jamila's armor to loosen, making her grunt with effort between sentences. "So we do hold at least a little responsibility for their safety." Finally, the chest piece came free, allowing both of them to sigh in relief. "Though, if they keep making things difficult, they have no one to blame but themselves if things get worse."

"Why would things get worse?" Donny was already done removing his armor. "What happened over there, anyway?"

We quickly explained what happened with the man who had been bitten, and that led to a long discussion about what we should do next. Obviously, no one had any idea about how a qi infection even existed in the first place, but it was a unanimous decision for all of us to stay in our full suits of armor and not allow ourselves to be bitten. Not that getting bitten by a walking corpse was near the top of any of our to-do lists in the first place. That this must have been a creation of the *nox* was never in question. I had no idea how they were doing it, but we would put an end to it somehow.

After cleaning up as best we could, and making sure our armor was back in top form, we quickly got fully dressed again. Considering the possibility of another sudden attack, sleeping without being completely protected was a bad idea none of us wanted to take a chance on.

I had problems getting comfortable at first, but after such a long period of no sleep I was quickly nodding off while trying to refine the qi in my cores. Chu volunteered for the first watch, and I was asleep not long after laying my helmeted head on the hard stone floor. My last thought before drifting off was about the necromancer. Instincts told me finding him would be the fastest way to put an end to this disease, so that had to be our priority. All we needed to do was find him.

CHAPTER TWENTY-FIVE

Orbs

———

I found myself once again on the other side of the bridge leading into the ancient city. Apparently, the gods didn't care how tired I was, they wanted me to see something. Since I knew there was no way out but through, I started walking.

The path through the gate was almost entirely rebuilt, forcing me to climb the wall to enter. I could see the fresh construction from the inside, and it was pretty clear the undead were poor builders. It wouldn't be hard to knock down the section on the left side of the gate. I filed away that information for later.

The guards on the walls were more numerous, and there were now undead beasts mixed in with the desiccated corpses. All of them were in much better condition than the opponents we had faced so far, and the ones capable of holding weapons all had much better versions. It would be a much harder fight to get through than I first thought.

After clearing the wall, I moved quickly toward the center of the city. There were signs of heavy foot traffic all throughout the major roadways, with more than one swept completely clean of the dust and detritus by the passage of hundreds of undead feet. It was a clear sign that we had only seen a fraction of the necromancer's forces.

Eventually, I climbed to the rooftop of a mostly-intact building near the edge of what used to be a courtyard for the central building. There was a perfectly carved qi gathering formation inside the remains of a massive fountain, and it was the source of the pull drawing in the dark and metal qi.

I had never seen a formation designed to target one specific type of qi before. In my first life, on the day I was betrayed by Ming and died, I thought I was using the most perfect formation for qi gathering in the Empire. I had most definitely been mistaken. That one, while it would gather in all the types of qi, couldn't do so evenly or consistently. Which was why I had needed piles of various elemental cores around me to keep the balance equal. The focused and concentrated swirls of black and silver energy inside the shallow basin were almost mesmerizing, but I could still see the carvings on the ancient marble bottom.

There was no way the young Hadad could have made this on his own. It must have been knowledge passed on from the *nox* he was possessed by. While I watched, a platoon of undead beasts marched into the square and circled the fountain. They took turns jumping into the fountain, taking a few moments to soak up as much of the qi as they could. So *that* was how they stayed animated. I knew it would have been impossible for a single cultivator to keep that many minions functioning without some kind of help.

While I was contemplating jumping down into the square to disrupt the qi gathering formation, the cloaked figure of the death cultivator stepped out of the central building. I still couldn't see his face, but this time I noticed how unhealthy his hands looked. They were almost skeletal, much like the figures I had seen in the basement of the dark temple all those years ago.

Clasped in his grip was the staff that looked like the grown-up version of the scepter contained in my storage belt.

He raised the staff vertically in front of him, and began drawing in the energy contained in the fountain. Once again, only one side began forming an orb of power. I couldn't be sure, but to me it looked like he was trying to force the metal qi to coalesce into the other end, instead of light qi. The metal qi just dissipated from the end of the staff and was slowly absorbed by either the formations in the fountain, or the cultivator himself.

The orb of dark qi had no problems, however. It quickly looked like a solid piece of black crystal, dripping with power. Hadad then spun the staff, driving the dark orb into the ground at his feet. It shattered, knocking him back a step, and the shards quickly dissipated and returned to the fountain. Instead of seeming disappointed, Hadad quickly knelt down to look at something. On the ground at his feet, there was a pea-sized spot of pure darkness. He dropped the staff and scooped up the small ball of energy with an actual spoon and fork, careful not to touch it with his bare hands.

Spinning in place, he hurried back inside the building, leaving the staff in the open. Before I could jump down to try and get a closer look at the object, a wall of darkness washed over me.

CHAPTER TWENTY-SIX

Consequences

As soon as I opened my eyes, I could hear angry shouts coming from the sailor's area headed our direction. Everyone else was already awake, stuffing their feet into boots and ensuring their armor was securely fastened. I peeked out the window near my mattress to see an actual mob of people coming toward us. Where in the stars did they find torches and pitchforks down here?

I was concerned enough that I spun up my brain core a little to provide me with a slight speed boost. Just as I dropped my helm's visor in place, the first man holding a torch stepped into the area we had marked off as our own. Maybe he thought all the swirling rune designs on the ground, wooden placards, formation plates, and clearly marked flags warning them not to enter were just for funsies. Well, let's just say he was quickly shown the error of his ways.

Donny had apparently gone a little overboard on the traps for the main path leading to our section, because the chain reaction the first guy set off was more than a little excessive. He was thrown straight up into the air, blasted with a wave of fire, and then slapped out of sight with an actual giant hand of stone. The hand made a very rude gesture in the general direction of the poor fellow before fading back into the ground. I needed to find out how Donny managed that last one.

After seeing the results of charging into our area, the rest of the mob seemed to be having second thoughts. Instead of charging forward, they clustered together at the edge of the not-so-imaginary line of our designated area.

Since it looked like no one else was going to try to win the 'King of Stupidity' award today, I went outside to see what they wanted and stopped spinning up my brain core.

"What did you do with them?!"

"Where's our friends, you jerks?!"

"Ragum fragum furger?!"

"How about you tell us what's going on, so we can answer your questions?" I looked around to try to find the last speaker. "Well, most of the questions."

"Don't play dumb, we know it was you!" I recognized the person talking as the man who had planned to steal our horses shortly before our two groups had separated on the surface. "Everyone heard about you trying to chain up Shoop, and now he and Bee Yang are missing!"

"I can assure you, none of us did anything to your friends. We haven't left our building since we tried to heal your friend." I was about to explain that our proof was the undisturbed ring of traps—which their compatriot had already verified—but he didn't let me finish.

"You think you're all high and mighty, struttin' around in your pretty armor, with your pretty horses, and your pretty ladies, and pretty… other stuff!" He drew the saber sheathed on his belt, and pointed it at me. "I knew I shoulda' finished you off after them goats didn't kill you, but I won't be makin' that mistake this time!"

The stiletto I carried in the storage stud at the small of my back was my favorite tool for carving fine detail into whatever material I was working on. It was also very well balanced. When it thudded into the base of the man's throat, I took a second to appreciate just how finely crafted it really was. For a plain steel weapon, it truly was a masterpiece.

"It was only a matter of time until I found out who knocked me into that stampede!" A quick flick of my wrist and flex of my willpower brought the thin blade back to me. No one had even noticed the spider-silk thin strand of air qi attached to the handle. They seemed shocked by the sudden turn of events, and the ones in the back had no idea what had transpired.

"Would anyone else like to admit to trying to kill our friend?" Jamila stepped in front of me, her weapons already in her hands. "How about more pointless accusations?"

"But—!"

"But nothing." She cut the speaker off. The attempted murderer finally dropped to his knees, his saber clattering to the cavern floor beside him. "This man openly stated he tried to kill our friend, and was here to finish the job. He deserved what he got."

"How about we all calm down here?" The captain finally decided to show his face, pushing his way up from the rear. When he finally reached the front, the body of his sailor was face-down in a slowly expanding pool of his own blood. "What in the gods—"

"Don't worry, captain, we found the man responsible for trying to kill Jim during the goat stampede you all brought back to us." Jamila sheathed her swords with a flourish. "I suggest you and your men return to your side of the camp, before more criminals in your ranks open their mouths to speak their own doom."

I couldn't help but give Jamila a sharp glance. 'Speak their own doom?' Maybe she was still suffering from the side effects of the dark qi saturation.

"I think it would be best if our two groups went their separate ways." The captain was gritting his teeth and clenching his fists, doing his best to keep from attacking us. I could see him carefully weighing his options. Apparently, trying to fight five heavily armed and armored cultivators surrounded by unknown traps was too much of a gamble for him. "I no longer think staying together is a good idea."

Before Jamila could say something else crazy, I cut in. "We didn't touch your men. I don't even know who Bee Yang is." I flipped up my faceplate so I could look the captain in the eye. "Stars, I don't even know your name, because you never even introduced yourself to us! At every opportunity imaginable, you have hindered us instead of helped. I understand you blame me for sinking the ship, but we would have been torn apart by Pilum Crabs if I hadn't killed them all. I warned you about Shoop, and your inability to listen to me probably cost the life of the other guy. Your actions have consequences. We're done holding your hands. You want us gone? Fine. We'll be gone in less than an hour."

I spun around and stomped off, mad enough to want to kill the man. I knew in my past life I would have just walked away feeling nothing but pity. But this wasn't my past life, it was now. I was still in the body of a teenager, and they weren't exactly well-known for their even tempers and good decisions. I didn't care. Right now, I reveled in my anger.

We packed quickly, making sure all our traps were collected as well. I left a thin line of barrier traps to cover the gate we had secured, but they would have to guard it themselves. As we walked away and Donny and I led the horses through the gate, the sailors lined up to watch us go. Only a handful seemed to realize the danger they were now in, but I couldn't manage to feel pity for them. They had built their house. Now, it was time to die while it burned around them.

"Where should we go now?" Donny was limping beside me as we walked into the tunnel. While we were packing, Scout had nudged a stack of heavy crates filled with blank copper formation plates that just so happened to land on his foot. I could feel him still using his wood qi focusing disk to help heal it. "We can get through the trap now without setting it off, but we don't know how much farther the horses can make it past that outpost."

"I hate to do it, but I think we are going to have to split up." He was wearing his helmet, so I could only see his eyes. I could tell he didn't like the idea, so I tried to explain. "Look, that next cavern has four tunnels leading out of it. Since we don't have unlimited food and water, we certainly can't search all of them one at a time over the next few days. Or even weeks. One person stays at camp, and the other four go check the tunnels. The one back at camp can run to help the others if needed."

"That sounds like a terrible idea." Donny was shaking his head. "It's never a good idea to split the party."

"We don't have a choice." I looked over at him. "And the part you won't like the most is that I think you should be the one to wait back at camp." Before he could argue, I held up a hand to stop him. "Think about it. The other three are a lower cultivation level, and can't sense qi fluctuations as far as you. With me down one tunnel, you can focus on the three that they use, and rush in to help if they need it."

"Why don't you be the one to wait with the horses then?" His tone told me he was angry, but there was more of a question than a challenge. "You have better senses than I do."

"I know you are strong, but we know one tunnel for sure will have enemies, and that means our strongest person should go there." It wasn't necessary for me to describe to him how necessary it was to put our strongest foot forward. Donny understood that already. "Once you have mastered better control of light and dark qi, I wouldn't have a problem sending you in by yourself. Besides, you can think of it as an opportunity to get some bonding time with Scout."

He didn't say anything after that, instead concentrating on healing his injured foot and completely ignoring my horse comment. It took us several hours to get through the trapped area without setting it off, and we managed to get to the outpost without incident. We placed more traps at both gates, and made sure to layer plenty of them along the approach. It would certainly be enough to slow down an army of skeletons, but the bigger monsters were large enough to soak up a lot of damage.

"Okay, I'll take the far left tunnel, and you three handle the others." Jamila, Valerie, and Chu were already on their way before I could even finish speaking. I turned and looked at Donny. "Be ready. There's no telling what's down here with us." He gave me a sharp nod, and I was off. That death cultivator had to be down here somewhere, and I was going to find him.

CHAPTER TWENTY-SEVEN

Alone

I was scouting by myself for the first time since running away from the rock troll. While I certainly didn't want to be alone all the time, it was kind of nice to enjoy the quiet. As I was moving deeper underground, I cast a wide net of qi threads to look for any hidden traps or passages. Finding another gas trap by myself would have been a real problem.

The tunnel I had chosen wasn't at random. It was the one with the least amount of dust and debris, which I hoped meant it was the most traveled by the undead army. From what I had seen during my dream walking, we had only seen a fraction of the things down here.

It was also becoming very clear to me why Wrath and Pride had sent me to the north. If all those creatures had a bite that could infect the living, a plague the likes of which the world had never seen was brewing under these cold, abandoned mountains. I would have to put a stop to it.

My threads found a six-inch circle divot on the right-hand wall almost an hour into my monotonous journey. The tunnel I was traveling down had several branches, but most appeared to be untouched. Considering I knew I had to go deeper to find the death cultivator, I didn't waste time checking them. The carved circle was the first item of interest I had detected the whole time. Something that perfect had to be man-made, so I knelt to inspect it. It was waist-height, and the center had three equal indentations. Three *very* familiar indentations.

It took a few minutes to find the three-clawed adamantine scepter in my belt, since I hadn't messed with it in a long time. The oily feeling seemed much worse. Considering the history of the hunk of metal, it might have been in my head. It was the device used as a focal point for a mass sacrifice, meant to open the door to a place the only thing worse than the *nox* called home. The devourers. The *vorare*.

An entire library from the place I found the scepter was in my belt, and I had never stopped working to translate the forgotten language when I had the occasional moment of free time. I was far from translating everything, but what I had learned wasn't good. While the *nox* turned everything to darkness, at least there was still *something* there. A chance to turn the dark back to light. But after the *vorare* had moved on, there was nothing. No darkness, no light, just emptiness. They were the locusts of the universe, leaving nothing in their wake but shrunken husks of lifeless rock. Why anyone would try to bring them into this world was beyond my understanding. Some people just wanted to destroy everything, and they were happy to lose themselves to that destruction.

I put the scepter in the keyhole and turned. There was a faint clicking sound, and a hiss of escaping air came from a section of wall a few feet back down the tunnel. The door was so well-hidden that my threads hadn't felt its outline.

Surprisingly, it didn't lead to a stairwell circling down into darkness. As I pushed open the door, glow stones that lined a short hallway lit up, illuminating a quaint little temple. There was a small altar, and six narrow stone benches where supplicants could sit. On the altar, there were two large globes that faintly emitted a pale light. The entire space was under almost an inch of undisturbed dust, and the corners were overflowing with piles of stacked dry scrolls. At the lightest touch, they would certainly crumble into nothing.

I couldn't see the floor because of the thick layer of dust, so I stood off to the side of the door and sent a tornado of wind qi inside. The cloud that shot into the tunnel was quickly dispersed by more qi strands, and I went back in to inspect it for any traps.

The first thing I noticed was how bright the two globes on the altar were. I didn't feel any energy coming from them, but they were certainly familiar. The two objects reminded me of the crystal used in the weather device the Southern Provincial King had used to control rainfall amounts, in his bid to lord over the food production for the region's clans and sects. I made sure it was safe to approach before walking over and inspecting them.

Upon closer inspection, I saw there were three neat grooves on the tops of each. The glow was coming from a set of swirling runes carved inside the crystal. I recognized them as a match to the style carved on both my scepter, and the necromancer's staff. It was obvious this was what the clawed ends were supposed to hold.

Before popping them on the ends of the oily metal, I double-checked the small temple to make sure I wasn't missing anything. The scrolls had turned into dust from the stiff wind like I thought, but they had been hiding small piles of the same ingots I had found at the dark temple. I stored them with the few I still had remaining in my belt, giving me enough to probably make at least two or three sets of armor. Or several more spears of solid adamantine.

I also found a stone tablet behind the altar, covered in the lost language of the *vorare* worshippers. The pitted and scarred writing was almost unreadable, but I stored it away as well. There was a chance I could still learn something when I had a free moment to look it over closely. A thorough search didn't uncover anything else, so I finally got ready to place the globes in the grip of the scepter.

With only some minor fumbling, I was able to seat the first crystal properly. I lifted it off the altar, and felt more than heard a shift in the stone near the base of the rectangular block. I moved to the other side, just in case there was a trap. The second globe slid into place, and I lifted it off the altar as well. This time, there was a definite thunking sound that came from the rear of the altar. I peeked over to see a small tray had popped free near the base.

Instead of opening it myself, I used a strand of earth qi to open the hidden drawer. My caution was well-founded, as a needle shot out hard enough to embed itself into the arched stone ceiling. That would have hurt.

A quick inspection of the drawer revealed a twisting three-bladed dagger and a small pouch of worked cores. This was the real treasure. Finally, after all this time. Ever since I had been reincarnated, I had been searching for a quality focusing stone. Now I had one of every element. And I do mean *every* element. I had never seen a dark or light qi focusing stone, and now they were in my hands. I felt like a toddler in a pastry shop. The clarity of these were extremely high, meaning the cores used in their creation must have been at least Sky quality, possibly Heaven. Not as good as Celestial, but those were almost never used to make focusing stones. Those were best used to power the few airships spread around the world.

With these, I could cultivate each element one at a time, instead of having to slowly distill the specific element I needed from the environmental energy I was surrounded by. Focusing stones turned whatever qi was in the area into the qi they were aspected toward, and allowed for a much larger amount to be absorbed through the meridians. It was similar to the difference between an irrigation ditch and a raging river. Both would water your crops, but one would manage to do it much faster. As long as you didn't drown.

Their discovery also reinforced my suspicions that the knowledge of light and dark qi had been suppressed by someone a long time ago. If there were focusing stones, what creatures made the cores they came from? Were they hunted to extinction before the founding of the Empire? Or were these formed artificially somehow? My intuition was telling me the answers might lay in the undecipherable language of the various writings I had found, but there was no way to know for sure. Maybe the next time I spoke with the gods, I could get some answers. Yeah, even I knew that wasn't likely. The gods were named for the sins of man, not exactly paragons of honesty and love.

Before I could try using any of the focusing stones, I heard a shuffling sound come from the tunnel outside. I stored the now-complete scepter, focusing stones, and the dagger in the treasury stud on my belt, and quietly moved to peek out to see what was coming.

The tunnel was filled with the undead. There were so many I couldn't even see the end of their orderly ranks, due to a bend up ahead. Finally, I found them. Well, they had found me, but the end would be the same.

I held back nothing. My right hand spun out a wrist-thick strand of wood qi, while my left spun out a dozen smaller strands to hold on to the solid adamantine spears I pulled from my belt. As I closed with the first rank of skeletons, I formed the runes for a popper along the length of the wood qi whip, giving my strikes a powerful boost in energy. I had to use the energy from my lower core to empower the runes, instead of ambient energy for the pebbles we normally had the runes carved on. I didn't care. I had two full batteries of qi to spare, and I couldn't risk letting any of these things getting behind me.

The first crack of my upgraded whip blasted the leading rank of skeletons into the one behind, slowing their advance. Then, I began reaping my enemies. I didn't bother using the spears with any kind of finesse, instead using them like the needles of the sewing machines found in the upscale districts of the capital. They were a blur, stabbing forward in a wave that mowed down brittle bones like stalks of dry wheat.

Such an expenditure of qi was quickly draining me, so I

started running forward to maximize the damage. Any time they tried to mount a defense, I cracked my wood qi whip forward, splintering any shields brought to bear against me. The life energy was anathema to the forces holding them together, and more than one undead backed away from the power.

After destroying over a hundred skeletons, the tunnel was becoming difficult to walk down. My pace was slowed, and I had to change tactics before I ran out of qi. I could see around the bend now, and up ahead there were over twenty of the desiccated corpses that carried the disease in their bite. Behind them came the real threat. The beasts.

I swapped a spear for a spiker from storage, and positioned it behind my shoulder. Three quick cracks from my whip bought me some space, so I used it to tilt the spears forward at an angle, like a row of pikemen ready to receive a cavalry charge. I jammed the butts of the shafts into the floor deep enough that I didn't need to hold them, and used the extra strands of qi to create a tube for the spiker to travel along. There wasn't much time to make my aim perfect, but with the strength of the runes carved along its length it wasn't necessary. Another blast of qi launched it toward the towering enemies in the rear, and a moment later the explosion rocked the tunnel.

The narrow confines meant the force could only go two directions, and I was very glad I had set the spears in place. A storm of bones and body parts were catapulted my way, and the shafts of metal blocked the worst of it from hitting me. There was an actual *wall* of... stuff... that was shoved against the spears. I used one of the new formation plates that emitted lava to burn it down, using the time I was stuck waiting to cultivate what energy I could. The occasional blast of wind qi kept the air clear enough to breathe, and most of the dry remains went up like kindling. It took a surprisingly long time to burn through all of it—especially the fresher pieces—but eventually I had a path forward.

I had to kick loose my spears, since the cooled lava had pooled at their bases. They had shown their usefulness, and I definitely didn't want to leave them behind. A quick inspection proved how tough they were as well. Besides a few discolorations from the heat, the oily metal still looked freshly forged.

Once I made it to the site where the spiker had impacted, I realized my mistake. From the remains of the undead beasts, I had taken out less than half. The remaining monsters had been blown the opposite direction, and there was no sign of them. They had escaped, and there was no telling how far they could have gotten while I was just sitting and waiting for the remains of their compatriots to burn. I needed to get back to the others, and make sure they were okay. Because if he didn't before, now the necromancer would soon know *exactly* where we were.

I made sure to heavily trap the tunnel the whole way back, and closed the entrance to the small temple. While I didn't relish the idea, it would make a great place to hide if necessary. There were no other incidents, and I reached our compound with little issue. As I approached the walls, I had a sinking feeling in my stomach. Something was wrong.

"Donny, we have a problem!" I shouted as I walked through the gate, only slowing once I finally realized what my senses were telling me. The compound was empty. A quick look through all the buildings confirmed my fears. Even the horses were missing, and there wasn't even a note to tell me where they had gone. My friends were missing. I was all alone.

CHAPTER TWENTY-EIGHT

Horses

I checked for any signs left behind, but there weren't any clues to Donny's whereabouts. Why he hadn't left a note or some other indicator telling me where to go was what had me worried. My four friends were very capable cultivators, but a well-executed ambush could get anyone. The only thing keeping me from worrying too much was the lack of Scout and Cloud. Wherever he had gone, it had been important enough for Donny to take the horses with him.

A cursory inspection of the surrounding area didn't show me any other clues, beyond the signs of the undead moving through the area. Whether that had been from before, or recently, I had no way of telling. I decided to just move out for the nearest tunnel to see if I could find any signs of Donny and the horses instead of waiting to see if anyone would return.

The tunnel closest to the one I had initially chosen was obviously less traveled, and the dusty footprints ended at a tunnel collapse a few minutes' walk down. It was clearly an old cave-in, so I turned around and headed back.

After exploring the third tunnel in line, I saw signs of extensive fighting that made seeing any tracks impossible. There were piles of bones and dismembered body parts, and the qi in the area seemed less dense. Considering the clean cuts, my guess was Jamila ran into a patrol of some kind. It was missing about half of the numbers I had seen, but it still would have been quite a fight for her. If she had made enough noise, this was where Donny should have run to help. I would have explored deeper, but a narrow part of the tunnel farther down stopped me. There was no way the horses would have been able to travel through this section.

By the time I made it back to the cavern to check the last tunnel, it had been over an hour since I had discovered everyone had gone missing. I double-checked that no one had returned while I was gone, and then took a quick break to eat some steamed dumplings I had stored in my belt. Finally, I headed into the remaining tunnel. There were no signs of fighting, and it was pretty clear from the dust layer that there hadn't been anyone in here for a long time before our arrival. The hoofprints and a disabled pitfall trap further down told me I was finally on the right track.

I had been walking around long enough by then for me to almost refill my cores. A quick internal inspection proved that I was getting even closer to reaching Sage, but I needed some time to dedicate toward compressing the qi in my system hard enough to forcibly expand the walls of my meridians. The channels used to absorb qi were too narrow, and Sage was an extremely important step forward.

When a cultivator advanced to Sage, their body was remade by qi. It was an exceedingly painful experience, but the cleansing made it possible to advance farther along the path of power. It also made it much harder to improve your physical self afterward. There were a few exceptions, like poison cultivation, but they weren't exactly easy to do no matter your level. I would have to do that one the hard way later. For now, I could at least prepare my body for the peak of what was possible before moving to the next step. Rushing would do me no favors.

The tunnel eventually opened up into another cavern, but

this one was far different than the ones we had seen in the past. It was some kind of transfer station, with over twenty tunnels leading in and out of it. There were tool marks along the walls, with several man-made support pillars spread around the area that were crumbling with age. It had probably been a wide spot in one of the tunnels that the former residents had expanded as they found more viable veins of ore in the surrounding area.

In the center of the room, there was a walled fort that was a fraction of the size of the ones we had seen so far. It was just a single squat, flat-roofed building surrounded by wide and sturdy-looking walls, with less than fifty feet between the two. When this place was active, it probably served as a checkpoint for miners to get their various assignments, or maybe as a place for them to rest between shifts.

The reason for my friends disappearing without leaving a note was pretty apparent. I could barely see it over the far side of the wall opposite from where I came in, but the stars-damned rock troll was here. Completely surrounding the walls was another horde of undead, with several more beasts mixed in than I had seen in one place down here so far. There was a steady trickle of more skeletons and desiccated corpses stum-bling out of the various tunnels, and all of them were converging on the square-shaped fort.

An arrow arched over the wall and exploded against the undead rock trolls, which sent dust shaking down from the ceil-ing. It didn't seem to do much against the monsters, but the shockwave knocked down a large portion of the undead that had crowded near the trolls.

That attack had to have come from Valerie, and if she was wasting qi like that, things must be getting desperate inside the walls. I needed to reduce some of the pressure on my friends, before it was too late.

I spun out a thick web of metal qi, in order to screen my approach from the undead. They didn't notice me until I had almost reached the walls, but by then I was close enough to jump up to the top of the small gatehouse. It was a mystery as to how the walls were even still standing. They hadn't handled the passage of time as well as the other outposts we had found. Either this section was much older, or the stones used to make it weren't as stable. Looking around at the crumbling pillars holding the ceiling of the cavern up, I decided it was probably a mixture of both.

"Jim! Thank the gods!" Donny was reloading his crossbow while using a strand of qi to hold his tower shield against a weak section of the wall next to me. "We were afraid you weren't going to find us in time!"

"Could use some help here!" Valerie jumped on the roof of the single building, using the extra height to rain flaming arrows down on whatever cluster of enemies she could find. "They are pushing in from the rear!" The undead she hit went up like dry kindling, igniting those nearby as they continued to march toward the walls.

"Got it!" Chu used a strand of life qi to knock the skeletons crawling over the wall back onto the other side. "Brace!" A formation plate went flying over the side, followed by an explosion that rained down more dust from the unstable ceiling.

I reformed my net of metal qi into a cone-shaped construct that I launched across the small compound, hitting the combined rock trolls hard enough to knock them away from the wall. Their stumble backward took the top section of the wall with them, but Jamila was there a moment later.

"Try not to destroy our only form of protection, please!" Her sarcasm was clear by her tone, but the quick work she did with earth qi to repair the damaged section showed extreme focus. "This won't hold forever. We need to change things up, before things get worse."

"How did you guys even end up down here?" I had to shout to be heard over the rattling roars of the aggravated rock trolls. "You were supposed to regroup back at the other outpost!"

"That's my fault." Jamila tossed a handful of poppers over the wall to discourage the mass of skeletons trying to approach. "I ran into a patrol, and took care of them. Then that big one came with another group, and I had to regroup with the others. It just shrugs off our attacks."

"They followed her down the tunnel, and the rest of us had already gotten back together by then!" Chu was shouting from the top of the wall, where he was using his mace to smash the skulls of any creatures that came into range. "The crazy horses ran down this tunnel before Donny could shut the gate, and you can figure out the rest. Valerie wouldn't let us just leave them."

"We aren't leaving Scout and Cloud!" The angry shout from the roof put an end to his complaints. She poked her head over the side, and tossed down a bag of poppers to Jamila. "They are making another run for the gate, push them back!"

They were still holding, but eventually we would run out of the tools and materials to keep them back. Or the rock trolls would just knock down the walls.

From inside the building, I heard Scout neighing louder than I had ever heard him. As Donny moved past an empty window, he was grabbed by the ear and yanked inside. That would teach him to keep his helmet on.

I thought at first the horse was just picking a terrible time to try to kill poor Donny again, but his lack of follow-up shouting meant this was something else.

Instead of helping him, I took his place on the wall. My instincts told me he would be back shortly. The forces arrayed against us were amassing along the cavern walls, and it would only be a matter of time until they rushed forward to drown us in a wave of bones and rotting flesh. Almost every tunnel leading to the cavern was now disgorging the necromancer's army in seemingly endless waves. The roar of the rock trolls across the compound from me wasn't anything to forget about either.

I spun out another dozen threads of metal qi, and used them to whip some carved copper plates across the cavern. The various attacks activated upon impact, shooting wind blades, earthen spears, and dropping groups of undead into newly formed pits of quicksand that hardened around them. It was like skipping stones into the ocean. The plates caused ripples, but they quickly disappeared into the mass of enemies we were facing. I needed a plan.

"Guys! Come quick!" The shout of Donny interrupted my thoughts. "You have to see this!"

"You guys go ahead, I'll hold them while you see what has him so excited." Valerie accentuated her point by tossing one of the plates that formed lava into the cluster of skeletons and desiccated corpses approaching the gate. "Don't take too long."

The rest of us dashed inside. It was immediately apparent why going into the building was so important. A large trap door hidden in the floor was lifted to the side, and a steep ramp led down into the darkness. Donny tossed a glow stone down, and it kept going for a long time. It eventually rolled to a stop when it hit the remains of a wheeled cart that had fallen onto its side. Well, now we knew the purpose of the building. This was the drop-off point for the ores the miners had unearthed.

"If this is an ore cart shaft, it has to go somewhere important, right?" Donny was already pulling out more glow stones to attach to the ends of some sticks for makeshift torches. The dry tunnel had none of the luminescent fungus or lichen to help light the way.

"It doesn't really matter where it goes." Chu pointedly looked out the door, where the flashes of light from Valerie's qi-infused arrows were slowly picking up speed. "As long as it takes us out of this death trap."

"I don't know, I think we can take them." Jamila gave her katanas a twirl to emphasize her point. "There isn't anything out there that can stop us."

"No, Chu is right." I tossed a wind blade formation plate deeper into the tunnel to stir up the stale air. No sense in suffocating. "We can't risk getting bit, and any of our large attacks might collapse this cavern on our heads. And we still don't know how many of these things there are. This could still just be a tiny portion of the forces headed to this tunnel."

She gave me a reluctant nod of agreement. "Okay. I'll agree

with you, especially about the cavern collapsing." I watched her eyes light up. "But we can use that! Chu, do you think you and Valerie can hold the walls by yourselves for a bit?" He gave her a sharp nod, and she turned to Donny and I. "Can you make some of those big spiker things go off after a certain amount of time, instead of on impact?"

"I can carve some runes that build up the energy before they activate." I pulled one free from my belt. "It would add a minute or two before exploding."

Jamila was almost bouncing with excitement. "That will have to work. The two of you make as many of them as you can. I'm going to go over the wall and get their attention."

Before I could argue, she was gone. Jamila could really lay on the speed when she wanted.

"What is she planning?" Chu was readjusting his helmet, making sure there were no openings around his neck. "Tell me she isn't planning what I think she is."

"Drop this cavern on the undead army? Yeah, pretty sure that's exactly what she is doing." I expanded my senses to try to get a better idea of the condition the ceiling was in. "I don't think we should drop the whole thing, but the entire rear portion is pretty unstable."

"Well, I'll hold the walls. You two get those spikers ready." He hefted his mace, and walked out the door. "Don't take too long."

"Okay." Donny had taken off his gauntlets to get the helm of his armor sealed in place. As it snapped into position, he held out his hand to me. "Hand me a couple of them, and we can get those runes carved before—"

The hoof that slammed into the back of his helmeted head launched Donny down the steep tunnel like an arrow loosed from a bow. I turned to look at Scout, who was clearly watching poor Donny skip down the ramp with an obvious grin.

"Really, Scout? Is now the best time for this?" I shook my finger at him, already casting a qi whip out of the other hand to grab the prone form of my cousin before he got too far away.

The horse looked at me, and tossed its head as if to say 'What do I know? I'm just a horse.' Maybe I was projecting, but I didn't think so.

"Don't give me that. I appreciate you finding the trap door and everything, but we still have a fight going on." I jerked my head toward the ramp. "Why don't you and Cloud head down there, and we can catch up in a minute." To my surprise, they both obediently walked down, with Scout walking across Donny's prone form. The clanking of horseshoe on plate armor woke the poor guy up and, to his credit, he held back from retaliating against his nemesis. I was beginning to wonder just how smart the horses really were. Their horseshoes couldn't be *that* enchanted. I yelled down at Donny when I saw him try to sit up. "Come on, we need to hurry." He looked back at me, and grasped the qi thread I had used to hold him in place to help him up the ramp.

One of these days, that horse was going to be the death of Donny.

CHAPTER TWENTY-NINE

Deeper

I had to help Donny to his feet once he made it back to the top. It only took the two of us a few minutes to carve the necessary designs into the four spikers I had picked, and we were as ready to go as we could be. Outside, the fighting was reaching a fevered pitch.

"Give me two, and you take the others. We should try and aim for the support columns." Donny smiled as he took the two I handed off to him. "I wish I could see the look on their faces when they go off."

"They are already dead, Donny. I don't think they'll care." I grinned at him to let Donny know I was mostly joking, and we moved out of the building into the maelstrom. It had only been a short time inside, but a lot had changed. The fluttering power surges from Valerie told me she was dangerously low on qi, and Chu wasn't much better. Jamila was doing well, but considering the other two were fighting more beasts than skeletons, it made sense. I moved to the side where the rock trolls were hammering against the crumbling wall. "You three, get down the ramp!"

"Better make this fast!" Chu sprinted past me into the building. "They'll be all over you in no time!"

I gave him a thumbs up to let him know I had heard, and he disappeared inside. Jamila helped an exhausted Valerie off the roof, and the two of them were gone. Donny jumped onto the roof and hurled his two spikers before tossing out some whip traps that laid into the approaching horde with strands of water qi. It wasn't as effective as wood qi would have been, but not many of our traps used the kind of energy that would heal as they hit.

"Okay, your turn!" Donny hopped down and moved for the doorway. "Make it fast!" I took my place on the roof after boosting my legs with a spin of my heart core, and immediately targeted the two farthest pillars on the side that had the weakest structure. "I'll see you in the tunnel!" After he saw me toss my two, he went inside.

The spikers were swiftly gathering energy, and I watched as they got close to detonating before flipping off the roof. While I was airborne, a chunk of the wall clipped my shoulder, activating my shielding and spinning me through the air. The rock troll had decided to use the thing blocking it as ammunition. All around the fort, undead started spilling over the walls into the open ground between the building and the walls.

When Donny's two spikers went off, it shook the whole area hard enough to knock everything standing in the cavern off its feet. Everything but the rock troll, of course. It did manage to throw off its aim, meaning the next chunk of wall meant for me smashed through the opposite side of the fort. I kipped back to my feet—not easy to do in heavy armor—and pulled out one of the throwing knives I had formed from adamantine. I wouldn't be getting this one back after I threw it, which hurt, but I didn't have any other choice.

Flicking it hard, I sprinted for the open doorway that led inside the building. There was no time to figure out which rune formation was on the knife I used, but the angry roar of the rock troll told me it had been a good choice. Right after that, the ground jumped hard enough that I went from sprint to face-first skid through the door. The explosion from my spikers was too much for the cavern to handle, and the ceiling started to come down.

I knew that the cavern wouldn't be around much longer because of the stonework around me swiftly crumbling into dust. I barely made it through the door when a large section of rock smashed down behind me, sealing me inside the room. The all-too-familiar roar of anger from the rock trolls was cut off abruptly, meaning they must have gotten a good bonk from the falling ceiling. Using a boost of qi from my heart core, I launched myself down the ramp in front of me. I tried to snag the block of stone that had covered the opening, doing my best to keep the falling debris from following me down the ramp.

"Jim!" Chu was waiting for me at the bottom of the ramp. "I thought you were only going to bring down part of the cavern."

"I'm not exactly an expert on underground rocks." The sharp rumbling from up above us caused dust to fall from the ceiling, and a few fist-sized rocks came tumbling down the ramp. "At least those rock trolls should be taken care of now." We both winced as soon as I said it. Tempting fate like that was a dumb move. I moved past the stupid comment and looked around in the dim light. "Where is everyone else?"

"Well, when the ground started shaking, the horses took off for parts unknown." Chu lifted a flickering torch over his head. "Everyone else ran to catch up to them, and they left me here to wait for you."

"That's not good." I activated the walking stick form of my spirit wood ring, and put a glow stone on the end for more light. From the difficulties Chu's torch was having, I was becoming concerned about air quality. "Everyone is very low on qi, and running into something nasty could mean real trouble."

"You don't have to tell me. That's why I'm the one waiting here. Jamila got clipped by a falling rock and I used up almost everything I had left healing her." Chu pulled out an alchemy pill meant to increase absorption rate and popped it in his mouth. "I don't think I could fight off a mildly upset kitten right now."

"Well, let's take it slow. Try to build up as much of a reserve as you can while we walk." I pulled a set of Basic-level cores from storage, one for each of the main six elements. After a moment of thought, I put the metal core back. "Here, you can use these. Since there is so much metal qi in the area, I left that one out. Now that you are actively pulling in dark and light qi, you need to make sure you stay balanced between those elements. Since you have help from the cores, you are only going to be limited by how much light qi you can absorb."

"Thanks." Chu took them from me, and tucked them up his sleeve so his armor didn't interfere with his cultivation. "That should make things much easier."

After making sure our light sources were good to go, and the cores in the back of our helmets still had enough charge to power the rivet shields, we headed deeper underground to search for our friends.

CHAPTER THIRTY

Lessons

The ramp continued to lead straight down at a constant angle for over five miles. My calf and shin muscles were starting to get sore by the time it leveled off. There had been several paths that trailed off the main tunnel, but a thin layer of dust over everything showed that no one had been down them in a long time. In fact, I was pretty sure even the necromancer might not know about this section. Or if he did, his undead army didn't use it.

Eventually, we found a fork in the tunnel, with one side blocked by a recent cave in. We probably caused it by dropping the cavern above. It was a worrying sight. There could be other tunnels affected, and I had no idea what the damage higher up might look like. The sailors might have had a very rough day.

"Do you think that collapsed before or after they went through?" Chu poked at the slabs of rock. "Because I don't see any tracks in the other tunnel."

"It was long enough ago that most of the dust settled, but I can't tell if it was before or after they came through. Moving or shifting things out of the way might only make it worse. We should check down the other side before we try getting through here." I started to go that way, and Chu quickly followed. "It could just be that the dust stirred up from the collapse covered up any sign of them going this way."

"Uh, Jim? I think we have a problem." I looked back to see Chu's torch gutter out, cutting the visibility to just the small circle of light put out by my glow stone. "The air is really thin down here."

"I noticed." I pulled out two more glow stones and passed them over to Chu. "There isn't much we can do about it though. I'll try something really quick, but it might not do much." I formed a construct using two parts wind and one part water qi, and shaped it like a large fan. Then I started spinning it, faster and faster as the dust in the tunnel started to fill the air. Chu and I lifted the visors on our helmets to cover our faces with a cloth, but I still ended up eating a mouthful of grit after a good five minutes of manipulating the construct. By the time the dust had all been blown away, it was definitely easier to breathe.

"That's better." Chu looked at the fan construct. "Do you think you can keep that thing spinning while we walk?"

"Probably, but then we wouldn't be able to see what's in front of us because of all the dust we will run into." I motioned to the bare floors. "And any tracks will get erased."

"Well, all the dust you just blasted down the tunnel didn't help, but I get your point." He tucked his handkerchief away, and changed the subject. "My qi is almost back to full. How is your level doing?"

"I'm almost to three quarters of what I can hold." I had a larger capacity, considering I was almost a full level higher than he was. "The batteries in my belt are both full, so we should be able to handle most situations."

He gave me a quick nod and we started walking again. After a few minutes, he pulled a fresh torch out of a storage device and lit it. "Just in case the air gets too thin again, the fire will give us some warning."

The two of us kept going for several hours. Neither of us said so, but we were starting to get worried. Our pace was drastically slowed because of the number of side tunnels we had to check, most of them ending in a blank wall of rock. It was like the people that made this place just decided to stop tunneling at random points. Without any clues, it was hard to guess why. I felt like it was because they were simply probing for ore, but Chu was convinced these were meant for temporary storage and sorting the ore that came down from above. Either way, it didn't really matter. Or, at least we felt like it didn't. Until we found the bodies.

A pile of dry bones and rusted armor at the end of one of the tunnels told the tale of an ancient battle. A group of seven bearing pickaxes and wearing little more than canvas clothing had fought against two warriors in heavy plate armor and ridiculously thick stone staffs. From the holes punched into the armor, it was plain the pickaxes had wounded them heavily. A dried strip of leather that almost covered the entire base of the tunnel looked like the desiccated remains of a giant worm. I had a thousand guesses as to how this could have played out, but none of them made very much sense. Had the men with pickaxes been fighting a giant worm, and the men with staffs shown up to defend the worm? Or was the worm with the miners, and the armored warriors stood against all of them?

"Take a look at this!" Chu was holding his torch over the floor at the end of the tunnel, where a hole that led somewhere else allowed a breeze to cause the flames to flicker and dance. "The air here smells… hot."

"From the odor, I think this might pass a lava flow deeper underground." I had seen the river of lava running past the city, and this might lead us straight there. Or, at least somewhere along the river. "What do you think happened here?"

"It looks to me like those two are guards, or maybe priests." Chu indicated the armored skeletons. "Why else would they have a staff as a weapon?"

"That does make sense, I suppose." I bent down to pick one up, and found it to be heavier than the solid metal spears I carried in my storage belt. Meaning it was nearing stupid levels of weight. There were runes spiraling down the full length, but they didn't accept any form of qi. It meant the runes were merely decoration, or the pattern had been broken at some point. "Then why were miners fighting priests?"

"Well, it looks to me like those miners were looking for something. That's why there were so many of these tunnels. They knew how far to dig, they just weren't sure where it intersected on the other side." Chu waved at the hole. "When they found it, those priests popped up through the ground and started fighting. I don't understand the worm, though."

"There are other tunnels farther down, meaning this discovery happened after they had already dug more of these. And like you said, what's up with the worm?" I tried to inspect the bodies for any clues or treasure, but everything either turned to dust when I touched it, or I just didn't see a use for it. What kind of miner didn't even have a coin pouch for a mug of ale after their shift? "I guess it doesn't really matter what happened. What does matter is I think we just found a direct route to the place where the necromancer has set up camp."

"Guess we need to find everybody, and get back here." Chu poked his torch deeper into the rough section that was still too dark to see down. "I can't tell how deep this goes, but it can't be too far from that lava. We might be able to end this whole thing in just a few more days."

"We need to backtrack to that collapse, and make sure the others are okay." I put one of the heavy stone staffs in my belt, but left everything else. The total storage space was about three thousand square feet, and I was actually starting to worry about it getting full. I needed to stop collecting everything that wasn't nailed down everywhere I went. Ah, who was I kidding? I might as well be considered one of the rare Dragon Rats. They were like Pack Rats, only with a larger hoard than a Storage Squirrel of the Apocalypse. And those had been hunted to extinction millennia ago, due to their plot to destroy the universe. Trying to steal the stars from the sky was a terrible choice, but some squirrels just had to learn the hard way. "Let's hurry, before the air gets too thin down here."

Chu led the way back, and I focused on pushing up my qi levels to the maximum of my capacity. We were about to dig through a large section of collapsed tunnel, and it would be important to have a reserve of power in case things came crashing down. It was impossible to know what could happen when you were shifting things hundreds of feet underground. I was tempted to try to use the focusing stones I had found in the altar of the small hidden temple, but waiting for a quiet time with no distractions was a better idea. The circumstances of my death in my first life flashed through my head, reminding me of just how risky it could be to use a new focusing stone without any safeguards in place.

"When you get a chance, I need you to fix my armor." Chu interrupted my cultivation by holding out his right arm. "I think the wire broke in that last fight, and now the shield doesn't work right."

"I'll take care of it once we find everyone." I examined the armor with a qi thread, trying to see where the wiring had broken. The orichalcum and mithril alloy didn't allow me to see anything. "I still think we need to look at a liquid qi option, but I'll worry about that later." We finally made it back to the tunnel collapse, and the two of us started poking at the rubble blocking the path.

"How do you think we should do this?" Chu picked up a rock the size of his head, then set it down gently after a cascade of rocks tumbled down around his feet. "This is really unstable."

"I have an idea. It sounds counter-intuitive, but we need to solidify this whole collapse first." I spun out a thick strand of earth qi, and started to combine the small rocks into a greater whole. "If we make all of this one piece, we can tunnel through it. There is still a chance things will come tumbling down on our heads, of course. It's impossible to know until we try."

"Sounds like as good of an idea as any." Chu reached out

and pushed earth qi through his hands, forcing the mound of rubble into a solid piece by smoothing it out from the bottom up. "I'll hit the bottom, you handle the sides."

We pushed out more and more qi, burning through our supply of energy as the loose pile slowly morphed into one solid piece. I had to push deep into the tunnel to reach the point where the rubble ended and open air marked the end of the collapse. Chu flopped down on the floor of the tunnel for a moment to catch his breath. I pulled in some extra qi from a battery to bring myself back up to a little over half, instead of just cultivating directly from the environment. We were too close to stop now, and the unbalanced environment made regular cultivation take too long.

"It's okay to catch your breath, but you need to stand up and stay close to me." I started shaping a narrow path straight through the blockage. "If the tunnel comes down, I won't be able to shield you from several feet away."

"Fine." Chu levered himself back to his feet. "I guess I need to improve my ability to cultivate on the move, anyway." He popped a medicinal pill in his mouth before walking over to me. "No time like the present for some more practice."

The two of us shuffled forward slowly, letting the wall of debris melt away as we walked. Since I was focusing on just earth qi, the occasional nugget of metal would drop to the ground. Most of it was iron ore, but a few various pieces of more rare materials tinkled to the floor. Chu collected them, so I could stay focused on what I was doing. It did give us some idea of what the original inhabitants were looking for down here. My bet was on the occasional pebble of gold, but that changed as soon as we found a fist-sized block of malachite poking out of the ceiling.

The almost glass-like material looked milky white with only a tint of green in its unprocessed form, but I had no doubt the rare, qi conductive material was their number one focus when digging. If there were more chunks this size, I was tempted to start a mining operation here myself. It would be one heck of a massive upgrade to my financial situation. Not that I was hurting or anything, I just knew how expensive things were going to get when five cultivators needed to get the materials to break through the Sage and Duke levels of cultivation. There was a reason why the most powerful in the Empire were also the most wealthy. It was almost impossible to have one without the other, especially when buying rare and precious materials at auctions. Then, add in the cost of having those same materials being made into pills and elixirs by a Grandmaster Alchemist, and you were talking about entire fortunes disappearing in the blink of an eye. Multiply that times five, and you get an idea of what we would soon be dealing with, especially considering we were reaching the limits of my own abilities in alchemy. Well, as far as qi cultivation went. I still had a lot of body cultivation formulas bouncing around in my head we could use once we made it to the Eastern Province.

After the distraction of the malachite, with Chu quietly mumbling future plans involving what sounded like a rather extensive plan to gain ownership of the mineral rights from the Empire, we finally broke through.

"Stars!" I activated the shields on my armor, and tried to move my spirit wood ring into place before the sneaking undead waiting for us could knock me back. Chu blasted an arc of wood qi over my shoulder toward the closest of the zombies, giving me a moment to react. In retrospect, it was something I should have been prepared for, but thinking about the malachite had me daydreaming instead of focusing on my surroundings. How I didn't sense them when I was exploring with my threads had to be from the increased ambient dark qi, because once I was exposed to them, the intensity from the energy animating their bodies was cloying in the tight space. "Back up, we need to get some room!"

Chu was quick to listen, immediately giving me the space I needed to shift back into the tight tunnel we had made. It meant they could only come at me one or two at a time, and a flare of light from Chu's torch behind me gave me a better look at what we were dealing with. The beak of a giant bird missing half its face peeked over the pair of skeletons trying to crowd their way inside, and I tossed a handful of poppers by reflex to try and separate the monster from my bony opponents. I immediately regretted throwing the tiny explosives, because the unsteady tunnel rained down a shower of dust and dirt on our heads. Since Chu and I were the only ones who needed to breathe, we were the only two distracted by the coughing fit it produced.

"Jim, take two big steps back, and then duck!" I immediately followed Chu's instructions, already crouching down and lifting my spirit wood shield to block the dark qi-infused bony fists that were pounding rhythmically against my hasty protection. "Now!" I dropped even lower, and barely cleared the scything wind blade that came from the trap plate Chu had placed at neck height in the tight tunnel wall. It held enough power to remove the skulls from the two skeletons crowding me, and their brittle remains crumbled in front of me as the dark qi holding them together was separated from the spinal column.

"I don't think you made it better." The bird creature, now unhindered by the skeletons, hit me hard enough that I skidded right up against Chu's leg trying to hold it back. An ominous cracking sound came from the spirit wood, and I spun up my heart core to empower the uppercut that I levered into the avian's rotting chest. My fist punched through the hollow bones, and I was covered in a wash of gore that made my qi shielding flare with a bright warning. There was something in the coagulated blood of the large bird that the warding identified as a powerful threat. Now that the skeletons were out of the way, and my shields were providing enough light to see by, I could finally tell that I was fighting some kind of oversized vulture with four wings instead of two. The upper pair buffeted against my helmet as they reached over my shield, and the beak slammed down once more, this time causing a visible crack to run from the center of the circle of spirit wood to the lower rim.

"That's it, carrion-eater. Don't you know it isn't nice to break peoples things?"

Before it could hit me again, I used a wood qi thread to pull an adamantine spear free and slam it through the base of its beak, nailing it to the ceiling above. It tried to pull itself free, and ripped its own damaged head off, dropping to the ground as its neck stump sprayed blood over me once more. The thin shielding that protected me flared once again, cooking the disgusting mess in a flash of light and heat that made the tight area stink bad enough I had to hold back a gag.

I noticed a small surge of dark qi tint the area around me for a split second as the smoke and vapor cleared, but it was gone before I could inspect it further. The memory of the infection inside the sailor I tried to save ran through my head, and I shivered at the thought of what could have just happened without the shields. I didn't even wince at the cost as I swapped out a fresh core in the back of my helmet. There was no way I wanted to risk my shields running out of power if that happened again.

"Well, that was disgusting." Chu looked over my shoulder as I morphed my spirit wood ring back into its ring form, trying to inspect it for damage as it sat around my finger. "Was that the last of those things?"

I shook my head, remembering what I had seen waiting for us deeper underground. "Not even close, Chu. Not even *close*."

CHAPTER THIRTY-ONE

Experiments

The two of us moved deeper into the tunnel, weaving through piles of rubble left behind by the collapse. There were two more sections we had to use our qi to push through; thankfully there were no more surprise attacks by the undead. We did manage to find several more hefty chunks of raw malachite, which invariably sparked conversations about what we could do to mine the region for profit. It was a way to pass the time while we searched for our friends, and Chu even stopped occasionally to scratch marks along the tunnel walls to make things easier if we ever came back.

"You have to know that the Emperor won't give up the mining rights to these mountains. At least, not without taking a large enough percentage that you won't see any true profits." I paused to let him catch up to me, after he had pushed a small glow stone into the wall to mark where he had been. "That's just how the Empire works. You have to give the Emperor his due, and then the King of the Province, and any officials between the two that might interrupt the process of getting—and keeping—mining approval."

"There's a simple solution, you know." Chu grinned, his

white teeth flashing in the dim light. "If they don't *know* about a mining operation up in the mountains, then they can't *tax* a mining operation up in the mountains." We both laughed quietly at the idea. I wasn't sure how serious he was being, but I knew once Ming became Emperor, there was no way an operation that brought in large amounts of malachite wouldn't be noticed. It was still a long time before we needed to worry about that. "I still haven't seen any tracks. Do you think we missed them somewhere?" Chu lifted his torch a little higher, trying to see deeper down the tunnel. The occasional pile of rubble would have made it impossible to see any farther than a few dozen yards, even if it had been brightly lit down here.

"I don't think we've passed them yet." I looked back the way we had come. "None of those piles of rubble were blocking a side path, so that means they must be deeper underground than we expected."

"Why would they take off like this, especially without leaving us some kind of note or sign to show what happened?" Chu took the lead position, picking up the pace a bit. "It isn't like leaving a few scratches on the wall is a hard thing to do."

"If they expected us to be right behind them, then they probably didn't see the point. And after the ceiling came down, they were probably trying to keep up with the frightened horses." I kicked at a pile of rocks on the ground, sending them bouncing deeper. "Those are enchanted horses, after all. They can move pretty fast when properly motivated. After being drained by the fighting, it was probably hard to—" A creaking sound echoed down the hall, cutting me off. It was some kind of hinge squealing in protest from someone—or something—interrupting its centuries-old rest.

Chu and I crept forward as silently as we could, while doing our best to limit the light we were using. No sense in announcing our arrival before we wanted whatever was ahead to know we were approaching. The air was lacking the tell-tale smell of rot and decay I was beginning to associate with the monsters down here, and finally the quiet ringing clop of a horseshoe on stone caused both of us to relax.

"About time we caught up to you guys!" Chu used a bit of wind qi to stir the air, causing his torch to flare up brightly. "You trying to leave us behind or something?"

"Oh, thank the stars! Jim and Chu are here!" The voice of Jamila came from the shadow left by a pile of rubble that, upon closer inspection, was clearly designed to help hide a stone door in the tunnel wall. "This way, guys." A glow stone was uncovered and provided enough light for us to see her standing in the doorway. She leaned out to whisper to the two of us. "You made it just in time. Valerie was about to try to cook something, and I was starting to worry about actually having to eat it."

"I heard that!" We all laughed, and Valerie poked her head out to get a look at us. "Jim, you need to get in here and look at Donny. He is looking pretty pale." The grimace on Jamila's face at Valerie's words made a tiny flutter of fear flicker in my stomach.

"What happened?" Instead of answering, the women motioned us forward, leading us deeper inside. The four of us made our way down a short set of stairs that ended at another doorway. This one made of wood so old it had petrified instead of rotted, and the tell-tale rust-colored metal used for the hinges, bands, and in the viewport meant it was made of orichalcum. A quick glance revealed this place to be some kind of prison or jail, with more bars of the mana-draining metal lining the back wall of a chamber the size of a great room in an inn. Donny was laid out on a bedroll with his armor in a haphazard pile next to him, while the horses were standing next to one another in the far corner, as far away as they could get from Donny. I paused in the doorway, feeling a wave of dark qi assault my senses as shadows crawled and pulsed along the walls from the braziers someone had lit to keep the darkness at bay. "Was he injured by something?"

"No, it wasn't that." Valerie led me over to her betrothed, and knelt down near his head. "There was some kind of vulture, and Donny managed to blast a part of its head off. When he did, a splatter of its blood hit him. His armor's shielding didn't activate for such a small thing, and it touched his skin. We were able to rinse it off right away, but he started feeling sick right after. Once we found this place, we stopped to set up camp. It was more defensible than the rest of the tunnel."

"That was smart." Chu moved to the side, pulling out the materials to start cooking. "I'll try to make something hearty, so he can recover faster. I think adding a few dried herbs to the broth would boost his healing ability."

"Good plan. You do that, and I'll see if I can figure out what's going on." I knelt next to Donny, who stirred when I placed my hand on his chest. I was hoping he would wake up, but it didn't happen. The moment my strand of wood qi touched his body, I knew instantly what the problem was.

A dark stain inside his meridians was spreading toward his core, trying to attack me the moment my strand was close enough for it to reach. This time, I knew what to expect, so I severed my connection and backed away. The thread erupted from the skin on the back of his hand, and tried to jump on my leg, where I was kneeling next to Donny. I was still in my armor, so it slid off the orichalcum and mithril alloy, making a screeching sound that I didn't hear with my ears.

I backed off and fired a pellet of light qi directly at the glob of corruption, and it bubbled into a mist that burned my sinuses. I worried the infection had passed to me somehow, but a quick scan showed I was clear. "Well, this isn't good."

"Oh gods, he has what that sailor had, doesn't he?" Valerie seemed to hunch in on herself, curling around Donny's head. "I... I don't..." She looked down at her betrothed, and her expression went blank. "He wouldn't want to become one of those things."

"And we won't let that happen." I immediately pulled out my pill cauldron, and walked over to the cages that lined the walls along the back of the room. "I'm not going to let this infection take away the person closer to me than a brother." I pulled out my stiletto blade and scraped some of the orichalcum lining the bars into the cauldron. "This is something that spreads through qi, so if we can shut down his system, it should slow it down long enough for us to find a cure."

"Give me one of the shackle sets, so I can put it on him." Jamila walked over and took a spare set from me, and clamped them around his wrists and ankles. "What else can we do?"

"We can try to reduce the amount of dark qi in the area. It seems to have its base in that element, so boosting the light around him might bother it." I tossed a few more braziers to Valerie for her to place around the area, along with a barrel of the lamp oil I had taken from the Auction House ship wreckage. "Set these up all around, but make sure you circulate the air from outside frequently. We don't want to kill ourselves by taking away all the good air."

"Give me all your glow stones, too. We can pile them up around him." I gave all I had to Valerie, who also took all of the ones in Jamila and Chu's storage as well. Pretty soon, the entire jail room was bright enough to hurt our eyes. The natural flow of dark qi wasn't affected much, but the amount of light qi that was produced started to balance things out. It would only last for as long as the oil-soaked wood in the braziers lasted, so I hurried back to the alchemy pill I was trying to produce. "He doesn't look any better, Jim. You should hurry."

I gave Valerie a quick nod and went back to pulling out ingredients. A few years back, I had taken everything from my uncle's alchemy shop in the southern capital, and there were several ingredients that I hadn't even touched yet due to their unique properties.

Most people would see these ingredients as only useful in poisons, or as counteragents to balance the effects of a concoction meant to expand qi absorption. If you took in too much all at once, it could damage your meridians, or stars-forbid, blow a hole through a core wall. To avoid that, you would need some kind of limiter to keep the effects spread out over an extended period of time instead of all at once. What I pulled out of storage was all of the limiter and poison ingredients I could find.

"Seven-Wind Severing Fruit, Flying Frog Lilypad, Brown Burgundy Blossom. All are poisonous unless used in tiny increments. If I can get the proportions evenly mixed with a double dose of Yellow Fire Grass, it shouldn't kill him right away." The sharp inhalation from Valerie made me realize I was speaking my thoughts out loud. Instead of stopping to explain myself, I raised my voice so it was audible to everyone. If they understood what I was trying to make, they might get a better idea of the side effects I wanted to create in Donny's cultivation network. "Those three ingredients will slow his breathing, heartbeat, and brain function to almost nothing. They *should* put him into a temporary coma that will stop any further damage to his body."

"I didn't think there was a cure for Brown Burgundy Blossom. What are you going to do if it is too much?" Chu was looking over from where he was cooking on the heating stone. "He won't ever wake up."

"While there might not be a cure, there are ways to treat the symptoms until it works its way out of his system." I patted my belt. "There are plenty of stimulants that can keep him alive long enough." I shoved a few items back in my belt to give myself some work space, and then pulled out the last two things I had that might work. "Barnacle Tree Root for reducing qi absorption, and two vials of Lavender Grape Liquid to help keep the ingredients from melding too deeply with his bloodstream. We want this to wear off quickly, after all."

Once I had the necessary ingredients, I started to heat up the cauldron with a controlled flame from the meridian in my left hand. Since I didn't want to take off my armor, it was necessary. I lifted the visor on my helm and used the meridian in my forehead to hold up the Seven-Wind Severing Fruit. A quick flick of my stiletto cut through the thick skin of the mango-like fruit, and I carved out a tiny sliver of the meat to drop it in the cauldron. Next, I added the Lavender Grape Liquid after allowing the fruit to sizzle and caramelize for a minute. Once it had reached a boil, I dropped in the Brown Burgundy Blossom and watched as it went from a burgundy flower to a brown liquid that bubbled and fizzed before blending evenly into the mixture. The Barnacle Tree Root shavings were quickly dissolved, and a light stir brought the orichalcum powder I had scraped from the prison bars swirling through the concoction in a red tornado. After the mixture was holding at a steady boil with the new ingredients, I added the crushed stem of the Flying Frog Lilypad. Once the ingredients were finally all blended properly, it was time for the hard part.

I swapped fire qi for water qi, rapidly cooling the mixture from the outside. I had to add a thread of wind qi into the liquid to keep it swirling and cooling evenly. It was necessary to skim the pulp and impurities off the top as the temperature dropped, and eventually I ended up with a purple-tinted milk-like substance. I put the lid on the cauldron, and started to heat it back up again. This time, I encapsulated the whole cauldron in fire, and used my willpower boosted by a concentrated dome of earth qi to increase the pressure inside the cauldron. As the pressure steadily built, it took more concentration to hold the lid closed and keep any steam from escaping. I felt a single drop of sweat trickle down my temple, and doubled down on the earth qi to increase the gravity bearing down on the cauldron. A rumbling sound started emanating from it, and the drain on my qi reserves spiked immensely. I was afraid I would have to start tapping into the qi batteries to make sure I didn't bottom out.

Suddenly, the rumbling stopped, and I knew the moment of truth had come. I spun up my brain core to speed up my perception, knowing it would be necessary. When the first explosion rocked the cauldron, I had to shift all of the earth qi in the dome to a small ring over the lid to help keep the seal. Since the explosion had unbalanced the heat levels, I had to shift a quarter of the fire qi heating the bottom to the upper half of the cauldron. A second explosion quickly followed, and I had to use a thread of metal qi to reinforce a weak spot on the side of the cauldron. It barely stayed intact, but barely was good enough.

When the third explosion came, it sent a deep rumble through everyone in the room. I lost control then, even with my perceptions cranked to the maximum I could manage. My ring of earth qi holding the lid in place shifted when the cauldron jumped, and the seal was broken. The mixture would have been a failure then, but luck was with us. Instead of the great pressure exerted on the lid blasting outward, the concoction chose that exact moment to coalesce. A strong suction pulled in all of the heat from the fire qi, the pressure from the steam, and the weight from the earth qi. Another quiet rumble signaled the mixture was complete. The cauldron went from glowing a cherry red from the heat, to completely cool to the touch. I dropped my hold on the creation and slumped in relief.

"Is it done?" Jamila walked over and poked at the cauldron. "What did you make? Will it work to heal Donny?"

"Not to worry anyone, but I don't think this pill has ever been made before." I pulled off the lid of the cauldron to reveal three pale violet pills about the size of the first section of my littlest finger. "At least, not that I have heard of."

"How will we know if these work or not?" Chu was still stirring whatever was in his own pot, occasionally adding ingredients to the meal. "If this is a new pill, how do you know it won't hurt him?"

"I don't know. This is all one big experiment." Valerie inhaled sharply at what I said, but otherwise kept quiet. I pulled out one of the pills and sniffed it. The power it held was undeniable, and I had to fight not to fall into a relaxed state. There wasn't time to sleep at the moment. "I'm pretty sure it's going to work, though. Once this takes effect, the qi infection should be halted in its tracks. That will give us enough time to figure out a cure."

"You mean, that wasn't the cure you were working on?" Valerie was clearly fighting back tears. "You wasted almost an hour, just to make a pill that wasn't going to fix him?" I could feel her aura pulsing in time with her heartbeat, and it most definitely wasn't happy. "The infection is getting close to his cores, and I don't think he can fight it much longer!"

"Please, just trust me. Think of this as the first step in making him better." I got up and placed a pill under his tongue to dissolve after prying his jaw open. Donny was obviously in a lot of pain. "Now, we just need to monitor him to make sure he keeps breathing." Valerie seemed to calm down a little, especially once his tense muscles started to relax. "I'll need you to get your healing medallion ready, in case the infection attacks Donny internally when I reach out to it." I passed over the two remaining pills. "If you use your medallion, it will probably remove the side effects of the pill, so give him another."

"Should you make more pills? There's only two left." Valerie already had her medallion out and ready, pressed against Donny's forehead. "What if we need to heal him more than twice?"

"You only have three charges on that medallion. We need one to heal him after the infection is cured, which means we only get two chances anyway. Neither myself nor Chu would know how to heal the damage this disease will likely leave behind. Our only real chance is that medallion." She gave me a sharp nod of agreement, and I knelt next to Donny. I paused for a moment to draw in a large portion of the qi stored in one of the batteries. "Enough talk, it's time to save his life."

CHAPTER THIRTY-TWO

Reactions

Seeing as how the infection literally fought back when you tried to kill it, I thought it prudent to set up a pair of shield formation plates that I could activate with a thought. They were two domes that would fit over Donny, one slightly larger than the other. If I timed it right, I could trap any attacks between the shields. That meant the dark mana goo couldn't get back to Donny, or reach me. All I had to do was make sure I timed it right.

Adjusting the runes so the plates would do what I wanted only took a few minutes, and a splash of liquid qi powered them enough to make the carvings glow a faint blue. Which was when I realized how low I was getting on liquid qi. The overwhelming presence of metal and dark qi in the area made the plates we used to collect liquid qi from the environment much slower than normal. I had an idea of how to fix it, but that would have to wait.

"Okay, I'm ready to start. Remember, be prepared to heal him if something goes wrong." Valerie gave me a thumbs up, and I spun up my cores. A quick inspection showed that my pill had done what I wanted for the most part, but it hadn't completely stopped the infection like I hoped. There was still a noticeable creep as the black sludge creeped farther along his meridians. It looked like the infection had started in his hands and face, and gone directly for his lower core. If it had tried to reach his brain core first, Donny would already be a member of the necromancer's army. It was chilling to see how close the mystery disease was to reaching its goal. Another thirty minutes, and it would all be over. Even more dangerous, the infection clearly possessed some form of basic intelligence, or possibly an instinct for maximum effectiveness. By reaching the lower core first, it would stop any further absorption of qi, and it could spread to the other cores through the central meridian channel that connected the three. I was more than a little concerned.

"How's it going?" Jamila came to stand next to us after refilling the oil in the braziers to keep the wood itself from burning. She was trying to stop herself from pacing back and forth, but her worry was still clear by the white knuckles gripping the hilts of her katanas. "Anything I can do to help?"

"Just be ready in case the black goo gets free of the shields. If you knock it clear or something, it might buy us the seconds we need to kill it." While I didn't think I would actually need her help, it was good to keep her busy. That, and I might actually need her to help me kill it once the disease was free of Donny's body. "Now, let me concentrate. There isn't much time left."

Everyone fell silent as I plunged my focus back into Donny's prone form. Considering I needed to get a better idea of what I was dealing with, I spun out a thread from each element and ran it into his body. I knew how it reacted to wood and light qi, but not the other elements.

The first one I used to touch the infection was earth qi. The two reacted like oil and water, completely unable to interact with one another. Wind qi was the same, as was water. Fire qi seemed to irritate the infection, but it only burrowed deeper inside Donny. I knew that light qi would kill it, but the interaction that would happen inside Donny might result in him being melted from the inside out. Unsurprisingly, metal qi was able to interact with it, but there wasn't anything it could do but swirl it around. That left me with the one option I knew brought about a violent reaction.

I swapped out the other elements for wood qi, and carefully started to push them against Donny's hands and face. The instant jolt from the disease sensing the wood qi caused his whole body to jerk as the black sludge attacked the life energy. It was like a ravenous beast, hunting for the life energy the way a hound sniffed after fresh blood. I activated the shields to trap the thick, tar-like substance as a much larger amount emerged from his body, and immediately killed it with light qi. The stone floor was etched by the resulting acidic sludge, and I held the shields in place until the vapor dissipated.

"Did it work? Is he better now?" Valerie leaned forward as the shields dropped to lay a hand on Donny, who groaned in pain at her touch. "Should I heal him?"

"No, but I think I figured out a way to handle this." I was scanning him with my senses, and the infection was far from gone. The good news was, it had pulled back from his cores in order to rush toward the pure life energy. It had only given us another thirty minutes or so of time, but I was hoping repeating the process over and over again would draw out all of the poison. It didn't escape me that the amount that came out of his body was not a reflection of what was inside, of course. I was only guessing, but it seemed like once the infection was in the open air, it expanded or grew somehow. I also noted the entire process seemed to drain him of his own vitality, causing his already pale skin to turn almost as white as bleached parchment. "This is going to take some time. Best to settle in for a long fight."

Chu brought over the meal he had been cooking, and we took a few minutes to eat a warm meal and cultivate what little qi we could. Everyone made sure to keep their draw on the environment slow and steady, to limit the impact in the area so the necromancer wouldn't notice. Valerie spooned the hearty broth into Donny's mouth, managing to get a good amount into his system. Considering the side effects of the pill I had given him, his body would take a while to digest the medicinal mixture. It did manage to improve his color a little, which made the mood lighten a small amount. For the rest of us, it provided a solid boost to our energy levels.

After handing over the bowls to be cleaned, we got back in position. Donny's infection had spread back to its former level, but it hadn't gained any new ground. Once again, I used wood qi to tempt the diseased dark qi out of his body, doing my best to get as much as I could to chase the life energy before activating the shields to isolate it. The growth of the sludge seemed to increase the longer it was outside of Donny's body, but it felt… frail. Instead of killing it with light qi right away, I left it trapped between the shields.

"Are you going to take care of it?" Jamila had a katana out and was ready to swing. "Or are we just going to wait for it to break free and infect someone else?"

"Just wait." I held up a hand to stop her from attacking, and watched as the black goo started to harden into a crusty lump that slowly shrank down into a brittle block of wrongness. "I think, when it is away from a host or source of life qi for too long, it dies." Everyone watched as it eventually collapsed in on itself, and turned into a pile of dust. I used a bit of fire qi to burn it just to be safe after dropping the shields.

"Well, that's good news at least." Jamila sheathed her sword, and took a step back from the burnt dust. "It can't survive to track us down later on."

"All we have to do is get it out of him, and he will be okay." Valerie sounded as if she was trying to force her version of reality into existence with her words, and from the underlying pain, I felt like it was my job to make it happen. "I'm going to be right here, okay Donny?" She caressed his face, and he shifted slightly at her touch.

"Okay, let's get back to it." I completely drained the batteries on my belt, refilling my cores to their maximum. It meant I didn't have anything in reserve if there was a fight, but this wasn't the time to be operating at a partial charge. "Be ready for anything."

After getting a chorus of acknowledgement from the people around me, I spun out a fresh set of wood qi threads to tempt the disease out of Donny. Instead of pushing them inside his body, I wrapped them around his wrists and forehead. The disease would have to push out of him to reach the life energy, hopefully taking the strain off of his system a little. This time, the response was far more swift. I didn't know if it was because the disease was sentient enough to remember that there was something outside its host that was tempting, or Donny's weakened form wasn't as appetizing as the pure energy resting on his skin. Either way, it rushed out of his meridians in a flood, trying to catch up to the power it hungered for. I cut my connection to the threads as soon as it erupted free instead of pulling it away this time, and activated the inner shield so it couldn't sink back into him. I drastically underestimated the expansion of the infection once it contacted the wood qi.

"Jamila!" I shouted for her support as I activated the second shield layer. It managed to capture most of the miasma, but a glob the size of a fist fell free onto the floor. The black goo took a quick jerk toward the kneeling Valerie before a katana wreathed in light qi sliced it in half. The infection burst into blue flames before dissolving into black acid and sizzled against the floor. "Well, we shouldn't do that again."

"You don't say." Jamila's dry tone made me wince. "Stop experimenting with it, and just kill this stuff already."

"Believe me, I didn't mean to do that. I was trying to lessen the strain on Donny." We all looked at him, and I was relieved to see he wasn't as pale as the last time. "I think this is going to be the best way to do it, otherwise he will be drained by the process before we get to the end. I think it replicates itself inside him when my threads are inside him, but it doesn't do that when a separate host presents itself nearby."

"That's fine, I'll be ready." Jamila gave her katana a spin, and a flicker of light qi ran over its edge. "I've got plenty of energy to spare."

"At least that answers why the undead make biting people a priority over killing them." Chu walked over, and hefted the reforged mace I had made for him. "The disease is focused on spreading to new hosts, not killing them. I bet that's why we saw those weird goats, and the trolls. There has to be tunnels leading to the surface somewhere, and the diseased hosts are attacking everything they can find. It's pushing the monsters out of the mountains and down into the Empire."

I smiled, realizing how stupid I had been to keep the knowledge of light and dark qi from my friends. They were competent and strong enough to handle the burden, and proved it to me over and over again. I couldn't help but wonder if my own mind still wasn't operating correctly after my reincarnation. Stuffing six and a half centuries into the gray matter of a pre-teen might have caused some problems I was only now beginning to recognize. Now wasn't the time to worry about it. I needed to focus on what was right in front of me, before second-guessing all my decisions over the past few years.

"I think you nailed it, Chu. I expect we will have quite a problem when we get out of these caves." He swallowed hard before nodding in agreement. I looked back at my patient. "Let's do this." I repeated the process once again, and the four of us gradually drained the sickness from Donny. It took four more iterations to get all but the tiniest bits of infected dark qi out, but then we ran into a problem.

"Why isn't it leaving?" Valerie was holding a second coma pill in one hand, and her healing medallion in the other. A large swirl of my wood qi was resting over each of Donny's palms, but the infection refused to part from his skin. "It's just sitting there."

"I don't know." I scanned him thoroughly, making sure there was none left in the rest of his body. Only a single globule of the infection rested in each of his hands, unwilling to leave him. "It must be aware enough to recognize that if it leaves now, he will be free of infection." As I watched, the lump of infection in his left hand expanded deeper a fraction of an inch, and Donny visibly paled. "It looks like it is draining him to make more of itself before it leaves."

"We can't let that happen." Chu knelt down and took a closer look at him. "If it drains him too much, I don't think he is going to make it." A strangled gasp from Valerie caused him to look up sharply. "Jim, I only see two choices. Cut his hands off, or use light qi inside his meridians and kill it inside him."

"Take his hands?" Valerie paled almost enough to match Donny. "What would he do without his hands?"

"Let's talk about this." Jamila tried to interpose herself between Chu and Donny, but he didn't budge. "He's already so weak, cutting parts off of him might kill him anyway."

"Whatever you choose, it had better be fast. It's only going to regrow more while we argue." Chu swapped out his mace for the heavy shield I had made, the sharp edge at the bottom ready to slam down with finality. "There isn't much time."

"I can make a Bone Regrowth pill to replace his hands if we can gather the necessary ingredients, but that won't happen until we get out of this place." I spun out two threads of light qi from my hands. "It would be hard to cut his hands off, though. Don't forget, you have been reinforcing your bodies for years. The trauma necessary to remove them would be much worse than a dose of internal acid." Chu relaxed, and I positioned the threads above his hands. "Valerie, get your medallion ready." She was already prepared, but took a deep breath to calm her nerves.

Thrusting the light qi inside his meridians was simple, but none of us were prepared for his reaction. The moment my light qi touched the infection, Donny sat straight up from his coma and screamed loud enough to tear his vocal cords. The palms of his hands melted as the acid was dragged out by my threads. I managed to keep any of it from getting into his bloodstream, but it was close. His sudden movement almost made me slip, but thankfully everyone else quickly held him down. After struggling for a few moments, Donny passed out again. His hands were in terrible shape, so Valerie activated a healing charge. For the first time since she had picked the item from the Roh Clan vaults, it failed to completely heal something.

"What's wrong with it?" Valerie used a second charge, but it didn't do much beyond making Donny's rest a little more restful. "His hands are all scarred up."

"I don't know." I picked up his right hand, and looked closely at it while Chu gave Donny another scan to make sure there wasn't any more infection hiding in his meridians. "It must be something about that acid. I think he will still be able to use his hands, but they will be stiff and sore until we find a way to fix him."

"He's still alive, and not crippled." Jamila placed a hand on Valerie's shoulder. "Donny's tough. Just let him rest a bit, and he'll be right back at it."

"Don't forget, as soon as he reaches Sage, his body will be reformed into its most perfect condition." I poked at the thick scars that pulled his hands into a claw-like shape. He wouldn't be able to open them completely, and carving formations might be a problem until he adjusted. Holding his axe and dagger should be easy enough. "Jamila's right. He's alive, and we all know this won't slow him down for long. Let's get some rest and get ready to track down the source of our problems." A flash of hot anger rushed through me, and I fought it back down under control. "That necromancer is going to pay for hurting him."

CHAPTER THIRTY-THREE

Onward

Before laying down to sleep, I grabbed a couple of the formation plates that collected liquid qi for us. With a few tweaks and a few spare scraps of copper, I made something new. It looked like a set of three concentric rings, with the center shaped like a funnel. The outer ring had six indentions connected by a solid ring of connected runes, with fittings to hold whatever was placed in the divots in position. The central ring was an adjusted formation that had a set of runes that would condense qi at a slower pace than our normal collection plates, but I left off the safety features that made it stop once a certain amount of qi was collected. It was wasteful on our other versions, but this one was different.

The funnel in the center was carved with a spiral of runes that angled down into the spout. They would make sure that the liquid qi didn't escape, and it slightly accelerated the qi so it wouldn't pool up. At the end of the funnel, I placed a large barrel that the new formation plate fit over like a lid. I didn't plan it to be that size, but I wasn't going to complain. A few runes lining the inside of the barrel that used to hold lamp oil meant it wouldn't evaporate. After getting everything ready, I placed the six normal element focusing stones I had found in the small temple's altar into the indentations on the formation plate. A quick flick of my wrist finished the final rune, and I stepped back as it flared to life.

"What's that?" Chu walked up, looking over the new device. "And where did you get the glowing rocks?"

"I found some focusing stones in an old altar. This should allow us to completely refill our liquid qi to power our formations by the time we wake up." I nodded at the swirls of dark and metal qi that were already forming over the top of the barrel. "The focusing stones can take in all this darkness and death, and turn it into equal parts of the six natural forms." I thought about adding the light and dark qi focusing stones, but the risk of forming mana from the perfect ratio mixture stopped me. That wasn't a risk I was ready to take. Also, it might have just given me some insight into why the knowledge of light and dark qi was suppressed. I swallowed hard at the thought of all the power-hungry people out there who wouldn't hesitate to use mana in a misbegotten attempt to improve their cultivation. They might destroy the world more efficiently than I ever had. My method had taken a long time to finish, after all. I looked over at Chu and motioned toward our bedrolls. "We should get some sleep." Valerie volunteered to take first watch, and the rest of us laid down.

After a few minutes of laying around, my brain finally calmed down enough to allow sleep to come. My dreams were filled with creatures trying to bite me, and for some reason, I saw Alya. She was the step-daughter to the Chancellor of the Southern King, who I had killed a few years ago. Also, a woman in Emperor Ming's harem that I had a very large crush on long ago. Several lifetimes worth of 'long ago.'

Alya was surrounded by a dark forest, and the trees were trying to grab her as she ran. This version of her was closer to the one from my memories of my first life. Too old to be the current Alya, but too young to be the woman from my first life. The things chasing her were cast in shadow, and I saw flashes of snarling, blood-filled mouths. But these weren't beasts, or some kind of monster. They were people. The veins of black running across their faces were easy to recognize as the infection I had just fought inside Donny, but it must have evolved beyond its current form to show on their faces. As Alya sprinted for a clearing brightened by rays of moonlight, a small darting figure broke free of the pack chasing her. It leapt off the side of a tree, tackling her just as she made it to the edge of the treeline. Filtering into the clearing from the other side was a man dressed in the clothes of a ship captain, and I knew it was the captain we had left behind. He was leading this pack, hunting down anyone not carrying the dark qi infection inside these woods. Then, the diseased child that had tackled Alya bit her upraised forearm, and she screamed loud enough that I jolted awake.

"What in the stars was that?" I tried to keep my voice down, but flailing around on my mattress was enough to rouse Jamila, who padded silently over to check on me. She must have relieved Valerie at some point on guard, because the white-haired girl was curled up against Donny.

"Are you okay?" Jamila had a trio of shuriken in her hand, and a flicker of light qi trailed over their sharp points. "You were really struggling."

"It was just a bad dream." I shook my head, trying to clear the fuzzy feeling that persisted. "This one was different from the times the gods have spoken to me. It felt more like a warning of what could happen, instead of something that was already going on."

"Could it be a premonition? Something from inside yourself, separate from the gods?" Jamila raised an eyebrow. "Maybe you are developing a new power."

"I don't think it's that." I shrugged my shoulders. "I've never shown a talent for precognition before. This is probably just my fears pushing to the surface."

"You aren't very old, Jim. Who knows what kind of abilities you might develop?" I barely held in the snort that tried to escape. "Well, tell me about it. Another perspective might help."

She put away her shuriken and sat down next to me before pulling out a flask of spirits. "Not like we are going anywhere."

I didn't have an argument for that, so I told her what I had seen. She sat silently for a time, so I walked over to check on the barrel. It was already over halfway filled, so I didn't mess with anything. When I returned to sit next to her, she started putting on the armor pieces that covered her legs.

"What are you doing?" I pulled out a rag to start cleaning my own armor. There was no way I was putting it back on with the way it smelled. "We can't go anywhere yet."

"If there is any one thing I have learned over the past few years, it's that we shouldn't ignore the signs dropped right in front of us." Jamila tightened down the straps that held her greaves onto her calves. "That dream might mean nothing, but it only costs us a little time to check on the sailors. I think it would be a good idea to look in on them, if only to make sure they understand what the infection really is. They deserve that warning."

"That's… fair." I hurried with my own cleaning, before starting to strap pieces of metal to me. "How were you thinking we should do this?"

"Just you and me, since we're the fastest. We make a run up to check on them while Chu and Valerie look after Donny." Jamila strapped her sabatons over her boots. "By the time we make it back, he should be well enough to move on. This way, we are doing something useful instead of just standing around, staring at Donny."

"I think it's a good plan. Before we go, we should cultivate as much as we can. I need to refill the batteries on my belt anyway." I pointed at where Chu was bundled up on the ground. "And you get to tell him we're leaving."

Jamila laughed at me, and walked off to wake up Chu after she finished strapping on the rest of her armor. I walked over to the six focusing stones collecting liquid qi and plucked them free. I started to use them one at a time to refill the batteries, adding in the light and dark qi stones to keep the balance intact.

Since I was able to draw directly on the dark and metal qi flowing by, the batteries were completely charged in less than an hour. They were effective enough that it was actually hard to limit the flow of energy so we didn't stand out in the area. I was more than a little amazed at how powerful the stones were, but I knew they wouldn't be nearly as impressive once we were above ground and the qi levels weren't so high. I also understood how important it would be to not let anyone know we had them. They wouldn't give up trying to take them until bloodshed persuaded them it was a bad idea to steal.

I put the stones back in the formation plate so it could finish filling the barrel. Refilling my own cores would still take some time, but taking too many shortcuts on my own cultivation path would only make the later stages more difficult. Sifting through the ambient qi using my own cores was the better option. And Jamila might choke me to death if she had to wait any longer. Her impatient glare was burning a hole between my shoulder blades.

"You two be safe." Chu followed us up to the door that led into the tunnel so he could reactivate the wards after we left. "And Jim, make sure you bring my fiancée back in one piece." His eyes betrayed his worry, and I gave him a sharp nod.

"Don't worry, we'll be safe. And neither of us will be taking off our armor the whole time." I looked over to Jamila to drive home the point. I knew the armor limited her movements more than she liked, but there wasn't any option given the circumstances. "Our shields will stay up the whole time, too. Burning through extra cores is a small price to pay for the extra safety."

"Good luck then, and I'll see you soon." We both gave Chu a thumbs up, and he sealed the door behind us. I turned and started heading back the way we came.

"Where are you going?" I turned to look at Jamila, who was walking the other direction. She pointed in the direction she was walking. "Did you forget the cavern we collapsed back there? We need to go this way." She had been down this tunnel before, so I didn't argue. Jamila obviously knew something I didn't. After another hour of comfortable silence as we moved deeper, we reached a sharp bend in the tunnel where a narrow tube branched off.

"I take it you scouted this far?" She nodded at my question, and moved to the small opening. It was a natural tunnel, carved by water over the centuries, until the mining operation obviously cut off the flow when they built the tunnel I was now standing in.

"This is as far as I went, but I smelled water down here. If my mental map is anything close to correct, we have been spiraling down. That means we should be able to climb up through the well that was in the center of the outpost, right into the middle of where the sailors are camping out." She didn't wait to discuss how accurate her mental map might be, and instead jumped into the tube and slid out of sight.

"Wow, great discussion. Glad we could talk about this before we jump into the dark, scary tunnel that might lead anywhere." I let out a mighty sigh as I followed her down the tube.

CHAPTER THIRTY-FOUR

Upward

Bouncing down the tube of slick rock might have been fun, if I wasn't in pure darkness, and wearing plate armor. Every twist and turn seemed to be at just the right angle to bounce my helmeted head off the side, or bang an elbow or knee, and I never saw it coming. I was cycling wood qi to keep the stars flashing across my vision from blinding me when I finally shot free of the tube.

Smacking into an underground lake of frigid, black water at extremely high speeds didn't make me any happier. On the positive side, the impact was hard enough to cause my shields to flare brightly, illuminating the space I found myself in for a split second before I went under. It was an onion-shaped cavern, and the ceiling was pockmarked with holes. I wasn't able to see much else before I went under water.

"Over here!" Jamila shouted to me as I struggled to the surface, and I started swimming in the direction of her voice. It was a struggle to stay afloat in armor, so I used a steady push of water qi from the meridians in my feet to help. A few seconds later, a burst of flames shot out and I saw where Jamila was waving for me on a small island in the center of the lake. "It gets shallow enough for you to stand once you get close!"

I paddled over to where she was standing, struggling to keep my head above water. The island made the small underground lake seem more like a donut, and I quickly made my way onto dry land. Jamila used the flame construct in her hand to light a torch, and we both peered at our surroundings while the cold water dripped loudly onto the rocky shore.

"Well, that was exciting." I made sure to lay the sarcasm on pretty thick. "I sure am glad we talked about what to do once we got through the tube, and discussed in detail what to look for once we arrived."

"Don't be such a wimp. I bet some people would pay good money just to go down a water-slicked tube at high speeds." Jamila pointed up to the general area we had come in from. "And the way you splashed down at the end? The only thing that could have made it any better was if I could have seen your face without your helmet on."

"Pay money for that? I think you're exaggerating a bit. Only a lunatic would have fun banging their head and body off a bunch of walls, just to slam into water hard enough it almost felt like hitting a brick wall." I shook my head, thinking about how ridiculous that would be. "Anyway, do you have any plans for getting out of here? I'm not seeing any obvious exits."

"See that?" She pointed to a pile of brittle fibers piled on the ground. "I think that used to be a rope." We both walked over to it, and I kicked at it. If it was an old rope, it was so old it had become unrecognizable. "Remember how that well was dry? I think this is why. Their mining operations cut off the flows that refilled this cave, and when the water dropped too low, their bucket hit this dry patch of ground."

"That would have to be one really long rope to be from the chamber we were in." I looked up, trying to see a corresponding tube that matched the location of the rope. "That means they probably had a very large bucket, to make it fewer times they had to haul it up the well."

"There, it has to be that one." Jamila pointed to a hole that was off-center, and larger than most of the others we could see. "It has marks along the rim, meaning something passed through it many times."

It was too high to check it closely, but it was the best option we had. We moved to the edge of the island and tried tossing some glow stones up to try and get a better look. It didn't reveal any new information, beyond showing us how difficult it was going to be to get up there.

"Well, we could lift the ground up to it, and use the climb to cultivate back the energy." I looked at the ground under my feet, trying to gauge how difficult it would be. "The island might be too small to provide a big enough platform for both of us, so we should—" Jamila's katana flashed past my face, imbedding itself in the rock above our heads. It was trailing a thin cord that led back to Jamila's hand. "Or, we could just climb up there."

"That's what I was thinking." She gave me a smirk, and started climbing up hand over hand. I waited until she reached the vertical shaft and began shuffling up to make room for me. The shaft was just large enough that she could push her shoulders against one side, and her feet on the other, managing to 'walk' up the slick rock. It looked very uncomfortable, and Jamila had to use her hands to keep herself from sliding down. Her armor wasn't the best at creating friction against the rock.

After I climbed up, I grabbed her katana and passed it up to her, angling myself like she had done. Since I was taller, it wasn't nearly as uncomfortable for me as I imagined it was for her. Fortunately, difficulty was never a deterrent to Jamila. She struggled upward, circulating the qi in her heart core to give her strength and to stave off exhaustion. We climbed for over an hour before stopping to take a break. I used my spirit wood ring to create a place for us to stand, balancing precariously on the walking stick form that I wedged against either side.

"I gotta say, this sucks. This is why you never skip leg day training." My thighs were trembling from the constant exertion, so I knew Jamila had to be suffering even more. Balancing on the walking stick wasn't much better, but it at least allowed us to stretch and move around a little. We could have made a platform using earth qi, however neither of us wanted to expend the energy for just a few minutes of rest since that could be extremely draining. Or let anything waiting above know a cultivator was manipulating qi nearby. "Tell me again why we're doing this?"

"Because leaving all of those sailors to die and their dead bodies to fill the ranks of our enemies is a terrible idea." Jamila was flexing her calf muscles, trying to keep them from cramping. "And this is great training. I haven't been pushed this hard outside of a battle in a long time."

"Well, we might need to rethink some of our training regimen then." I smiled, thinking of the complaining Chu would have been doing this whole time. "Can you imagine throwing in something like this once or twice a week? Chu would probably plan a revolt!"

"No, I don't think so." Jamila chuckled quietly. "He would put something in our food, so we would sleep through the whole day we were supposed to do it." We both laughed, and went back to balancing. After drinking some water and splitting a hunk of cheese, the two of us started the uncomfortable climb once again.

I was starting to doubt if we would ever reach the end of the shaft when the faint smell of smoke reached our noses. Both of us picked up the pace, pushing toward the top with a purpose. The lack of light coming from the opening Jamila disappeared through told me what we would find. There was no way the sailors would still be there in the dark. I emerged from the well and rolled into a crouch, extending my senses in case of an attack. Jamila was nowhere to be found, but I hadn't heard a scuffle so I imagined she had immediately moved to the top of a nearby building. Deciding it was a good decision, I did the same.

Remembering the layout of the area, I made it to a rooftop

in less than a minute. The smell of smoke was heavy in the pure darkness, and I could tell it wasn't from a recent fire. Whatever had happened, it was at least several hours ago. Dead silence made my own breathing seem loud in the darkness. After waiting for a few minutes, I finally pulled out several glow stones and tossed them around the area. Jamila gave me a wave from two buildings over, and tossed out a few light sources to help illuminate the area as well. Once we could finally see, it was obvious what had happened.

"You check the buildings." I motioned for the new opening in the side of the cavern, where an invading force had punched through. "I'll go see about that." Jamila gave me a thumbs up and hopped down. I used a tiny burst of qi to launch myself over the burnt remains of the makeshift gate the sailors had set up, and pulled an adamantine spear from my storage belt.

There were a few streaks of blood leading back into the new tunnel, telling me that at least a few sailors had been injured before getting dragged away. Whatever had made the new tunnel hadn't used qi, and I made an educated guess that the undead had simply chipped away at the rock in an adjacent tunnel until they made a new way into the cavern. I turned back to see what Jamila had found, but dropped an alarm formation that would alert us if something came through the area.

"So, was there anything on your end?" I poked my head inside the building I felt Jamila exploring, and it was obvious a hard battle had been fought here. This was where they had set up their makeshift hospital, and the stack of bodies and bones piled up at the opposite entrance matched up with the new incursion into the cavern. The lack of tactical planning by the undead was mildly surprising, given that the door I was walking in didn't have a single body. It was like they got close enough to sense the living, chipped their way through the stone, and came straight at the largest cluster of life qi they could find. To me, it meant this group wasn't being controlled in any way. They had just been left free to wander and attack whatever they could find.

"There aren't any bodies of the sailors in this mess." Jamila was poking at the pile in front of the door. "I think they killed everything attacking them at this point." She pulled out a charred skull, and tossed it to me. "They lit the gate on fire when they couldn't hold it, and pulled back to this point. The skeletons and zombies marched straight through the flames, and I think the sailors won."

"I found drag marks at the new tunnel, so some of them are probably still alive." I rethought the circumstances of the battle. If they had fought off the group trying to kill them, that meant the smears of blood were from the sailors moving out of the area. "We should probably follow their trail, to see where they went."

"You and I both know the odds are high that more than one of them were infected." Jamila's grip on her katana made her knuckles turn white. "If they don't listen this time, we might have to kill them before they make it back to the surface."

"I know." I put my spear back in storage. "Either way, we need to catch up with them." I activated the walking stick function of my spirit wood ring, and tied a large glow stone to the end of it so we could follow the blood trails. "Hopefully, we can save at least a few of them."

CHAPTER THIRTY-FIVE

Blood Trails

The two of us followed the drag marks until we decided to stop for a quick meal. It had died down to only an occasional drop of blood here and there, but we didn't have a problem following it. The new entrance that the undead had made was only a short tunnel that led into a regularly formed tunnel, and the sailors had chosen to travel in the direction with a slight incline.

"How far in front of us do you think they are?" Jamila was eating a Perfect Prime Pear, the juices dripping down her chin and making a mess on her armor. The vibrantly green fruit was something Chu must have picked up somewhere, because I certainly didn't have one. It helped rejuvenate lost qi, and the energy it provided would keep her from needing to circulate her own qi for several hours.

"They have wounded with them, and I would say the battle was only a day or two old. That means we should catch up soon." I watched as she took another bite. "Have any more of those pears?"

"Nope." She took another large bite, finishing off most of it. "This was my last one." I sighed as I gnawed some more on my dry biscuit. I didn't want to take the time to warm up any of the things I had stored away, and most of my other food items needed at least some form of preparation to be an improvement over what I was currently eating. "Tough luck, Jim. I guess you could eat some of those Murder Goats you won the competition with."

"Ah, I see how it is." Her sharp grin meant this was her form of revenge for beating her in the hunting competition we had weeks ago. "Just couldn't let that one go, huh?"

"It's a pride thing." She tossed the core behind her, and got to her feet. "Should we get back to it?"

The path wound upward for a good thirty minutes before we finally found where the sailors had holed up after their fight with the undead. It was another set of ruins left behind by former occupants of the caves, but these were more recent. They had carved into the side of a small cavern, creating a series of shelves they had built long, rough stone buildings on. They looked barely large enough to stand upright in, and none of the construction had the same sense of age and majesty the other ruins held. Spots along the edges of the shelves were stained where waste had dripped down the walls, and dark splotches of soot on the ceiling marked the places cooking fires had been located. These ruins must have been made in more recent times, possibly from a group that used it to explore deeper. It would explain the lack of proper plumbing, especially if they didn't intend to stay here long-term.

Jamila and I were able to make it halfway into the cavern before anyone noticed us. Extinguishing our lights, we crept closer to better measure what we were dealing with. Two sailors were huddled around a small fire, both of them barely awake on their feet. Exhaustion painted their features, and I could sense neither had much qi remaining in their cores. The saturated qi in the area had lessened the higher we went, but it must have still been enough to stifle their ability to cultivate properly. We both silently agreed to approach their fire carefully with our hands exposed, not wanting to startle the poor men overly much.

"They've found us! Get ready to attack!" One of the sailors unsheathed a cutlass, and the other sprinted for the only building with light coming from its open doorway. The one who had shouted stood his ground as he swung his curved blade from side to side. "Back! Back, you evil things!"

"Whoa there, sailor. I've been called many things, but evil is a bit of a stretch." I lit a torch, allowing the tired man to get a better look at us. "We tracked you here from the outpost. It looked like you had quite a battle."

"All's clear! It's the passengers, not more of those monsters!" The sailor shouted back over his shoulder and lowered his weapon. I noticed that he didn't put it away, or relax his posture. "Only the two of you still alive? Or are the other three sneaking up from some other direction?"

"They are still alive." I lowered my free hand, and tucked my thumb behind the buckle of my belt as I raised the torch a little higher. "It's just the two of us here at the moment, though. The others are recovering from an attack by the undead."

"Sure they are." The sailor lifted his weapon again, aiming it toward me. "Why don't you go back to wherever you came from, and leave us alone? Ain't none of us trust you, and the captain ain't around no more to protect you."

"That's why we came to check on you." Jamila stepped forward, her hands raised and empty. "After we suffered a serious attack, we decided to come and make sure you were okay." She looked over the man's shoulder, where a group of four more sailors were approaching. She raised her voice, so they could all hear her. "Jim found a way to cure one of us who was infected by those things. If any of your people are sick, we might be able to help."

"Help? We don't need more of your *help*." The largest of the men approaching was holding a hunk of broken stalactite like a club, and I could feel a strong aura of earth qi coming from him. While only a Body cultivator, he had a strong connection to his chosen element, making the sailor more formidable than the average person at his level. And making his improvised weapon a realistic threat. "Those things took the captain, along with most of the crew. There are less than ten of us now, and we wouldn't even be here if it wasn't for you!" I could feel his heart core spinning, sending power through his body. "If I were you, I wouldn't be standing around here for much longer."

"Which way did they take the others?" I tried to impose myself between Jamila and the sailor preparing to attack us, but she wasn't willing to back down. Deciding she could handle herself, I stopped trying. "We can try to see if any of them can be saved."

"Saved? *Saved?* Is that what you are trying to do?" The large man's knuckles turned white as he gripped his stone club hard. "You sure confused me, because all I have seen are ways you keep managing to kill us!"

"Well, the feeling is pretty damned mutual, then!" My own anger started spiking, and I had to keep my cores from spinning up in preparation to attack. "You blamed me for the ship sinking, but if I hadn't done anything, we would have been torn apart anyway. Then, you drag an Angry Murder Goat stampede—didn't think I'd ever say that out loud, by the way—down on our heads, and try to get me trampled to death. Now, we come here to try and help you, and all you do is threaten me?" My outburst left me feeling tired, and I moved to leave. "We'll go, and leave you to it then."

"Wait." He looked down at his feet for a moment to think. "Fine. I don't agree with everything you said, but you did come here to help. That counts for something." The sailor tapped one of the men standing next to him on the shoulder. "Bring Roberts out here, and let's see how genuine this kid is." I sighed at him calling me 'kid,' but it was just one of those things I had to deal with. From his perspective, I was a lucky young cultivator who was favored by a powerful group, and he was a man who had most likely come up on the docks with no help but what his own hard work could earn. "Roberts hasn't been doing well ever since the last fight. He wasn't even wounded that bad."

Jamila and I stood back to wait for the man to arrive, and I pulled out the two formation plates that I used for shielding while working on Donny. When they stepped into the firelight while dragging the man, it was hard to hold back a wince. The black veins had webbed across his face in a thick net, and I knew it would be much harder to save him. Considering how hard the process had been on Donny's body, I didn't have much hope that Roberts would make it.

"Lay him down on the ground. I'll get started immediately." I stepped back to give them some room. "Could you point Jamila in the direction the others were taken? She could scout, and hopefully report back what happened."

"Okay. I'll take her there, but you better get him fixed while we're gone." The sailor left, taking another of his shipmates with him to help guide Jamila. I wasn't worried about them trying to do anything to her. They would regret it if they tried. The three cultivators headed for the exit, and I crouched over the injured man to use a pair of qi threads to look him over.

"Are any of you good at healing?" I glanced up to see his friends all shaking their heads. "Well then, I'm sure this won't go horribly." Grimacing, I looked back down at the man I knew was on the brink of death. My initial inspection revealed he already had the qi infection in his lower core, and it had spread throughout his entire meridian system. The only thing keeping him from trying to eat my face off was the lack of qi in his heart core. Apparently, the infection needed qi to be present for it to move through the body, and his heart core was almost completely void of energy. "He is in bad shape. I can't promise that I can save him, but I'm willing to try."

"Do your best." The sailor who had been on guard dropped to one knee next to me. "Is there anything I can do to help?"

"Be ready to give him this." I handed him two pills, one that helped with qi absorption, and the other that boosted the body's natural healing speed. They were both lesser pills, because I didn't want to overwhelm his system if he survived. "I'm going to get started. Fair warning, it's going to get pretty weird, and you should make sure to not let the infection touch you as I draw it out."

"What do you mean?" The sailor immediately jumped back as the first glob of black goo erupted from a wound on Roberts' forearm. "Gah! What in all the constellations is that!"

"It's the infection. The thing I tried to warn your captain about, but he ignored me." I activated the double layer of shields to isolate the gunk. "I've been trying to help you guys this whole time, but everyone thinks I'm either lying, or outright attempting to sabotage them. Even though I have no reason to do so." After it was isolated, I let it expand and die off. Then, I repeated the process, drawing out as much as I could with some wood qi. "I mean, really, how does me hurting you help in any way?"

The group fell into silence, either ignoring me or just disgusted and mesmerized by what I was doing. I zoned out after a while, the repetitive nature of my actions making it difficult to stay focused. It was the same thing over and over; draw out the infection, activate the shields, starve it, deactivate the shields, and then start again.

My patient's condition didn't seem to improve as time passed, and I was afraid he would die before I could finish. I hadn't seen what the process looked liked up close as someone died and the infection took over. It was certain to be unpleasant, and having the double shields in place was a necessity if it happened.

"Jim!" I looked up with a start, and Jamila was standing at the entrance, her armor's shields sparking with dissipating energy. "We have a problem."

CHAPTER THIRTY-SIX

Scraps

Jamila rushed back out of the chamber, not bothering to tell me what was going on. I checked Roberts, and I was happy to see the infection had cleared out of his cores. The lack of qi in his body must have made the infection even more hungry for the wood qi I had been using. It also explained why the infection had attacked Donny so much faster. Donny had more qi, giving the infection more fuel to absorb as it traveled through his system. It meant the disease was more dangerous to those who were more powerful. If I was a dark mana demon that wanted to take over the world, I would definitely want to take out the most powerful cultivators to make things easier on me. I looked back down to Roberts, and he still had plenty of the black sludge in his meridians, but I had bought some time before he was turned.

"I have him stable, but he isn't healed yet." I stood, brushing off my knees. "Try to get him comfortable, and make sure he doesn't try to cultivate. It only feeds the infection." I checked the core that powered the shields on my armor and went to check on Jamila. "I'll be back to finish healing him when I figure out what is going on."

The remaining sailors all gave me a somewhat unenthusiastic acknowledgement and piled more fuel on their fire. I ducked into the tunnel and made my way deeper underground. Right away, I could hear the sounds of battle. A flickering light in the distance flared brightly, as if a fireball had exploded. I started sprinting, and activated my armor's shields.

As I ran, the tunnel expanded into a larger section that had been artificially expanded. If it hadn't been for the flames, I would have completely missed the crack in the wall to my right. After squeezing through the gap, I almost ran into the back of the sailor who had led Jamila away. He was gasping for breath, leaning against the rough stone and clutching a bleeding wound on his upper arm. His clothing was smoking, and he smelled like burnt hair. I didn't have time to ask what was happening before he hurriedly told me what was going on.

"We ran right into them!" He pointed with his good arm, just in time for another blast of fire to wash over the two of us. I shielded him from the flames, letting my shields take the brunt of the attack. "They must have been looking for us, and when we walked up, they just attacked!"

"Stay here, I'll see what I can do." I turned sideways to make my way through the tight spot in front of me, and popped free into another cavern that was very similar to the one the sailors were currently using as a base. The biggest differences were the reduced number of buildings built into the walls, and the ceiling was much lower. Oh, and the giant undead lizard the size of a freight wagon breathing fire at my friend. That was definitely not the same.

"About time you showed up!" Jamila was standing over the second sailor, who looked a little crispy. She had tossed a handful of shield formation plates out, and the undead fire-breathing lizard was doing his best to wear them down. "Mind giving me a hand?"

Behind the lizard, a group of undead skeletons were standing in three lines of five. They seemed to be waiting for the lizard to get out of the way, or possibly they understood that moving in front of a fire-breathing monster was bad for their long-term un-health.

Normally, I would be able to tell what kind of beast I was dealing with, but rot and decay made it almost impossible to figure out if this was an adolescent mighty Lava Wyrm, or just a run-of-the-mill Fire Gecko. There were a dozen more options between the two extremes, and I gave up trying to guess when the skeletons finally noticed me.

"Try using some spike plates to push that thing back, and get that sailor out of here!" I shouted instructions to Jamila, and then focused my attention on the fifteen skeletons approaching me. While they weren't much of a risk while I was wearing my armor, they would certainly get in the way when I tried fighting the lizard. I boosted a jump up to the second shelf of low houses, and used the few seconds it bought me to pull out my silver bow and a full quiver. Charging it with earth qi made the arrows it would fire extra heavy, and I clipped the quiver to my belt. Trying to put them down quickly, I started loosing arrows at the skeletons as quickly as I could line up shots.

My jumping around had distracted the fire lizard, and it shifted to look at me with its undead, milky eyes. A single spike plate thrown by Jamila forced it back in surprise, and she took advantage of the space it provided and rushed past it into the crack with the sailor flung over her shoulder. The lizard spun in anger, its thick tail knocking a skeleton that had gotten too close into flying bone shrapnel.

Seeing an opening, I loosed an arrow at the hip joint of the lizard. The heavy arrow easily punched through the dead scales, and a loud crack of bone caused the beast to stumble and fall backward. That brought its attention back to me, so Jamila had time to get clear.

While I was distracting the lizard, a pair of skeletons had managed to clamber up the steep ramp to the shelf I was standing on. I took a half-step forward and loosed a single arrow that passed through the head of the first skeleton and clipped the jawbone of the second. The dark qi holding the closest skeleton together escaped through the hole in its skull, and it collapsed like a puppet with its strings cut. The second skeleton didn't fall apart, but the hit caused it to tip over the edge of the shelf and it dropped ten feet to the ground. Its leg bones shattered, and it started trying to pull itself up the wall using its arms. A quick count told me there were still ten skeletons moving around, so I lined up a shot to try for another two-for-one special. Instead, I got interrupted.

Fire washed over me, causing my shields to shimmer into visible light. It was only a brief moment of heat, but that was enough to suck the air out of my lungs and make my armor uncomfortably hot. The arrow I had nocked burst into flames, and I threw it away before the bowstring was damaged. I guess it was time to switch weapons.

I swapped my bow for an adamantine spear, and hucked it as hard as I could at the lizard's face. It tried another blast of fire to knock the spear off course, but it wasn't enough to stop it from nailing the beast's lower jaw to the ground. The lizard tried to pull away, and managed to split its rotting mandible in half. The fire streaming from its throat fanned out from the bottom of its mouth, carpeting the ground in a layer of flames. Dry skin and bones caught fire, lighting up the cavern, forcing me to squint as my eyes watered from the bright flares when the skeletons lit up like candles. The lizard was more… juicy, so it only smoldered, filling the cavern with a thick and noxious smoke.

Somehow, the skeletons kept coming for me despite being on fire. I couldn't help but admire their dedication. Backing away, I started forming a qi construct similar to the one I had used on the rock trolls. This time, I shaped a pillar with air qi and filled it with fire qi. Instead of shaping blades as I set it spinning, I just left slits in the sides of the pillar and sent it toward the skeletons. Blue flames spit out the sides, creating disks of destruction that sliced into the skeletons that tried to climb up the ramp, adding to the fire already eating away at their dry bones.

Having taken care of the skeletons, I refocused on the beast. It had rolled around on the ground to put out its smoldering flesh, and then immediately made the same mistake of trying to breathe fire and coating the ground in flames from the split in its jaw. Occasionally, the stupidity of your enemies was the thing you didn't even know you needed in your life.

Considering the size of the undead beast, I decided to use another qi construct to finish it off. Long ago, I had dealt with a nest of Magma Newts, and a strong air qi attack had increased the temperature of their own fire attacks so much that it overwhelmed their high resistance to heat. Becoming an undead had obviously reduced much of the fire resistance this beast had when alive, so a smaller version of the same attack should work.

Building a construct of air qi in the form of a nine-sided pagoda around the lizard only took a few heartbeats, and I filled its framework with more wind qi. It was a ghostly-blue version of a building you might see anywhere in the south. A simple roof was held up by thin pillars, and a few subconscious decorations made its basic form look very similar to one of my favorite meditation locations inside the gardens of the Imperial Palace. It sat around the lizard like a cage, keeping the undead creature from escaping. I left the base of each pillar holding up the construct unsealed, and the moment the lizard spit fire all over the floor, the leaking qi interacted violently.

The almost smoky-red flames of the fire lizard ignited into a flare of yellow and blue. The interaction of wind qi with the undead creature's fire qi attack blended into a violent reaction. Spots danced in my vision, and I blinked rapidly to adjust to the new level of light in the chamber. By now, the skeletons were all destroyed. The undead lizard was bouncing between the pillars of the pagoda, shaking the construct. All it managed to do was increase the speed with which it was burnt to cinders. I watched impassively as it went from undead to completely dead.

"Well, that took you long enough." Jamila stepped through the crack in the cave wall, hands on her hips and a sarcastic smile on her face. "I can't believe that thing gave you so much trouble."

"It wasn't giving me too many problems. With the walls already cracking in this place, I didn't want to risk a collapse." I pointed out the long-running crack that almost bisected the ceiling. "That would be a very bad thing."

"Sure, tell yourself whatever you want. Either way, thank you for the assist. At first, it was only the skeletons, but while I was getting you, that fire beast showed up, and I was afraid I wouldn't be able to save the two sailors." She motioned for me to follow her back through the narrow opening. "Let me show you what we found. Those things interrupted us before we could finish looking things over."

I hopped down and collected my slightly-singed spear before joining her. When we got to the wide tunnel, the two sailors were slumped against the far wall. Both looked exhausted, and the one who had been injured was covered in a purple ointment that stank of herbs and vinegar. I knew that it helped with his burns, but that didn't mean I was going to stand next to him in a confined space. At least, not for longer than I had to.

"You finished them off?" The relatively uninjured sailor climbed to his feet. The other man didn't even wake up. "We were getting a little worried. Not many beasts spit fire." It was hard not to snort. Fire-breathing creatures were so common that I had literally been unable to figure out which one I had been dealing with. I supposed someone who spent most of his time on the ocean wouldn't know that, though. "You ready to see what happened?"

"Sure. Jamila was about to show me what you had found." I stepped closer to the smelly sailor, and used a strand of wood qi to look him over. "I can help your friend some before we go." I fixed the worst of the damage, and cleared up a nasty venereal disease I wasn't too surprised to find. Sailors tended to find the more exotic diseases, considering their profession. I left the more minor issues to be corrected by his ointment. If he was going to suffer from the stink, he might as well receive the benefits from it. I also noted how poorly he had layered the qi elements through his body, causing a harsh imbalance toward wind and water qi. It explained why he had been so sensitive to the fire qi. "There we go. That should help things along nicely."

"Thank you." The sailor looked his friend over. "How long do you think it will take for him to wake up?" He nudged him with his foot, and the man slumped over onto the floor.

"Healing can take a lot out of someone. It will probably take an hour or two, and he will be hungry and thirsty when he wakes up." I handed the man a set of rations from my belt. "You should probably take him back to your camp while we go check whatever it is you found." He nodded in agreement, and I followed Jamila deeper into the tunnel.

"It's over here." She pointed out the tell-tale signs of a large group traveling through the area. We continued walking for almost half a mile before she stopped and pointed. She led me to a small alcove carved into the side of the tunnel. "I think this is where they must have tried to fight back against the undead."

"And didn't win." I winced as I looked over the scraps of bone and flesh that marked the remains of the people we had sailed with. They had been torn apart, and it was clear the undead had *chewed* on their remains. "There isn't much left."

"I think it's impossible to tell how many died here. It would take a long time to sort through all this and try to piece them together." Jamila nudged a pile of fabric, revealing a bare leg missing chunks out of it. "If we even could piece anyone together."

"Let's just look for some sign of the captain, and try to use the clothing to guess how many are here." The two of us did our best to poke around, but our concerns were proven true. The shreds of clothing were so similar to one another that it was impossible to know if they came from different people or not. We could be digging through the remains of five people, or fifty. What we didn't find was anything that might point to the ship captain being among the dead. I decided to call it quits after ten minutes. "I don't see the point in continuing. We should head back, so I can heal the infected sailor the rest of the way, and we can get back to our friends."

"What do you want to do about the survivors?" Jamila dropped the piece of skull bone she was inspecting and brushed her hands together. "I don't think they will be willing to go deeper underground with us."

"I'll talk to their leader about it. We can leave a trail for them to follow if they want to go our direction, but I bet they head for the surface." I looked at the markings left on the wide tunnel floor. The group of undead that had walked through here had probably been even larger than the one I had hopefully wiped out in the higher tunnels. "Since they are a smaller group, they might manage to make it past the bigger patrols of undead wandering around down here."

The two of us walked back toward the sailors, and I did my best not to think about the dream I had involving the ship captain. Dreaming of the new future I had helped to shape seemed impossible, but I was beginning to understand that 'impossible' didn't mean much anymore. The addition of dark and light qi in my cultivation had already caused me to change, and dreaming of the future might be another side effect. It didn't seem to be the same kind of dream walking I got from the gods. Seeing Alya die made me unreasonably angry, considering we were little more than strangers in this timeline. A romantic relationship with her was only hypothetical at this point, and I wasn't expecting to be back in the Southern Kingdom for a long time.

Ultimately, it didn't matter. As long as I could kill the necromancer and stop the infection from spreading, that version of the future wouldn't come to pass. It was time to head deeper underground, and finish this task from the gods. No more distractions.

"Hey Jim, where did all the sailors go?" Jamila's question caused me to pay attention to our surroundings. We had made it back to their camp, and no one was home. I cast out my senses, trying to sense any form of life nearby. Jamila hopped up to the low buildings built onto the stone shelves and searched them while I inspected all the nearby exits. "It looks like they just up and left. There isn't anything left to prove they were here at all."

"I didn't find anything either. There are tracks at every exit, and we don't have time to follow all of them to figure out where they went." I moved to go back toward the tunnel that led to the well. "Let's go."

"What about the infected sailor?" Jamila jumped down and joined me. She was dragging her feet, slowing us down. "Are you just going to let him die?"

"I didn't *let* him do anything." I picked up the pace, lengthening my stride and forcing her to do the same. "They made their choice, and we have a death cultivator and *nox* to take down. No more distractions. We need to finish this, before it's too late." The image of Alya being run down like prey ran through my head, and I grit my teeth in determination. "Too many lives depend on us to allow any more delays." I felt an invisible clock ticking away, and the pressure to bring down the necromancer seemed to grow with every moment. Whether it came from the gods, or my own subconscious, it didn't matter. "We need to regroup with the others, and check on Donny." It felt like we had wasted time here, after all.

"Fine." Mentioning our friends made Jamila speed up the pace even more, forcing me to jog to keep up. "Stop being so slow then, and let's go." I snorted in amusement, and the two of us broke into a run, racing each other to see who could be the first to jump down a well.

My life was weird.

CHAPTER THIRTY-SEVEN

Bread

.

"How are the hands?" I was inspecting the damage to Donny, once again getting rebuffed by the scar tissue. Jamila and I had returned to our little hideout without any issues, and checking my cousin's injuries was the first thing I wanted to do. "I haven't seen anything like this before. Something about the infection makes the scar tissue seem more… resistant. I can't even soften it to make the scars more flexible."

"It's a little painful, but nothing I can't handle." Donny winced as he flexed his hands. "They are just really stiff. Some practice fighting and stretching should help."

"Don't forget to practice carving formations a bit before you try it on the real thing." I gave up trying to heal the damage, and stood to get my skewer of roasted murder goat meat and vegetables from Chu. "Making a mistake on a plate you want to power up could lead to some real problems."

"I will, don't worry." Donny grabbed his own skewer of food, and used it to point at a pile of stone disks sitting nearby. "I was practicing while you were gone. The only thing I really need to watch out for is how deep I carve the runes. My hands aren't as sensitive, so going too deep is easy to do."

"He isn't giving himself enough credit." Chu flopped down next to me, two skewers clutched tightly in his hands. "He hasn't taken a break since waking up. I bet he will be carving and fighting circles around the rest of us again in no time."

"That just means the rest of us can't slack off." Valerie came over to join us. She carried two skewers as well, but handed half of one to Donny before sitting next to him. "I have to admit, I think the strain of cultivating with all of this dark and metal qi around us has forced me to improve my rate of absorption to a new level."

"I noticed that too." Jamila snatched a piece of goat meat off the end of Chu's skewer and popped it into her mouth. She only grinned as he glared at her in silent protest. "Well, don't cook so good if you don't want people to eat it."

"Fair." Chu smiled at the compliment, but angled his skewers so she couldn't steal any more from him. "I agree about the cultivation speed, too. It might suck to be stuck underground, but it has definitely forced all of us to get better at collecting the different elements, no matter how faint they are."

"That's what separates the good from the great." I took a bite from my own skewer. "Finding the advantage even in a terrible situation to make sure you improve yourself is the way to always move forward in life." I stood up and went to check on the barrel that I had set out to collect condensed liquid qi. It was close to overflowing, so I plucked the focusing stones out of the formation plate and stored them away. The funnel-shaped formation plate went into a different storage stud on my belt, and I sealed the barrel before any of the liquid qi could start evaporating. "Is everyone about ready to go? I want to check over your armor and then we need to head out."

"Just a few minutes!" Chu jumped up and went to go and store his cooking implements. "Are we going to that tunnel we found?"

"That's the plan." I eyed the horses, trying to think of a way to get them through the small entrance. "It might take some work to get us all down. And I think we need to come up with a way to protect us all from roaming bands of undead, especially the horses. Do you remember those expanding blocks of wood meant to patch holes in ships?"

"Sure. We should still have several pieces left." Valerie was packing up the hay and water trough left out for the horses. "What are you thinking? A wagon or something?"

"There is something they use in the North called a battle wagon. Field generals use them as a kind of mobile command center." I used my finger to draw a rough sketch on the dusty floor. "They aren't utilized very often, because they move so slow. I want to try to make a smaller version. Something that only two horses could manage to pull. Instead of focusing on communication and offensive formations like they use, we could do only defensive formations." Another rough sketch beside the first outlined what I was picturing. "The wood won't be very strong, so we will have to interlock the designs on plates instead of carving into it directly. Powering them will be a strain, but we can use the liquid qi for the more basic designs. If we—"

"How about you take a breath, and check this over?" Donny dropped his armor next to me, the clatter cutting me off. "We can worry about that once we get to the lower level. For now, make sure we are good to go, and then we can move forward."

"Right." I picked up his gear, and sat down again. "I'll focus on one thing at a time. You guys make sure everything is packed up." I shook my head, trying to clear my thoughts. The invisible clock ticking away inside my head was making it hard to think straight. I shoved down the pressing urge to go sprinting off on my own to kill the necromancer and meticulously checked over everyone's armor. The thin lines of malachite that transferred energy from the core on the back of the helms were all showing signs of scorching. They weren't thick enough to handle the amount of power needed to empower the shield formations on the oversized rivets. I patched in some additional wire to make them more robust. It was only a temporary fix, meant to get us through the next few battles. That was all I was hoping we would need before we got back to the surface. "That should do it. Everyone just do their best to avoid overloading too much damage in one place. Spreading out the strain should help keep the wires from burning out."

"We will try." Chu gave me a sharp nod before strapping his armor into place. "If we stick together this time, we can watch out for one another better."

It was a subtle dig at my decision to split us up earlier, and I could only give him a chagrined smile. Maybe I was expecting too much from my friends. They weren't me, and depending on one another in combat had become second nature for them. I needed to keep that in mind for future training sessions.

"Okay, no more splitting the party. Can we go now?" Jamila was already leading Cloud for the door to coax the horse up the stairs. She had her armor on much faster than the others. "We are supposed to be in a hurry."

The rest of us strapped our stuff on, and made our way toward the small tunnel that led toward the river of lava. After several minutes of walking, we reached it without having to fight any undead. The tunnel was more of a hole in the floor, which required us taking turns to widen it enough for Scout and Cloud to fit. Taking our time to reinforce the surrounding stone was an exhausting endeavor, and we all took long breaks to cultivate in between. I made sure to top off the charge on my batteries while I was at it, but it wasn't easy keeping the balance right in the thick environment of dark and metal qi. We managed, but it took longer than any of us liked. Shaping a ramp took even more effort, and by the time we were finished, it was past time for another meal.

"I don't think we should stop to cook something. Cold rations while we explore deeper." The others nodded in agreement, and we headed down. We emerged into another cavern, this one with a steep-sided canyon splitting it neatly in the center. It was shaped like someone had dropped a rectangular box on top of a floor with a thick crack running through the middle. It was obvious the space was artificially shaped, and I was a little curious why they had built it to capture so much heat. The stink of sulfur combined with a stifling heat that rose in waves from a small stream of lava far below the ledge we came out on. It made the whole place almost unbearable, but we continued over to the edge to inspect what we were dealing with.

"Guys, just throwing this out there, but you probably shouldn't trip." Chu kicked a small pebble over the edge, where it disappeared into the slow-moving trickle of molten rock. "I don't think our armor would hold up to that."

"You don't say!" Jamila thumped him on the shoulder with a smile tugging at the corners of her mouth. "You are over-flowing with good ideas, you know that?"

"I aim to please, my future wife." Chu's comment was said in fun, but Jamila's sudden blush caused him to redden in return. "I mean, uhhh…"

"What he means is he is going to shut up now." Donny shook his head at the two. "What are you two doing, anyway? This isn't some love story. You are warriors, not blushing brides. Let's go kill something so you can get it out of your systems." We all had a laugh, and backed away from the stream of lava.

"There doesn't seem to be anything on the other side, but those ancient dead skeletons up above had to come from some-where." Valerie pointed to the dark corners of the cavern on the opposite side. "I'll check those with Donny, and you guys check this side for an exit."

"Wait, what about not splitting the team up?" I said it with a wide grin, and everyone just stared back at me like I was the dumb one now. Eh. Everyone's a critic.

I felt Donny and Valerie spin up their cores before leaping across, the light from the lava gleaming on their armor in dramatic fashion. Chu and Jamila went to check upstream, and I went downstream. The chamber was small enough that a loud shout would bring us all running to help each other. Scout and Cloud stayed by the ramp we had shaped leading down, clearly not enjoying the smell of this new space.

The section I was searching didn't have any exits or tunnels, so I turned to head back and pulled out a trail ration to eat. As I chewed on dry biscuit laced with some kind of herb meant to fortify the body, I felt a cool breeze brush past my face. Freezing in place so I didn't lose it, my eyes drifted to the wall near the canyon.

"It was a bakery!" I jerked my head around at the sound of Chu's shout. "This whole place, it was a giant bakery! The walls are lined with ovens!" I inspected my part of the wall, but I didn't see any ovens.

"It's the same over here!" Donny jumped back across the narrow canyon, a large stone long-handled peel in his hand. "There were a few of these just laying around. I think it's some kind of spatula to take loaves out of the ovens."

"Peel," Valerie corrected him as she jumped over the canyon. "The big spatula with a long handle is called a peel."

"Well, whatever it is, it means this place was basically a giant oven. They must have had a *lot* of people underground to need all this." Chu took the hunk of stone from Donny to inspect it. "The question is, how do you get out of here? And why were there guards protecting an oven that a bunch of miners broke into?"

"Maybe they were low on food, and the miners were hungry?" Jamila took the peel away from Chu and stored it in a ring. "If they were using this as some kind of industrial bakery, it had to have been controlled by some important people. My guess is, being underground like this would make food production a vital part of life. Control the food, and you control the people."

"That's... pretty dark." Donny flexed his hands, stretching the scar tissue. "Do you think hunger was what made the people that built these ruins leave?"

"It's as good a reason as any." I didn't expound on the idea with my friends. They had never been in a position where food was scarce. More than one winter campaign in the North I had been on had run low on provisions. The shipments of food from the South were frequently interrupted by storms, and I knew exactly the kinds of problems empty bellies could cause for those in a position of leadership. "If they were running out of food, it could have led to riots, and eventually the people would have left for greener pastures. Literally."

"I'm sure all of that was important a *really* long time ago, but what do you say we find a way out of here? It isn't getting any cooler in here." Valerie nodded at the horses. "They won't be able to put up with the heat forever."

"Well, they had to get the bread in and out somehow, and keeping in the heat to bake things means there has to be a door. That side doesn't have any ovens on it, and I think I felt a breeze." I moved toward the area I had been searching. "This has to be where we need to go. If we search, there has to be some kind of lever or something to open it."

The five of us spread out along the wall, looking for anything to indicate a mechanism to open a part of the wall. After searching the soot-stained floor, I noticed faint parallel lines from a cart or wagon running along the edge of the canyon. At some point, there had been a bridge running over the chasm, and it led from there straight up to the blank wall I had felt the breeze from. After ten long minutes of searching, Donny gave up and knocked a big hole in the wall.

"Well, that's one way to do it." Chu looked through the gap in the wall as chunks fell from the ceiling around him. "Oh, there it is." He stepped through the hole and a loud crack echoed through the chamber. The sound of gears thunking heavily into place somewhere under our feet caused dust to fall from the ceiling, and the entire wall section slowly lowered into the floor. "I guess it was only on this side."

"I don't know about you guys, but I'm ready to get out of this heat." Jamila led the way forward, her katanas unsheathed and ready for a fight. "I'll scout forward while you bring the horses up."

Valerie was already heading back to get them, but Scout and Cloud were more than ready to get out of the giant oven we had been standing in. The two horses walked right past her, chuffing in aggravation as they stepped into the much cooler tunnel that angled deeper underground.

"I guess we should follow them." Donny shrugged, and quickly followed behind. I was going to shout a warning for him to stay clear of Scout's hooves, but he made sure not to get *too* close to the violent horse. I guess he was starting to learn his lesson.

CHAPTER THIRTY-EIGHT

Construction

As we went deeper, the air only got more stale and the stink of sulfur permeated everything. It was also warmer than the higher levels, but thankfully wasn't as hot as the oven chamber. The density of dark and metal qi finally started to give way to some earth and fire qi, but it was more of an increase of the latter than a reduction of the former. It was still a pervasive and cloying feeling the moment I started to pull in the energy, and maintaining the balance in my cores caused them to ache with the strain. That internal clock warning me that time was running out kept ticking away, making me feel more anxious than I had in a century. I mentally asked the gods to knock it off, but I got no reply, and the clock didn't stop. As we came to the next chamber, I called a halt.

"Okay, I think this is as good a place as any to stop and make the battle wagon." I looked around, making sure the area would work for our project. This chamber had a narrow path running past a trio of buildings shaped in a triangle, a low wall surrounding them on two sides, with the back of the cavern serving as the rear wall. They were only a single story tall, and they looked extra thick. It was probably the guard station for those that protected the food production. I pulled out all the chunks of expanding patch wood I had, and piled them in front of me. "This looks like another guard outpost or something, so we can eat some hot food and get some rest before we make the final run." The clock ticked, and I shook my head. "Not too long though. Something is telling me we need to get down there soon."

"What do we need to do first?" Donny picked up a rectangular block of wood the size of his palm and slowly started expanding it with qi until it had reached the size of a barrel. "Just expand all of these to see what we are working with?"

"That's a start, but I would rather you work on the plates that will attach to the outside." I pointed at the oversized grains of wood, and the formations that already existed that allowed it to expand. "Carving into this will weaken it even more, and foreign mana running through it will risk ruining the runes already there. Even though the wood is meant to be cut and shaped to patch holes in ships, it isn't meant to be a permanent fix. It's already weaker than normal wood. That's why we need to mount the plates." I pulled a few examples of what I wanted out of my belt. "We need mostly shield plates, about twenty would be good, and I think five or six wind plates to freshen the air would be good. Especially if it gets worse as we go deeper."

After a few seconds of thought, I pulled out a blank plate and carved a quick formation that combined air, water, fire, and wood qi runes. There were twice as many air and water runes, which would combine to create a cool mist that sprayed over us. The fire would keep it from turning to ice, and the wood would ensure they didn't react strongly enough to make steam. The lack of control runes would keep it from forming anything beyond a condensed aura of the elements we wanted. "Make three of these, one for the front and one for each side. The combination should allow us to maintain a constant temperature around us, so that way we don't over-heat again. We will have to power them with the condensed liquid qi, considering the lack of everything but fire in the area."

"Got it." Donny took them from me, and walked over to where Chu was setting up his cooking stone again. "I'll make several of them, in case some burn out."

"What about us?" Jamila walked over from getting the horses settled in one of the buildings. "Do we get to help build this crazy wagon?"

"Sure. Let me draw out a better image of what we need, and then we can build it." I pulled out my carving stiletto and scratched what I wanted right into the floor. "Imagine a long rectangle, with a hollow center. We will build two harnesses into the center, side-by-side, and that's where the horses will be. For them, it's like pulling a wagon, but it is around them instead of behind them." I outlined two divots, front and back, where someone could sit on the top, with a hatch that opened up to the inside of the hollow box. "We have a front and rear guard, who will fight off anything that attacks." On the rear wall of the large box, I drew two shelves that would serve as bunks. "This is where the replacement guards rest and cultivate so they can swap out." The front area had enough space for someone to walk, and I drew a horizontal slit that ran the length of the wall. A circular bracket was mounted to the right, with a groove that ran the whole circumference of the box in a slight spiral to give it a downhill slope. "This is where we will place the barrel of liquid qi, and the person steering the horses will be responsible for pouring it in this groove so it powers the formation plates we will place around the outside. Once the plates start to dim, they can add more as needed."

"Basically, we are making a box with wheels." Valerie wiped away the dust over the part where it allowed the guards to swap out. She had walked up while I was finishing the explanation. "Do you think the horses will cooperate? I can't imagine them wanting to walk without seeing where they are going."

"It will take some practice, but I think we will be okay." I pointed at the slit in the front. "If it becomes a problem, we can widen the view port so they can see out as well. I just don't want to leave a big gap if we don't have to."

"Why are we doing this again?" Jamila eyed the narrow shelves, where we would be resting in shifts. She obviously didn't think much of the design. "I mean, why can't we just walk down there like we have been doing?"

"Yeah, and what happens if we get to a tunnel where the wagon doesn't fit?" Valerie motioned back to where we had expanded the hole that led deeper underground. "Remember the pain it was to get down here?"

"That's the genius of using these." I picked up a square piece of wood and expanded it to twice its size. "If the tunnel gets too tight, we just shrink it." I set it on the ground before answering Jamila. "As for why we are building it in the first place…" I thought for a moment. "We need something that will let us punch through the army of undead the necromancer has, without risking getting separated. I think we could do it without the battle wagon, but not as one group. This gives us the best chance." I took a deep breath, and winced at the smell. "Plus, it would be nice to not worry about fresh air, or what temperature it is."

"Okay, but I'm still not happy about being trapped inside with the horses for long periods of time." Jamila pointed at the shelves in the back. "And I am telling you right now, I am going to complain about sleeping on those."

"Fair enough." We all laughed, and then I picked up a wooden rod that was meant to replace a spar on a ship. "I will start with the axles and wheels. How about you guys work on the walls and roof?"

After everyone had their tasks, the wagon came together rather quickly. The part that took the longest was figuring out how to get the harness for the horses in place. Donny mounted the formation plates to the sides after we figured it out, and tossed a few spares of each kind into a crate he nailed in place opposite the barrel of liquid qi. The whole thing looked like it would fall apart if it got hit with a stiff breeze, and we ended up not making the hatches for the front and rear guards because there weren't any hinges available. They would have to crawl along the roof and drop through a hole we made on the top. It wasn't a perfect solution, but it was what we had to work with. The single line of formation plates ran in a slanted line along the outside, making the whole thing look like it was tilting. Maybe it was tilting.

"Does it look crooked to you?" Chu handed out plates with an assortment of dumplings to everyone while eyeballing the wooden hulk. "I think it's leaning to the left a bit."

"Nah, that's just the optical illusion of the formation plate line not being straight." Donny walked over and pushed against the side. "See? Steady as a rock." We all nodded in agreement, collectively agreeing to completely ignore the concerning sway it had produced.

"It only has to get us to the necromancer." I looked over at Jamila and Valerie. "Why don't we get the horses hooked up, and then we can start moving."

Donny shrank the rear wall so the horses could walk in and get fastened into place, while Chu and I got in position on the roof. We would be taking the first shift, with a rotating change every four hours to keep us fresh. I felt the wagon lurch as the horses got settled, and after a few thumps and shouts from below, we got underway.

CHAPTER THIRTY-NINE

Destruction

"Get down!" A spray of razor-sharp stone shrapnel exploded across the roof as the wagon hit a low-hanging stalactite, the overloaded shields allowing several pieces through that embedded themselves into the wood. My own armor's shields were able to keep any from hitting me, but the loud crack from the wood was concerning. I didn't know how many impacts like that it could take before it finally gave out. "Try to stay in the middle! There aren't as many things to hit!"

"Easy for you to say!" Chu's shout from under me was barely audible over the background noise of the running battle raging around us, but I could picture him staring up at me with a frustrated look on his face through the roof where he knew I was standing, yelling at the top of his lungs as he sprinted to keep from being trampled by the horses that were running right behind him. "Want to switch so you can steer?"

"Nope!" I used a simple fireball construct laced with wood qi to blast the clump of undead waiting at an intersection in front of us. It exploded with a 'whump,' clearing enough space for us to shoot the gap. "Too busy at the moment to swap!"

We had been traveling for a full day before we ran into the

first of the patrols. It had consisted of a single beast and thirty skeletons, similar to what we had dealt with when looking for the lost sailors. Now I realized that was what a regular patrol consisted of, but at the time we hadn't known what we were dealing with. Our pace had slowed considerably after the first encounter so we could be better prepared, which we quickly came to regret. Playing it safe had given the necromancer's forces time to figure out exactly where we were. That led to a running battle through twisting tunnels as we tried to break through their screen, while they tried to corner us in a place where their numbers could overwhelm us. It was a race against time, one we had been fighting for longer than I wanted to think about. Eventually, they would either succeed, or the horses would run out of energy. Even their incredible stamina and enchantments had a limit.

"There!" Valerie was poking her head up through the hole in the roof, occasionally shooting her bow as targets presented themselves. "On the right!"

I twisted to see what she was talking about, and I was pleased to see a wider tunnel that angled downward. We had been looking for something leading down for the last two shift changes. Ever since the first encounter, the breaks had been coming shorter and shorter. With Valerie using the hole in the roof to support the two people on the roof with archer backup, that meant only one person could rest at a time. She was using the least amount of qi, but she hadn't taken a break at all yet. The other four of us rotated out as soon as we dropped below half of our capacity to try to cultivate what we could.

Donny and I were both Saints, meaning we could last a little longer than Chu and Jamila, but even we needed the occasional break. The meridians in my hands were throbbing with overuse, and I winced as I charged another construct to block a side tunnel from some kind of undead squid that was crawling on the ceiling toward us. The disk of fire and metal qi that snapped into place would turn it into rotten calamari steaks, so I focused back on the path in front of us.

"Hard turn, hold onto your butts!" Chu's muffled shout was all the warning we had before the wagon whipped around a particularly large pair of stalagmites. A chain of metal qi that must have been cast by Chu whipped around the nearest spike of stone, helping the solid wood wheels slide around the turn that led to the tunnel we needed to go toward. Poor Donny was only hanging on by one hand off the back as we drifted around the turn. I was worried for a second that the horses might have been injured, but the steady clop of shod hooves on rock continued with only a slight pause. "By the stars, we're still in one piece! Is everyone okay up there?"

"How about we don't do that again!" Donny had pulled himself up to the roof and shouted down into the wagon. "I'm going to need a break after that."

"On my way!" Jamila squeezed through the hole and Donny slipped away out of sight. "You guys look tired!"

"Thanks!" I spun some wood qi through my body to try to clear away the exhaustion that was creeping up on me. It didn't do much for my aching meridians, but my thoughts did clear up a bit. "Hey, does the sulfur smell seem stronger to you?"

"I think so." Valerie gave a few deep sniffs, sticking her head up a little farther to try to clear the wind formation range to get a whiff of what it smelled like without their interference. "It does stink more than it did before."

"That means we must be getting close!" I drew on my stores of light qi and fired a tight beam of energy at another side tunnel as we rumbled past. Something in the darkness screamed in rage and anger, vindicating my choice to shoot blindly into the narrow opening. "We should slow down, just in case. The main tunnel has too many obstacles for us to make it at this speed!"

"Okay!" Valerie ducked out of sight, relaying my instructions to Chu. She popped back through the hole and gave me a thumbs up. "We're slowing down!"

The sound of wood squealing against wood signified the manual brake lever was getting pulled hard, and we gradually dropped from a barely controlled sprint to a slow trot. The shift in speed gave me a minor case of vertigo for a moment, and I almost tumbled off the front of the wagon.

"Woah there, Jim. I don't think you want to test how resilient your armor is *that* way." Jamila stalked back to her own spot at the rear, and immediately tossed out a bevy of formation plates to cover our trail.

Her speed and reflexes were steadily improving, and I was pretty sure she would be the next one to reach Saint. Chu was right behind her, with Valerie trailing a little. She usually fought at a distance, reducing her near-death experiences compared to the others. Those were important for a cultivator forged in battle to have. It helped strengthen their foundation to know that they were only one battle away from death. Valerie had a certain kind of determination though, one the others hadn't quite found for themselves. It would give her an edge when she needed to push to Sage.

"That's it!" Chu's shout brought my head back around, and I saw what he was talking about. "This has to be the place Jim saw in his dreams!" He took a less dramatic turn to lead us into a larger tunnel.

Chu was definitely correct. The blue-green glow illuminating the maw-like chamber thickly studded with stalactites and stalagmites was exactly what I had seen in the dream I had when our ship was sunk. A thick stream of dark and metal qi traveled down the center of the path, leading the way toward the dead city where the necromancer made his lair.

"I'm glad we finally found it and everything, but do you think we could speed up again?" Valerie loosed a pair of glowing arrows behind us, where a flash of light illuminated hundreds of undead shambling after us. "They are starting to gain on us."

"If we go any faster, we'll end up slamming into one of those stone spikes again." Donny hopped back up on the roof, his axe in his hands. He was unconsciously flexing his scarred appendages as he held the weapon out in front of him. "Someone needs to slow them down."

"This is the entire reason why we built this shit-box." I shuffled back toward the hole so I didn't have to shout. The roof was pretty crowded with four of us on it, so I had to hang halfway off the side. "It was made so we didn't have to split up. So sorry, but no glorious self-sacrifice for you. We already lost Kory from that. I don't want to lose my cousin—the man I consider my brother—in the same fashion."

"Yes, what Jim said." Valerie reached up and pulled Donny back down into the wagon with her. "I'm not willing to lose my betrothed to a bunch of moldy skeletons who forgot to play dead. You can stay right here, and fight them off with the rest of us."

"Guys, I'm sure this is important and all, but can you kill stuff while you talk?" Chu could only hear the rattling approach of the undead, which was getting loud enough to be concerning. "Either that, or clear us a path!"

"Why don't we do both?" Jamila threw a handful of shuriken at the desiccated corpses getting dangerously close to us. The throwing stars exploded on impact, engulfing the zombies in bright yellow flames. "Jim and I can fight from back here, while Donny and Valerie knock a path free for the wagon to get through easier."

"Better than nothing. Get to it!" Chu dumped another ladle of liquid qi in the groove that powered the formation plates, causing the shields to flicker brightly in the dim cavern.

We all jumped into action, with Valerie loosing arrows as fast as she could pull back her bowstring. Each one hit with a resounding crack, shattering the base of the stalagmites that blocked a straight run to the underground city. Donny sprinted ahead of us, using his axe to shove the fallen chunks of stone out of the way.

I could tell both of them were burning through their qi at a ridiculous rate, but I knew from my dream that once we made it deep enough, we could use the area where the stalagmites and stalactites were growing together to stage a counter-ambush. All we had to do was get there.

Jamila and I commenced with the destruction of the undead rushing us from behind. I could see in the flashes from the explosions that there were much larger undead hanging back, but the hundreds of skeletons, desiccated corpses, and fresh zombies trailing us took up all of our immediate attention. The more intelligent and bigger ones were probably hoping we would get worn down by all the lesser undead, and they could swoop in and crush us once we were out of qi. I was excited to disappoint them.

While Jamila kept tossing out our supply of trap plates, I started forming the most intricate braid of threads I had made since being reincarnated. I wrapped a triple strand of light, wood, and fire qi strands together from each hand until they were over eight feet long, and thicker than my thumb. Then, I mentally carved a series of runes along the last two feet of each. They were all meant to enhance the speed of the strands, and the ones at the very end were runes that mimicked my poppers. I had them ready to use in less than a minute.

"Jamila, could you form a platform a foot off the ground on the back of the wagon for me?" I hopped down as soon as it formed below us. "Thank you."

The whips trailed behind the wagon, their tips bouncing off the ground with small pops as they bounced around. Without Jamila dropping wind blades, quicksand traps, and spike plates, the undead started to gain ground again. The faster-moving desiccated corpses and zombies quickly grouped together directly behind us, with the slower skeletons fanning out behind. I waited until they were literally tripping over my threads of qi before I rolled my wrists, snapping the whips backward and forward in a steady rhythm. The results were everything I had hoped for.

"Yes!" Jamila whooped behind me, pumping her fists in excitement. "Get those rotting bastards!"

The first hits landed high, slicing through skulls and

upraised arms like a burning brand through fog. Every body part hit by the tips of the qi strands exploded outward in a storm of shrapnel that cleaved through the nearby undead with sharp cracks of shattered bone. I snapped my whips up and out to the sides, hitting the stalactites we passed. The heavy stones crushed those trailing behind the front line, and created more obstacles for the monsters hiding in the back. A horizontal swipe from my right-hand whip took out those still in range at the knees, and the reverse swipe from my left-hand whip dug a furrow almost a foot deep through the ground along our trail. We picked up our speed again, and none of those still standing could keep up with us.

"I think that should work." Jamila gave me a hand back up on the roof as I reabsorbed my threads. Using them had burned through a quarter of my reserves, and I only got a small fraction of it back. It was still worth it. "When are you going to show me how to do that?"

"Probably after you reach mid-Sage. You should have enough practice splitting your focus by then to maintain at least one braid with no problem." I shook out my aching hands, and looked back at the horde that was slowly falling behind. "I will warn you, it isn't an easy technique to master, and the strain on your meridians can be painful."

"I bet you two gold I am ready by Low Saint." She arched her eyebrow, and held out her hand for me to shake on the bet.

I laughed at her competitive nature, and shook her hand. "Deal. I probably just lost two gold."

"You know it." Jamila turned to look in front of us, where Valerie and Donny were still clearing the way for us. "How much longer until we are clear?"

"Considering I was walking this in my dream instead of riding a speeding battle wagon, I would say another five minutes at most." I looked back at the undead following us. "If we can get a few minutes to prepare, I think we can finish off this group before moving on to the city."

"How do you want to stage it?" Jamila pulled out an almost

empty bag that had contained the majority of our formation plates. "We are running low on everything but alarm plates. I guess we could—"

"What's that?" I cut her off, and pointed behind us. The dim light emitted by the lichen was hard to see at this distance, but it was slowly disappearing as something approached. A heartbeat later, my heart felt like it dropped into the pit of my stomach. "Donny, get back here!" I shouted at the top of my lungs, using a thread of air qi to enhance my voice by reflex. "Dark qi wave incoming!" The all-encompassing wave of darkness was rushing toward us like a tidal wave destined to destroy everything in its path. Which, traveling at these speeds, was exactly what would happen once we weren't able to see anymore. "Chu, stop the wagon *now*! Everyone inside!"

I saw Donny staring at us wide-eyed as we thundered downhill, the wagon heading straight for him. Chu slammed on the brake lever hard, the friction immediately causing the smell of woodsmoke to drift up from the wheels. Looking back, the last thing I saw was the glowing eyes of the undead following us brighten from a dull purple to a shining violet color as the element that gave the infection they carried life washed over them. Then, the sound of an axle snapping, and we started skidding sideways, straight for Donny and a row of unbroken stone pillars. The flood of dark qi washed over us, and all the light that allowed us to see went with it.

CHAPTER FORTY

Instincts

The crunch of impact with the stalagmites threw all of us into the side of the wagon with incredible force. I was expecting to see flares of light from our armor shields activating, but the pervasive darkness absorbed even that. The core on the back of my helm shattered with a wave of heat, the power draw sucking it dry instantly. I moved my arms and legs to inspect them for damage, happy to find I was only bruised. The groans from the others around me told me everyone inside was okay, but the screaming whinny from one of the horses indicated they hadn't been as lucky.

"I've got it!" Valerie's voice seemed muffled by the thick dark qi surrounding us, like she was talking to us through a thick door. The muttered curses of her thumping around in the dark made it easy to track her progress to the horses, where she must have used two of the three charges on her healing amulet to bring them back to full health. "I think the horses are okay. Make sure Donny doesn't get near them. We can't tell which one is Scout right now."

"Where is Donny?" Chu's voice came from the front of the wagon. I was sure the makeshift battle wagon wasn't going anywhere anymore, but at least the wooden contraption seemed to still be in one piece. "I didn't see him make it inside."

"Donny!" Valerie's shout was loud enough to overpower the muffling effect of the dark qi. "Donny, where are you!"

"Keep it down! I'm fine." We all let out a collective sigh of relief when he spoke, his voice coming from somewhere outside. "They'll hear you."

"Stars!" Chu immediately dropped his volume, and I could hear him shuffling around. "I don't know what happened to the barrel of qi, but we still have the box of spare shield plates."

"Don't worry about that. Everyone just quiet down, and try not to make any loud movements." I popped a fresh core into the back of my helm, and felt the hum of power pass through my armor. "Make sure you have a fresh core to power your armor, and stand against the wall we hit. If the undead make it inside, we should only have to fight what is right in front of us. As long as you are fighting forward, you aren't accidentally hitting each other in the dark."

"Shhh…" Donny's quiet shushing was immediately followed by the scrape of bone on rock. Dozens of skeletal feet were shuffling past us, somehow walking right past our broken wagon. Finding out they too were blinded by the flood of dark qi was a relief. I had no idea how they could miss the giant battle wagon parked in the middle of the tunnel, but they managed it.

Recalling how long the last blinding wave of dark qi had lasted, I was surprised this one was still ongoing. It was likely that because we were deeper underground, the amount collected from the various tunnels through the region created a longer-lasting flood. We had only experienced a portion of the actual amount collected by the death cultivator when we were farther up.

A thudding stomp just outside the wagon marked the arrival of the undead beasts that had been hanging back, waiting for us to run out of energy. I tensed up, ready to fight. My senses were distorted by the dense power washing past us, but I thought I could feel my friends doing the same. We all waited for the inevitable fight to kick off, but nothing happened. The plodding steps of the unknown beast walked right past us, followed by a parade of other monsters.

We obviously couldn't see them, but we could hear their various limbs and appendages thumping, scratching, fluttering, and slithering past. It was worse not being able to see what they were. My imagination tried filling in the images each sound represented, and a veritable menagerie of horrors paraded past us in my mind's eye. Intellectually, I understood that unless there was a Duke-level monster walking past, the five of us could easily defeat whatever was out there. That didn't mean my instincts weren't screaming for me to do something. I took a deep breath through my nose, reminding myself that I wasn't some pushover ready to get squished by some unknowable evil. The goddess Wrath surely wasn't one of the monsters outside, after all.

I smirked at my own joke, doing my best to break myself out of the instinctive drive to lash out at the monsters walking past. Luck was with us. The horses mercifully stayed quiet, not even letting loose a quiet nicker of fear. The sounds of the infected undead eventually passed us by, and we settled down onto the floor.

"What just happened?" Jamila still spoke in a whisper, considering we didn't know how far away our enemies had traveled. "How did they not find us?"

"It has to be what the wagon is made from." A groan of wood announced Donny climbing through the hole in the top of the wagon. The crunch of his boots on the grit of the ground meant he had dropped safely inside. "Think about it. They are animated and controlled by darkness and death. This wagon is made from wood qi. Life energy. Their instincts must have walked them right past the thing that hurts them the most."

"That makes sense." I touched the wood I was leaning against, feeling the faint aura of wood qi contained within.

"Although, I don't like what this means. If the uncontrolled undead have survival instincts, it means they might survive the death of the necromancer. That means we will have to hunt down every single carrier of the infection before we can leave these caves. Otherwise, the infection could spread like a wildfire."

"Do we?" Valerie's voice carried a slight hint of frustration. "When does the leadership of the Empire step up and start handling these threats? The sects? The clans? The Kings and the Emperor? Don't they have some responsibility to protect the people that make up their organizations? I can understand the mission to stop the *nox*, but if we have to *also* correct everything they unleash on the world, we won't ever have a moment of rest." We all silently contemplated her statement for a few heartbeats. "I say we warn the General of the North about the qi infection at the same time we tell him about the *nox*. He will have the manpower and organization to handle a threat this big, especially if he works quickly. Before it can spread."

I actually knew the current General of the North from my future-past, and she was absolutely correct. The man could certainly handle the infection if he took the threat seriously. That was the big 'if.' Ignoring us, or underestimating the threat, would mean the dream I had involving Alya might actually come true.

"We will just have to make sure he understands the gravity of the situation." Chu must have moved some, because his voice came from the opposite side from where we had been leaning. "If he doesn't, maybe seeing some of the bottled dark qi would convince him."

"No, that is something we can *never* do." I lowered my tone, surprised at my own vehemence. "Telling our secrets to someone who hoards power… They would kill you just for the secrets you know. And if they are in charge of something like an entire kingdom, they definitely hoard power. Even the best of them do it by reflex." I took out a wineskin and took a long drink before continuing. "I imagine the giant influx of powerful beasts that have been dislodged from their territories by the undead will serve as proof."

"That's true." Chu yawned, causing a chain reaction for the rest of us. "I don't know about you guys, but I'm exhausted, and this darkness doesn't seem to be going away." He was right, of course. This wave of darkness did seem longer than I had first thought might be possible.

"Rotate through a quick nap? Even half an hour would do us some good." Valerie was closest to the horses, and I could hear the distinctive sound of her brushing them. "Even if the dark qi wave goes away, we can probably risk thirty minutes or so."

"You guys go first. I'm not exactly ready for sleep after almost getting crushed by the wagon. If those stalagmites had broken, I would have been dead." Donny's voice moved to join Valerie. "We will tend to the horses, and wake you up in thirty minutes."

"Fine, but also wake us if the dark qi goes away. We should at least find out where the undead are as soon as we can." I heard grunts of approval, and did my best to make myself comfortable. It wasn't easy, but the exhaustion of the last few days overwhelmed me, and I nodded off.

CHAPTER FORTY-ONE

Deal with a Devil

I groaned as I opened my eyes. Apparently, the gods decided I didn't need a nap. Instead, I needed to go dream walking and look at stuff. It was probably punishment for making a joke about Wrath.

As I looked around my new environment, I realized I was standing on the edge of the roof on a building overlooking the fountain I had seen the necromancer using as a dark qi collection point. The only reason I was able to see was because the flood of dark qi was being sucked into the fountain like a drain had been plucked from the base of a tub of water. The courtyard was awash in energy, the spinning power almost hypnotizing as it was drawn in and condensed inside the stone basin. Where I had appeared was right on the edge of the qi, and the rest of the city was covered. It made it feel like I was standing on the edge of an island surrounded by darkness, the only things visible were the peaks of the tallest buildings surrounding the fountain.

While I watched, the necromancer came stumbling out of

the building across from me. He seemed disheveled and unsteady, leaning heavily on his staff to help him make it out the door of the crumbling palace or temple he was holed up in.

After making his way down the stairs, he leaned heavily on the lip of the fountain and shoved the end of the staff into the condensing qi. It created another vortex, drawing in the power much faster than the fountain's formation. Just like before, it slowly condensed into an orb that fit into the end of the staff.

"This time will work. It *has* to work…" Hadad's voice was more like the croak of a frog than a human. I imagine being by yourself for a long time with no one to talk to made it easy to not talk for long periods of time. "I'll show you. You'll see what happens to liars!"

He pulled the staff out of the fountain when it had shifted from a glowing violet to a throbbing indigo. With the speed of a striking snake, he spun and smashed the freshly-formed orb on the ground hard enough to chip the cobblestones. It shattered like glass, spraying chips across the courtyard in a fan of crackling energy. An orb the size of an acorn rolled free, emitting the indigo light with a throbbing pulse. Once again being careful not to touch it, Hadad bent over the glowing gem with a spoon and fork to pick it up off the ground.

Before he could walk back inside, he was struck by a series of tremors that shook his body hard. The acorn-sized gem fell off the spoon, bounced, and rolled against the rim of the fountain. Hadad didn't stop shaking, and suddenly threw himself down on the hard ground with bruising force.

"You think to change our arrangement, *my bag of skin and bones?"* The rasping voice that came from the death cultivator's mouth was completely different from the dry croak I had heard before. Hadad writhed in pain on the ground, and I finally got to see his face as his hood fell away. He looked younger than I expected, no older than my friends and I. His gaunt features were smudged with dirt, and his long black hair was clumped with grime. Hadad probably had a deep tan complexion before coming underground, but now he was so pale I could see his

veins running under his skin. *"I think it's time for me to show you the cost of insubordination."*

"No!" The dry croaking voice of Hadad broke through whatever hold had been on him, then he immediately vomited blood in a spray that coated the ground in front of him. "You *lied*, demon!" He got back to his hands and knees, but wavered, too weak to stand. "I'm not the one who broke our deal!"

"*Wrong.*" The rasping voice returned, and Hadad climbed to his feet, any former issues with instability gone with the weird laughter that shook his shoulders with mirth. *"Your family will be returned to you. It isn't my fault that you are too weak to perform the ceremony now. I have no doubt my experiments will return them to full life once we can power the runes and ingredients with increased levels of power."* The necromancer turned and walked with fluid steps back to the building he had come from. *"Next time you make a bargain with a demon, you should remember to include a time limit. Now, we have things to prepare. The light sends its agents, and we want to properly greet them."*

As I watched, the possessed cultivator walked back into the arched doorway just as the levels of dark qi started to lower. Hadad stumbled once, turning back to look at the gem created from dark qi before he disappeared inside.

My mind raced trying to understand what I had seen. Hadad seemed to have control of himself only part of the time. He must have made a deal with a *nox* when his ship wrecked to bring his family back from the dead, but the demon had only been interested in creating an undead army to sweep the Empire. The only thing I didn't understand was the gem he had created with his staff. It reminded me of the dark qi cores I had collected from some of the lesser *nox* creatures I had killed, but far more powerful and pure. What purpose did it serve? Was he trying to kill the *nox* inside himself with it somehow? He had certainly been afraid to touch it. Before I could hop down and inspect the small gem, I was pulled back into darkness.

CHAPTER FORTY-TWO

Mid to High

Donny was shaking me awake. The fact that I could see him meant the dark qi was gone. I sat up and saw the extensive damage to our battle wagon. The walls were more of a collection of splinters held together by the shield plates than an actual solid piece of wood. My aching body reminded me that I hadn't healed the bruising from the wreck yet, so I spun some wood qi through my body to relieve the pain.

"You good?" Donny was holding a strip of dried meat out to me, so I took it with a grunt of thanks. "The wave passed by a few minutes ago, but waking you up was a chore. Valerie already checked for the undead, but she didn't see anything when she poked her head out."

"It was so hard to wake me up because I had another dream. It turns out, things aren't exactly what we thought." Everyone gathered around me, and I explained what I had seen. "So, what do you think?"

"Sounds to me like we need to help him." Chu looked around, seeking approval from the others. "I mean, he lost his family. The *nox* took advantage of that, and it seems to me like he has been trying to get free ever since."

"Not just that." Jamila pulled out a jug containing some kind of fruit juice and started passing it around. "If he has figured out a way to kill a *nox*, but save the host, don't you think we should at least try it? That knowledge could come in handy."

"I thought you had to have a stained soul for the *nox* to join with you?" Valerie frowned sharply, looking down at her hands that slowly curled into fists. "That means he wasn't a good person before his family died, right?"

"There is a big difference between being the stuck-up chosen brat of some clan, and a necromancer possessed by a demon hell-bent on twisting the world to darkness." Donny yawned, not having the advantage of getting a nap yet. "No matter what, I say our safety comes first. If we can get the *nox* out, that's great. If not, then so be it. Either way, our lives are more important."

"I couldn't have said it better myself." I climbed to my feet. "We help him if we can, and kill him if we can't." I took a moment to take a closer look at everyone around me, gauging their current readiness. "We know the *nox* is preparing something for us, but charging in right now would be stupid. All of us could use some time to recharge, especially Donny and Valerie. They could use a nap." Both of them gave me a nod of thanks. "The three of us will cultivate while you rest."

"Jim, I'm pretty sure you are ready for the jump to High Saint. Your qi is almost to the liquid stage without you even needing to compress it." Chu's eyes flashed as he spun qi through them to see my meridian flows better. "If we were to take a longer break, you could probably make the leap before we go in."

"No." I shook my head, and spun my cores to move the qi through my system. He was right, but I didn't want to make the change right now. "The qi in this area is too unbalanced. I don't want to risk going from fog to liquid in this environment."

"It might happen in the middle of the fight whether you want to or not. Remember the fight with those cannibal things at that roadside inn? You were forced to ascend at the worst moment possible." Jamila pulled out a bunch of cores she must have been holding on to. "I have a lot of the elements here. The only thing you would be short on was light qi, and I think you could handle that."

"Do it." Donny's scarred hand landed heavily on my shoulder. "A stage jump isn't as big of a power difference as a whole level ascension, but it could make all the difference."

"Fine." I sighed in defeat. They weren't wrong, but neither was I. Any change in your cultivation base should be done while in as balanced an environment as possible in order to avoid future problems. "I have enough cores stored away that I don't need your stockpile, Jamila."

"We will stand guard. Go as quickly as you can, but don't compromise your stability for this." Chu stood and made his way outside, where the horses must have been moved. Jamila followed quickly behind, storing the cores she had offered, while Donny and Valerie laid down next to each other near the back of the former wagon.

I laid down a qi concentration plate and sat cross-legged in front of it. Placing a handful of elemental cores around me improved the energy balance. I only needed to use wood, air, and water. Earth, fire, metal, and dark qi were already heavily represented, and I didn't have any light qi cores to help. What I *did* have was a light qi focusing stone. It would turn a portion of whatever I absorbed into light qi, hopefully making the end result as balanced as I could manage in a place like this.

After setting aside my trusty wood qi focus, I held the new stone in my right hand. You could only use one focusing stone at a time, so I would be without my slow healing for a little bit. That made me pause, and I stood up to place some alarm plates around the area just to be safe.

Now feeling more secure, pulled off my armor to allow me use of all my meridians for the first time in days. I let loose a groan of relief as they reflexively pulled in the energy leaking from the cores around me. It was almost like stretching after being stuck hunched over for a long time.

I sat back down and started drawing in a steady flow of qi. It wasn't the maximum I could pull in, but it was as much as I could comfortably handle without using my brain core's ability to speed up my perception of time.

The qi flowed through me, saturating my meridians as it circulated through my lower core. After making sure all of my meridians were flowing at a smooth and steady pace, I started to spin my heart core. Once it was at the same speed as my lower core and everything was still moving properly, I spun up my brain core. I felt the world around me start to slow, and I was careful to keep my breathing slow and even.

After ensuring all parts of my cultivation were in perfect sync, I felt a thrum of power run through my body with every heartbeat. This level of balance and perfection was impossible to maintain for long, so instead of enjoying the sensation, I doubled down my focus on the task. As I hummed with energy, I concentrated my willpower and *squeezed*.

Contracting my cores and meridians all at once forced the qi spinning through me to go from a thick fog to a liquid, the glowing energy finally making the jump in quality that separated the middle stage from the high stage. The increased density created more room in my system, and my meridians dragged in all of the energy they could in a vortex of power that quickly refilled my cores.

No one ever wanted to talk about how painful it was to contract your cultivation system. It was why most people only did it one core at a time. The process was drawn out over a much longer time, but it didn't hurt nearly as much. I didn't have the time or inclination to waste the hours or days it would take.

A quick inspection showed that I would need to bolster my body with some extra wind and water qi to bring my balance back to perfect, but the small amount of adjustment necessary wasn't nearly as bad as I had feared it might end up. I could probably correct it in a few weeks of concentrated cultivation.

I opened my eyes, not sure how much time it had taken to make the change. The first thing I noticed was that all the cores were used up. I must have drained them dry. The second thing was that my friends were gone.

Putting my armor back on didn't take long, and I made sure to put my wood qi focusing stone back in place. After cleaning up my area, I made my way outside.

"Ah, done already?" Chu stood up from where he had been sitting next to the wagon. "The others went to investigate some strange noises we were hearing."

"How long was I cultivating?" I was still feeling a mixture of the high from my system being perfectly in sync, and the pain from contracting my meridians and cores so hard. "Did everyone else get some time to rest?"

"It's only been a couple of hours. We let Donny and Valerie sleep for a full hour, and then woke them up when we heard the scratching sounds." Chu nodded toward the area we had traveled through already. "It is hard to tell with the acoustics down here, but we were all pretty sure they came from that way. It was the same direction the horses had wandered off to stretch after all that running, so they were concerned. They went to find them so we would be ready when you were done."

"Well, let's go see if they found them, and then we can get back on task." I led the way, and quickly noticed the poor air quality. I looked back at Chu as I used the meridian in my forehead to try to improve the air directly around my face. "Hey, did you say you found spares of the plates that we used on the battle wagon?"

"Yes." He rummaged through his storage rings for a moment before pulling out an old shirt that had been converted into a bag. "There are three of those kind, and nine of the shield plates. That's all I could find. And the barrel of liquid qi was shattered."

"It's better than nothing." I took one of the formations from him, and shifted my spirit wood ring into its shield form. I tied the formation in place with a few strands of some twine and poured one of the few remaining vials of liquid qi over it to power the formation. "That should improve things some."

"Good plan." Chu gave me a thumbs up and moved to walk behind me to take advantage of the trail of cleaner air I was creating. After only a few minutes of walking, he grabbed my arm to pull me to a stop. "Did you hear that?"

"No. Where did it come from?" I cast out my senses around us, trying to see if I could feel anything. My improved cultivation level allowed me to feel things more clearly, even with the dense qi in the area causing some interference. "I'm not detecting anything."

"I think it came from above." Chu squinted in the dim light as he looked up, the light from the lichen not providing enough light to see anything clearly. "Somewhere over there."

"Careful, it could be something dangerous." I prepared a wind construct in the shape of a globe and filled it with light qi. The whole thing formed almost as fast as I could think, proving that my friends had been right for me to take the time to upgrade. After it was filled, I cast the construct straight up above us.

Which was when millions of tiny spiders rained down around us.

CHAPTER FORTY-THREE

Carpet

"Gah! What in the stars-damned hell!" Chu stumbled backward, spitting. "I got some in my mouth!"

"Use fire!" I didn't bother trying to form anything specific. I just blasted fire qi from both of my hands, washing the area around me in flames, my shield quickly changing back into a ring and the plate on the front dropped to the ground. Feeling dozens of the spiders crawling around under my armor, I forced more fire to explode out of my meridians that were covered. My skin instantly started burning as my clothing caught fire, so I switched to water qi before it got bad. The stink of burned hair caused my eyes to water, but the lack of spiders crawling all over me was worth the discomfort. "We need to get out of here!"

"Baaaah!" Chu didn't need my prompting. He had seen what I had done with fire, and had copied me. He just hadn't swapped to water qi fast enough, and the hair on his head had caught fire. He sprinted back toward the wagon, smoke trailing him as he pulled out a waterskin to dump over his head. "I *hate* spiders!"

"Me too!" I took off after him, doing my best not to slip on the guts of the spiders I was stepping on. More continued to fall in sheets around me, and I activated my armor's shields to protect me from any that might land on my head. "Get on top of the wagon!" I wasn't sure if Chu had heard me or not, but I was sure he would think to do the same thing. In the blink of an eye, the floor of the tunnel had turned from rock to a moving carpet of spiders. I continued to kill as many as I could while I ran, using my newly concentrated qi to increase the heat of my flames to the point it made even those spiders not directly touched by fire burst open.

"Jim!" My head whipped around when I heard my name. I looked back to see Valerie leading the horses single file, with Donny in the rear. Leading the group was Jamila, who was the one who had shouted. She was hunched over, lifting and dropping a plank of wood as they walked closer. Dense clusters of spiders rained down on them, only to be shunted away a few feet above their heads. To the front and sides, drifts of the arachnids were shoved to the side, as if there was an invisible snow shovel being pushed in front of them. "I told you it would work!"

"Great! Follow me!" I had no idea what she was talking about, so I turned and ran for the wagon. Its shields still held enough of a charge to keep the spiders from swarming over it, but they were drifting higher and higher. Eventually, they would reach the edge of the protection, and swarm inside. Chu was already on top of the wagon, completely naked and hairless, with reddened skin on the brink of blistering. His armor was strewn about him, and he was slapping himself all over. "Am I interrupting something?"

"Shut up, would you? I can feel them crawling all over me!" He continued to slap his back and arms, swatting at nothing. "Maybe you could help, instead of just standing there and watching?"

"Chu, take a breath, and use some wood qi to heal yourself. Nothing is there." I watched as he calmed down. The redness went away, and even some stubble started growing back on his head and face. The whole time I was still casting flames around, cutting down on the spiders trying to swarm us and doing the best I could to avoid seeing anything I couldn't unsee. "Now, that's better. You might want to put some clothes on, before the others get here."

"What?" He looked up sharply, finally noticing everyone else coming up quickly. "Ah!" He ducked inside the wagon, scooping up his armor on the way. He poked his head back up for a second. "I'll be out as soon as I get dressed."

"Go ahead, I've got this." To give my meridians a break, I tossed a few poppers around. Their small explosions sent bug guts flying. "There are a lot of them, but they are only spiders."

While I waited for the others to come closer, I got a closer look at one of them. I snatched one off the ground as it walked past the edge of my armor's shields and inspected it closely.

The first thing that I noticed was the faint smell of vinegar and decay. It was smaller than the tip of my pinky finger, and its tiny fangs weren't long or sharp enough to puncture my toughened skin. It made them essentially harmless, as long as they didn't get in our eyes, ears, mouths, or noses. That didn't mean the little thing gave up. It kept trying to bite me over and over, determined to inject me with whatever venom it carried. The fine hairs that covered it were a mix of black and gray, making it easy for them to blend into the walls of the caves. When I squished it between my thumb and middle finger, I flicked its remains away. After smelling the rot on my fingers, I finally realized what we were dealing with.

"It's an attack! These things are all undead!" I cleaned my fingers off with fire, then quickly healed the damage. "We need to get out of here!"

"Hold on, we'll be there soon!" Donny's shout was immediately followed by explosions as he tossed his own supply of poppers off to the sides. The others were only a hundred feet away now, but their pace didn't speed up any. Whatever they were doing to protect themselves, it was making a clear path that the spiders couldn't cross over.

"Okay, let's kill some creepy crawlies!" Chu jumped back on top of the wagon, and the roof immediately gave way, causing him to tumble back inside. "Stars-damn it!"

"Quit goofing off and get out here. I need to check you for the qi infection, since they got in your mouth. Their fangs aren't long enough to pierce our skin, but that's a different story if you swallow one." I also didn't mention that the roof collapsing meant that the shield formations were running out of energy. "Hurry up!"

"Jim, Chu, come to us!" Valerie was waving us over, and she pointed to the thing Jamila was using. "We have a way to make it through this!"

"Alright, I'm here." Chu had jumped out of the wagon, and immediately joined me in blasting the undead spiders around us with fire. "Check me, please."

"Sure." I let him take over our defense, and ran a thorough scan over his body. I healed the few scratches he had gotten in the fall, but I didn't sense any infection. "I think you're good."

"Thank the gods! I was pretty sure I didn't feel any bites inside my mouth, but you kind of freaked me out there." He paused his bursts of fire to swap out the core that powered his armor's shields from an earth element to fire. "There. Now I should be good to go. Even if they push through my shields, they will get cooked in the process."

"Smart." I quickly did the same, and the two of us shuffled to intersect with the others' path. When we burned our way to them, I was the first to speak. "Quick, everyone swap their armor cores to a fire element."

"Why? With this, we don't need to worry." Jamila held up the piece of wood I had seen her with earlier. "I knew I could do it."

"What did you do?" Chu moved closer to inspect what his fiancée had made, blocking it from my view.

The narrow space free of spiders forced us to shuffle past

one another, so I let Chu look it over first since he was blocking my view anyway. Instead, I looked down at our feet, where a repeating series of runes was perfectly carved into the floor. It would take hours—maybe days—to do this, but they had managed it at a walking pace. "I don't believe it. You successfully made a stamp, didn't you?"

"Yep!" Jamila pulled it out of Chu's hands and passed it over, obviously proud of her accomplishment. "I used some light qi to carve and reinforce the dragon jade Chu picked up from the Auction House, and fitted it into a piece of the fire wood those sailors didn't burn up when we first entered the caves. I guess the materials were rare enough to hold up to the demands of shaping a formation, huh?" I heard a groan escape from Chu when hearing her describe having used his dragon jade. Of course, he only thought of it as *his*. I knew how wrong his assumption was from the wisdom I had secured over my very long life. He would figure it out as he got older. Once you are in a relationship, everything becomes *ours*.

"I guess so. I'm glad I was proven wrong, because this thing might have just saved us all." What I didn't say was that I *knew* it shouldn't be working. Dragon jade was expensive, but not particularly rare. The plank of wood she had used was even more common. The two combined should have either fallen apart or exploded the third or fourth time she had used the stamp to make a formation. It had to be that she used light qi to reinforce it while making the stamp. There were still so many things that I didn't know when it came to the new types of qi. It drove home the point that there might be a whole bunch of preconceived notions of cultivation I had that were outright wrong now that two more elements could be included.

"Well, I think we have a city to visit." Donny tossed out a few fire whip traps that wiped out entire sections of the spider carpet that was growing thicker around us. "How about we knock on the front gate?"

"Sounds like a good idea to me." I handed the stamp back to Jamila, and took position in front of Valerie in the middle of our ragged line. "I have a feeling they are expecting us." I tossed a ball of flames at the battle wagon as we passed by, the concentrated impact of energy finally bringing the shields down and lighting it on fire. Thousands of spiders were incinerated, but it barely put a dent in the tiny monsters swarming us. "We wouldn't want to disappoint our host."

CHAPTER FORTY-FOUR

Knock Knock

As much as I would have loved to go charging into the huge cavern that housed the undead city, we ended up having to walk. The stamp took a few seconds to activate, and it only lasted for about fifteen minutes without adding more qi to power the formation.

We found that out when we paused to eat a small snack, plan, and top off our cores by cultivating whatever we could. The trail behind us had started to fill in with spiders, and they rushed forward in a surge that we had to scramble to burn away. It certainly ended any breaks. At least we could still make plans while walking.

"How much longer?" Chu was still occasionally slapping himself, his mind playing tricks on him as he looked out over the millions of spiders crawling all over each other. "I *really* want this to be over with."

"Not long." I tossed another formation plate to the side, where it immediately started whipping around five strands of metal qi that cut through the mounds of spiders around it. Using metal meant that the trap would stay powered longer, considering the abundance of the element in the area. Then I pulled out a fresh one to finish the project Donny and I were working on. "Those big pillars up ahead mark the entrance."

Everyone paused to look at the thick columns that were backlit by a faint glow from up ahead. I knew the light came from the river of lava that separated the tunnel we were in from the city. We would probably have a hard fight to get over the bridge, but it was the only way across. It was good things were ending soon, because we were almost completely out of formation plates. This whole trip had been an expensive endeavor.

After another ten minutes of walking, we stepped out into the cavern. It was muggy with the steam of water hitting the lava far below, and the smell of sulfur was strong enough to make me want to gag.

"Ugh, talk about a vacation destination, huh?" Chu stepped up next to Jamila, who was stamping another formation into the rock at our feet. "This place sucks."

"We aren't here to see the sights." Donny put the stone plate he had been carving in the pouch on his belt, and pulled another blank one out of a storage ring. "This is the last one. Once it's finished, we should be able to rush the bridge."

"Finally!" Jamila stood and stretched out her back, the constant need to be hunched over for so long obviously straining even her cultivation-enhanced body. "Next time, I'm using a broomstick for a handle, that way I can stand and use this thing."

"I don't know why you are complaining. You're the one who wouldn't let anyone take over." Chu held out a waterskin for her to drink. "Any of us could have taken over."

"And run the risk of someone messing it up? I don't think so. The light qi has to be applied just right, or it doesn't work." Jamila took a drink and handed it back. "After this, we should all make a few. Having a variety might come in handy for the future."

"We'll work on it, don't worry." Valerie dodged a nip from Scout, and handed the ornery horse an apple to get it to behave. "I want to make one that specifically kills bugs. All kinds of bugs."

"I'm done." Donny tossed his pouch of plates he had been working on over the horses, and I caught it with my free hand. My own stack of plates were balanced in my left hand, so I used a thread of wood qi to open the bag and add his own stack to mine. "Be careful. You don't want to be holding those when they activate."

"That's why I'm using wood qi. Don't worry." Once I had the stack balanced, I counted to make sure there was an even thirty. "Okay, everyone should get ready. Once they hit, things are going to move fast." I spun out thirty metal threads and wrapped them around the plates. "Here we go!"

Fire so hot it was blue erupted from the hands of everyone, incinerating the swarms of spiders drifting around us. I carefully cast the thirty plates behind us, filling every space between the pillars that marked the opening into the chamber. They activated the moment they touched the ground, and a bright light of orange flames connected them together. A solid wall of fire rose straight up, plugging the gaps between pillars and burning any spiders that passed through to ash.

"Now!" The five of us turned and sprinted, the bridge almost a quarter mile away from our current position. Valerie mounted Scout, but stayed with us instead of ranging ahead. Jamila, seeing what she had done, hopped on Cloud. The two women spread out a little to give us some room. While we ran, I noticed the reconstruction of the wall surrounding the city had been completed. I had seen steady improvements being made while dream walking, but I had hoped to reach the city before it was completed. My stars-damned luck just didn't allow it to happen. There would be no easy entrance without siege machines. Going over it was our only real option.

The gate cranked open, and a flood of the necromancer's minions poured out. The faster-moving zombies and corpses reached the opposite end of the bridge at the same time we got to ours. Valerie swung out to our left and started loosing arrows at the undead beasts that were beginning to come out of the gate now that the skeletons were out of the way. Jamila dismounted and fell in behind the three of us.

"Forward!" I was the first person on the bridge, my spirit wood shield shifting into place over my left arm. I spun out a fire, air, and wood qi whip, the combination burning hot enough that I could feel it through my armor. Donny and Chu had their tower shields out and leading, axe and mace in hand, and Jamila brought up the rear with a glowing katana in either hand. "Attack!"

The impact of our two groups was hard enough to shake dust loose from the bridge. I was bounced back a half step, but the undead zombie wearing rusty plate armor was bowled over into the corpses rushing behind him. My whip snapped forward, slicing through everything that stood in front of me. Donny, who was on my left, was using his shield to knock undead over the side of the bridge as fast as they came into range. Chu was doing the same, but his mace was knocking them off in chunks instead of in one piece.

"Push!" Donny dropped his shoulder and plowed into the enemies in front of him. It bought us another three feet of room, and we lashed out once again to keep our gains. We kept pushing, smashing, and crushing our way to the middle part of the bridge.

"On your left!" Jamila shot past me as I pulled my whip back, slipping between the two zombies in front of me. They were wearing rotting furs, and looked to be more recent victims of the infection. Both of their heads went flying as she ran past, her katanas a blur around her that removed limbs and heads with abandon. Her entrance into the fight signaled Valerie, who appeared by my side as if by magic.

"We've got this. Now's your chance!" She loosed an arrow that knocked a particularly large zombie into a group of skeletons waiting to join the fray, and the whole bunch went over the side. "Go!"

I took a step back and started running out a single thread

from each hand. The rising heat from the river of lava below us caused them to flutter in the breeze. I kept spinning them out, longer and longer, until the updraft started to cause them to rise. As they grew, I started to lift off the ground. Just like the spiders we had killed, I was using my threads the same way they used their silk to fly.

I used a blast of air qi from the meridians in my feet to help boost me higher, and the updraft carried me over the thousands of undead that were waiting for their turn to try and kill my friends. Looking back, I saw how small they appeared compared to all the forces arrayed against them.

That was why we had waited until we reached the thinnest part of the bridge. It was barely wide enough for a single wagon to travel across safely, meaning their numbers counted for nothing. Without ranged attackers, the undead would have to fight on a more even footing. The two sides were too close to one another for volleys of arrows anyway. As long as they didn't run out of qi, my friends would be able to hold.

Splitting up was the opposite of what I wanted to do, but without the wagon we had been forced to adjust. I was our best shot at reaching the necromancer, and as long as I could take him down, we had a chance.

After only a few minutes, I floated over the wall. It was just in time, because I had been losing momentum rapidly the farther I had gotten from the source of heat that had created the updraft. I landed on top of a flat roof two rows back from the wall, and I immediately dropped low to assess my situation. As I peeked over the roof, I was almost hit in the face by a flying rock. A familiar roar shook the roof I was standing on, and a two-headed, eight-limbed, undead monster stomped out into the intersection below me.

"You have *got* to be kidding me." My nemesis, the stars-damned troll. "Oh, I am so going to enjoy this, you son of a—" Another rock went flying my way, and I was forced to jump to the side as it obliterated the section of building I had been standing on. "You suck, you know that?"

All I got was another roar as a response, so I pulled out three spikers and hurled them at the monster. The troll had been undead for a little while now, and its reflexes weren't what they used to be. All three hit it dead center, blowing huge chunks off the pair in a spray of gravel and rotting, black blood. It stumbled from the impact, and fell against the side of a building. I pulled out another spiker, and took my time aiming this time.

It hit the one troll in the face, blasting the two apart with a horrible sound of ripping flesh. I stared in macabre fascination as the two trolls got back on their feet. The one that had been facing away from me had taken the brunt of the first three spikers, and it was missing a good portion of its mass. The one that had taken a spiker to the face only had half a skull remaining, but somehow it was still up and moving, its one eye fixated on me with a single malevolently glowing violet orb.

"I bet I hate you more." Shockingly, its only answer was another roar of rage. I pulled out my bow, and used wood qi to empower a single arrow. My newly condensed energy was almost too powerful for the weapon, and it hummed dangerously in my hands. I lined up my shot, and let go of the bowstring. "Everybody hates trolls."

The arrow hit the monster in the eye, cracking into the death energy orb located in the skull that animated the undead. Life energy from the arrow interacted with it in explosive fashion, and the troll's head blew apart in a shower of gore. I repeated the trick with the other troll as it turned to run, piercing it through the back of its head and sending it to oblivion.

"Thank the gods that's over with. I hope I never have to deal with trolls again." Considering my luck, it probably wouldn't be the case, but I could always hope. "Now, time to find a *nox*."

I dashed across the city, using the rooftops as a way to avoid the streets that were overflowing with undead. It didn't take me long to find the courtyard that contained the fountain, and I dropped down to pick up the gem Hadad dropped in my dream. I made sure not to touch it with my bare hands, instead using a scrap of cloth before dropping it in an empty pouch.

A pair of monsters that looked like giant wingless crows guarded the door to the building in front of me, so I used a pair of whip trap plates to rip them apart. I climbed the steps to the entrance, and threw another spiker into the heavy stone doors that blocked my path. They shattered upon impact, blowing chunks of stone deep into the building. I stepped inside, waving away the dust that filled the entrance.

"Knock knock, star sucker. Anybody home?"

CHAPTER FORTY-FIVE

Necromancer

The entrance was in shambles, and I was pretty sure it wasn't all my fault. Trash, dirty clothes, discarded weapons, scrap armor, and piles of random trinkets filled the room. One corner had a pile of cores, and another was filled with jewelry and treasure that looked like it was actually worth something. Everything else was useless. It took me a bit to realize what I was looking at, but then it clicked. This is what he had pulled off of the dead.

"Necromancer!" My rage-filled shout almost tore my vocal cords. I must have been hanging around angry trolls too much. "Come and face me, you stars-damned piece of garbage!"

"Wait! It isn't what you think!" Hadad came stumbling into the room, a gash on his forehead causing blood to run down the side of his face. "It was this thing—a demon—and it possessed me! I didn't want to do all this. It would be in control right now if you hadn't knocked it out with that explosion."

"I know all about it, Hadad. That's why I brought that little rock you left outside." I held up the pouch holding it. The look of shock on his face quickly faded, replaced by relief. "I take it you know how to get rid of the *nox* then?"

"The demon calls itself a 'scientist,' and it has been experimenting for months with formations." He pointed back toward the hallway behind him. "I have been learning a lot while it was in control. I think I found a way to contain it in a chunk of condensed dark qi. At the very least, it should give me control over the undead, so I can stop everything that's been going on."

"You mean you can't control them?" I flexed my hand, the urge to just kill him before my friends could be overrun almost overpowering. "My friends can't fight those things forever."

"They only listen to me if they don't have any orders from the *nox* already implanted in their head. I can't stop them otherwise." I lifted my hand, preparing a wind blade that would remove his head. "No! Wait! The formation will work! All I need is five minutes and the stone."

"You have three." I dropped my hand and tossed him the pouch. "Better move fast. Your life depends on it." I didn't trust this kid, but considering how weak he seemed to be, I held off from killing him. Could it have been from reading through his father's journal, and I formed some kind of attachment to him? That he was a victim in all this? I kept my cores spinning, ready in case he tried anything.

He nodded quickly and took off running. I followed right behind, walking down a hallway and into a room that looked like it had once been a study, considering the stone desk and empty bookshelves along one wall. Hadad plucked the gem out of the pouch with a pair of sticks, and placed it delicately in the center of a circle of carvings on the floor that took up half the room. The runes lit up brightly, and I was forced to look away. Which was when I saw the scratches on the floor I was standing on light up as well.

"*Wow. I can't believe that worked.*" The raspy voice of the *nox* caused me to look up sharply. "*Oh, please help me, I'm so innocent!*" Mad laughter not meant to be made by the throat of a human made me grit my teeth in frustration. "*If you think this host is worth saving, you have it all wrong. His dreams are filled with conquest and destruction. He already has plans to use what I have taught him to take over your tiny little empire the moment he breaks our pact.*"

"And I'm just supposed to believe you? You are literally a demon, *nox*." I tried pushing against the formation that trapped me in place, only managing to shock myself hard enough for my whole right arm to go numb.

"Ah ah ah. I wouldn't recommend that. Those runes are powered by death qi. You will die the moment something vital touches the containment field." The *nox* sat on the edge of the desk that had been pushed up against the wall, kicking his feet back and forth like an over-sized child. Though, he was barely more than a kid, after all. Well, the body was at least. I had no way to know if the kid was still even inside there. Not like I was going to believe the *nox* again so easily.

"Why am I still alive then, *nox*?" I started spinning my cores harder, preparing to try something stupid. "You could have just as easily built a lethal trap."

"I'm not like my brothers and sisters, in case you couldn't tell. Don't get me wrong, all of us are more concerned with ourselves than following orders from the higher ups." The demon shrugged. *"Some are trying to take this world for the Dark, but that's so... boring. There are so many things a world still in the Light can tell us, if we were just left alone long enough, to experiment."* Hadad's face twisted into a sadistic smile.

"What are you saying?" I clasped my left hand over my numb right arm, pulling it tight against my body to hide what I was doing. "Are you looking for some kind of alliance?"

"An alliance? I think we can both agree that there is no need for me to offer such a thing." The demon waved at the stone sitting in the middle of the formation. *"What I'm offering is the lives of your friends, in return for your body. I can contain your soul inside the stone, and be rid of this weak form once and for all. No struggle for dominance, no poorly balanced body unable to manipulate other elements. I can experiment in peace, and you can spend the next few centuries asleep."*

"Besides the lives of my friends, I'm not seeing much in this for me." I was almost ready, all I needed was another minute. All I needed the *nox* to do was keep talking. These things loved to reveal their evil plans with little to no prompting anyway.

"Why should I sign up for a death that doesn't even allow me to return to the wheel of reincarnation?"

"*Oh, returning your body once I'm done with it won't be a problem. I'm sure once my brethren finally quit their power struggles long enough to band together and crack this realm open like a rotten egg, I won't need it anymore.*" It motioned to the stone again. "*Being inside there for so long would actually help you! You would be able to survive in the new world, without your body melting into goo from all the power fluctuations that would result. I know of several places you could go and live out whatever life you had left in peace.*" It almost sounded like it could have been a shifty merchant, instead of a scientist. Would that make it easier to kill? Nah. Not my luck.

"You know what?" I looked at the stone, and activated the spirit wood ring I had been cramming full of life energy for the past few minutes. I selected the spear form as I activated it, and it punched straight through the energy holding me in place with a snap of black lightning, and I jumped clear before it could reform. I looked the *nox* straight in the eye, and angled my spear at its head. "I'm going to have to decline."

"*Fool!*" The *nox* lunged to the side, barely dodging the thrust of my spear. "*Fine, I'll just have to force you!*" He waved his hands, forming a dome of metal qi that would protect him from my attacks.

"Stars-dammit." I looked around me quickly, while he couldn't see through the opaque metal qi dome. I found what I needed, but it felt like a real dumb idea. I didn't have time to think of anything better, and just went with it. "Force me? Nope." I spun one more burst of wood qi into the spirit wood, and threw it into the formation that held the solid gem of dark qi. "I don't think so."

The spirit wood ring had been with me for a long time, and I felt a pang of regret for overloading it. Its structure could only contain a certain amount of energy, and I had just surpassed that limit by almost double. Another bright flash of light erupted from the formation, and the spear detonated.

I was thrown through the stone wall next to the doorway,

creating a new Jim-shaped exit. The shields on my armor over-loaded, and I felt the malachite strands burn out all at once. I really would need to come up with a better design. Climbing back to my feet took some effort, and I just stood there swaying gently as I tried to gather my wits. There was blood running out of my ears, the explosion bursting my eardrums. They popped as I spun more wood qi through my body, healing the worst of the damage. More than one rib had cracked, so breathing was a lesson in agony until they were healed as well. Now that I was relatively back in one piece, I looked around to inspect the damage.

"How are you still alive?" The necromancer was lying in a heap on the opposite side of the room. There was no sign of the gem at first, until I noticed shards of it embedded in his face, along with splinters of wood from my spear. I glanced around the room and saw more splinters of both embedded into the stone wall where he had been standing. Looking down at my chest armor, I didn't see anything sticking out of me. I counted my blessings to have survived that blast with no dark qi shards using me as a pin cushion. I pulled out an adamantine spear and hefted it in my left hand. My right still wasn't working yet. He opened his eyes as I approached with the spear raised.

"Wait!" Hadad's croaking voice made me pause. "It worked. The spirit of the demon is trapped in the shards of the stone. You don't have to kill me anymore." He sat up, rubbing at the wounds in his face. The splinters of wood fell free, but the shards of gem stayed in place. I found that odd to say the least. Then I felt a twinge in my gut, my instincts warning me that this was almost too easy. Scientist or not. I hadn't listened to my gut the first time, so I was more inclined to do so now. Not that I had any idea what getting struck by dark qi shards would do to a *nox*, but I suppose it could be trapped in them. I still had so much to learn about these two new elements.

"Was what the *nox* said true? Do you have plans to take over the empire?" I watched his eyes and probed his aura carefully, looking for any signs of deception.

"I-I don't! I mean, I thought about it a few times, but I would never do that! In fact, I've already ordered the army to stop attacking your friends!" He swallowed hard, the lump on his throat bobbing in fear, and then he tried for a weak smile. "I'm not a monster like he said I was."

"Okay." I lowered my spear. "One more question. What was the *nox* planning to do with all the gold and jewelry in the other room?"

He looked up at me, the fear melting away from his features, and flicked his wrist. I tried to deflect a small rock that looked suspiciously like one of my poppers with the butt of my spear, but the impact threw me back into the wall right next to the Jim-shaped hole I had already made. He had taken my poppers, and enhanced them somehow.

"The gold? He didn't have any plans for it." Hadad stood up, stretching his back. "The demon doesn't understand what it means to rule. It just wanted to experiment, testing what it could do. It didn't understand how to *use* what it created." He stepped over the rubble at his feet, massaging the shards of crystal sticking out of his face. "The gold will help to start the uprising I will lead. To be Emperor is to be the most powerful, and with the tools I have, that's now me. I was the most promising cultivator of my generation, and now I will take what I am owed. It's too bad you won't be there to see it."

A swirl of dark qi erupted from his fists, blended with the heavy presence of death qi. A construct slowly took the form of a headless humanoid, wielding a sword nearly as large as I was.

"You are owed nothing, Hadad. I had thought to spare you, but I already knew that only a soul stained with darkness can properly bond a demon." I stood and pushed out my own construct of life and light qi, forming a simple orb with a shell of fire qi to contain it. "Your pride will be your downfall."

His construct rushed forward, ready to slash my body in half. The orb of qi I had formed intercepted it, exploding on impact and the two constructs canceled each other out in a flare of power. The alloy my armor was made from shielded me from the worst of the blast, but Hadad had no such protection. He was thrown back against the remains of the desk, and I heard the loud crack of breaking bone.

As I approached, he looked up at me, his eyes wide with fear and pain. He gasped, and held out a hand to stop me. "Wait."

I thrust my spear through his chest as I spun up my heart core for added strength and pinned him to the wall. "No. This is the end." His face twisted in a grimace of pain and rage as blood bubbled out of the corner of his mouth. He tried to form an attack with his upraised hand, building another swirl of darkness in his palm. I let go of the spear holding him in place before I quickly spun a rod of braided light and dark qi out of my left hand and pushed it straight through his eye. The combination both melted and incinerated his head at the same time. The dark qi shards interacted with the light qi and caused an explosion which ripped what was left of his body apart. I braced myself as I saw it happening, and thankfully my armor held. To be safe, I could take no chances of the *nox* even remotely being 'alive' in those shards. Now I felt better seeing them and his body destroyed. One more *nox* down, however many left to go.

I turned to leave, pulling my spear free and letting what was left of him slump to the floor. My armor would need a good scrub down after today. I paused at the door, burning him to ash. Leaving any part of a necromancer around was asking for trouble. I also found his staff in the rubble, confirming it was just a larger form of the scepter I already carried. A few extra carvings along its length meant it had a different purpose, so I stored it for study later.

Before I walked out of the building to rejoin my friends, I made sure to take all of the treasure from the entryway he had collected. I *did* have a war to fight, and every little bit helped. Saving the world was going to be expensive.

EPILOGUE

The window closed, and Wrath leaned back in her chair. Pride was sitting across from her, his eyes shining blue as brightly as the stars behind him. Their chairs sat above a constellation of stars that flickered as Pride stood up to pace the room.

"He isn't growing fast enough. At this rate, he won't even make it to the East." The god turned to face Wrath, his perfect face showing worry lines for the first time in a thousand years. "What can we do?"

"By the time they make it back to the surface, the other pieces will be in place. Just give it some time." Wrath held out her hand and the window reopened, showing an image of imposing mountain peaks that stretched out of sight in all directions. Thousands of creatures swarmed forward, following in the wake of something just out of sight. "You focus only on one part of the plan because it shines the brightest, and forget all the others that have been staged."

"You think it will be enough?" He waved his hand, opening his own window. It showed a haggard Jim stumbling out of the gates of a dead city, uncontrolled undead running away from him to hide deeper in the city. His four compatriots looked even worse, but all of them were still standing. "Look how weak he looks."

"He either will be, or he won't. All we can do is set the stage." Wrath willed both windows closed, and turned to look off into the distance. "And how long have you been watching?"

Exposed by the goddess, a man with long hair twisted up in a high ponytail stepped into sight. His body and hair resembled white marble, a sibling to Wrath and Pride's perfect form. The chief difference was the excessive amount of jewelry layered on his chest, arms, and fingers. Each piece glowed with hidden power, making the solid green eyes of the man gleam in the darkness of space.

"What do you want, Greed?"

"What do I want, little sister? I want… everything." His chuckle made Wrath frown, and the stars in her empty black eye sockets swirled. Pride stepped forward, placing himself between the two.

"Is your part done?" Pride's eyes pulsed blue, and another chair appeared so the new arrival could sit. "Tell us what you have in place."

"Oh, you know me, big brother. When have I ever failed a mission?" Greed raised his hand to cut off Wrath, who was more than willing to list a litany of things that the god felt didn't need repeating. "An important one." Wrath sat back, her face returning to its neutral cast.

"So it's done, then?" Pride pulled a bottle and three glasses out of nowhere, and started filling them. "You are sure?"

"Oh, I'm sure." Greed took his glass first, snatching it from Pride's hand before he could offer it. "The rebirth is complete, and the new creature is hungry." All three gods leaned back and sipped the drink Pride had passed around, thinking over the many plans they had laid to ensure the ending they wanted. None of them seemed willing to break the silence.

Wrath finished her drink first, and her glass disappeared as she set it down. She stood and turned to leave, other tasks calling for her attention. Before she left, Wrath looked at the empty space where the window had been, and mumbled something under her breath. Far away, a whisper reached the ears of those meant to hear it.

"The Phoenix rises."

AUTHOR'S NOTE

Well folks, I hoped you liked this one. Life got pretty crazy there for a bit, but I finally got it done. It's too much to get into here. Just know that I'm incredibly glad I was able to continue doing what I have come to love to do—write books. If you have gotten this far, I sure hope you love reading the stuff I put out there.

I know you have probably seen the ask for reviews a hundred times, so I won't go into how important it can be, or how much it helps me sell books, which allows me to keep the lights on and write even more books for you to enjoy. I won't even mention how important a five star review is, especially when it comes to counteracting those hated trolls who love to tank a book's rankings with one or two stars. I certainly won't talk about how big of a deal it is to actually *write* a review, because they hold more weight than a star ranking alone does. I'm definitely *not* going to do that.

What I am going to do is thank my wife for how awesome she is. I'm also going to say how much I love my three daughters. They are pretty freaking awesome. And I would appreciate them not ambushing me with lightsabers any more.

Eric, thanks again. You are the best.

Dakota, Danielle, and everyone else at MDP, I appreciate your patience and support through all the things.

Travis Baldree, if you read this far back in the book, just know I think you are amazing.

Last, but not least, thank you readers. Your support means the world to me, and I can't tell you how much it means. The adjectives don't exist. Trust me, I checked.

If you stick around a little longer, I've got more to show you. So, so much more.

-Michael Head

AUTHOR'S NOTE TWO

On a completely unrelated note, I'm going to take a shot in the dark, and hope for the best. Recently—according to rumors—a movie based on a book made it into theaters because the author put in the back of his story that any person helping to get them a movie deal would receive three percent of their personal income from the movie royalties. I'm going to up the ante, and put it out there that any one person who can get any of my books a movie deal will earn five percent of all movie royalties I earn, for as long as that person lives, or for as long as there are royalty payments. That's one heck of a sweet deal. All you have to do is get my book through the door, and if a contract gets signed and a movie/anime/TV show is made, you get five percent of my earnings from that project for the rest of your life. Maybe you have a cousin, or uncle, or niece—whoever—that works in the industry. If you can tap that resource and something awesome comes from it, we all win. And I do love it when everybody wins.

I can be reached through all kinds of avenues, including Facebook, my website michaelheadauthor.com, and, of course, Mountaindale Press.

Once again, that's five percent of my personal royalty payments from any movie/anime/TV show deal that results in an actual product created by a reputable company (not a college group production that ends up on YouTube). I genuinely hope to hear from you soon!

-Michael Head

www.ingramcontent.com/pod-product-compliance
Lightning Source LLC
Chambersburg PA
CBHW070757190726
48292CB00002B/570